Praise for *Really Good, Actually*

'Painfully funny, beautifully written, heartbreakingly real. You will fall in love with this protagonist and you will fall in love with Monica Heisey's writing. I couldn't put it down'
DOLLY ALDERTON, author of *Everything I Know About Love*

'The kind of book you miss when you finish but that also leaves you feeling so deliciously content and satisfied. Heisey's pen is by turns relentlessly sharp, incisively funny, sneakily disarming and heartbreakingly tender ... Maggie felt like a chaotic friend I adore and Heisey tells her story beautifully' BOLU BABALOLA, author of *Honey and Spice*

'I am twenty years older than Maggie but really felt I was reading a book about me, taking the piss – kindly and lovingly – out of myself ... A smart, funny and warm debut with such a strong voice'
CATHY RENTZENBRINK, author of *Everyone Is Still Alive*

'One of the most hilarious and barbed accounts of unexpectedly starting over I've ever read. If you've ever felt lost and hoped that it was leading towards wisdom, *Really Good, Actually* is your novel'
STEPHANIE DANLER, author of *Sweetbitter*

'Made me both laugh and feel sick in recognition. Painfully real and so, so funny – it will console any reader, divorced or otherwise' LAURA KAY, author of *Tell Me Everything*

'If I wanted to highlight all the laugh out loud one-liners I would have ended up highlighting the whole book'

EMMA GANNON, author of *Olive*

'Monica Heisey is so funny and entertaining it might be tempting to call her a humourist. But all the best humourists transcend the label, and she is one of those'

LAUREN OYLER, author of *Fake Accounts*

'A book about break-ups that doesn't ever sour into being anti-love is a real magic trick ... really, really funny'

JOEL GOLBY, author of *Brilliant, Brilliant, Brilliant Brilliant Brilliant*

'The book everyone is talking about, and it absolutely deserves the hype: funny, addictive and profoundly relatable. I can't believe it's a debut'

SOPHIE IRWIN, author of *A Lady's Guide to Fortune-Hunting*

'A goddamn delight. Heisey doesn't shy away from any of the hard stuff, showcasing the myriad ways people turn into little monsters when their hearts get broken and they lose sight of themselves. This novel is wildly funny and compulsively readable, the kind of book you immediately share with your best friend'

KRISTEN ARNETT, author of *With Teeth*

'Brilliant and honest and so funny'

JENNY COLGAN, author of *An Island Wedding*

really
good,
actually

really good, good, actually

MONICA HEISEY

4th ESTATE • London

4th Estate
An imprint of HarperCollins*Publishers*
1 London Bridge Street
London SE1 9GF

www.4thestate.co.uk

HarperCollins*Publishers*
Macken House, 39/40 Mayor Street Upper
Dublin 1, D01 C9W8, Ireland

First published in Great Britain in 2023 by 4th Estate

1

A catalogue record for this book is
available from the British Library

ISBN 978-0-00-851172-2 (hardback)
ISBN 978-0-00-851173-9 (trade paperback)

Lines from 'Telemachus' Detachment', from *Meadowlands* by Louise Glück
© 1996 by Louise Glück. Used by permission of HarperCollins*Publishers*

Quote on page 98 is taken from 'Gracelands' by Paul Simon
Quote on page 127 is taken from 'The Last Saturday in Ulster' by Nick Laird
Quotes on page 195 are taken from *When Things Fall Apart: Heart
Advice for Difficult Times* by Pema Chödrön

Set in Adobe Garamond Pro
Printed and bound in the UK using 100%
renewable electricity at CPI Group (UK) Ltd

To Louise, with thanks

When I was a child looking
at my parents' lives, you know
what I thought? I thought
heartbreaking. Now I think
heartbreaking, but also
insane. Also
very funny.

– Louise Glück,
'Telemachus' Detachment'

My marriage ended because I was cruel. Or because I ate in bed. Or because he liked electronic music and difficult films about men in nature. Or because I did not. Or because I was anxious, and this made me controlling. Or because red wine makes me critical. Or because hunger, stress and white wine make me critical, too. Or because I was clingy at parties. Or because he smoked weed every day, and I did not think it was 'actually the same thing' as my drinking two cups of coffee in the morning. Or because we fell in love too young, and how could our actual lives compare to the idea we'd had of what our lives could be when we were barely twenty and our bodies were almost impossibly firm? Or because we tried non-monogamy for three months in 2011, and it was just fine, not great. Or because he put hot sauce on everything, without tasting it, even if I'd spent hours balancing the flavours from a recipe I'd had to scroll past a long and detailed story about some woman's holiday to find. Or because he forgot our anniversary once. Or because I did our laundry never. Or because his large Greek family had not quite accepted me as one of their own, even

after I learned his yiayia's favourite poem for her birthday. Or because he walked in on me pooping that time. Or because, in 2015, we attended nine weddings and got carried away, and a big party where everyone told us we were geniuses for loving each other and gave us $3,000 seemed like a great idea. Or because we went to Paris and had an argument instead of falling more in love or at least rimming each other. Or because I'd stopped imagining what our children might look like. Or because he'd never started. Or because I was insecure and sometimes petty. Or because he kept insisting we go vegan, then sneaking pizzas into the apartment while I slept. Or because we finished watching *The Sopranos* and never started *The Wire*. Or because when we were first getting together, I'd kissed someone else, and sometimes still thought about her. Or because he was needlessly combative, with a pretentious streak. Or because I was a coward, whose work did not 'actively seek to dismantle the state'. Or because I scoffed when he said that and asked about the socialist impact of his latest Burger King commercial. Or because he called me a cunt. Or because sometimes, I was one. Anyway, it was over.

Kind of. He'd moved out, taking the cat (for now) and a gaming system and three acoustic guitars. The idea of Jon writing breakup songs in some dark sublet filled me with equal parts deep despair and incredible relief – despair, to think that I had caused him such pain he'd been driven to experimental songwriting; relief that I wouldn't have to listen to it.

Not that I begrudged him the impulse. This morning, after he left, I had almost immediately taken a photo of

myself, wanting to 'preserve the moment' and entertaining grandiose ideas about this horrible loss marking the start of a very creatively generative time. Maybe I'd take a photo of my face on every significant day for the rest of my life, compiling a gallery's worth in time for a show on my eightieth birthday: my big potato head smiling at a PhD ceremony, weeping at my mother's funeral, chewing thoughtfully on the first food my child ever cooked; a few boundary-pushing close-ups during orgasm to generate some buzz, etc. Instead I took the picture, saw the bags under my eyes, and downloaded Facetune. The dark circles felt right, in person. Looking in the mirror I would see them and think, *there is a twenty-eight-year-old who has seen some shit.* But in the photo, I realised, I wanted to look hot.

Having him properly out of the house was a relief, not because things felt better or calmer without him, but because the two weeks between 'I am going to move out' and 'I have rented a van' were some of the longest and slowest of my life. It had been so inconsistent: one day tiptoeing around each other, speaking in the stilted tones of new colleagues on a work retreat, then slipping into old habits and kissing goodbye, eating off each other's plates, fucking. Every time we fell back into some old way of being – so easy, so familiar – I wondered if we were going to write off the whole thing as a few bad months, but one night he came home with some boxes, and we had to decide whose records were whose and what to do about the piece of crap couch we'd bought barely a year ago. The warranty on history's worst sofa had outlasted our marriage.

We swore neither of us had Seen It Coming. After all, we did not have the major problems that led to this kind of thing. There were *some* problems, sure: in addition to the eating in bed, I had no indoor voice and did not respect his fridge organisation system; he had a temper and wanted us to take up running. But we weren't unhappy, just unsatisfied ... until suddenly we were so, so unhappy, and we couldn't laugh, and we couldn't have sex, and we couldn't order Thai food without looking at the other person like, *who are you?* staring at the stranger we'd chosen at age nineteen and nineteen and a half, respectively, and not hating them, exactly, but wondering if they died without warning – of natural causes or in some kind of horrible accident, not that that would be good, of course, it would be a tragedy ... but if it *did* happen – if maybe life would be easier. The words slipped out of my mouth one night at dinner: 'Is this working?' Neither of us had an answer, which seemed an answer in itself.

It had been working, or appeared to be working, for almost a decade. Jon and I fell in love at university, his cheerful nihilism a surprising complement to my chronic overthinking. We'd been friends first (important, everyone says!) and even had exciting, slutty freshman years before realising sometime in the first semester of sophomore year that not only did we get along great, we were also deliriously horny for each other. We attached ourselves at the mouths and genitals and didn't unlatch until graduation. We liked enough of the same things and made each other laugh, and our arguments were only as dramatic as the arguments of all our other twentysomething friends. We

took modest vacations and met each other's parents. Eventually we moved in together – we'd been dating the right amount of time and neither of us could afford to live alone. We painted part of a wall with chalkboard paint. There were poorly judged birthday gifts and petty jealousies and one or two mild betrayals, but mostly there was comfort and an easy understanding. After six years of date nights and pet ownership and learning how to make a carbonara, there was simply nothing else to do. Jon said, 'What do you think, Maggie?' and I said, 'Yeah, okay'; and so we got married, because everyone else was, and because nothing being particularly wrong felt, at the time, like everything was right.

It had always been slightly surreal to me that we were legally wed. When I said 'my husband' to people, their eyebrows would raise and I would think, *totally, yes, how bizarre*. Jon did not find it strange at all. It was not that he was a romantic per se, but his were the last set of mutually enamoured parents on earth, so he had above-average faith in the institution. To him, marriage was a natural response to being in love for an extended period. When we checked into the honeymoon suite at our budget Italian hotel, the chatty American concierge had shrieked, 'Oh my *god*, you're like a child bride!' and Jon had laughed, but I felt weirdly bashful. There was something naïve about it. Hadn't I crunched the numbers? Did I really think our marriage would last, when so many didn't? Maybe I felt embarrassed because yes, I really did. I wanted to tap that version of myself on the shoulder: *honey, if you're embarrassed now …*

The first morning without him, I swear to god I woke up crying. My pillow was wet, at any rate, and instead of flipping it over or changing the pillowcase, I rolled out of bed and let myself land heavily on the floor. *Even if we handle it as well as possible*, I thought, *it's still going to be terrible.* Even though we were going to be well-behaved exes, the type who didn't gossip about each other, or have sex with that one coworker the other's always been jealous of, or post vindictive thirst traps on social media, or tweet excessively about our exciting new lives as single people, it was still going to feel awful for years, possibly forever. It certainly felt that way now.

It was important to me that we have a Good Divorce. As we'd packed his clothes away, we'd agreed that handling whatever came next with kindness would be a nice way to honour what we meant to each other (or had meant). We'd composed a little speech to say to friends – 'we just grew in different directions' – that was true, but also meaningless, and promised to stay in touch – for the first while, anyway. He'd been gone twenty-four hours, and we'd both checked in a few times already via text, variations on how are you and i'm sorry it's like this and have you told your parents. In time, I could see us being the type of exes who went to each other's birthday parties, stayed for a tasteful number of drinks, hugged the new partner, and left before things got messy. But for now I couldn't see anything, except how badly we'd fucked it up, how quiet the apartment was without him, and how few plans I had for the weekend.

I stayed on the floor until mid-afternoon. It didn't feel great, but it was the kind of thing you were supposed to do

when your marriage fell apart. In the movies when you got divorced you lay down on the floor, and then you got drunk, and then you picked yourself up by the sweater shawl and learned to love yourself again at a beach house rented from a charming and handsome older man whose first wife died, and although he clearly still loves her in a respectful way, he feels like he might be ready to move on, like the two of you might help each other heal. In the movies when you get divorced, you have a big fight with lawyers, and it's very painful because the children resent you and you can't decide who gets the house – the big, beautiful house you spent years decorating together, into which you have poured your life's savings and where you raised several children or at least one sizeable dog. In the movies you are Diane Lane, or Keaton, or possibly Kruger, a beautiful middle-aged Diane who is her own boss and knows about the good kind of white wine. Usually, you do not continue living with your ex for weeks because you can't make the rent on your dusty one-bedroom apartment alone. Generally, you are not a glorified research assistant and an advertising copywriter, respectively, whose most important shared financial asset is your one friend who always gets free phones from work. Certainly, you are not supposed to be twenty-eight years old and actively planning a birthday party with the dress code 'Jimmy Buffett sluts'.

But there I was, semi-prone, texting the group chat about how much a banner reading PARROTHEAD PUSSY would cost, and whether a margarita-flavoured cake was within the scope of Clive's baking abilities. It was widely agreed that he could handle it, and not only that but it was

surely something his enemy, a handsome television chef who had recently taught viewers how to 'make' corn on the cob, could not achieve. Further, Amirah had found a party bus that had wipe-clean seating inside: it seems like it's probably used for some kind of bang-bus scenario rather than birthday parties normally, but it's cheaper than the other one by almost $100 ... Lauren, whose birthday it was, wrote back: maybe we don't think about it too much and spend the extra cash on booze? The rest of us agreed.

The group chat comprised my four closest friends from university: Amirah, a lightly frazzled, emotionally turbulent nurse I had met in residence halls; Clive, a large and elegant gay man who was always describing himself as 'chaotic' for doing normal things like paying for cabs in cash; and two Laurens – one who cried at everything and another who maintained she had cried only once in her entire life, when McDonald's stopped doing pizza. For simplicity's sake, we called the former 'Emotional Lauren'.

I had not confessed to the group chat that Jon had left. They knew we were considering separation – that things had not been great lately – but I couldn't bring myself to type the words he's gone. I think part of me assumed we would get back together, even after we agreed he'd go, even after everything. I couldn't envision it lasting, this time apart. Who would I complain to about the speed of the wifi? What would he do when he needed to remember his mom's birthday? By whom would I run every single decision I made every day of my life? What about Sundays, what would we *do*? I assumed he would eventually come back and we'd both

say, *that was exhausting, ha, ha,* and then we'd get stoned and watch *The Great British Bake Off,* an activity that constitutes, as far as I can tell, a full 60% of all marriages.

I had also not told them because it felt unbelievably stupid. It is hard to explain exactly how mortifying it is to have had a wedding when your marriage ends almost instantly thereafter. The relationship had been longer than the marriage – much longer – but so what? To have that all-eyes-on-you, congratulations-on-your-big-moment, till-death-do-you-part day, with its attendant preparation and fights with family and guest list issues and thousands of dollars, turn out to simply have been a very expensive Tinder photoshoot for your friends is … well, it's not ideal. And you don't even get to use the photos for Tinder yourself; first, because you do not know how Tinder works, and second, because you are wearing a wedding dress in all of them.

Instead of confessing, I entertained: telling stories about funny dogs I'd seen, or a recent medical appointment where I'd taunted my doctor with tales of my healthy, active lifestyle as she blinked confusedly and tapped the orange-to-red section of the BMI chart on her clipboard. don't get Maggie started on BMI, wrote Lauren. we'll be here all night. Clive told us he'd recently decided that it really stood for 'Beautiful Man Index', which made sense, because his was so high. Emotional Lauren said she'd heard a podcast recently that would change our lives. Amirah sent a link to a video of a seagull shoplifting, and then we were off, riffing about marine animal gangs, gossiping about acquaintances, and complaining with equal vigour about real injustices in

the world and the corniness of a Toronto micro-celebrity's social media presence.

Eventually, I knew, I would have to tell them, but I was waiting until I found the right opening. I couldn't face their questions before I had the answers myself. Was I ready to be single again? Where would I live? What was I going to do about money? I had some money, sure, but Jon had lots of it – from his job, his family, his savvy financial habits. He knew how to save and how to invest and how not to spend a long-awaited freelance check on risky crop tops or a new kind of fancy cat food. He had subsidised my rent and paid for our groceries, and when we went on holidays, he'd pay for everything except my flight, which I was 'allowed' to pay for the way children who clear their plates at Thanksgiving 'help' with the dishes. A few weeks before our wedding, I'd joked that I was running out of time to get him to sign that prenup; what if we split and he took me for everything I was worth? He told me I could keep my $80. (That used to be a funny story.)

———

Days passed, and I haunted the house like a reverse-Havisham, wandering aimlessly from room to room. As I looked around our silent, empty home – half empty, anyway – I realised my husband ('ex-husband') had paid for the TV and the art on the walls and the kitchen chairs and the thing we put our feet up on when we sat on our appalling couch. Most of the stuff in our apartment was, by definition, his. Though I'd encouraged him to take

everything he'd purchased, he left some of it behind, so the place was technically functional, but felt wrong: a too-spacious bedroom closet with no shoe storage, a cutlery drawer without any big knives, a kitchen table you could not sit at. I dropped onto the terrible hardness of our couch, set my drink on the floor where our bar cart had been, and sobbed my little eyes out.

I didn't know where to look, what to think about, or how to spend my time. Every item in the house was dripping with significance. The toaster was a wedding present, so I ate bread at room temperature. The fridge door ephemera – receipts, grocery lists, notes about bananas and eggs and plans to buy a bike lock – was too painful to look at, so I took my coffee without milk. I taped a piece of paper over a framed photo in the bathroom, not quite ready to take it down, but not ready to face it yet either. A banner left over from our engagement party glittered on a wall above the space where some of Jon's art had hung. C O N G R A T U L A T I O N shone in gold calligraphy. The s had fallen off at some point but we'd kept it up, liked it better that way, thought it was kind of fun. Looking at it now was unbelievably depressing.

There were positive discoveries too: without any pressure to blend our two styles, I realised I had disliked almost every decorative item my husband had brought into our home. Anything I'd ever looked at and thought, *we'll have to replace that eventually*, had been his – or something we had settled on, defining compromise as 'an object we both hate equally'. Now most of these objects were gone. The sparseness of my possessions gave the house a slightly

threadbare quality, and I hadn't kept any of the big towels, but there were no band posters on the walls, no novelty shot glasses in the kitchen, no lightly mouldering wooden bath mat he'd gotten high and ordered on eBay. Now there was space to display my little knick-knacks, to light the candle Jon thought 'smelled weird', to play the nineties pop music he found boring and generic. Of course, it did not feel better to burn a tobacco and juniper candle and listen to the Backstreet Boys than it had felt to be loved.

Every article and forum I'd found through grim googling (tips for divorce; marriage breakdown young; first time alone how) had told me to prepare for sleeplessness, but I had not realised how long the nights would feel. Another surprise was that I could still stomach food. I'd been led to believe that heartbreak spoiled the appetite. As a teenager I had heavily anticipated the breakup – inevitable, teen soaps about handsome vampires and their underage lovers had taught me – that would leave me unable to eat, wasting beautifully away, so thin and wronged and absolutely thrilled to hell about it. To have had a boyfriend, then lose that boyfriend and several dress sizes, perhaps enough to fit into one of the cursed polo shirts Abercrombie sold in its dank, perfumed mall caves? I could not imagine anything better.

Tragically, I was the victim of a supportive home life which had led to an alarmingly robust self-esteem, and went to an arts-friendly high school that channelled most of my latent sexual energy into overwrought plays about middle-aged women with oral fixations. And so I did not date, and remained chubby and happy until roughly twelfth

grade, when not having been laid was enough heartbreak to make me lose, rapidly and with no real effort except abstention from solid food and constant monitoring and recording of my caloric intake, fifty-five pounds. Everyone was very happy for me until I fainted in math class after having a Popsicle for lunch.

The truth is, if you start your eating disorder even slightly overweight, no one will notice until things are very much at the 'what if two meals a day were soup' stage. There was some tutting and discussion about nutrition and balance, then I went to a hypnotist who told me to imagine being beautiful in a bathing suit and I was cured. Just kidding. Really what happened was I fell in love and I forgot about it for a bit. These days I was comfortably soft-bodied, the kind of woman people condescendingly referred to as 'shapely' or 'curvy' or, more often, 'confident', the word practically buckling under its euphemistic load. Sometimes, during periods of stress or after reading too many magazines or listening to a much thinner friend complain about the size of her legs, I could feel myself tiptoe back toward counting, consuming an egg and thinking: *seventy*. But, I reasoned, no one has a completely healthy relationship with food and exercise, at least not anybody who came of age during the period when the cover story of every supermarket tabloid was some variation on 'This Beach Hag Has Cellulite'. As long as I wasn't writing out the daily caloric inventories of my teenage years, I considered myself more or less healthy.

However, the temptation in this moment to dust off the ol' ED – to become one of those heroines in novels whose

bones begin to jut concerningly, frightening their friends and rendering them absolutely gorgeous with grief – was strong. 'Her big eyes somehow more blue for the dark smudges beneath them, Maggie was too sad to eat, because too many people wanted to have sex with her,' or whatever. I was not about to be the first woman alive to experience emotional devastation without the sudden, dramatic emergence of my collarbones.

But I had recovered too well in that area, was annoyingly committed to nourishing myself, and so my soft butt and I stayed fed. Meals were the only thing that broke up the long, slow hours of that first week without Jon. I worked my way through our cupboards, unearthing long-forgotten curry pastes and the instant noodles we stockpiled 'for emergencies'. Every time I tucked into a comforting stir-fry or cut open an oozing homemade quesadilla, I'd imagine David Attenborough's tranquil narration: *even in the darkest times, life … goes on.* Eventually, I knew, I would run out of food, which was stressful, because I could not imagine leaving the house to acquire more.

Not sleeping was less concerning; no one sleeps well anymore. The world is falling apart, and our phones are just there, glowing in our faces, full of news about what the president has said and which of our exes have recently had a haircut. If I really craved rest, I could always drink or take sleeping pills. Jon had told me he was taking them before he left, though I thought maybe this was because the couch was so uncomfortable. He offered me one when he was moving out. I wanted to say yes but felt like it was some kind of statement about How I Was Doing to say no, and

so I stayed up most nights watching British murder television on Netflix.

Previously I had found these shows too scary – we (I) lived in a ground-floor apartment with very suspect window fittings, and we (I) slept lightly and frightened easily. Now I found them soothing. There was a pattern to them, a clear hierarchy of right and wrong. Maybe the troubled detective inspector drank too much and cheated on his wife, but he was not a murderer-paedophile living in some kind of pervert's bunker in Swansea. The murderer-paedophile was always caught eventually, and the beleaguered partner always had to admit the detective inspector was bloody good at his job. It was nice to feel that the difference between guilty and not guilty could be so clear. It was nice to hear David Tennant swearing. Also, a lot of the tension had been drained from these dramas when I realised the murderer is always whoever speaks slowest.

When I did manage to sleep, I would wake up in the middle of the night, groggy and confused. I'd reach across the now-enormous bed, my hands searching for the warm, familiar lump of Jon's body … and feel nothing. Fear would course through me and my eyes would spring open, struggling to adjust in the dark. I'd break into a sweat, confused and scared and a little irked. Had I missed a text? We were supposed to communicate about this stuff! Telling one another when you were going to be home late was one of the main Things of marriage! Then, of course, I would remember.

When this happened, I felt, in order: stupid; sad; embarrassed; disappointed; vindicated when I remembered

something similar had happened to Joan Didion in *The Year of Magical Thinking*; embarrassed again that I'd grasped at this connection to Joan Didion; quietly proud, like maybe there were some similarities; then more sad; and, eventually, tired. But I was not an incredibly chic voice of a generation who had lost her life's love. I could not even figure out the new pant shape, and my greatest work was an incomplete PhD dissertation about the 'lived history of objects' in early modern theatre. Even when it was finished, no one would read it. Plus I hadn't lost my husband, I had left him. Or, rather, I had suggested he leave, and he had taken me up on this incredibly quickly. In many ways it was the last thing we agreed on.

And so our marriage was over, six hundred and eight days after it began. One day we were in love, and the next it had curdled. Suddenly we only had two settings: quiet and exasperated. When we weren't making light, self-consciously upbeat small talk, we were having hundreds, thousands of arguments, rolling our eyes and sighing and sniping at each other about:

- career satisfaction, lack thereof;
- emotional labour, definition of;
- who had used the last of the coffee;
- who had paid the last three utility bills;
- who was really condescending to whom, actually;
- whether it's acceptable, maybe even very normal,
 to stay up till four a.m. playing video games with
 angry teenagers in Europe;
- our parents, our friends as parents, the spectre of
 us as parents;

- the possibility of pornography as a feminist enterprise;
- relevance of feminist porn argument to one straight man's Pornhub premium account;
- toenails, length and disposal locations of;
- whether moving out of Toronto was 'giving up';
- 'Barcelona', pronunciation of;
- why the bedroom was still purple, we moved in years ago, said we would paint;
- that one time he called me an 'adjacent professor' by accident, and it was completely innocent, the word being truly very close to 'adjunct', but because I was already so hurt all the time, I took it as a slight about my lack of professional seniority, and because I was hungry and exhausted and premenstrual, I cried about it in public, and because we were sick of each other, we said snide things we didn't mean and wounded things we did, and the whole thing lasted a full day longer than the four or five seconds it would have taken to correct him and move on, and I never admitted it was my fault, even later when he apologised.

An underwhelming breakup. No affair; no big, blowout moment. Just a series of small fires that we let burn out around us, clutching our coffees like the dog from the internet: THIS IS FINE.

And now I was alone on a hot June evening, eating bread and butter in my wedding lingerie because the rest of my underwear was dirty. I sprinkled some salt on a hunk of

baguette and said, 'Divorce,' out loud, to see how it felt or maybe just to be dramatic. I picked at an expensive, lacy wedgie and wondered, as I had almost hourly for the past week or so, if maybe it had all been a huge mistake. It was so easy to move through the world as a pair – splitting the cost of things and sharing big sweaters and having someone to stand in line with at the bank.

Jon and I had recently started to make Couple Friends, going to dinner in groups of four or six to lightly tease each other over small plates, then go home and have pointed sex after deciding that Ben and Esther probably never did it. The couples were all slightly older married people Jon knew from work; he'd keep them like he'd kept our tea towels, and I would never be invited to a casual dinner party again. Right when brussels sprouts were finally having their moment in the sun! I chuckled thinking this, and wished I could text the joke to Jon. I'd already used my daily check-in, but there was nothing more satisfying than making him laugh.

This whole situation had the air of a joke, like any moment now one or both of us would call each other, tears streaming down our cheeks: *oh my god, you should have seen your face.* Although I hated pranks, Jon loved them. After we got engaged he started doing this thing where he would pretend to die if I left the room. I'd come back to find him sprawled on the couch or slumped over the kitchen table, his dark eyes vacant and lifeless. I told him it creeped me out. He said the outcome of marriage, best-case scenario, was one of you finding the other's corpse. Since women usually outlived their husbands and he took significantly

worse care of his body (his words), it would certainly be me finding him and not the other way around. This way, he reasoned, his death – ostensibly one of the worst moments of my life – would be something funny and shared, an inside joke. No one I told about this ever agreed, but I thought it was sweet.

It is horrible to be sad in the summer.

Google Searches, 10 June

dark circles pale skin

korean skincare routine fewer steps

veins coming to surface

non-medicinal sleep aids

skin looks grey?

watch instagram stories anonymous

kate bush not on itunes

kate bush this woman's work

kate bush youtube rip

canadian divorce law what

does sleeping on your front cause wrinkles

legal definition intolerable

bell hooks pdf

jacquard pantsuit

botox for double chin

bill hader divorce

bill hader wearing t-shirt

bill hader warm laugh

normal person marries celebrity

gua sha videos

what is 'jacquard'

how stay friends after breakup

breast exercises

rules of tinder

population toronto

male population toronto

bloor and ossington liquor store hours

risotto recipe easy

arborio rice replacement
parmesan cheese past expiry ok to eat
24 hour delivery toronto
dial a bottle toronto
what is tiktok
kate bush this woman's work karaoke
how delebe tiktok

That first month alone passed in a haze. A typical day involved waking up after one, then lying in bed joylessly masturbating while *The Last Five Years* soundtrack (original off-Broadway cast recording) played in the background. My afternoons consisted mostly of trying to work, then giving up and posting Instagram Stories containing oblique references to my emotional state. At some point in there, I turned twenty-nine.

It was this that had forced me to confess to my friends. As a group, we went hard for occasions, and a birthday should have been no exception. We had agreed months earlier to celebrate with a trip to Toronto Island's nude beach, bringing cake and cocktails and nothing else. The chat was deep in discussion about the importance of sunscreen and the merits of various private water taxis when I cracked. need to postpone, I wrote, jon moved out ... permanently i think? An unbearable few minutes of silence followed, then Clive wrote, be there in thirty.

I fell back on my bed and stared at a patch of water damage on the ceiling until I heard him bounding up the

front steps. I got up, fixed my hair, and went to the door, and for a moment I did not want to let him in. He would see my bare apartment, the missing books on shelves, the piles of takeout for one. If I showed this to Clive, I would eventually have to show everyone else. I would have to walk around and be in the world, alone.

I screwed my courage near the sticking place and unlocked the door.

'Out of ten, how ready are you to joke about this?' he asked.

I mulled. 'Six?'

'Right,' he said. 'So we'll get into the eyebrows another time.'

Clive and I had met in the university's drama society in second year, and became close when we played each other's love interests in what he termed a 'chubs-only' production of *The Music Man*. He still occasionally yelled 'MADAM LIBRARIAN!' and pulled me in for a wet kiss after a few too many drinks. We leaned against the kitchen table (I would need to buy some chairs) while I tinted my eyebrows with beard dye and Clive told me I'd be back to normal in no time.

'These things happen,' he said. 'If you had committed to everything you wanted when you were nineteen, you'd still be wearing that little vest. And anyway, the happiest people on earth, statistically, are childless, unmarried women. You did it!' He clasped both my hands like our Little League team had just won the big game.

To be blasé about something like this was classically Clive. The only things he took seriously in life were cook-

ing, his job as a producer of structured reality television, and his 2011 New Year's resolution to 'become famous', which he was still working on. Around the same time as the resolution (and potentially in service of it), he had asked us to start calling him Clive instead of Brandon, which was his given name, and although it took some getting used to, ultimately we agreed that stylish Brandons were thin on the ground, so the change was fair enough.

Clive and I split a bag of jagged low-calorie chips and toasted the beginning of my 'ho phase', though my lip started to quiver as our glasses clinked, forcing him to walk it back and remind me that every ho must take things at a pace that works for her. When his assistant texted that they were in danger of losing Scott Moir as a guest judge on a new show where hockey players were paired with professional ice dancers, Clive ran off, promising to check in on me tomorrow.

Amirah arrived an hour or so later, distracting me from my own circumstances with one of her classic workplace embroilments. Although she had been happily partnered for over a year, Amirah was constantly stoking emotional affairs with men at the hospital who then became obsessed with her. The latest of these poor fuckers was an orderly called Brian.

'It's getting bad,' said Amirah, half sorry and half loving it. 'Last week he made me a playlist. He keeps asking if I've listened to it, but to me, that is where I draw the line.'

'At listening to the playlist.'

'Yes,' she said gravely. 'Who knows what could be on there?'

It was easy to understand how Amirah was wreaking romantic havoc on C-Wing. She was casually gorgeous, even in scrubs, and a little bit mean in a way men were obsessed with. When I moved into my dorm, she was already fully installed in her room across the hall, adjusting the angle of a Pussycat Dolls poster near the window. I'd said, 'Do the non-Nicole ones even have names?' and she'd said, 'Maybe they're *all* called Nicole,' and that was it.

'How are your parents taking it?' she asked after we had scoped Brian's track list (handwritten on heavy paper, high-lighting relevant lyrics … *oh, Brian*). I told her they were following my lead, which meant we were not talking much. My mother had offered, instantly, to come down to Toronto and get me, to take me back to Kingston for as long as I needed and feed me all kinds of comfortingly nostalgic baked goods, but I stayed where I was. In a way it was a relief that my family – mom, dad, younger-but-wiser sister Hannah – was safely stowed a few hours out of town, the depth of their worry revealing itself only in my father's daily text: alive? y/n.

Anyone trying to comfort me had been dealt an impossible task: too much attention and care felt like pity, not enough was proof that I was worthless and no one wanted to be around me. I told Amirah my ideal situation (to the extent that any of this could be considered ideal) would be for everyone to know about the divorce without my having to tell them, and for me to lie in some kind of hyperbaric de-stressing chamber until I was ready to re-enter society. I needed a few weeks to be disgusting on my own and adjust to my new life as an unlovable husk. Amirah curled her

long legs underneath herself, and I could tell she was going to say something annoying.

'Do you want my mom's therapist's number?'

I did not. It was only a divorce, and not a particularly juicy one. I hadn't even had any significant dreams – what would we talk about?

'I don't think I'm very "therapy" in general,' I said. 'Doesn't seem like a fit.'

I meant it. The only therapist I'd ever met was Jon's cousin Penelope, a small woman with lank blonde dreadlocks who ran workshops where participants dug their own graves and were buried in them to experience ego death.

'I don't think this would be … like that,' Amirah said. She held a finger to her lips and bit the corner of a hangnail, looking at me pensively while she ripped it off with her teeth. 'But it feels like, if there was ever time for a li'l *soupçon* of therapy, this would be it, right?'

'I'm good,' I promised. 'I downloaded this meditation app thing, and I'm gonna do more running … Hey, does Tom know about Brian?'

Tom was Amirah's lumbering boyfriend, a man with enormous hands and a booming laugh who had some important, hip job at a downtown brewery. They had met on a dating app last spring and been inseparable ever since. Their love language seemed to be tagging each other in flattering photos captioned with long descriptions of their friendship and the way life together felt like an adventure. Their favourite adventure was going to restaurants. First Tom would post Amirah holding a glass of crisp white –

fridays with this one – then when mains arrived, Amirah would post Tom – big boy loves a slice – after which Tom would repost her photo of him, with Amirah finally closing the circuit by sharing the original 'fridays' post to her Story. In this way, everyone they knew got to see every side of the table at which they had eaten. This behaviour was very, very unlike Amirah, but love makes people corny and a bit absurd, and that is just how it is.

I was curious how she felt the embroilments fit into the photoshoots, the oyster nights, the big boy himself.

'I'm not doing anything with these guys,' said Amirah. 'And Tom's only a boyfriend, so far.'

I had forgotten about Amirah's unorthodox definition of the word, which she felt implied no real commitment outside time spent together. Amirah was always ruthlessly casual until the instant she decided a man was the One. There had been two Ones so far – a high school boyfriend and a med student who still texted sometimes – but Tom seemed due a promotion.

'Anyway,' said Amirah. 'One is real life, and one is, like, a *frisson*. I know what I want long term, but sometimes in the moment you really need to know someone has never seen anything better than your ass.'

That did sound nice. Maybe I could have a *frisson* or two, even if my long-term trajectory was irreversibly 'husk'. Amirah received a text asking her to cover for someone at work. 'Do you mind if I go?' she asked. 'I'm trying to build up goodwill so I don't have to work New Year's. Plus there's a patient I promised I'd make friendship bracelets with.'

'Should I be jealous?' I asked.

'Well, she's a seven-year-old with bone cancer, so probably not,' said Amirah.

I sucked the insides of my cheeks between my teeth. 'Fuuuuuck!' I said. '*Fuck*. I meant, like—'

'I know what you meant,' she laughed. 'And this patient's prognosis is pretty good. Chill out.'

I was always amazed at how lightly Amirah wore the day-to-day heaviness of her work, how she could go into the hospital and deliver difficult news to parents or help children manage pain they would be dealing with for their entire lives, then come to dinner and listen to the rest of us complain about bad email etiquette. Whenever she revealed some harrowing detail about the hospital, the rest of us would panic, though as she'd pointed out many times it was not a competition, and Clive's professional stress was not less valid just because it was mostly caused by the tumultuous personal lives of minor Canadian sports personalities. ('Are we … sure about that?' Clive had asked at the time. I still was not.)

'God, that's so intense,' I said. 'I don't know how you aren't constantly having a breakdown.'

'There is actually a crying room on the third floor,' said Amirah. 'But it's mostly nice to be able to be there for people going through a hard time. Like it's difficult, but it's good. I'm sure that's how you feel when you … explain *Macbeth*, or … honestly, I have no idea what your job entails.'

'Like half of it is coming up with puns for the pre-colon part of paper titles,' I said. 'But in many ways that is similar to helping children with cancer, you're right.' I stood and

started rummaging through my cupboards. 'Let me feed you before you go.'

I took out ingredients for her favourite sandwich, a disturbing combination of pickles and hummus with honey and Dijon mustard. Amirah stood behind me as I assembled it, swiping her index finger into open jars before closing them and putting them back in the fridge.

'Why don't you text the Laurens,' she said, taking a first, soggy bite. 'Don't sit around your apartment alone. It sucks in here without Janet.'

To avoid crying at the mention of my cat, I shouted, 'GREAT IDEA!' with unconvincing vigour and pulled out my phone. It turned out the Laurens were convening shortly at a bar near Emotional Lauren's office that offered wine by the ounce. I told Amirah I did not feel particularly sociable but did want to drink several thousand ounces of wine.

'Perfect!' she said. 'You can walk me to work.'

She grabbed her bag and we headed to the hallway, where I tried to make myself presentable with a stray mascara I'd left on the shelf near my keys. I poked at the bags under my eyes and sighed loudly.

'Shame this had to happen right as I lost my last shred of youthful beauty,' I said.

'Don't talk that way,' said Amirah, pulling on a pair of decorated plastic clogs. 'Ugh, I could kill Jon. I'm so mad at him.'

'It's not his fault,' I said, shoving my keys into a purse and opening the door. 'Really. It's my fault, if anything.'

Amirah made a face. 'How is it your fault?'

I didn't really know; that was just how it felt.

The next day I was supposed to go to work but could not bring myself to do it. For one thing, Toronto's humidity levels had switched from June's traditional 'Coca-Cola misting zone' to a 'world's armpit' scenario we usually didn't struggle through until August, and for another, I looked like shit and was sad all the time.

Although I didn't teach in the summer, I normally worked a few days a month at my cramped desk in the English department as a research assistant for Merris, the elderly and understanding early modernist who had supervised my master's thesis and occupied a place in my imagination somewhere between feared-yet-beloved aunt and powerful elder witch. I had not come in for the last two Wednesdays, texting her vague and unconvincing excuses each time. This Wednesday, she called.

'Merris, hi – sorry, I—'

'What is it today, grandmother's emergency dentist appointment?'

I liked working for Merris. She was the most knowledgeable person I had ever met, and she never made other people feel stupid, though sometimes, as now, she could not resist toying with them a little bit. I could see her sitting at her desk, smiling wryly, long fingers wrapping the cord of her office phone around her knobbly left thumb. She was probably wearing a pair of reading glasses with another perched on top of her head. Sometimes there was a third pair on a stylish chain around her neck.

'I think I'm getting a divorce,' I told her. 'I mean, I am getting one, but I don't know when or how, exactly.'

'Ah.'

I hadn't loved telling anyone about this development, but breaking the news to Merris felt spectacularly silly. I was a twentysomething going through a breakup, so what? Merris had been married twice, divorced once, and was now widowed and living what she called her 'best life', sharing a large duplex in the east end with two other professors in a kind of highbrow *Golden Girls* situation.

'I'm sorry,' she said. 'Work from home for now and come in again when you're ready.'

I told her that might be never. Merris laughed and tried to pass it off as a hiccup. 'Take as long as you need,' she said, 'as long as you only need until September.'

Merris had not cared for Jon, based largely on her feeling that he'd lectured her about French Canadian cinema for 'several hours' at a department function a few years ago. When I asked Jon about this, he told me they'd spoken for under fifteen minutes, during which he'd said almost nothing about film, except to mention he'd recently been to a showing of Xavier Dolan's *Mommy*. I suspect they were both being low-level insufferable and disliked seeing their own pretension mirrored in the other. At our wedding, he had tried to ingratiate himself with her by quoting Sonnet 18, and she'd said, 'Shakespeare, for weddings? You might be on to something.' Like everyone I've ever loved, both of them were capable of being a Bit Much.

After Merris and I hung up, I returned to my usual activities: working, eating and thinking up reasons to avoid taking a shower. Most days, after a few hours of carefully scrutinising plays from the 1500s that had been unpopular

even then, I'd reward and/or punish myself by looking at Jon's various social media profiles. He had recently scaled back our already minimal communication, something I was trying to take with a casual grace while freaking out about it internally. In an effort to seem breezy, I'd also suggested we block each other on social media, to 'facilitate our transition out of each other's lives'. He had done so unnervingly quickly, though neither of us had blocked the joint Instagram account we'd created for our cat.

If I logged out of my own account and in to @perfectjanetgoodgirl, there was Jon: not posting much on main, but certainly playing the piano and singing (!) in his Stories, broadcast from some darkened basement. I'd poke around in his tagged photos and watch his friends' Stories, looking for something painful – audio of him laughing at a party, a video of a concert where he was standing close to a woman I didn't know – evidence of joy or satisfaction in his new life as Not My Husband. It was objectively unhinged behaviour, this cyberstalking via pet account, but I was comforted that Janet occasionally watched my Stories too, meaning Jon was doing the same thing to me.

We had not yet decided who would get the cat, easily our most precious shared possession. She was technically his, but we (Janet and I) had lived together for as long as we (Jon and I) had, and I loved her fiercely, even if her main hobbies were screaming and vomiting on my clothing and furniture. She was tough and enormous, a big streetwise tabby with scraggly grey-brown fur and intelligent green eyes. When I read student papers in bed she would sneak into the room, attracted by the sound of rustling paper. By

the time I realised she was headed for me, it was too late: she'd already be midflight, soaring up from the floor to land directly on top of the essay in my hands. I had apologetically returned more than one crumpled, punctured term paper to a confused student, but I would have let that cat destroy everything I owned – which she did occasionally seem on a mission to do. The house was so quiet without her. It was weird not to have to check on top of the fridge when I entered the kitchen (she had a small pouncing-on-people's-heads problem); every unopened packet of foul-smelling treats in the cupboard broke my heart. Jon and I had agreed to take some time to think about what would be best for her, with an eye to a potential shared custody situation. Like many things about my old life, I missed her often.

I spent the evenings watching my murder shows (having ploughed through England's offerings, I was now exploring the sex-based killings of Scandinavia), and thinking about being alone, and sometimes just putting my feet on the floor and sighing. If I was feeling ambitious, I would brush my hair, open and close the windows, and fill online shopping carts with expensive outfits for invented functions. The group chat checked in regularly, but I never had any updates for them, and I knew they were busy enjoying their own lives – they didn't need some loser divorcée dragging them down. I slept poorly but napped often. I'd eat lightly during the day, then start a bolognese or fajitas or some other ambitious dinner concept, and give up and eat cereal while watching someone called Anders or Lars skulk around Helsinki or Stockholm, furious at their ex-wives for having

the audacity to be murdered. I found cooking for one exhausting and depressing.

I tried the mindfulness app but couldn't make it stick. I did not want to be grounded in this moment. This moment was miserable! I tried to reminisce about past triumphs – graduating from university, say, or giving a blow job once in the South of France – but my entire life had been witnessed by Jon. I had to go back to high school to avoid him, and those memories were boring. Almost nothing had happened to me before we'd known each other. Meeting him had felt like the most significant event in my life, and until a few weeks ago, every year that passed had only reinforced that this was true. *Now what?* I thought. There are only so many times a person can read 'One Art' by Elizabeth Bishop. It took three to four minutes, plus a few extra for crying. I'd do that and be back, instantly, to *now what?* Now what, indeed.

Along with Janet, Jon had taken most of the better items in our bar cart (to say nothing of the bar cart itself), so I'd make cocktails from Cointreau and lemon juice and soda water, eventually using regular water, eventually drinking straight Cointreau. Once the Cointreau kicked in, I'd be ravenous for whatever dinner I'd abandoned, and took to ordering something I called 'Night Burgers' from the only place that my delivery app offered at four a.m., a generic chain pub with a gigantic menu that included history's most middling hamburger. A Night Burger was exactly this item, plain, with a pickle and French fries. It was bland and stodgy and always arrived cold, but I did not want the food to be an experience. I wanted it to look and taste how I felt,

which was like nothing. I wanted a tepid meat puck, and I got one, often.

It was my first time, ever, living alone. Growing up with my parents, sister, two dogs, and a rotating series of doomed hamsters, our house was bustling. It was barely a transition to move to the din of university residence halls, where the boys wrenched the doors off stalls in the inexplicably co-ed bathrooms and rolled melted tubs of ice cream down the eleven-storey back staircase, staining it pink and shutting down half the hallway for a week. As soon as we could, Amirah and Lauren and I moved in together, watching reality television and getting briefly into day-weed and never ever cleaning the bathroom.

After graduation we ventured further into Toronto, and Emotional Lauren and I became the fifth and sixth residents of an enormous house in the west end, crammed with artists and baristas and grad students and – we found out after we moved in – one bat in the basement that someone's boyfriend's landlord had caught him keeping at his own place.

When Jon and I moved in together, it was the smallest number of people I'd ever lived with, and I loved it. I was twenty-three when we got our first apartment. Most of my peers were still in grubby shared houses (Emotional Lauren still had a bat in her basement). I felt impossibly adult. I liked coming home to one person – my person; liked making cupcakes at ten p.m.; liked putting on some weird

album of Jon's and vacuuming the rug so we could have sex on it. When I *was* in the house alone, if Jon was stuck at work or away with friends for the weekend, I savoured it as a treat, knowing he'd be home soon to disrupt the quiet or drag me out of the bath. After we got married, I sometimes felt it was a shame that I'd never get to experience living alone but concluded I wouldn't be very good at it. It seemed, so far, I had been right.

Still, there were a few benefits to my Personal Situation: I'd been given essentially unlimited bail privileges on account of it, and I exercised these with relish. I bailed on my own birthday, family events, coffee dates with colleagues and friends from high school I'd been meaning to catch up with for years. I attended only things I really wanted to, which meant I attended almost nothing, not even Lauren's Jimmy Buffett Bang-Bus Birthstravaganza. Lauren had been understanding. Emotional Lauren texted to say she'd added my name to the card: i copied your handwriting from that time we did MASH drunk ... it says you're going to have four husbands ... tho apparently your future car is a toilet :(. Part of me felt it was rude, avoidant maybe, to be ditching out on so much, but wasn't this the kind of thing women were supposed to be doing, saying no?

The Old Me might have worried this would make people hate me. In the past I was worried about basically everything, basically all the time. Now my constant, low-level anxiety was replaced by a feeling of dull invincibility I referred to as 'haha, so what'. Concerned you might be coming down with a cold? No illness could be worse

than this new, gaping emptiness at the core of your very being, haha. Feel like you said the wrong thing at a party? The person who promised, in front of everyone you know, to love you for the rest of your life didn't make it two years, so what! Missed a deadline for work? The thing is that life is actually a joke, and nothing is guaranteed to us, and anything you think *is* guaranteed will probably be taken from you unexpectedly, and also it seems like deep down you may be an unlovable shrew, which is probably a bigger problem than some late assignment – let's give that a big haha, so what!!

When we were married, Jon rarely stayed out late. On the few occasions he did, I would enjoy my evening until about two, then lie awake staring at the ceiling, thinking about all the things that could go wrong. What if the power went out, and I needed to know how to interact with that big box in the basement? Our back door was rickety and unreliable. No matter how carefully I closed the bolts, checked and double-checked that I'd done it, fear would keep me awake. I'd get up to redo it ten times in the night in case someone was about to break in and kill me. I didn't worry about that anymore. *Maybe someone will break in and kill me*, I'd think. *Perfect.*

To: j——@gmail.com
From: m——@gmail.com
Sent: 28 June, 1:12 a.m.

Hi Jon –

I know we're supposed to be 'giving each other space', and I get that, I'm only emailing because I spoke to Lauren's aunt's friend, who I maybe mentioned is a divorce lawyer ... it turns out to get a divorce, we need to prove we've been legally separated for a year, which means we can't file for one until next spring. There's also a bunch of other paperwork etc. that I'd hoped we could avoid since we don't, like, own anything of value, but apparently not, so there's a lot to do in the next few weeks/months, and you probably do have to email me back at some point.

I'm sorry if this email feels abrupt, or overly businesslike, but I think it's important to get the ball rolling, especially with this waiting period I didn't know about. This is, obviously, not the ideal situation for either of us, but I keep thinking about what you said when you moved out: I want us to do this the nicest way possible. I hope this email can count as an official declaration of our intention to divorce, a kind of start date for our year of separation ... weird, right? Life is so weird.

I love you, I'm sorry,
M

Sent from my iPhone

To: j——@gmail.com
From: m——@gmail.com
Sent: 28 June, 1:16 a.m.

Oh my god, I just realised I left the 'sent from my iPhone' thing on the bottom. I promise I took the time to actually compose this email on my computer, I just sent it from my phone because I was sitting on the toilet looking at it in my drafts and thought, 'you have to send it, right now, or you never will.' I'm really sorry and I hope you don't think I was leaving it in there as, like, a casual-guy power move. Same thing for telling you about the toilet, it's just where I was at the time. It's just the truth.

This has been one of the most difficult periods of my life, and I know it's hard for you too, and I just would hate to think that you think it's not a big deal for me. It is.

Sent from my iPhone

To: j——@gmail.com
From: m——@gmail.com
Sent: 28 June, 2:40 a.m.

Fuck. Sorry.

It was a real blow to learn you couldn't just *have* a divorce – there was a waiting period and many forms and some business involving tax returns to wade through first. Further blows from the same meeting included: finding out how much a lawyer cost, bringing a cup of cold water to my lips and missing, and having to show my bank balance to a woman who charged $215 an hour. I told the lawyer, a kind-faced, soft-spoken family friend of a friend called Lori, that I supposed Jon and I could use some of the money we'd been given as wedding presents to cover our various legal fees. She laughed – a short, sharp honk – then grew very serious: 'Ah, you're not joking.'

Lori opened one of several folders as a young woman wearing the kind of trousers that are begging to be called 'slacks' brought her a coffee. 'Thanks, Lindsey,' she said, taking a sip. Lindsey left, grabbing a few folders as she did. From my limited time at the offices of Janson Parker Stevenson, LLP, it seemed that the legal profession was essentially a very sophisticated folder management system. Lori's walls were lined with shelves displaying certificates

and leather-bound books and photographs of smiling children I took to be hers. I shifted in my chair, trying to appear competent and grown up and like I wasn't wearing a stretched-out tankini top as a bra.

'Well, I suppose that's one benefit of separating, what is it … two years? After the marriage? Less than, oh dear. Well, not to worry,' she said. 'You know, they say the average person files for divorce about two years after the first time they think about doing it. Sorry, I don't know why I said that.'

After the lawyer visit, I spoke to Merris about taking on some extra work. She promised to ask around, though demand for someone with my specific set of skills (reasonably proficient with JSTOR, the ability to tell the difference between a long *S* and minuscule *F*, almost nothing else) was not, shall we say, through the roof. I reminded her I was also good at making copies of things and tactfully telling undergraduates when it was clear that they had plagiarised their essays from the introductions of easily searchable books on the same subject, and she said she'd see what she could do.

I missed the occasional copywriting work Jon used to wrangle for me, coming up with slogans for running shoes and frozen pizzas and 'offering a woman's perspective' on fibre-packed weight loss cereals. Initially, I'd been annoyed to discover I was alright at this sort of thing, that it felt similar, somehow, to coming up with reasons anyone should look twice at a seventeenth-century play where all five senses went on trial after the concept of language challenged them to decide who was best. In many ways, it was easier to see the value in explaining to women aged thirty-

five to sixty-five that with Earth Eve's fibre-packed weight loss cereal, you'll be surprised what you *gain*.

At home alone I ordered Night Burgers, browsed rental listings and had nightmares about Jon's parents telling me I was a bad person before morphing into two girls I'd worked with at an ice-cream store the summer after ninth grade. Most days I felt like a wrung-out old dishcloth, but then out of nowhere a good day would take me by surprise. They were rare, but they happened. I would say I was operating at about 98.9% long, bad, lonely days, then once in a while, despite the restless sleep and all-beef diet and nights spent sitting directly in the glow of my phone, I would wake up and feel calm – like things would be okay, even if I didn't know how.

On these mornings I often became what Amirah had started to call 'dangerously reflective', stretching and putting lemon in hot water (to … alkalise … it?) and going on tearful, meditative walks. I'd been reading a lot of books I'd seen on stylish women's Instagrams, propped up in the sun next to a crystal. They were full of long, descriptive sentences and whimsical digressions about old movies I had never heard of. Normally I found these books a bit corny – all that vulnerability, all those florid descriptions of sunlight – but these days I couldn't get enough of them.

I would open one and put a flower on top of it, then take a picture and imagine changing everything about my personality and core friendship group to allow myself to post that image online. Then I would read something like 'You are not broken because someone tried to break you' and think, *wow, exactly*, despite not having even one single

life experience to relate to a statement like that. The books were very much the gateway to the creative efforts that followed, and to several other soft blunders besides.

I had become doggedly committed to 'taking my broken heart and turning it into art', mostly via the medium of collage, an activity these books tacitly encouraged. Suddenly all I wanted was to sit on my floor and cut out images about my feelings, to wear a nightgown that looked like a curtain and know things about attachment styles. To this end, I invited the group chat over for a 'solstice celebration', with promises of some kind of moon ceremony.

wasn't the solstice last week? wrote Emotional Lauren.

daughter of the witches they failed to burn alert!!! texted Amirah.

oh fuck off, said Emotional Lauren.

bring sage please, I wrote.

────────

When they arrived they found me rummaging through my spice drawer, pulling out anything green. 'Turns out smudging is cultural appropriation,' I said. I had found an article. 'Maybe we could use herbes de Provence?' It did not bundle well, so we rolled some of it in a paper towel and set it alight in a bowl on the kitchen table.

I sniffed the air. 'Smells like …'

'Chicken,' said Clive. 'Are we having chicken?'

I shook my head. We were having what we always had: a pile of assorted bits.

'Well,' said Lauren. 'Very powerful so far. Are we doing anything else? What does this ceremony involve?'

I hadn't really looked into it, so I improvised, suggesting we all think of something we wanted to let go of and then spit it into the bowl.

'Oh, I don't want to—' Amirah started, before Emotional Lauren stopped her. Amirah rolled her eyes and spat into the bowl. Dubious eye contact ricocheted through the group, but god bless them, they all did it. I closed my eyes and imagined all of it – my shame and sadness, a petty fantasy I'd had about one of Jon's female friends falling off her bike – rising up through my body, ready to be expelled. I worked my tongue around my mouth a few times, building an amount of spit that seemed like enough, then horked it into the bowl. I opened my eyes and confronted an unholy cocktail of singed rosemary, a rubber band, a smouldering paper towel and the saliva of five adults.

'Actually,' I said, 'I think maybe this is incredibly gross?'

My friends agreed. We doused the fire and cleaned the bowl thoroughly, and Emotional Lauren, the light mystic of the group, read everyone's tarot cards while Clive assembled and then took pictures of an enormous pile of snacks. Lauren cracked a bottle of Lambrusco and told us about a colleague who was crowdfunding to finance a photography series 'reclaiming the human ass', largely via photos of his own. I left the room to grab some ice, and when I came back Amirah had taken my spot on the couch. Without any other sitting furniture in the room, I curled up at her feet like Janet.

'Just take your nudes in your bedroom like the rest of us!' she screamed, then showed us a particularly impressive

one she'd sent Tom the other day, which she worried had been ruined by the presence of a half-empty soup bowl in the background. 'I don't want him to think I paused huffing some broccoli and cheddar to take a sexy picture for him,' she said, although that is exactly what she'd done.

We passed our phones around, sharing our favourite naked self-portraiture, reclaiming our human asses together. We all agreed nudes were getting more complicated as our twenties dwindled. Our poses were getting increasingly contorted as we tried to whittle and protrude the right things, no longer content to stand in front of a mirror and let the flash obscure our faces. It was increasingly appealing to leave the bra on.

'I know what you mean,' said Clive. 'The other day this guy asked for a pic, and I wanted to do something kind of artful or coy, but I was feeling crappy about my body and couldn't make it work, so I gave up and sent full hole.'

We consulted Lauren's colleague's crowdfunding page and had to admit the man knew his angles. I mentally bookmarked a lying down/side twist pretzel thing he was doing. Lauren said crowdfunding was a 'slippery slope', and that probably we as a species had experienced 'all the web series we could ever need about white people doing polyamory', and that if you weren't careful, someone you went to elementary school with would be asking you for $12 a month to make feminist watercolours. Emotional Lauren said she'd probably buy a feminist watercolour, then we all got distracted because someone we didn't like had posted a series of bizarre engagement photos on Instagram. A small fight erupted when Lauren pointed out that Amirah's Tom

posts were only a few degrees off the photo set we'd scrolled through, featuring the bride-to-be mostly submerged in a lake, her future husband wading in to rescue her, King Arthur in a polo shirt. After we'd all been unequivocally bitchy for an hour or so, I explained 'haha, so what' to the group, with an emphasis on how liberated I was feeling.

'I used to be so preoccupied with what I looked like or what people thought of me,' I said. 'But the other day, I went to a coffee shop in old pyjamas and last night's makeup, and when I ran into someone from work, I simply told them I was having a hard time. It was very freeing.' I wrapped a cheese cube in salami and popped it into my mouth. When nobody asked a follow-up question, I continued: 'It's good! It's like, I don't need to dig my own grave to know that ultimately, nothing is that important and we all die alone. I don't know why you guys are being so serious about this. I mean it in, like, a fun way.'

My friends looked more sceptical than they had about the spit potion, but I was undaunted. I told them the stakes of being alive had been pleasantly lowered, since nothing could be as disastrous as this breakup, and that I'd been sleeping better – in fact, sleeping often – and eating with less worry about things like nutritional value or whether I'd be exercising later.

I felt pleasantly disconnected from everything around me, as though observing life underwater, which allowed me to take my time before responding to stressors and to fret less about the things that were ultimately insignificant. I was sure this was the way forward and happy to have finally arrived here, even if I'd had to undergo a traumatic event to

do so. Everyone listened carefully, nodding like a group of NPR hosts. Lauren dipped an endive in yogurt, wiped the side of her mouth, and said politely, curiously, 'Isn't that, like, exactly how people describe depression?'

———

After they left, I piled the dishes in the sink alongside the ones from yesterday and the day before. The night had been mostly wonderful, and it was reassuring to have the house feel full again. I imagined the upstairs neighbours poking each other with excitement: *No Kate Bush tonight! And is that ... the laughter of others?* Still, I was frustrated by what Lauren had said about my new outlook. It didn't feel like depression. It felt like burrowing down in a positive way. The next day, I cleared out the self-help section of the used bookstore down the street, working my way through my purchases with a pen, underlining passages and annotating the margins with !!!s, ????s, and YOU DO NOT NEED TO ASK PERMISSIONs. Everything felt heightened: making tea was a ritual, the time I spent ignoring work emails was sacred, buying a garish lipstick I would never use was an important act of self-care.

Summer carried on. I worked from home and allowed myself to rest and tried almost aggressively to let the soft animal of my body love what it loved, which mostly at that point was potatoes. I spent distracted time with the self-help authors, agreeing furiously with whatever was in front of me and forgetting it moments later. I almost booked a spot on a ten-day silent retreat dozens of times. The collages

got weird, and I hung them up around my house, thinking, *this is good. I am building a temple to my grief.* And then thinking, *oh, for god's sake*, but leaving them there anyway. I subscribed to a lot of newsletters about feelings.

One day after some particularly intense decoupage, I looked down and noticed my hands. Noticing Things had become a major pastime of mine. I'd noticed, recently: that coffee was warm, that sunlight was bright, and that I felt sad. This morning, I noticed my hands and had a thought that had become increasingly frequent in recent years: *my mother was right.* This time, she was right about the hands themselves. They were exactly her hands. The brittle, nubby nails and the too-long-to-be-stubby, too-short-to-be-elegant length of the fingers, the soft knuckles and small palms.

My mother pointed this out often in my teen years, gasping and holding up her hand against mine. 'Look at that,' she'd say, as if suddenly remembering that this person in her kitchen was someone she'd made with her own body. 'There they are.'

I hadn't paid much attention to it. I was very busy deciding how to get my hands and the rest of me looking as terrible as possible, using Wite-Out as nail polish and scribbling absolute nonsense all over my arms and palms so that a boy who talked about pop punk too much might one day talk too much about pop punk to me. I hadn't paid enough attention to that or anything else my mom had said when I was young.

And so, that night, I wrote her an email. It was long and emotional and mostly about our hands. I told her I loved seeing mine and remembering they were hers too – that she

had made them and, with her own hands, had raised me and fed me and shaped me into a person. As I wrote it, I imagined her being moved by my honesty, my eloquence and gratitude. I pictured her finishing the email, taking a minute, and thinking, *you know, she was more difficult than her sister, but she turned out okay. Finally, I know for sure that she understands everything I've done for her.* I pictured her shedding a single tear. I pictured her looking up the word 'inchoate' in a dictionary. I meant everything I said in the email and took pains to express it clearly and with maximum emotional impact.

Maybe this was the hidden blessing of a breakup: not 'haha, so what', but a new tenderness, an opening up. An ability to say the things that hadn't been said but should have been. Maybe it was all worth it, the disappointment and heartbreak a crash course in sitting in my feelings, observing them without fear. As I'd recently read in a six-thousand-word advice column addressed to a terminally ill woman whose struggle with her impending fate I considered relevant to my current personal tumult, maybe I was sublime right now, walking in the moonlight of my glorious, complicated selfhood. Maybe I *was* a warrior. At the very least, I was a fucking *great* daughter. I pressed 'send' so full of love and positivity, I felt it must be seeping out of my pores. I breathed deeply and went to sleep, smiling and satisfied.

I woke the next morning to a text from my sister: mom says we have to check on you, apparently you're having some kind of breakdown?

Well-Meaning Conversations with Loved Ones, Truncated at the Exact Moment They Start to Bring Up Kintsugi

'I think the time apart will be good for you. You'll find your way back to each other. Nine years is a big investment! There was a reason you were together. And sometimes, something that's a little broken can be even more beautiful. Did you know in Japanese pottery there's this thing—'

'Sorry, but he can't get mad at you for being bitchy. He married you knowing you're a bitch. It would be so unfair to divorce you over it. And it's not official yet – legally speaking, you're still his bitch wife who he loves. He'll get over it. He'll get over it, and he'll come back, and you can figure out what to do with the posters or whatever, but eventually it'll make you guys so much stronger. After I had that thing with that guy in college, I thought Greg would never forgive me, but we worked through it, and now we only fight about it, like, once a year, maybe twice if we get really drunk. I don't even think I'd take it back. Going through all that made us as strong as we are now. We went to this exhibit at the AGO, and—'

'Have you thought about couples therapy? I know he can be difficult ... and don't take this the wrong way ... but I feel like being with you is probably not a cakewalk either. I mean that as a compliment, like you know what you want. I think if anything, I'd love to be more that way, but I also think it would drive Ade bananas and honestly might do

the same for me. I think you should call him. He might surprise you. The other day I went to this craft fair with my mom, and this woman selling these gorgeous earthenware centrepieces told us about—'

'He *still* hasn't answered your email? Men are trash. Every single man alive is a pile of actual trash. Why don't I set you up with someone? My cousin is single. He's got a decent job and he's a total sweetie, and the only downside is that he's definitely one of those white guys who's too obsessed with Japan. Always going on about … actually, you might find this interesting—'

'God, I had no idea it was so hard to get a divorce. When Sammy and I broke up she just, like, took her loom and was out of there. But I guess it gives you some time to get super-hot and show up to sign the papers like, *Sorry, who are you?* You should get some big earrings. Also remind me to send you a link to this video I saw somewhere, I'll have to find it. It's about the concept that you can embrace the cracks in things, like if you—'

'Man, sorry to hear that. I had no idea. I ran into him the other day. He looked pretty good, I'm sorry to say. He was with a wo— Hey, have you ever heard of k—'

In July the landlord started emailing. Someone in the building had told her Jon moved out, and she wanted to know if I would be changing the lease – for my own security, and also because the lease change fee was £70. I wondered if she was nervous about my ability to make rent. Our initial application had made us list our separate salaries in addition to our joint income total; maybe she had correctly intuited that Jon had shouldered more of our monthly living expenses, in accordance with how much more he earned. Now, *her* income was threatened by the presence of the weak link in one of her mid-tier one-bedrooms.

I logged in to my bank account: I had $200 and a credit card statement that was mostly burgers. Instead of emailing her back, I went online to homeware shops and clothing stores and little accessory boutiques I'd seen on Instagram, filling cart after cart, drinking wine and imagining the kind of life I'd lead if only I owned these items.

Sometimes I went practical, sometimes whimsical, sometimes extravagant. I'd conjure an important event – the

Oscars, a second wedding – and craft the perfect outfit or bundle of accessories to stand out in a way that ensured I fit in more than everyone else. I'd decide an Italian villa was in my future and design a bedroom for it in the sale section of Urban Outfitters, ducking past the 'vintage' items that threw back to my not-that-distant childhood in search of the perfect duvet to nap under while my focaccia rose in the other room. It was nice to imagine that owning the right nightdress could help, even if it would actually just put me in very stylish credit card debt. I only hit 'purchase' about 20% of the time, but still managed to rack up an impressive number of orders.

For instance: I bought a SAD lamp. I bought a posture-correcting harness. I bought a $113 candle, later returned. I bought new, humongous underwear. I bought a robe. I bought a set of watercolour paints, sat down with my pathetic little cup of water before realising I hadn't bought a brush. I bought a big, aggressive vibrator, then a less ambitious one. I bought dinner. I bought a $90 vial of acid to put on my face. I bought a sleep app. I bought plants. I bought a yoga mat, dumbbells, resistance bands. I bought an experimental nail polish. I bought Korean pimple patches in the shape of hearts. I bought a hair mask and a face mask and a hand mask. I bought little plastic bags to put on my feet and waited until the skin sloughed off. I hoped it would all be in one long, large chunk, like a snake moulting, but instead it was like walking around on two open shakers of processed parmesan cheese.

I bought a consultation with a psychic who spent thirty minutes drawing me a picture of a man: 'Is this person

meaningful to you?' It was not a good drawing; it felt impossible to say. I lied and said yes, he looked very meaningful. She said that was because he would be there when I died. I bought a beautiful, sculptural coffeemaker that took forever to complete its one job. I bought coffee in takeout cups from the café down the street while I waited for my expensive kitchen object to make more. I preferred the coffee from the café.

I bought wine. I bought a lavender 'sleep spray' for my pillows and pulse points. I bought a bikini wax, which bled lightly, looked smooth for three hours the next day, then erupted into an angry rash packed with future ingrown hairs. I bought a mineral sunscreen that didn't work. I bought some loose trousers I saw on Instagram. I bought the shirt to go with them. I bought extra storage in the Cloud. I bought a chipped cocktail shaker from Value Village and then a less chipped one I found when I went back the next week.

I bought an expensive dress online, realised the $350 I'd agreed to pay was a first instalment – that the store expected to receive three more – sent a panicked email, and got my money back. I bought a sleep tea and a laxative tea and a hormone-balancing tea. I bought a hundred books on being alone, cooking alone, inhabiting your body alone, and on exercise. I bought scarves for a future winter and hats for a dwindling summer and a set of cocktail glasses for a glamorous anniversary party I would never have.

When my credit card bill came, I returned almost everything, then cancelled the card and started looking, in earnest, for a new place to live. Everywhere was too expen-

sive and unpleasant to look at or think about. I made a few calls, responded to a few craigslist ads and Facebook posts. There was something wrong with everyone I spoke to – too cheerful, curt, young, old, too close to my own age and situation, too different from it – and every place I looked at – cramped, mouldy, too many roommates, not close enough to the subway, 'looked like the kind of place where a neighbour has drums'.

Ever ready for a project, Lauren forwarded me links with thoughtful notations (near me!; has cat!; owner sounds hot???), but I was uncompelled. I had envisioned some sunny, minimalist loft or verdant, divorcée-ready one-bedroom, but it was all crumbling 1960s houses with cement front yards and four 'happy, sociable graphic designers' living in three bedrooms and a den.

Lauren forced me to contact a few of these, but I found it impossible to explain who I was or what I was looking for to the friendly Christophers and Brianas and Evanys who emailed back asking about my 'vibe' and hygiene habits. What mattered to me? Was I messy, or had I just been messier than Jon, who was very tidy? Did I like to go out or prefer to stay in? Would I call myself a 'morning person'? Jon liked to sleep late, while I woke up most days at 8:15 no matter what I did.

Thinking outside of a comparative context was a challenge. I was less of a partier than Jon had been, but could I really call myself a homebody in my own right? In marriage I had traded in my essential traits for a series of comparisons: I was the Cranky One, the Bookish One, the One Who Cares If the Towels Are Damp. I wanted a place where

I could figure out who I might be next, but every potential landlord or roommate wanted to know About Me, now.

I tried my best: *I am an average-height, redheaded academic with anaemia. I'm halfway to being a vegetarian, on weekends. I'm left-handed and short-sighted. Technically speaking, I am an 'average-sized' woman – still, it is very difficult for me to buy trousers, like it seems impossibly hard, and I don't totally understand who trousers are for, if not average-sized people in general. I have no opinion on 'the outdoors'. My politics are leftist, which so far has mostly meant that I sign a lot of petitions and donate small amounts of money to people who are working harder than me at solving the Problems or go to protests and attempt to stand in solidarity with people the Problems are happening to. I go to one festival a year despite not liking live music. I'm not sure I'm bisexual enough to 'count'. I'm an ENFJ or an INFJ or an ENFP – I have taken the test many times. I read a lot of books and own a number of tote bags that makes that clear. I cycle. I'm the baby of my family (not by birth order, but you know). I'm jealous of people in more useful careers, even though useful careers seem like a lot more work. I think most intelligent people are a little bit mean, and all nice people are a little bit stupid. I wish I didn't think that. I'm working on not thinking that. I have bad posture and good blood pressure. I'm heartbroken.*

I didn't get a lot of responses and didn't open the ones I did. I went to exactly one viewing, cold, for a house three doors down from me. An older man lived there – after his wife had died the previous winter, he'd found himself with too much space and converted a back annex of his home into a 'junior one-bedroom, with all the modern conveniences'.

At $1,000 per month, it was the only close to affordable place I'd seen where I could live alone in the neighbourhood of my choosing. In the pictures it was incredibly clean, although a single, healthy pothos plant was doing a lot of work to give a raised platform bed over a hotplate and dorm fridge a homey atmosphere. It wasn't bad, exactly – by the standards of Toronto rental listings it was a real find – but there was no denying that it looked like the second-nicest room in a very humane Scandinavian prison.

When I got there, I realised the older man expected us to share a bathroom.

'I'm very respectful,' he said with a laugh, 'but if you come in without knocking, you're responsible for anything you see!'

I told the group chat this experience had put me off house hunting, that it might make sense to wait things out a little bit. Maybe I could Airbnb my place on weekends, staying on friends' couches while a wealthy couple I didn't know fought or fucked in my bedroom. Maybe I could get another job. Maybe my parents would help me out. Mostly, I could not imagine leaving, not yet. We'd properly decorated the living room this year, had recently risked our deposit to put three nails in a wall. Two of these were now bare, sticking out by a window like metal indictments. I had made a promise to this place. Maybe I couldn't keep all my promises, but I would try to keep this one.

I logged back in to my bank account and gave my landlord seventy of my remaining dollars. She wrote back confirming receipt of payment, adding: Sorry to hear you're going through a tough time. It's always darkest

before the dawn. :) If you meet someone new and want to add another person to the lease, a new $70 charge will apply.

REALLY GOOD, ACTUALLY

To: CustServ@Treatza.com
From: m——@gmail.com
Sent: 30 July, 4:12 a.m.

To Whom It May Concern,

I am writing to complain about your phone-first policy, which your driver, Erik, assures me is standard across all Treatza deliveries. As you can probably see on my customer profile, I have been especially active on your app recently. I just looked, and I've placed 15 orders over the last 20 days, so I'm in a particularly strong position, I think, to deliver some constructive criticism.

Basically, it's really, really important that you tell people you're going to call them before you even try ringing the doorbell. I live on the ground floor of my apartment building, so I can usually see and hear when someone arrives. I go outside, collect my food, and come back in without the bell or my phone ever ringing. As I say, I've done this almost every day for the past three weeks without incident.

Tonight, after placing my order, I got in the shower. I don't know why or how he was so fast, but Erik must have arrived within minutes of me turning on the taps. I didn't hear anyone on the landing, because of the shower, and Erik didn't ring the bell, knock, call out, or text. What he did do was call my ex-husband four times and leave three voicemails.

I'm sure I don't need to explain why this was less than ideal, but unfortunately that was not the end of it. When I called my ex-husband to apologise, he told me it was not a big deal to receive four calls from a delivery driver at 4 a.m. because he was at this point 'pretty used to it', and the only thing he found disturbing was the volume of my beef consumption. Erik had not been the first driver to call before trying the doorbell. In fact, it turns out that *every single delivery person who has been to my home since our breakup has called my ex's number before coming to the door.* He says one of them even told him it was 'always burgers', which feels grossly unprofessional. Surely there is some kind of confidentiality clause in your employee contract? My deliveries are none of his or anyone else's business!!!!

I ask that you amend the phone-first policy (or at least make it VERY CLEAR in the app), remove the number 647-xxx-xxxx from my user profile, and credit my account $15, in light of emotional damages. Also, if there's any way to add a tip to Erik's bill now, I would like to do so. I didn't do it at the time, because I was so flustered and upset in the moment, and I really regret it. I know the gig economy is super precarious and you guys refuse to let your workers unionise, which in the long run is probably a way bigger deal than this burger mishap, plus he's a good guy. Very kind eyes.

Thank you for your time. And to be clear, my dog is on a special diet where he can only eat ground beef, so that's what all the burgers are for.

Margaret

To: CustServ@Treatza.com
From: m——@gmail.com
Sent: 30 July, 4:25 a.m.

P.S. The vet said my dog has to eat at very specific times of night, which is why the orders are all so late. It's a bit inconvenient, but I am a very devoted dog parent.

To: CustServ@Treatza.com
From: m——@gmail.com
Sent: 30 July, 4:37 a.m.

Look, I thought about it some more, and I really shouldn't have been in touch. Please don't get Erik in trouble over this, he doesn't deserve that. I only emailed because I wanted to make sure other people weren't affected by this policy, which, for the reasons outlined above, has the potential to hurt a lot of people, or at least really ruin their day. I just care a lot (maybe too much, haha!) about my dog's well-being and want to do right by Fozz (a Pekingese-Schnauzer mix I rescued from Puerto Rico through a charity). Anyway, I'm sorry to bother you. Please use my $15 credit to tip Erik, and we'll call it a day.

Thanks,
M

The grocery store was a minefield. So was my favourite coffee shop, local subway station, and the bar I'd spent every birthday in since turning twenty-three. Toronto is too small a city to get divorced in, really. My recommendation, if you live in Toronto and your marriage is not working, is to stick it out or move away.

At first I avoided Jon (or the potential of him) by staying inside, but lately I had begun to venture out, taking my heart in my hands each time. Once, thinking I saw him, I ducked behind a bush like the heroine of a screwball comedy, if heroines of screwball comedies wore old camp sweatpants with the words AUG '02 – WE FREAKY across the butt. It was hard to know if I was seeing Jon everywhere because I missed him, my subconscious longing morphing the faces around me, or because every second man between Ossington and Dovercourt was an average-height white guy with a dark brown beard.

Still, the grocery store loomed largest in those early months, it being the most necessary to visit and often the only outdoor activity in my day. Sometimes I would

shower, primping in the mirror as if the midsized grocery chain a block from my house were a new lover. (Obviously, the idea of an actual new lover was out of the question, I was simply too old and disgusting and would never feel the touch of another or love again. I would die alone, probably sooner than expected, maybe tomorrow.) Other times I looked terrible and that was fine.

The five-minute walk down my quiet, tree-lined street felt long and slow and exposed. Couples were an affront, single people with their shit together equally so. I walked with a bereaved shuffle, blinking at the brightness of the sun, sweating in my leisurewear, and hoping not to run into anyone I knew. I always, always ran into someone I knew.

It's actually very hard to live in the west end of Toronto and escape a daily unplanned social encounter, harder still to avoid someone you're hoping not to see. I ran into students, relatives, elementary school classmates, and acquaintances from three jobs ago, each time doing grim mental equations regarding whether they knew and didn't care, knew and did care, didn't know and would like to, or didn't know and wouldn't care to find out.

All options were bad. If they did know, I had to buckle up for Soft Eyes, a concerned tilt of the head, and a drawn-out 'How you holding up?' Their compassion felt terrible. The more maternal women and optimistically horny men would reach out for a shoulder rub, patting me like a child who'd done a bad job at kickball, instead of a woman whose plan for her life had fallen apart one day over mediocre pad thai. If they didn't know they would ask after Jon, and I

would have to say, in a voice I hoped sounded wise and resigned and maybe a little European, that we were 'taking some time apart'.

This was where I felt older divorcées had a competitive edge. It was hard to seem worldly and accepting when so little had happened to make me that way. I wanted to project the image of a together, independent woman, puffing a cigarette like, *Ah, life!* and then doing something cool like blowing a smoke ring or ashing without making a mess everywhere. Saying 'I am getting a divorce' made me feel like a child clomping around in enormous shoes, my mother's lipstick all over my face. I had been in love only once before meeting Jon. I'd legitimately assumed he and I would be together forever. Every encounter revealed my naïveté, put me in a pillory with a sign next to it: BELIEVED FULLY IN ROMANTIC LOVE AND THE POSSIBILITY OF ETERNAL COMMITMENT (IN THIS DAY AND AGE!!).

My first real run-in came a few weeks after Jon moved out. It was with an acquaintance called Gaby, who worked at an art gallery and dressed in such a way that if you saw her on the street you'd be like, *I bet that girl works at an art gallery*, which I think was how she liked it. I found her in the condiments aisle comparing two identical jars of tahini. She looked up while I was trying to figure out how to escape, a shared flash of *god, I wish I hadn't made eye contact* passing between us as we both smiled and started the high-pitched, drawn-out 'hiiiiiiis' of the reluctantly encountered.

When I asked how it was going, she said, 'Oh, you know … terrible. Haha!' I sighed in a way I hoped sounded

empathetic, and for a moment I wasn't sure I'd tell her. She hadn't asked, and for a real, full second, I lived in the gentle delusion that I was a woman capable of not saying, in one breath, without stopping, all of the following: 'Ohmy husbandandIaretakingsometimeapartandIdothinkit'sfor thebestbutit'shard,harderthanIexpected,actually,andI justfeellikeabitofafailureandliketheyoungestpersonto evergetdivorced,whodoesthatattwentyeight,youknow,like mostofmyclosefriendsarentevenmarried,andhereIamracking updivorcebillsandputtingonmakeupincaseIrunintothe formerloveofmylifeinthecerealaisle,hahahaha,buthonestly it'stheworstI'veeverfelt.' I paused, waiting for Gaby to reply with a comforting platitude, something like 'Change is hard,' or 'Hopefully it's for the best,' or 'It will get better in time.' She looked at me with pity, but something else too, before putting both tahini jars back on the shelf and saying briskly:

'Right. Well, my dad's dying! So, you know, everything sucks for everybody.' As she turned away, I noticed how red her eyes were.

Later I looked Gaby up on Facebook and sent her a message, saying I was sorry I'd been so thoughtless, so wrapped up in my non-tragedy tragedy, that things felt very large at the moment, even though I knew, somewhere, that they weren't, and she'd reminded me of that, and if I'd seemed out of sorts it was just that City Market was Jon's and my classic spot to pick up the fancier bits we couldn't get at FreshCo, and every time I went in there I found myself thinking, *in another world, would we still be here, considering impulse-splurging on fresh tagliatelle?* If it makes

you feel better, I wrote, I realised when I got home that I'd bought a bunch of food I didn't want to eat.

Although I hated eggplant, Jon was obsessed with it, and now I had two gorgeous, disgusting nightshade vegetables sitting in my fridge, mocking me for prioritising the dietary preferences of a man who did not love me anymore. If she wanted some free eggplant or a big bundle of cilantro (another Jon favourite I detested), she knew where to find me.

She didn't write back. The message rested, 'seen', under the last message I'd sent her, seven years earlier: SUCH a fun birthday, thanks so much for the invite, gotta do it again soon girlie! I didn't remember the birthday, or a version of myself that used the word 'girlie', but I guess both things had happened at some point. A few weeks later I saw on Instagram that her dad had passed away. Her post said it was pancreatic cancer and that he'd been her best friend, forever Scrabble partner, and biggest champion. I started ordering my groceries online.

———

It was hardest to run into Jon's friends. They knew the best bits of what I was missing. Still had access to it, even: Jon's sense of humour; his warm, woody smell; the way he rubbed your feet when you sat down next to him. (He probably wasn't rubbing the feet of his friends in my absence, but my arches hurt like hell, and when I figured out why – that he'd been rubbing them probably three times a week for my entire adult life – I burst into tears.)

Plus, I assumed his friends all hated my guts. Some of them hadn't cared much about me to begin with; others I mourned alongside everything else, one more part of the life I'd counted on now dissolved. There is a safe, easy intimacy between a woman and her male partner's friends, or there can be. Before we moved in together, Jon had a number of goofy roommates I'd particularly loved, with whom it was easy to be the kid sister, the lone civilising influence, the person playing Mario Kart with a generous handicap.

Once, I'd arrived at Jon's while he was still in class and found them all playing some cowboy video game; they were chasing down a sheriff who'd bountied them, stealing gold and cattle as they went. Still, they said, the world was so well designed, you could do anything: shoot your father, catch fish in a stream with your hands, fall in love. They handed over the controls, and I got stoned and spent an hour picking flowers in a field to give to my horse. It was how I imagined it might feel to have brothers.

The best of all these not-quite-siblings had been Calvin. Essentially a large Labradoodle turned human, Calvin was a friendly, unmotivated man with curly blond hair and an easy smile. He had been Jon's roommate in the early years of university, the two of them sharing a legendarily gross basement off King Street that the sun did not touch, where they pioneered dishes like 'curry pizza' (exactly what it sounds like), 'all-day egg buffet' (scrambled for breakfast, boiled for lunch, fried for dinner) and 'dumpling surprise' (a frying pan full of dumplings, with a few pierogis thrown in 'to keep us on our toes').

Jon and Calvin were always having fun in ways that I thought were stupid and was secretly desperate to be a part of: hotboxing motorcycle helmets and shooting pellet guns at each other in armour made of stuff they'd found, or, in later years, an actual suit of armour Jon had stolen from the set of a pasta sauce commercial. They loved each other and seemed proud of their ability to say so, making showy displays of being the kind of men who could hug easily and support each other emotionally, but also beat each other up in a game of 'full-contact croquet' or start a metal band called Gorgo's Ass.

In our third year they moved above ground, somewhere not much better. Jon and I were an established couple by then, so we spent a lot of time lounging around their crumbling Kensington Market town house, eating cereal and skipping all our morning classes. We had always been wryly amused to meet whatever beautiful woman had come home with Calvin after his serving job at an upscale restaurant in the Financial District. Some made repeat appearances, but not many. None seemed to mind, they were just happy to be there, eating toaster hash browns in an unwashed kitchen with a man who called all women 'bud' so he'd never get caught having forgotten their name. One summer he time-shared three girlfriends who all knew about each other, dating them on rotating nights. The entire experiment culminated in a debauched group trip to Port Hope, after which none of them spoke again. All of this is, I guess, a long way to say that Calvin, famously, fucked.

Which somehow made it extra surprising to find him standing inside the studio where I had begun attending a

restorative yoga class since learning by happy accident that it was basically structured lying down. After a few months of lying prone in my bed, I wanted to get out there and lie prone somewhere else. I was grabbing a few more bolsters than I needed, feeling like this class might be one of the ones where I napped, or maybe cried lightly with a lavender pillow over my eyes, when there was Calvin, wearing flimsy athletic shorts and a T-shirt from something called GUY FIERI'S DINERS, DRIVE-INS, AND DAVES.

'Bachelor party,' he explained. 'My cousin Dave. Kind of a lame guy, but honestly? Killer weekend.'

I laughed, slipping for a moment into an old way of being, when I could respond casually to a friend of Jon's and not attempt to project *doing great, thanks!!* with every cell in my body. I straightened my posture and instinctively wiped the area under my eyes. No black flecks – good. Calvin explained he was here because of a snowboarding injury and asked if I was 'surviving', which I'm sure he meant as a kindness, but the gentleness of his tone made me feel caught out and embarrassed, the neighbourhood sad sack. I wondered what Jon had told him.

The class was as quiet and uneventful as it always was, led by a gorgeous pregnant woman whose balayage was the colour of the oat milk lattes she drank in the foyer before class, and attended mostly by senior citizens and women who had visibly taken at least one aerial hooping class. And this time there was Calvin, twisting into lightly stretched positions, making forts out of bolsters and blocks and large cloth straps on the mat next to mine. Around the support-ive bridge portion, I got the sense he was sneaking looks at

me. Something had shifted the way I felt in my compression leggings and the too-tight sports bra I'd had since high school. I kept tucking unruly bits of back fat into the band, trying to keep everything sleek. I made a big show of rolling up vertebrae by vertebrae, and the teacher complimented the depth of my sleeping pigeon, something that had never happened in my lengthy but intermittent yoga career.

It was exciting to be noticed, I thought, to notice someone noticing me … it *was* exciting, until I remembered this was not an original thought of mine, but a lyric from a song about 'dangerous girls' that played on every dance floor I was part of, every year of university. Realising this, I felt old and tired – a divorcée in yoga pants lusting after some guy with a moustache because it seemed like maybe he was checking me out. Pathetic.

After class, Calvin stood in line with me while I got a green tea and kept walking alongside as I turned up the street in the direction of home. I asked if he still lived in his old spot, and he said that he did, but on his own now, and added that he had 'really done the place up', with a projector for movies and a rug and everything.

'You guys should come see it,' Calvin said. 'Fuck, sorry.'

I told him it was alright; I made the same mistake all the time. 'I hadn't even realised I'd become a "we" person,' I said. 'Not sure which is more embarrassing, using it during the relationship or using it after the relationship is over.'

'Probably after,' he said, completely earnest.

I sat on my front steps and asked Calvin the question I'd been strenuously avoiding since the instant I saw him.

'Oh … yeah, I mean, he's been down,' he said, weirdly bashful. 'We haven't exactly gotten into it, but, uh, he's smoking, I would say, more weed than usual, although I think he's been seeing s— I probably shouldn't get into it.'

I agreed that he probably shouldn't, though didn't mention that he probably shouldn't have been outside my house in the first place. It was nice to talk to him; it felt familiar, like good times past, but the change in my circumstances also hung between us. Being alone – even single – felt, for the first time, intriguing.

He came inside, and we drank the beers that had been coming since we'd first encountered each other, sitting too close together on the couch and laughing about cottage weekends and house parties gone by, his sex life (robust) and mine (nonexistent, doomed). I confessed I'd been staying up too late and crying myself to sleep like a jilted woman in a film. Calvin said it would all work out eventually. He really seemed to believe it, and I wondered, aloud, if maybe it would. Breaks could be healing. People did that, separated and returned to each other. You sometimes heard about couples, apart for years, remarrying decades later. Calvin let out a loud, amicable laugh:

'Oh my god, that's not what I meant at *all*,' he said. He laughed harder. 'Are you kidding?! That guy is *never* coming back. You guys are OVER. I meant, like, you'll both move on with your lives. Oh my god. Imagine!'

I realised as he said it that of course this was true, and of course at that moment he leaned in to kiss me. I let him, for a few seconds, enjoying the novelty of this new mouth, its sugary, beer-inflected breath and bizarrely solid tongue.

Having someone casually name what was happening, without pity or reverence, was a foreign feeling too. My marriage was over! That didn't have to be bad! It could even be funny! At least, it could be okay.

I stopped the kissing almost immediately. Sleeping with the man who had read Neruda at our wedding seemed like it would be *very* satisfying in a way that felt vulgar and dangerous, but it was certainly not the mature way of doing things. I imagined Lauren making a pass at Jon and felt my throat constrict. If I was going to move on, it couldn't be with Calvin, and not only because an ex of his had told me he gave her 'every strain' of HPV. I hadn't spent enough time thinking about how to be with someone new. (And, although it was not a key factor in my decision, it occurred to me that I hadn't trimmed my pubes since April.)

'I think, probably not …' I said, sinking back into my corner of the couch. Calvin was so undaunted by the rejection I felt like maybe I'd imagined his attempt. The mood in the room didn't even shift.

'Weed?' he asked, traipsing over to the stove and lighting a joint before I'd even said yes.

We smoked and drank until late in the evening. I played him a recording of my sessions with the psychic, and he swore the man she'd drawn looked like his uncle. We ordered a pizza and showed each other important YouTube videos: a clip from a documentary where a woman has sex with the Eiffel Tower (me) and an eleven-minute supercut of Jason Derulo singing his own name (him). Sometime after midnight, I asked him to sleep over.

'I can't stress how non-sexually I mean this,' I said. 'But it's been nice having you in the house and I'd like it if you stayed.'

Calvin agreed, with one condition.

Later, when I was taking him through each step of my skincare routine, I asked if this was his regular move with women. 'Oh, definitely,' he said. 'Doesn't it make me seem sensitive?'

We double cleansed and applied an acid, serum, and night cream. It was the first time I'd done my full skincare routine since Jon had left. I fell asleep in my pyjamas, a foot away from Calvin in his boxers and T-shirt, Guy Fieri smiling out at me over the rim of his little shades.

I woke up alone and glowing.

A Fantasy

I am at a karaoke bar, and I look amazing. Better than normal, but in a casual way, like I just got a haircut that affected my whole body. The bar is packed, and although I am the only person singing, everyone is on board with that and thinks it's fun. In fact, I am taking requests.

The outfit I'm wearing is casual but looks special, like it's not sparkling but I am, like 'wearing sequins' is a vibe and I'm dressed head to toe in that vibe exactly. I am carrying myself with the easy confidence of a woman who both has a tax-free savings account and understands how one works. I sound great.

All the songs I'm singing are about heartbreak, and the raw emotion of my recent experience informs each number. People are so moved – some of them are weeping. Much of the audience is made up of enthralled strangers, all of whom find me mysterious and alluring. The friends I came with are dumbstruck. No one can believe that I've been hiding this voice, that I've been so humble about it.

'We thought all her grief would be for nothing,' one whispers to another. 'But look what she's done with it. She's like Nora Ephron, if Nora Ephron had the voice of Adele.'

Onstage, the pianist (there's a band) gives me a little wink. A stranger leans over to my friends, 'Sorry, do you know her?'

They beam. 'We do.'

Everyone is smoking indoors, and it feels glamorous instead of like one of those old-man bars where the lights are always on full blast and someone's chalking a pool cue

for much too long while impossibly aged men read out-of-date newspapers and swear in Portuguese.

'What's cool about Maggie,' a friend tells a stranger, 'is that she's divorced, but in like, a really fun way.'

'Divorced?' the stranger says. 'So young? That *is* fun. Good for her.'

Suddenly, from somewhere: nuggets.

Women should not be out here promising to buy the flowers themselves. I learned this the hard way, having woken up absolutely determined to do something thoughtful for my friends, in recognition of the food they'd cooked, the pep talks they'd given, and the maudlin slideshows of Janet pics they'd sat through since Jon's official move out two months ago. They had better things to do – family gatherings, protests for or against various causes, brunches hosted by drag queens – and yet they'd rallied, taking me to the park to drink rosé, sending texts like plz shower ... you can be depressed AND smell good, and even coaxing me out one night in August for a belated birthday celebration. It was time to repay their kindness (and, I thought, to build up further goodwill, since I was not done wallowing and would probably need to be babied for another month or so).

Lately I had been trying to lean into my little errands, framing everyday tasks as reprieves from sitting around thinking about my breakup. At the flower shop, this was not possible. The place was a temple to romantic love, full of thoughtful gifts, heart-shaped stationery, and balloons

reading UR THE 1. The unexpected kiss from Calvin had bolstered my romantic self-esteem for a week or two, leading to a few late-night DMs to people I knew at university and one spectacularly misjudged smile at a pretty barista. But I flirted like a baby deer learning to walk – falteringly, without any clear direction – and when my first efforts went unrewarded, I gave up. Now I was back to my resting state: assuming I would be alone forever.

I stood behind some pampas grass and watched a wave of suitors consider tasteful potted plants, select arrangements, furrow their brows over the right message for the flimsy free card. It struck me that I was buying my loner's bouquets at the same place my former husband had frequented for other flower occasions: Valentine's Day, our anniversary, my birthday, a fight. The morning I turned twenty-five, he'd woken me up with the same number of bright, hopeful daisies.

I shook off the image and moved away from a shelf of cutesy picture frames. I was not interested in preserving these thoughts 'in the amber of my memory' or anywhere else. Behind the counter, a middle-aged man with rolled-up sleeves and an apron stretched across a friendly, daddish paunch was fussing over an explosion of orange and yellow ranunculus. The store's website had said small arrangements were $49 each, which was more than I was looking to spend, so I approached the man and asked if they offered discounts on bulk orders.

'Oh, absolutely,' he said. 'We do lots of corporate work. Above fifty units and we throw in a few fully free arrangements.'

'Great,' I said. 'Good to know.'

The man cocked his head to the side, presumably waiting for me to place a large order on behalf of my company. Inoffensive jazz tinkled from the store's speakers as I tried to think of something to say.

'I'm going to look around for a bit,' I offered, unconvincingly fingering a monstera leaf. The florist maintained his cheerful demeanour. I could tell he saw he was losing the sale, or perhaps that the sale had never been there to begin with. He gave me a resigned smile and went back to his bouquet.

Maybe I didn't need to buy my friends anything. After all, I had been there for them, too: Lauren once had a breakup so bad we got in her car and drove to Montreal that same day; Jon and I provided a couch for Amirah during her final fight with the med student; it was me who nursed Clive back to health after a summer romance flew back to Brazil without warning; Emotional Lauren had never broken up with anyone, but was constantly having some minor meltdown in the bathrooms at work, and as the least regularly employed person in the group chat, I often fielded these as well.

I told myself they had just been doing what friends did, that maybe it was even my turn to become a kind of emotional labour vacuum, sucking up whatever they had to give. But I knew this was bullshit – and further, that it was not only the group chat who had gone above and beyond. My parents and sister deserved flowers too. And Merris, and my landlady, and the barista who'd let me down gently, and the upstairs neighbour who'd said, 'It'll get better,' so

quietly, almost under her breath, one morning as we passed in the hall. The divorce had made me so beholden to others, I would have to bankrupt myself at this florist. I was going to be here every week.

'We have some tulips at the front,' the man said, scratching his bald head almost bashfully. 'If that's more what you're looking for?'

I wandered to the front of the store, a little bell above the door clanging as I opened it. Outside, the air was hot and the patios were full, and that guy who hangs around downtown dressed like Spider-Man was haranguing people from his skateboard. The tulips were plentiful and vibrant and, crucially, $10 per bunch. As the florist wrapped them up – two purple, one pink – I expressed my gratitude by promising to leave an incredible online review for his establishment.

'Do what you like,' he said. 'I'm just an employee.'

'I'll mention you in the review,' I said. 'Superlative city.'

'Very generous,' said the man, a hint of something other than warmth in his voice. He handed me the tulips, wrapped in a crinkled sheet of brown paper. 'Have a lovely day.'

I strolled home and put the flowers on the kitchen table, dividing the bunches into six mixed bouquets, four for the group chat and two for whoever did the next kind thing. I considered the dishes in the sink, but the pile was enormous and there was a threatening crust on one of them, so I sat down and opened my laptop.

I was still working mostly from bed, which was isolating and surely doing something appalling to my spine, but I

could not go back to the office until I looked and felt better. All the burgers and liqueurs and late-night crime shows had left me bloated and pimply, my skin a blur of greys and pinks and yellows.

A few weeks ago, I had posted on our department's virtual message board that I was looking for a new place to live, and Jiro, a pretentiously dapper professor in his forties, sent me a link to a palatial two-bedroom it turned out he not only owned, but rented to others for profit. It was wildly out of my price range, and the idea of my rent cheques directly funding Jiro's pocket square collection made me want to hurl. I accepted the viewing he offered anyway, thinking it might send a message to my colleagues that I was doing alright.

'Are you okay?' Jiro asked as soon as he saw me. 'Seriously, you look *wiped*.'

He showed me around his income property, pointing out its wood floors and big windows, the charming if nonfunctional fireplaces. I pretended to appraise it all and said I would let him know. At the door, Jiro rested both hands on my shoulders and told me 'no good marriage ever ended in divorce', which I found somewhat presumptuous; this was our first ever non-work interaction, and he had called me 'Magda' at the start of it. As I waited for the streetcar, I wondered whether he was right – if I'd had a bad marriage – or if Jiro was just kind of a dick.

I settled on the latter. If he was so rich, why didn't he give me a discount on his giant apartment, or better yet, let me live in it for free? I wouldn't need it long, and that type of thing was always happening to wan, melancholy women

in the novels I read on vacation. Now that I was down and out, weren't Jiro and his wife supposed to invite me into their summer house – and, eventually, their marriage? They could at least offer up a gorgeous, unused loft in New York for a couple of weeks!

I explained this to Clive when I went by his place to drop off the tulips, the second and last of my floral delivery stops after I'd called from outside Lauren's house and discovered she and Amirah were with him.

'Don't even think about it,' he said, showily eyeing up his own loft apartment, purchased years ago after the death of a childless great-aunt. It was small and charming, with exposed beams, built-in shelves, and one big, south-facing window in the mint-green kitchen. The rest of us were committed renters, so we treated Clive's spot, with its tiny balcony and deposit-free interior, as a kind of clubhouse – our shared home. We had spent many Sunday evenings like this one, clustered on his sofa with snacks or foot masks or six bottles of wine and a movie.

'You're so lucky you own this place,' I said, leaning back on some vaguely nautical throw pillows. Lauren took my hand and placed it on her head, a gesture I knew well. I put my drink on the coffee table and started separating her hair into sections for French braids.

'I'm lucky the rest of my cousins are so garbage,' said Clive, kicking Amirah's legs off him and standing up author-itatively, a man with a plan, even when the plan was vodka tonics. 'Thanks, Aunt Grace! Eat a dick, Jordan and Luke!'

Amirah had spent the entire evening stretched across us on the couch, distracted by a text-based argument with

Tom about a dinner reservation he had forgotten to reschedule.

'It's like he doesn't want me to nag him,' she said. 'And then when I don't ...'

'You have to eat at a different restaurant?' said Lauren. '*Nightmare.*'

'Exactly, thank you,' said Amirah. Then, 'Oh, fuck off,' when she realised Lauren was mocking her. 'I'm meeting his parents, okay? I'm nervous.'

Amirah had nothing to worry about. She was universally adored by parents, still on holiday card terms with several exes' families. It was rare for her to fret like this, another of many recent signs she was starting to consider Tom a serious romantic partner rather than a mere boyfriend.

'Do you think it's too soon?' she asked.

Clive shrugged, emerging from the recesses of his fridge with three limes. 'Famously, I either want to meet your grandma on the second date or do not bother with last names.'

Lauren nodded knowingly. 'Can't help you,' she said. 'The apps have destroyed my idea of what's normal. I had to break it off with that guy I was seeing – remember he said he was agoraphobic, so we always had to meet at his house? Turns out he's totally fine, he just doesn't like coming to the west end.'

'Holy shit,' I said.

'Stealing that,' said Clive.

Lauren got up to examine her braids in the mirror. 'Not your best work, no offence,' she said.

Amirah threw her phone into some pillows and let out an anguished sound. 'What do I dooooooooo?' she wailed, falling onto the couch and burying her face in my shoulder.

I said I wasn't the right person to ask; at the rate I was speeding through rites of passage, I would shortly be retiring, then enjoying some time in a seniors' facility before my funeral at forty. Clive snorted as he plopped a tray of chilled glasses on his coffee table.

'Oh, whatever,' said Lauren, carefully undoing her braids. 'It's weirder to be married young than it is to be divorced. Before when we went out I'd have to be like, "This is my friend, Someone's Wife." Now you're like, reset.'

I told them I wished I were a widow. 'I feel like when you get a divorce, everyone's wondering how you ruined it all, what made you so unbearable to be with. If your husband dies, at least people feel bad for you.'

Amirah perked up at this, perhaps realising she had been disengaged from a crucial support moment and seeing an opportunity to get back in the fray. She leaned forward to soothingly pat my head and looked at me very earnestly.

'Oh, babe, do *not* worry,' she said. 'People feel very bad for you.'

Unanswered Texts, 6–16 August

hey, I've got some mail of yours. do you want me to send it to your new place? hope all's well over there.

did you get my email? we still have to settle on a date of separation ...

hey, do you know what shoegaze is?

just saw eli from your work, i think. could also have just been ... a guy haha

sorry to bug, but I really think we need to discuss next steps and get the ball rolling with the legal stuff. how is janet doing? hope you're both well.

it's your sister's birthday today, fyi! i'm sure you don't need me to remind you, but in case you did need me to remind you: it is.

saw that pottery barn spot you wrote ... the actress they cast is like fourteen and her husband's fifty, but it's really good otherwise!! great job :)

haven't heard from you in a while ... thought i'd check in about your mail and the cat and the separation date, blah blah. let me know when you get a sec! hope you're well!

hey, did you scrub your instagram? i accidentally saw it when i was trying to log out of janet's account and saw you deleted everything ... there's like four pictures of food and nothing else. is everything ok? hope you're well xo

????

...

please, jon, i really don't want to send one of those long, deranged block-of-text messages.

Getting back to me about our cat is not that much to ask. And I'm going to start looking for new apartments soon, and eventually I'll move, and your mail will be going to a house where strangers live. Also since when do you subscribe to Architectural Digest? It is really painful to keep having stuff with your name on it show up at the door. It sucks, honestly. And by not getting back to me, you're making it worse. I don't want us to be one of those couples who has to hate each other to split up properly, but you're being selfish and honestly a bit cruel. I can't believe I'm saying this, i actually hate that you've driven me here, but look at Gwyneth Paltrow. All I'm asking is that you get back to me regarding your mail, and what a timeline might look like for divorcing. If you wanted to exchange a few pleasantries now and then, about life or whatever, that would be nice too. Oh also, re: Janet, I am still hoping to share custody (this works great for Gwyneth and Chris, even though he is now with Dakota Johnson). Janet could handle

it. She's really adaptable – if you remember, we took her to Lauren's cottage that time and it was no problem. I'm trying so, so hard to be reasonable here and I barely feel like you're doing anything to help. I also need to talk to you about something else, nothing huge, but something that happened that I do think we should talk about, and I hope you haven't been talking to other people about it somewhere else, and that you're not avoiding me because of it, because that would be really unfair, and I promise it's not what you think. I know you're not supposed to 'bring up the vows' at a time like this, but we did say we'd love each other for better or worse, and this is obviously much, much worse than we expected, but can't we still try to be kind? It's really starting to piss me off that the division of our entwined lives can be like, a non-event for you and an enormous administrative chore for me.

really do hope you're well.

Amirah set me up for a commiseration evening with a colleague of hers who had recently been involved in what she called a 'category five divorce'. People in general were very keen to suggest I hang out with other people they knew who'd divorced before they'd gotten grey hair. Sometimes it felt like a gesture of support, and sometimes it felt like loading all the corpses on the same cart so the rest of the village didn't get the plague.

My summer had been peppered with these arranged evenings, which always involved alcohol and usually involved crying, and each was odd in a different way. Being united only by one grim fact of your life left a lot of other points upon which two people could be incompatible. It was like constantly going for drinks with someone who had also lost an uncle, or whose roommate had moved out unexpectedly, or who'd recently ripped a cherished pair of jeans. This woman's name was Amy.

Amy had been with her husband for four years. They were married for three. I did not tell her that I thought it was objectively stupid to marry someone you'd known for

one year, age twenty-seven, even though that is how I felt. Amy was beautiful and small and very, very mad. Her fury radiated off her in nearly visible lines, like bad smells in cartoons.

'It's fucking ridiculous,' she said. 'He's such a fucking *loser*.'

Amy's husband had left her for a younger woman, which was the kind of thing she thought didn't happen until you were, like, actually old. His new girlfriend was twenty-one, and taught Pilates with one of those machines that look like they're for sex but are really for thin women to pulse on. Amy had considered taking one of her classes but assumed her ex's new girlfriend knew what she looked like, because of social media and because of Toronto. Instead she had started going to a different Pilates studio, waking up at five to take the six and seven a.m. classes back to back.

'You sort of need to do two hours to feel any impact,' she said, which I suspected would not be true in my case. Amy felt washed up now, at thirty.

I envied the clarity of Amy's anger. Deciding your ex was a villain seemed like an easier way to go through a breakup. I flip-flopped hourly between hating Jon and wanting to go easy on him. After all, he had not done anything terrifically wrong; his major crime was not fighting me when I suggested the marriage was not working, and I couldn't blame him for that (... could I?).

'I think he freaked out because we got married and he realised that was it, no new puss till he died,' Amy said. 'He got weird as soon as we got back from our honeymoon. I don't get it. Being married didn't feel any different to me.'

The night before our wedding, Jon had wondered aloud whether something would change, if we would feel different as man and wife. After the ceremony, I asked him if he did.

'Not really,' he said. 'Still love you a lot like normal.'

Then he said, 'My waiiiife,' in the Borat voice and ran off after a server holding a tray of chicken sliders. I felt different, though: calmer, safer. Buckled in.

Amy said she would not go back to her husband in 'more than a billion years'. She said my ex was a definite idiot with a probable small penis. She suggested I put on a sexy dress, go somewhere I knew he would be, and 'show him what he's missing'.

Jon and I had been together almost ten years, I told her. He could draw what he was missing from memory. Plus, he didn't seem to be missing it that much. I confessed that he hadn't responded to my text messages in nearly a month.

'That's actually so toxic. It's harassment,' said Amy, pouring us another glass each of natural wine.

I felt like a persistent lack of contact was, if anything, the opposite of harassment, but stayed quiet and sipped my drink, the sourness of it stinging my throat. When the server first dropped off the wine list, Amy had asked him to 'challenge her'. I told her that Jon had once told me he considered all wine bourgeois. Amy's mouth dropped open: 'So he's a fucking asshole.' She loved it.

Amy was fun. She swore a lot and went to the corner store to buy cigarettes after we finished our first bottle of challenging wine. Amy talked such merciless shit about her ex-husband I felt free to think about how annoying Jon was

during election seasons, how he acted like it was reasonable to spend nine hours on the toilet (an approximate figure, but still), how he sometimes acted like working in advertising was a noble higher calling. Hadn't I chosen to cut him loose? I felt again the euphoric freedom that had washed over me when Calvin had laughed and said, 'That guy is *never* coming back.' Maybe this was not a life-defining tragedy. Maybe I was a smart woman who knew her worth, or at least knew she deserved more than being shredded to death by a junior ad executive's gnarled toenails every night. Amy said she'd never felt better, on days when she didn't feel the worst she ever had.

Still, she couldn't get over the fact that one day her ex-husband would die, and she would have no idea. 'I was supposed to be at that funeral,' she said with a hiccup. 'Or I guess also dead, but, like, nearby.'

I thought about Jon dying one day, an old man with millions of newly accumulated experiences, none of which would have anything to do with me, darkly sweet death prank long forgotten. In the scope of his life, the near decade we'd spent together wasn't much. I'd occupy a space in his mind similar to elementary school: a thing that had happened, from which few memories remained. What would stay? Would he remember our first apartment, the shower you couldn't stand up in, the vintage posters we were weirdly proud of, the time we got locked out in the dead of winter, the look on the landlord's son's face when he came to rescue us at two a.m.? Would he remember that we'd loved each other, changed each other; how we'd compromised on bedroom decor and gone halfsies on a

mattress that was cooling for his night sweats and rock hard for my back problems? He'd learned to handle a kitchen knife at a cooking class I'd bought him for our anniversary. Would he think of me when he chopped garlic, at least?

'This is bumming me out,' Amy said. 'Let's get nachos.'

We moved bars and ate melted processed cheese under a neon tiger as Amy told me about her dating life. She was seeing three different people, all of whom she had met 'on the apps'. The most exciting was a twenty-four-year-old aspiring actor who was already famous in certain corners of the internet for stunt videos where he climbed improbably tall, out-of-the-way buildings. We watched a few. They were stressful and impressive. Amy said he was amazing in bed and that he 'specialised in divorcées' because he travelled a lot and didn't have time to settle down. Also, because he was mature for his age.

Amy said that lots of men were into divorced women: 'The damage makes you kind of sexy, so they're more likely to stick around instead of ghosting or having sex with your friend to prove it's casual.'

I countered that Amy's great bod and fun attitude were probably what made her appealing to men.

She grabbed my phone, held it up to my face to unlock it, and said, 'No, it's divorce,' while downloading Tinder.

I told her about the incident with Calvin, how I didn't feel ready to meet anyone yet.

Amy clicked her tongue: 'You don't have to marry the guy. Plus, it's so cool that you fucked his friend, like … burn.'

I tried to explain that we hadn't fucked, just platonically shared a bed in which my boob had slipped out of my sleeping tank only once, but she was no longer listening. As she swiped through my photos, not even blinking at the dozens of mortifying sadness selfies I'd amassed, I felt pleasantly powerless.

Amy settled on a three-year-old picture of me smiling with friends on a patio in Collingwood before saying, without malice, 'You should maybe grow out your bangs.' She paused for a moment, then cropped a conspicuously attractive friend out of the picture and made it my profile image.

'You'll like dating,' she said. 'Everyone eats ass now.'

Amy and I workshopped opening lines as couples started to pack it in around us, established pairs walking out holding hands, newer ones politely hugging and heading in separate directions or exchanging too much eye contact before coyly agreeing to share a cab. I looked them over: how many of these people were happy, how many were unhappy and didn't know it, how many were pretending to be happy even though they knew damn well they were miserable ... and when would they be single, if so? I tried to imagine myself joining them. The last time I had been available, dating meant putting on a Going-Out Top and sneaking Smirnoff Ices into a movie theatre. I thought about the jolt of one knee purposefully touching another, lingering in the street after last call, two bodies making excuses to move closer. I probably still had one of those tops somewhere.

Amy and I soldiered on, decamping to the bar's patio and switching, ill-advisedly, to cocktails as we compared

breakup stories. Amy's family had been handling it badly – they loved her ex. Her mother was even occasionally still in touch! Mine were being as supportive as they could from Kingston. 'I feel like they don't really know what to say,' I said. I had recently asked my mother whether any of my family had seen this coming, and she had texted back: define 'seen'.

Amy's parents were still together, which meant, she felt, that they saw her as a failure. More than thirty years of marriage they'd managed, and their daughter couldn't hold it together for three. My parents separated when I was a child but did not formally divorce until we were adults, leaving my sister and me to grow up in a limbo state I'm sure had no ramifications for our adult approaches to intimacy.

For her divorce, Amy had gone out in a blaze of glory, not quite keying his car ('I was tempted, because of Carrie Underwood'), but definitely not being careful as she lugged her things down the driveway past his souped-up Toyota Yaris. Their condo had been everything to her, she told me. The day she left it was her 'personal 9/11'.

Still, Amy's lawyer was sure she would be vindicated.

'We're going to take that fucker to court, and he'll have to go live with his mother in *Orangeville*,' she cackled. 'Orangeville! Can you even?'

I said Jon and I were hoping to avoid lawyers for anything more than paperwork purposes; we'd already divided up almost everything, so there wasn't much to fight about. I explained that taking the high road felt important, that we owed it to our younger selves to be kind. Amy

drained her martini and puffed her cigarette, looking more divorced than anyone in history: 'Good luck.'

The night carried on. I felt myself cross the threshold between fun drunk and 'about to quote a song lyric from my past', but there was nothing to be done except drink through it. I told Amy everything I posted online felt like a PR exercise, like I was trying to broadcast to friends, colleagues, acquaintances, and a few friends' dogs that I was doing well, possibly even thriving. I had found myself putting on makeup before watching a movie, then posting a few front-facing camera videos to Instagram, cracking dumb jokes about the films. Always, I chose movies Jon had loved (still loved, presumably). Always, I deleted the videos in the morning.

Amy said the pursuit of a glow up was only natural. I should come to spin with her if I really wanted to get the word out. Her studio had a mirror that said STRONG AS A WOMAN on it, and she loved the way it made her butt look in selfies.

'There's only one winner of a breakup,' Amy said. 'Why shouldn't everyone know it's you?'

I had to admit that it did have the air of a competition, all this being observed. The experience of my marriage ending felt like the closest I would ever come to a kind of grim local celebrity: I imagined our wider circle tracking my movements, studying my posts, wondering in groups about my dating life. I felt super visible – supervised, even. If everyone was going to look, why shouldn't I have, like, a six-pack when they did?

I told Amy I would try cycling, but would not attempt

to 'win' the breakup. Amy, one false eyelash starting to peel away from the corner of her eye, looked at me like I was the dumbest idiot alive.

'Why do you think they make you wait a year?' she asked, slurring only slightly. 'So you have time to look amazing at the mediation. I bought this top that's going to kill him.' She smiled, and I saw a tear building in her left eye.

By the time the bar closed, Amy and I had each cried twice. We stood outside waiting for her Uber, and I couldn't believe how pretty she still looked, with her dainty features and long, shiny hair and her flippy wrap dress with the ruffle down the front. I had caught a glimpse of my face in the mirror during a trip to the bathroom and could not say the same for me. Why didn't she have wine teeth? How did she keep her hair like that? She exhaled the last of her cigarette and said, 'I hate being someone's ex-wife. It's so random.'

I said it did feel pretty unexpected.

Amy laughed bitterly, the first time she'd sounded rueful all night. 'When did you ever hear a good story about an ex-wife? They're horrible, all of them. This chain around a man's neck. But he made me one. If he didn't want to deal with an ex-wife, he shouldn't have fucking made me one.'

Amy looked at me and smiled shyly before throwing up a little into her hand. Her car arrived and she threw up again, properly this time, before climbing inside. I heard her telling the driver not to worry about it, though he did seem very worried, and fair enough. I walked home, listening to breakup songs and feeling like a loser for relating to

them all. *Losing love* is *like a window in your heart*, I thought. I tweeted, everybody sees you're blown apart, then deleted it, then found the lyric on a Paul Simon fan account and retweeted it from there. As I walked, I opened Tinder and swiped right on everyone, feeling an unbelievable rush of self-esteem or something like it when matches came up, not speaking to any of them. No harm in looking. I could delete it in the morning.

Clicking 'show men and women' was exciting. My bisexuality until now had been largely theoretical, based on one university hookup and a few drunken kisses. I'd had a number of charged same-sex 'friendships', one spectacularly botched threesome, and my preferred genre of porn was some variation on one or many women bullying another in a sexual way, but none of this felt substantial enough for me to proclaim it part of my identity. Though I'd always felt at least 35% gay, whenever my orientation came up in conversation, I felt inexperienced and sheepish. Now if I told someone I liked women, I could back it up with supporting evidence. I scrolled through some profiles, drawn to ones with pithy, lowercase bios: pile of human garbage seeks same; looking for a partner in crime (i plan to commit many crimes); run. The women's profiles were on the whole more subdued than the men's, except when they were many times more intense – badly lit close-up selfies in the bathroom of those clubs where there is a pool and you wear a bikini, bios seeking someone who was willing to get real and was NOT about drama.

It was nice to feel my phone vibrate, to see the looping, exclamatory cursive, like a wedding invitation: It's a Match!

I swiped on tall women and short men, women with nose rings and men with tattoos, men in large, anonymous groups or standing alone on top of mountains, gesturing vaguely to the outdoors like, *get a load of this*. There were men holding babies (don't worry, she's not mine!) and women at house parties with their tongues out and men next to big, sedated jungle cats. Women who were too into having a bicycle, men in suits who were looking for no-strings fun, sepia-toned shots of attractive androgynous people with half their faces obscured, winking from behind a dog filter or in heavy makeup. Nobody was terribly appealing. I kept swiping for hours.

The next day I had a hangover and forty-seven new matches. I was scrolling through my options when Amy texted:

such a fun night, babe!!!

main thing to know about the apps is

nobody actually likes anyone else on there

just breathe and remember:

hakuna matata :)

Selected Correspondence, Tinder, 20 August

what's up, how's your day going

cute pics

hi

hey beautiful how's your day going? lovely curvy figure

hi haha hows it going

i don't like to waste time messaging on here, want to go for a drink? you look hot :)

so u work at a university, nerdy but sexy haha

heyyyyyy

if you could travel anywhere in the world, where would you go? just got back from peru, it's so rad there. crazy foreign and everything's dirt cheap. can rec some places if you want

hi baby what are you looking for on here, i'm casual

redheads not really my type haha but maybe you can change my mind in person

hola chica ;) i'm lisa

nice to meet u, hows ur day? want to be super upfront and say my girlfriend doesn't know i'm on here

hey, looking for fun on here, hbu

did you go to macdonald high school? thought you were married. it's danny haha

Hi Maggie! You seem like a pretty and fun person with a very interesting job :) I'd like to get to know you better and buy you a drink or dinner. Just to be sure we are compatible, could you send pics of feet? I'd love to give them a massage and some kisses and licks. All the best!

i think ur my TA lol

can never think of an opening line for these things but, hi, you seem kewl B-)

big legs

I showed up to work, in person, for the first time in late August. Merris must have told everyone why I'd been gone because it was Soft Eyes all around. Most people were nice about it, but the arm patting and head tilting wore on me, and people kept asking if I thought I'd ever get married again, which seemed like a quick turnaround.

Olivia, a quiet medievalist with a gentle, academic-seeming lisp, had gotten engaged during my time away and was incredibly bashful, as though matrimony had a one-in, one-out policy and the start of her marriage had directly brought about the end of my own. Jiro stopped me in the hall to tell me about an event his sister's church organised for young singles.

'Relatively young,' he corrected himself. 'What are you, thirty-four?'

I started closing the door to my office.

Now it was September, and Jon had not answered a single text, call, or email since the Night Burgers incident, when he had been half asleep and seemed confused about who I was and why I was calling, eventually saying, 'Don't worry about

it, honestly,' and hanging up. At some point, he'd blocked the cat's Instagram too. I texted Calvin to ask if he had confessed about our evening together, and he wrote back, SO sorry, who's this? then no, when I clarified. I asked my lawyer if we needed Jon to get in touch for some legal something or other, but apparently with 'so few assets on the table' (thanks, Lori), there was unlikely to be much back and forth.

I kept busy with my collages and self-help books and a few more tentative forays into socialising. I was preparing for a new round of students, and Merris's latest book had some big, unanswered questions at the heart of it that had me spending a lot of time alone in the library, and it was unbelievable how normal it all felt until I went home and no one was there, or something funny would happen and I'd go to text Jon and remember we didn't do that anymore. Sometimes I texted anyway.

It felt humiliating to admit it, but without a partner to dissect things with, the big and small events of life seemed flimsy. I had accepted that it was over, that it would never be how it was again – even, possibly, that it was for the best, but I would have paid a million dollars for one more cab ride home from a party, drunkenly touching each other's legs and poring over the night's events – who had said what about what or accidentally offended whom, who was too drunk and going home with a new person, whether there had been enough snacks and if it seemed like the hosts were going to have an argument later – thrilled to have been out with so many people and more thrilled to be alone, now, just the two of us, on our way home to fuck and laugh and drink cold, cold water.

But! Better not to think about it. Work was a helpful distraction, usually, though my situation – the confused longing and self-flagellating nostalgia, the constant down-loading and deleting of Tinder – found ways to seep in there too. One day, sifting through Alciato's *Emblemata* for references to rivers, I was ambushed. 'Sometimes sweet things become bitter,' he wrote after someone was attacked by bees. *Wow*, I thought. *So true.* 'I unhappily bear the fruit of my own destruction,' a chestnut tree said after being shaken by some children. It was disorienting to find that this, too, was about me, a voice reaching across centuries and an ocean to say, *sorry about your divorce.* When I reached Emblem 192, 'That respect is to be sought in marriage,' I had to close the book and take a break, texting the group chat once again about my hair.

The desire to cut and bleach my hair was extremely strong and getting stronger by the day. The group chat had already sheepishly admitted to the formation of a second, separate group chat mostly dedicated to tagging in who was going to talk me down that week from a home dye job. I understood the argument against it: how trite, to get a dramatic haircut during a breakup. I wanted to resist. Amy had recently gotten a tattoo of the word BREATHE, and Amirah had joked that it might as well read DIVORCED. Did I want everyone around me to know, on sight, that I was Going Through Something?

Maybe I didn't, but there was something alluring about it anyway, the temptation of a fresh start. The image of the runaway in a gas station bathroom with scissors and perox-ide, becoming new. Only my pride at the idea of Jon

finding out caused me to hesitate – and even then, if I could pull it off, turn into a sexy-stranger version of the woman he'd known … well.

I was collating photos of Drew Barrymore in the nineties to support my case when I received an email:

Thanks for your inquiry regarding Janet's annual checkup. Per our records, Jon arranged it and brought her in last week. You'll be happy to know she's perfectly healthy and all her shots are now up to date. While he was here, Jon updated Janet's account with us and removed your contact info and status as primary caregiver. Was this done in error? If so, we are unable to make further changes without Jon's input, so you'll have to get in touch with him. Sorry I can't be of more assistance. Please have Jon send us a message, and we can amend Janet's file.

The vet signed off with her name and a little picture of a paw print. It looked like a small cartoon cat was giving me the finger. As I blinked at the monitor, Olivia came in, a bag of lean protein in her hand.

'Everything okay?' she asked, fishing around in her Ziploc for the first of two wet-looking eggs. I told her everything was alright, I was only tired, and she nodded like she knew what I meant, though I suspected she was rarely tired, and as soon as she was, she'd take a reasonable twenty-minute nap and awake refreshed and hydrated.

Olivia ran marathons, which was why she had the eggs. She was always knocking back some protein between meals, uncomplainingly chewing through turkey jerky or count-

ing out eight almonds. The Pocket Eggs were her worst snack by far – a seemingly endless supply of damp hard-boiled eggs she carried around and whipped out at inopportune moments to peel and unselfconsciously eat.

'So,' she said perkily, fingernails digging into the shell of the first egg. 'What's new?'

I think possibly my husband has stolen our cat, or is going to move somewhere new without telling me and bring her with him, or simply hates my guts and wants me to struggle, or the cat is a hostage, or this is an elaborate scheme to win me back, or maybe he's gone insane, and this is a cry for help, and I need to find h—

'Not much.'

Olivia laughed: 'Same old, same old!' She said this with enthusiasm, like it was a fun new phrase she was trying out. I tried to turn back to my computer, but she was clearly in the mood for a chatty little break. The thought crossed my mind that she might have come in here, with this attitude, on purpose, to cheer me up – horrific.

The problem was that Olivia was a wonderful, considerate person, and she always brought extra almonds in case anyone wanted some, and she'd never asked me to do a 10k with her even though she was always doing them and had once asked Merris if she'd like to join. Merris had not joined, and we sometimes had a little laugh about the Pocket Eggs, but it was not pleasurable or even really possible to dislike Olivia, so you had to take the eggs as part of it.

'… which isn't terrible or anything, but it's not my job to field those kinds of questions when Google would answer

faster than me,' she finished, making me realise I hadn't been listening, just staring at her hands picking haphazardly at an eggshell. It was not peeling easy – the egg beneath was pocked and uneven, the shell chipping and pulling little chunks of white along with it. I felt sick.

Olivia continued: 'There's this one girl who emails me almost every day, and on the one hand, I empathise, and I hope she's got friends or loved ones or, you know, people in her life, but it's not really my job to be there for her like that ...'

Was this because I emailed his parents? It was only to say thank you for welcoming me into their family, and that I would miss them, and that if they wanted to hang out sometime, surely, we still could? What was so wrong with that? They hadn't responded, and I'd only followed up once.

Olivia was still going. 'I'm being so mean ... but if I responded to every lonely student with no boundaries, it would be another full-time job, and I basically already have three. Are you sure you're okay?' Olivia seasoned her second egg with a limp little salt and pepper packet that was also in the bag. 'Can I get you a coffee or something?'

She took a big bite, and I imagined her at home, wiped from a day of mountain biking with her fiancé, filling a twelve-gallon pot of water to boil a thousand eggs.

'I know you're going through a hard time,' she said.

I shrugged and said I was okay, a bit bored and broke mostly. 'Don't worry,' I said, adopting a faux-brave expression. 'I'm only suicidal on Mondays.'

Olivia's face was suddenly very grave.

'I'm kidding,' I said. 'I'm fine.'

Olivia folded the plastic bag the eggs came in and put it back in her pocket.

'Change can be so difficult,' she said. 'Are you getting out of the house? Seeing friends?'

I said something about doing my best. Her head was tilted so far to the side it looked uncomfortable.

'Listen, if it ever feels like too much, if you ever start to feel like you might, you know, if you need someone, in an … emergency situation …'

'Jesus, Olivia, it was a *joke*,' I said. 'Come on.'

Olivia swallowed. 'Of course it was,' she said. 'But you have to do your due diligence with these things, and you've been looking so … anyway. If you ever want to talk to someone, for any reason, I'm here. Just don't tell my students, right?'

She tittered nervously and turned to leave, looking back at me with such genuine concern I blushed. I turned my focus to my computer. Dozens of Drew Barrymores grinned back at me, sticking out their tongues and flashing David Letterman. They looked good but their eyes were empty.

I tried to remember the last time I'd been in touch with Jon. A voicemail a week ago, because Bean Pun, our favourite coffee shop, was turning into a Starbucks. Text messages the week before that said, i don't know what happened to us, then sorry, that was stupid, then haha, hope you're well!! But what *had* happened to us? Weren't we going to do this the nice way? At the very least, wasn't the cat conversation fucking ongoing?

He didn't get to slink away in the night with the animal I had jokingly but also incredibly seriously referred to as my only child. I would not be denied a final boop on her soft nose, or a bittersweet moment where Jon and I wished each other well and exchanged platitudes about growth, where maybe he wistfully kissed my forehead. We had decided it was over, yes, but we were supposed to work together to end it properly.

Merris came in, wearing one of her jazzier sweater shawls. She was holding a small baggie of eggs. 'You have unsettled Olivia,' she said, putting them down in front of me. 'Apparently B12 will help.'

'He took the cat,' I said.

Merris patted my back, an uncharacteristically maternal gesture. 'Well,' she said, 'at least you won't be coming to work with vomit on your shirt anymore. Not cat vomit, at any rate.' She chuckled, and it really felt like I was going to laugh too – the sound started the right way. Instead, I let out a loud and unexpected wail and felt myself crumple in half. My head dropped first, then the rest of my body, a little pile of woman where a competent human had been. Merris seemed to be expecting this, pulling my head to her shoulder with one hand and closing my office door with the other.

I had cried a lot since Jon moved out, but this was different, intense and animal. It was all spilling out, at work, to my boss: Jon's refusal to return my calls, my relief that he was leaving and immediate regret when he did, the Cointreau and burgers and reckless credit card activity, the hours on Instagram and the impossible rent and the rapidly dwindling bank account. The fact that my parents were

hours away, that I knew my friends were already finding me a bit much, that my lawyer seemed unconcerned about the biggest decision in my young life, that I was writing poems again. And worst of all, the knowledge that none of these were real problems, that spending every moment dwelling on them probably made me a very bad or at least preposterously boring person who would never accomplish anything or help anyone, who would die of climate-related flooding or cancer or famine, alone and hated.

I wiped my nose, and the silence of a crossed boundary settled.

'Well,' said Merris, before I could finish the apology my mouth was forming. 'I hope you can take some comfort in the idea that I think you did the right thing. You're not supposed to say that, in case a couple gets back together, but that doesn't seem much of a risk here.'

I told her I was continually surprised by how horrible I felt. When my first boyfriend and I broke up, at eighteen, it cured my fear of death – eternal nothingness seemed preferable to the cavity wound in my chest that Adam had left when he chose a different university (despite an *express* agreement to move to Toronto together!). I'd assumed, a full decade later, that heartbreak would feel different, that I would have acquired some skills to manage it with grace and dignity. But no. In a post-breakup email, I'd told Adam it felt like he'd ripped open my rib cage and shit inside me. This felt almost exactly the same – worse, if anything, because of its familiarity – and here I was, crying at my desk in the middle of the day, being given pity eggs by younger colleagues.

Merris tutted. 'They're fine eggs.'

I told her I'd liked the idea that marriage was hard to get out of at the time – had even found it romantic. It seemed like it should be hard to leave, because it would probably be hard to stay at points. An aunt had jokingly said, 'The best marriage advice I can give you: *make sure you each want the divorce at different times.*' I had assumed that challenge would come later.

'Seems like a tremendous idea in the moment, doesn't it?' Merris said. 'And look, it probably was. I'm sure you loved each other then, and it's not a crime to change your mind. I won't patronise you by suggesting you learned everything you needed from each other. Sometimes a relationship just loses its way.'

I told Merris she was right. I did feel lost. And stupid. The whole thing was embarrassing. And demoralising, and hopeless, and, and, and. I said I felt too old to move on and too young to be divorced, like I'd stranded myself in the gap between experience and maturity.

Merris sat us both up straight. 'One day,' she said, 'and it will surprise you how soon this day will come, but one day you will wake up and feel good. It won't last long, but then you'll have another day where you barely remember this abjection, and another, and another, until that's just your life. But for now, it will be hard. This is the part that's hard.'

I smiled weakly: 'God, you're wise.'

'I'm old,' she said. 'And a divorcée *and* a widow … you certainly came to the right place. Now go home, you're not fit. Get some sleep, down some triple sec or what have you,

and come back tomorrow, better. And maybe leave the man alone.'

I squeezed Merris's arm and looked away, wanting to spare her any further emotional displays. Though we were relatively friendly colleagues, this afternoon had demanded more intimacy from her than the entirety of our relationship to this point. She stood and smoothed the linen of her shift dress.

'I'm going to forward you an article,' she said. 'It's a compilation of autocorrect mishaps. People texting "nipple" for "dimple", that sort of thing. Bit of light humour might take your mind off it all.'

After Merris left, I gathered my things and stepped into the oppressive haze of another too-warm September. I walked along College Street, serene enough to get through five minutes of a fifteen-minute 'mindful walking' meditation. Listening to it was awful, but clicking on it felt transformative, the first step on the path toward meaningful growth. I turned it off when the too-soothing voice asked me to notice the way my toes felt in my shoes.

Merris's advice had been thoughtful and mature. *How lucky*, I thought, to have access to such a generous model on which to base my way of thinking. *How sad*, that her words meant nothing to me, that I was filled instead with a white-hot rage that would not be sated until I had won this divorce and reduced the man who hurt me to rubble, razed his cities to the ground and salted the earth so nothing would ever grow there. Merris had been correct in every way, but that was not the way we would proceed.

Rather than mindfully noticing the leaves on the trees, the smells and sounds of the street, I meditated on how much I despised my husband, his intensity and pretensions and taste in music, the bump on his nose from a high school hockey injury. I hated his back hair and his mother's cooking and how he was too tall to be technically short but not really, actually tall, and certainly not 'close to six feet' as he claimed. I recited like mantras my pet hates, lingered over every time he'd disappointed me, hurt my feelings, expressed anger. I thought about moments I'd looked at him and felt, *Jesus, this person?* – times he'd humiliated me at the grocery store, broke a mug in anger, cut someone off in traffic. I ran through my twenties thus far, blaming him for every negative experience, paving over birthdays, trips, Saturday mornings, dinners and movies and Christmases with family. I reshaped our happy memories until they were revealed for what they truly were: false moments of hope concealing the truth. This was a man who would promise to love you and lie about it. This was a man who would steal your cat.

I got drunk and had sex with Calvin.

Google Searches, 4 September

feminist dating apps
is B12 important
dating apps no couples
tracy anderson arms video free
good memes
global extinction likelihood
does recycling help
nicole kidman leaving divorce lawyer's office
fast track divorce ontario
watch instagram stories anonymous
toronto bars good lighting
STIs 2018
eating ass dangerous?
what's going on with bees
exercises for dowager's hump
spaghetti squash why
toronto housing crisis
HPV tongue to butt
catherine zeta jones divorce
graphic designer fergus toronto leslieville
graphic designer tess toronto vegan
graphic designer photographer bartender ali toronto
the four agreements cult?
weird nub on thumb
early onset arthritis from phone
fillers for hands
romantic speech TV supercut
sense and sensibility emma thompson willoughby

posture correcting harness scam?
blue light glasses scam?
natural deodorant scam?
academic jobs early modernism north america
fast track teaching degree
taylor swift breakup songs
one direction early videos
saturn return

When classes began again, I promised myself I'd stop thinking about Jon. This turned out to be surprisingly easy; all it required was 100% of my energy, 100% of the time. I stayed busy with work and meetings, going to friends' houses to gossip and text through movies, and obligatory calls to my family to tell them that, yes, I was okay, no, I still did not want to move home for a while to 'sort some things out'.

I avoided thinking about him on my commute to work, crammed onto the bus with my headphones in, occasionally looking at attractive strangers with an expression Lauren called 'Missed Connection eyes'. I barely thought about him while trawling rental listings in my office or fielding students' half-assed questions – more comments than questions, really – about Spenser or whoever. I did not think about him during long weeknights alone, sitting on the living-room floor marking papers or doing probably unhelpful facial tightening exercises, or lighting my one fancy candle for an allotted thirty minutes before blowing it out again.

I didn't know exactly what the plan was; all I knew at this stage was that staying occupied meant staying distracted and therefore something close to happy. If I emerged from this period with a better body, cooler life, cuter face, and incredibly hot, possibly famous new partner, so be it. In service of those goals, I started a 'squats challenge' and made a resolution to cycle more and possibly save up for preventative Botox. I stopped crying all the time – in fact I hadn't cried in weeks – and made jokes online about my fabulous, wild life, spending my weekends drinking and dancing and dating. Because it provided the most instant distraction, I focused most heavily on the dating.

My friends feared I was moving too quickly, warning that my first time with a new person might feel messy and emotional. It had actually been alright – minus a few instances of erectile dysfunction from Calvin – though I had resolved not to tell anyone about that particular life choice. Having a sexual secret felt kind of fun and soapy, but I was also fairly ashamed of myself. So I feigned interest in their advice about taking it slow, while secretly hoping to take it as fast as possible, to push Calvin swiftly down the scroll of my sexual history. I was impatient, too, because being excited or nervous or horny was better than being sad.

'This is what I'm supposed to be doing,' I told my friends one evening at Clive's. 'Getting back out there. I'm on Tinder and I think I'm going to try Hinge.'

Lauren laughed ruefully and said, 'Godspeed.'

Amirah pointed out, not necessarily helpfully, that I'd barely been 'out there' to begin with. Having dated Jon

since I was nineteen, I wasn't making some grand come-back to single life. This was my debut.

My first date was with a twenty-seven-year-old bartender called Sofia, from whom I got the idea to use normal-to-average photos of myself on my dating profiles. She had seemed pretty enough online – short and strong, with bold eyebrows and little Marie Antoinette boobs – but when we met in real life, and I first saw her walking toward the patio where I was guarding two ciders while trying not to be sweaty, she looked so beautiful that I thought briefly about running away. Instead, I wiped my clammy palms on my jeans and, before I could stop myself, shook her hand like this was some kind of sexual and emotional job interview, which I guess in a way it was.

Sofia took my hand with a sly smile and said, 'How's it going, Maggie?' and we spent three hours drinking cider and talking about our core wounds before getting to second base in Trinity Bellwoods. The date was so successful I spent a week or so entertaining the idea that I was done with men for good, but then on another date a musician called Tyler lifted me up onto his washing machine, and I was forced to admit I was pretty much interested in whoever was inter-ested in me.

It took an enormous amount of time, all the swiping around, matching, picking a charming yet aloof opening line ... then the banter, the scheduling, the rescheduling, the cancelling and finding someone new. Sometimes I would let Olivia or Amirah swipe around for me. People in committed relationships got a real kick out of 'the apps', not because, as many seemed to think, they were jealous or

wistful about new, high-tech methods of meeting and mating. They approached it more like war correspondents, as if they had a duty to impartially observe the horror. I could see it in their eyes when a profile popped up featuring the bottom two-thirds of a man's face incredibly close up in three different locations, or a woman I'd been speaking to for four days revealed she had a boyfriend and was looking for a fun surprise for their anniversary, or when a man messaged, u suck cock? with the emoji of a monkey bashfully covering its eyes. There was an excitement there, an eagerness to rush back and report to their partner from the front lines of modern dating: *you wouldn't believe it, babe, it's a nightmare out there.*

It was not always a nightmare. Sofia was lovely, and we saw each other two more times before she sent me a long message full of compliments and ending with the information that she was getting back together with her ex. Lauren and I went on a double date with a pair of cousins who got us free tickets to several basketball games, and a woman called Gretchen made me squirt, something I had previously thought impossible. Even when a date was bad – the man who flossed at the table, the woman who asked if she could use some of my pubic hair for 'non-dark sexual magick' – it didn't matter. There were, as promised, many more fish in the sea. Lots of these fish were even attractive. Some were fun to talk to, and really the only thing that mattered was that all of them were technically available. Once you matched with someone and parsed the obligatory how's your day goings and what you looking for on heres, you were between twelve hours and two weeks from a first date.

I was always surprised by how forthcoming new matches were before we'd even met in person. In these ten-minute preliminary chats, I learned about people's peccadilloes, parental relationships and least favourite coworkers before I knew their last names or how tall they really were. For my part, I preferred to drop the divorce bomb in person, though I was never sure how to approach this disclosure. I asked a friend with herpes for pointers and was told she'd rather date a guy with an STI than 'that level of emotional baggage'.

I said I was the total package: dead inside, plus I got cold sores.

'Oh, if it's just cold sores you don't have to tell them,' she said. 'HSV-1 is not the headline herpes.'

Far from being a problem, my marital status provided a fun talking point. Most people reacted with amused surprise, as if I'd told them I'd had a secret life as a famous children's performer or an international spy. It was also a neat segue into both parties discussing what had gone wrong in their last relationships, an activity that comprised a full 50% of the app dates I went on. Amy was right: it made me seem exciting, even mysterious. Also – and perhaps most importantly – it made me seem unlikely to seek commitment, something I quickly learned most men did not want and most women wanted immediately but seemed to love being denied.

Noticing this made me feel like I was living in one of those sitcoms where characters are always saying, 'It's the nineties!' but I could not deny the pattern that evolved. Men were apparently freed by the thought that a woman

actively trying to disentangle herself from one man would not be quick to jump into a serious relationship with another, and women found it either romantically tragic or relatable. If they didn't want to save me, at least we could trade war stories – not everyone is divorced, but everyone's had their heart broken.

A younger woman I met on Hinge told me my marital status was 'honestly kind of chic', adding that it functioned 'like an age reset, because you don't look young, no offence, but you look *very* young to be divorced.' Later that night she – Harriet, I think? maybe Hali? – got her period so hard that the blood seeped through my sheets, staining my mattress. A few days after that I made a joke over text about medieval virginity tests, saying my father, the king, had been pleased to see it, but she didn't get it, or if she did, she didn't like it. Either way, she didn't respond.

Clive told me Gen Z rarely wasted time breaking things off in full.

'I think it's a best-case scenario,' he said. 'Old guys are so clingy. With young people, they like you or you never hear from them again.'

This would very much prove to be true. In my first month on the apps I went on six first dates, three second dates, and one third date. I didn't see anyone a fourth time. It was nice to be busy, to have places to be and reasons to shower. It was nice, too, to have a good reason to look at my phone. Suddenly sitting at home scrolling mindlessly on Twitter felt like biding time between important texts. My phone was not only a food delivery portal or scrapbook full of heartbreaking pictures and videos. It was a hub of

sexual affirmation and potential romantic connection! Being on it for hours just made sense.

But as the weeks went on and the novelty of the all-you-can-fuck human buffet wore off, I realised my favourite part of these dates was the hour or so before they started. I liked the ritual of date preparation: showering and moisturising languidly, trimming my armpit hair (she's a feminist!) and shaving my leg hair (a low-key one!), working a lightly scented oil through the ends of my head hair while the ice melted in a little pre-date pick-me-up on the radiator.

I'd stream something to get me in the mood to be alluring, singing along as blasé women crooned through my phone's tinny speakers, eating a light snack to absorb alcohol but avoid bloat. I'd run through the evening in my head, idly rehearsing my dumb jokes, trying to remember if this person was the one I'd already told about the devastating sunburn of 2005, or if that had been someone else who also wore glasses and enjoyed travel.

I read in some grim article I'd googled about dating in 2018 that men didn't like it when you wore trousers on dates, so when seeing them I stuck to dresses and skirts, though I didn't own many. I worried initially that if I met a man I liked, I'd run out of clean versions of my woman costume, but of course shortly discovered this would not be an issue. The real danger was seeing too many other bi women and going home to spend four hours considering the acquisition of a septum piercing.

Most of these dates were pleasant enough. Only one was terrible – a man who arrived thirty minutes late, barefoot,

and lectured me about women's usurpation of the 'natural masculine role' – and two were very fun. We would go to bars or sit in the park at sunset or occasionally do an activity, bolstered by three to seven drinks, relative anonymity, and the tacit understanding that we were equally attracted to each other, or at least equally horny.

It occurred to me – while straining with every fibre of my being to avoid getting my phone out while a girl was in the bathroom – that by your late twenties you could probably have a satisfactory first date with almost anyone: everyone had a big breakup or two under their belt, most had acquired a semi-reliable source of income and could afford a drink or two (or at least knew a bartender) at the kind of place where the servers were resolute in their bralessness and you just knew there was a taxidermied something somewhere.

That the bars all looked the same was not an issue. There is too much data about millennial tastes in the world; everywhere we go looks like math. But although I'd assumed the apps would broaden my romantic horizons, an incredibly homogenous figure emerged as the type I most often matched with, chatted to, and met for dates. The men tended to be bearded and left-leaning and got too excited if you mentioned Harry Nilsson. All of them thought Bernie would have won. An alarming number were thinking about getting into stand-up comedy. None of them had curtains.

While the women were marginally more varied (different haircuts, different styles of dress, different routes to the idea of 'finding the Jim to one's Pam'), the size of the queer

dating pool in Toronto meant I also knew a lot of them: saw them in yoga, held doors for them at friends' parties, passed them in the hallways of the university. The women were too close and obsessed with letting the world know they were 'tender'. The men, while strangers to me, had disgusting bathrooms and were bad on text. Tinder was not as fun as nobody had said it was.

It turned out not to matter. Just as I was tiring of the app-based dating cycle (meet, two dates, sex, delay third date, reschedule, cancel, and, finally, ghost), I noticed something else at work. Some kind of 'I'm vulnerable' bat signal had gone out to the almost-encounters of my past – people I'd wanted to sleep with at university, acquaintances I'd always found cute, flirty coworkers from old bar jobs – and they were getting in touch in massive numbers.

They would like an old tweet, or comment under a photo, or drop a casual text to say something they'd seen had made them think of me: an ad for a restaurant we'd joked about six years ago, a flower the same colour as my hair. A British man I'd almost kissed at a party in 2017 sent me a picture of a bean-covered baked potato with the cryptically menacing caption, ur the beans.

Amy, with whom I had stayed in touch and sometimes met for coffee when I'd already complained about Jon too much to my other friends, said these figures from my past could 'tell' I was single from my social media activity.

'It's instinctual,' she said. 'That Story you posted the other day? Your nipples were *visibly* hard. Women in relationships simply do not post like that. And that's something these people would know.'

She showed me a Boomerang of a man adding powder to a water bottle and shaking it vigorously. 'This to me has big single energy,' she said. 'The way he's eye-fucking the camera? And look.' She tapped his profile and scrolled through his photos, tutting. 'Hasn't put the girlfriend on main in three months. I mean, this is Great Wall of China-level single. You could see that this guy is single from space.'

Part of me was horrified to be in the same camp as the hulkingly horny protein man. Was I really so obvious? I felt like a baboon waggling my big, swollen ass at some other baboon I'd attended a conference with five years earlier. But mostly I was thrilled by the messages, at the external valida-tion, the chance to try something I already knew I liked.

Meeting new people felt like starting over: daunting and depressing, a challenge for someone fallen on romantic hard times. Reconnecting with paths not taken was easier and seemed more purposeful. These were the people my relationship had been holding me back from being with! The right ones were there all along! It was comforting to think that being with Jon had been the mistake, not losing him or letting him go. If I was supposed to be with one of these near-flames of my past, then breaking it off with my husband had been an important step toward finding real love, instead of what it usually felt like: a failure.

Coming home from a date with an old colleague, distantly flirtatious acquaintance, or friend of a friend with whom there'd always been tension, I felt a satisfaction and pride bordering on mania. Realising that other people – lots of people! – liked me or thought I was pretty or wanted to fuck me was spectacular. I had hoped that Jon would

love me forever, sure, but a part of me had also assumed he was the only person who really wanted to try.

Back at my apartment at four a.m., I'd pass the hall mirror and catch my own eye: a person beguiling enough to be asked out, hot enough to be frenched in the back of an Uber, 'good on text' enough to acquire a second and possibly third date. Spewing my little anecdotes and doing some eyeliner and discreetly finding opportunities to touch whoever's back had worked. I was, according to the objective opinion of an outside body, worthy of time, and what was the saying? 'Time is how you spend your love'? Take it up with Zadie Smith!

That loving and supporting someone for many years was not the same as eating pizza with them for two hours in a bar full of pinball machines did not really register. I was fucking lovable, actually. I was fine.

A Fantasy

I am walking home from doing something productive and morally good, like spinning. I have recently showered, and my hair has dried exactly right. I am not wearing makeup, but I don't need to be, my skin is dewy like I've done three simultaneous sheet masks. I look French. I *feel* French. I am not even listening to a podcast while I walk, because I am the type of person who wants to Experience Life.

The sun is setting, and I breathe deeply, the way people do when they are internally settled and have nothing to prove. No part of my boob is popping over the top of my sports bra, which I am wearing as a shirt, a decision no one has noticed, because I am pulling it off with such ease.

As I walk up the street, lit beautifully, someone hands me a smoothie: 'You should have this, miss.' They don't even *think* to say 'ma'am', and why would they, I am young. I drink the smoothie and the wheatgrass in it settles in my body, energising it or pulling out toxins or whatever wheatgrass is about.

I hum to myself and skip a little way down the pavement, I feel so light. When I get home, I will burn incense and read a book, and my phone will be in another room and I won't even remember which one, because I am so unbothered to be away from it. I will moisturise my body and feel neutral about my cellulite, which is okay to have, everyone has it, even someone who is doing as well as me.

As I walk up the street I will know, deep within my body, that I am loved. By friends, family, and even—

Suddenly, there he is. Jon, red-eyed and tired-looking, wandering aimlessly like a person who has made many bad decisions in life, one of which haunts him in particular. I see him long before he sees me, and I think, *how tragic*.

It is hard to see him struggle when I am doing, in the words of our friends, acquaintances, and one surprisingly personal but nonetheless correct front-page newspaper article, 'incredibly well'.

I think maybe it would be kinder to avoid him, and so I measure my pace to put more distance between us. I'm walking so slowly, but it is not enough. The way he's trudging – resignedly, with devastation – means I've almost caught up. I'm trying to imagine the kindest way to say *I've met someone* when:

'Maggie! Maggie!'

I turn at the same time Jon does. We both see the man immediately – can't miss him, because of the crowd that's formed. He runs toward us in his massive, experimental trousers, smiling and waving.

'There she is,' says Harry Styles, slipping a stylish, tattooed arm around my waist.

Jon clocks it immediately: our easy intimacy, the flush in my cheeks. I feel a flicker of compassion for the man who was once my husband. I want to ask Harry Styles to be a little less familiar, to show some respect for the awkward situation. I want to say, *Harry Styles, please*. But I know I can't stop him – he's too excited, it's all so new. Jon's face falls, but he reaches out to shake the hand of the international superstar I met by chance on an airplane and

charmed by pretending to be unfamiliar with his discography.

'Better not, mate,' says Harry Styles. 'I've spent all morning fingering your wife.'

The activities frenzy took over sometime in mid-autumn, and even I could tell it was a bad sign.

'Absolutely not,' Lauren said, after I suggested we sign up for a krav maga intensive Olivia promised would wreck us. 'No adult starts a hobby from a good place.'

She was right. It didn't matter if it was a buzzy new fitness trend or an aspirationally useful class or something fun and specific, like life drawing or an Italian conversation group – everyone involved in adult learning was running from something.

I'd learned this firsthand, having got the idea to take up a hobby from reading wikiHow's advice for managing a divorce during a particularly pathetic dark night of the soul. The list featured eighteen tips, though the final seven pertained to the raising of children in a joint-custody arrangement and were therefore not relevant. 'Get a Hobby' was tip number four, right above 'Revisit Old Passions', a heading accompanied by an illustration of a woman stirring something beige in a frying pan while imagining an alarm clock. A hobby seemed less confusing,

and the sixth tip, 'Get a Therapist If Needed', did not apply to me.

I could not sell Lauren on Israeli martial arts, but I did convince her to join a singles bowling league on the grounds that there might be a few hot guys in attendance. This was a deception. I knew there would be maybe one eligible man among the bunch, even in a best-case scenario. Every class I signed up for – every group workout, creative writing seminar or weekend workshop on making your own essential oil blends – was wall-to-wall with the recently dumped, most of them women, all of them much older than me.

Once, at an extremely ambitious 'introduction to bouldering' evening I'd found on Groupon, I saw two women near my age and got excited, thinking, *this is it, this is how you make friends in your thirties.* But it transpired that they were not amateur rock-climbing enthusiasts hoping to make connections; they were sisters, there to support their mom, who was – you guessed it – deep in the middle of her second divorce.

'It's hard,' one of them said, putting chalk all over her hands in a way I found inscrutable and weirdly alluring. 'She keeps saying, "We must admit that the heterosexual experiment has failed." And like, I agree with her, but she's not a lesbian, so … I don't know what she thinks the plan is.'

Later, when I was sitting on the floor of the rock-climbing gym watching the supportive-if-cynical daughter clamber up the simulated cliff face, her mother sat down nearby, offered me a Capri Sun, and sighed so long and loudly that I dusted myself off and left.

Outside of bouldering, I tried a macramé class, a 'stitch and bitch' evening, and a pottery night where everyone around me frantically shaped clay into little breasts for plant pots; there was a tie-dyeing workshop, a pan-Asian cooking weekend, and a group fitness class where we were encouraged to scream throughout, releasing our rage and whatever was holding us back from our undefined, individual goals. This I left after the instructor hollered, 'There are more important things than MONEY!!' and the entire class cheered, even though it had cost them all $47 to be there.

It had cost me nothing, and a big reason I was so into my new hobby of 'having hobbies' was that most activities allowed you to attend a first class for free. The city was teeming with opportunities to try crafts and athletic hybrid activities at no charge. If you had enough time on your hands and weren't fussy about things like studio cleanliness or instructor expertise, you could take multiple free yoga classes any day of the week.

I continued attending my local studio's restorative class (Calvin never reappeared), but otherwise shopped around, taking hot yoga, yoga for runners, and something called 'Rihanna yoga' in different but nearly identical storefronts across the city. I would zip to Mixed Level Movement before my 10:30 seminar ('Enter Wet: Weather on the Elizabethan Stage'), then walk into the gloomy, windowless room where I taught, my head held conspicuously high. After class I'd disengage my core and slump over my desk for seven hours before stopping in for another round of subsidised chaturangas on the way home.

Most of my non-yoga efforts were centred around unlocking some untapped but prolifically talented creative side that various leaflets and online class descriptions assured me lay dormant within us all. My apartment slowly filled with tangled yarn 'plant hangers', lopsided clay sculptures, and a miniature Zen garden resembling a litter box with a small takeout fork attached.

I did the majority of this alone. My friends were anti-activities on principle, and I could no longer invoke their sympathy in the same way I had earlier in the summer. They were used to it by now – I was going through a breakup and would be for the foreseeable. They couldn't be expected to drop everything and come to my side whenever I felt bad. I felt bad all the time! Occasionally, as I struggled with glue and yarn or cut up little bits of fabric to sew onto a bigger bit of fabric, I would imagine my contented friends: Emotional Lauren snuggled up with her laid-back boyfriend, Nour, watching nature documentaries and crying about baby animals; Lauren coming home from an F45 class to her perfectly appointed apartment for one, ready to order fancy delivery; Amirah and Tom finding their light over tapas; Clive watching a movie with the handsome older dudes with whom he was in a kind of throuple situation. And there I was, tie-dyeing a towel.

Eventually even my single friends were not single enough for the path I was on. Clive ducked out after the fitness class I had brought him to turned out to include a jazz dance component. Lauren broke at paint night as we stood side by side, drinking wine with twelve other women all outlining the same image of a city skyline at sunset. She

added a few swipes of pink to the corner of a fading sky and said, 'This is self-harm. This is worse than when my boss made us go axe throwing.'

———

I could not sell anyone from the group chat on axe throwing, and Amy had spent the last two weeks holed up in a loft with some finance guy, alternating between texting this is IT!!!! and ignoring me for days. Instead, I took Nathan, a bearded, muscular man I'd met several years ago at a house party, who had recently responded to one of my Instagram Stories at three a.m. with lol.

Nathan was the kind of man who would have been considered vaguely alternative ten or even five years ago, but whose signifiers now combined to make clear that he was a former suburbanite who had moved to the city, gone vegan, and taken a job in music PR.

'People think it's all grain bowls and açai,' he said, taking a wide stance and eyeing the axe in his tattooed hand. His flannel shirt and ripped jeans seemed fused to his body, like someone had vacuum-packed Kurt Cobain to store over winter. 'But I'm living proof that you can eat like crap and still live a plant-based life. Ask me which Doritos are vegan,' he said, winding up. 'It's not all of them, but it's more than you'd think.'

The fact that he got a bull's-eye instantly, and several more thereafter, I found oddly depressing. Dating has a way of making incompatibility feel like personal failure; there was nothing technically *wrong* with Nathan, except

that I did not like him or want to spend any more time with him, which, in the context of us having paid $45 for an hour of axe throwing and one draught beer each, was a problem. When he told me I seemed like I had a 'great shape under there', I offered to go to the bar.

The venue did not only host axe throwing. Adults above the drinking age could come here to enjoy any number of loosely camp-themed activities: tug-of-war, shuffleboard, and that classic camp pastime, enormous video arcade games. I skirted around a large, rowdy group as they jostled each other over indoor lawn bowling, their opponents insisting, yes, Scott had put his foot over the line, he had – he had! – they'd all seen it.

What were they all doing here? What were they hoping to feel, these adults engaged in games from their real or imagined pasts? Distracting themselves, I guessed. This was the conclusion my ongoing hobby experiment seemed to be working toward. Skiing weekends, bowling, after-work volleyball leagues, knowing about professional sports … all activities seemed to be transparent efforts in void-avoidance, when actually nothing drove home the meaninglessness of life more than watching thousands of people desperately cheer as one millionaire tried to get a ball across another millionaire's line. The only activity that has ever really interested me is sitting around with my friends in flattering lighting, eating food and talking about who wanted to kiss us, and what we were wearing when they did.

I thought about this as I watched a group of twenty-something girls cheering while one of their friends whacked

a pinball machine. They were having a level of fun I'd never seen outside of a commercial for a chain restaurant. Maybe I was wrong. Maybe avoidance was the way forward. I considered joining them to cheer on their friend, who wasn't even doing that well at pinball, not that you would know from the onslaught of support she was receiving from her rowdy companions. She had just landed in a fifty-point pocket when the dart pierced my leg.

What happened was this: a woman shrieked, and when I looked for the source of the sound, three people were staring at me with their hands clapped over their mouths.

I looked down at my thigh. The skirt I was wearing (leather, a big swing) and the tights (double layered for extra smoothing and support) had helped, but there was nonetheless a small lawn dart impaled in my upper leg.

'Ohhhhh my god,' one of the women yelled. 'Oh my *god*, are you okay?!'

I didn't know how to answer. The dart did not appear deeply embedded, but what if it was plugging a vein? What if, when I pulled it out, I spurted blood all over everything, like in movies where someone gets nicked in the, what was it, jugular? Wasn't there a major artery in the leg somewhere? The key was probably not to panic, to keep my heart rate low, but that didn't feel like something that was up to me. What was the breathing thing – four, eight, five?

'Do you mind if I have a look at that?'

The voice belonged to a curly-haired man wearing a concerned expression and a shawl collar cardigan. 'Are you a doctor?' I asked.

'Better,' the drunk woman said, grabbing me by the arms and giving me what she must have felt was a reassuring shake. 'He's my *boss*.'

'Are *you* a doctor?'

'Maybe!' she said.

'You absolutely are not,' the man said, gently pushing her away. 'Go get some water, okay?'

Over her shoulder the woman yelled, '6Bites ER! CODE RED!'

Formerly called Taste of T.O., 6Bites was one of a number of new media ventures that dived in headfirst when a child actor turned rapper suggested we start calling our city 'the 6ix'. It ran restaurant reviews and interviews with local chefs and the occasional exposé about 'toxic kitchen culture', but mostly it seemed to make its living via videos of disembodied hands cooking completely inedible recipes and listicles about where to get a Bloody Mary with a burger in it.

'I'm sorry about her and everything else about this,' said the man, kneeling to examine my leg. 'A disaster, start to finish.'

An ambient awareness that he was quite handsome solidified into stress about whether all the tights and leather had given me swamp crotch.

'We gave the new hires a bar tab,' he said. 'This is the worst it's been, but believe me when I say you are not the first casualty of this dart game. Maybe I could ...' He reached tentatively for the dart.

'Shouldn't we get an employee or something?' I asked.

'They're all, like, nineteen and stoned,' he said. 'I think I'm your best shot. Plus, it looks like it's not – I mean, that's barely in there. Just let me ...'

His fingertips made contact with the body of the dart. I flinched and looked away, unable to bear it. My face was still scrunched, body tensed, eyes averted, when I heard it clink to the ground. I examined my skirt: it hadn't even pierced the lining.

'I'm Simon,' he said, smiling as he got up off the ground. He had the calmly confident demeanour typical of the attractive, but there was an openness to him that suggested something else: an insistently supportive home environ- ment maybe, or a religious upbringing. He looked like someone who thought heaven was real.

Simon offered to buy me a drink to make up for the injury. I pointed out that there had not, in the end, been any injury at all. He said, 'Still,' and started walking toward the bar.

I didn't know how to process the straightforwardness of his flirtation. It was my understanding that romantic (or at least casually sexual) intent was communicated with a series of tongue-in-cheek digs about the other person's clothing, habits, or character, maybe some social media interaction conducted at a conspicuous hour. This earnest 'can I buy you a drink?' approach was new and disconcerting. Still, he was very good-looking, and I had ignored weirder feelings than novelty in the name of a few minutes' conversation with someone hot.

Simon got to the bar, made easy small talk with the person behind it, and ordered a drink I'd never heard of,

with bourbon and Campari and some third ingredient I didn't catch. It was bright red and tasted sweet and bitter, with a cherry in it. He thanked and tipped the bartender. I watched them absorb his easy smile. Then he turned to me.

We conversed easily and without any uncomfortable pauses for twenty minutes or so. I discovered that he was thirty-one, single, and lived nearby. He was almost impossibly straight – the button-down shirt, the assumed camaraderie with the bartender, the fervent support of a soccer team I didn't even know Toronto had – but no immediate red flags presented themselves. He seemed to be a kind, soft-spoken man who felt at home in this bar and presumably every other place he'd ever been. The yelling of drunk people and clattering of various lawn games made it hard to hear each other, and although I liked having to press my face near his ear to speak, I wanted to talk more intimately and in private.

'Are you allowed to ditch your interns?' I asked. It was unusual of me to 'put myself out there' like this, but I had already noticed myself trotting out reliable flirt techniques: an exaggeratedly girlish version of my regular laugh, insults that were really compliments, some slutty straw work I was not proud of. It didn't feel like a risk to show this man interest; for reasons unclear (to me at least), he was visibly interested already.

'Technically no,' he said. 'Although I do hate it here. Do you need to get back to your group at some point?'

I looked back at my booth, where Nathan was chatting happily with another table, presumably about seitan. 'Not really.'

'Great,' he said. 'Would you like to come home with me?'

Simon had biked there. He fiddled with a U-lock while I sent Nathan a text saying I'd had to leave due to an unspecified emergency I heavily implied was diarrhoea. His bike freed, Simon offered to walk beside me, then said, 'Wait, no,' taking off his sweater and bunching it over his pannier rack to form a crappy cushion: 'Get on.'

I rolled my eyes – the whole thing seeming kind of *Aladdin*. But I did get on, and we coasted down Dovercourt and the autumn wind whipped my hair back, and I thought that if this was how Princess Jasmine felt, she was probably having a pretty good time. Then I opened my mouth wide and a bug flew into it.

When we stepped inside his apartment, I yelped.

'You have to tell me what's going on with curtains,' I said. 'I've been going on all these dates and no men have them? What is that? Do you hate sleep? Privacy? I recently gave a blow job in full view of some teens jumping on a trampoline.'

'Jesus.'

'The man had no curtains!' I said. 'There was literally no other option.'

'Guess you could have not given the blow job,' he said, taking off his coat and hanging it on a neat row of hooks by the door. 'I moved in here at somewhat short notice, and there were these terrible plastic blinds, so I took those down and haven't replaced them yet. I'm going to.'

'When did you move in?'

'Four months ago.'

I walked past him into the living room; it was mid-century modern, like everyone else's. Something smelled good, either his apartment or him. I peeked into the bedroom to make sure there were sheets on the bed (not always a guarantee, Tinder had taught me). Not only were there sheets, the bed was made.

His closet didn't have a door, and I could see a row of crisp blue collared shirts, exactly like the one he was wearing now. I wondered what this meant about his personality, if he was risk averse or wealthy or had merely found out Uniqlo was going to stop making a particularly well-loved style of Oxford. This Snoop's Math was one of the best parts of being single, and the reason I rarely invited anyone back to my place. I wanted to nose around the other person's home, drawing conclusions from their drinking vessels, knick-knack placement, toilet-paper ply; the idea of someone doing this to me made my blood run cold.

I wandered back into the living room, where Simon was rummaging in his cupboards.

'Snack situation dire, I'm sorry to say,' he said. 'Want a beer?'

I nodded. His fridge was clean and sparse and sad: a few Mexican beers, some Polaroid film, three kinds of hot sauce, and dog food.

'Do you not eat at home?' I asked.

'Not often.'

'Do you have a dog?'

'I did, yeah.'

Simon and his girlfriend of four years had broken up last spring. To deal with the loneliness he had adopted an ancient

chihuahua called Bartholomew who died more or less instantly thereafter. Simon had spent the summer grieving the ex and the animal, and now he was in therapy, excavating what he wanted from life, his shortcomings as a person, the ways he'd failed and been failed in his relationship.

This was more information than I'd wanted, about the dog or his emotional history. He looked away wistfully, and it seemed like he might cry. I really, really didn't want him to.

'All I'm hearing is that dog food's been in there for three months at least,' I said.

Simon pursed his lips in mock-annoyance. 'Do you want this beer or not?'

I took it and thanked him, leaning over to awkwardly clink the base of my beer with his. He was farther away than anticipated, and the amount of effort expended to reach him was made immediately pathetic by the dull thud of glass barely tapped against glass.

'What about you?' he asked. 'When was your last relationship?'

I paused for a moment, then said it had been a while since I'd seen anyone. Even so, my love life wasn't that interesting. Nothing major to report.

'Really?' he asked. 'No big loves? No "one that got away"?'

'Nope.' I shrugged. 'Not a relationship person, I guess.' I told him I'd recently deleted Tinder for the fourth time and hoped it would stick.

Simon had not ventured onto the apps. He had been casually seeing a friend of a friend, and their time together

seemed to be running its course. She had been asking, with increased frequency, for him to slap her in the face while they had sex.

'I want to give her what she wants, obviously,' he said. 'But it feels a bit … soon maybe? I'm trying to figure out how to do it in a respectful way.'

I told him that might be missing the point. There was an unpleasant moment in which Simon was obviously thinking over how to say something, and then he came out with it: 'I don't know if it's a good idea to sleep together.'

'You don't have to slap *me*,' I said. 'I mean, you could. I've never tried that, but I'm sure it's, like, a step up from hair pulling, which at this point in the discourse is basically kissing, right?'

'It's not that,' he said.

I was starting to feel embarrassed. He was the one who invited me here! What had he thought was going to happen? I recalled a phrase I had been shocked to learn was common parlance in Australia: 'I'm not here to fuck spiders.' I had first heard of this saying from a bisexual polyamorist from Melbourne, with whom I'd shared a drink and a conversation about whether I'd be an appropriate participant in the threesome she and her husband were hoping to arrange. We did not have the threesome, in the end, but it's always fun to learn something new about language.

It occurred to me that I had read the entire situation wrong. Maybe this man did not find me incredibly compelling, as his behaviour, speech and body language had suggested. Maybe he was only trying to avoid a lawsuit for

6Bites. Maybe he was 'too nice', and this kind of misunderstanding happened to him all the time, his friends always warning him to stop inviting strange women back to his place for a long talk and no sex over one beer. Maybe he had a bad penis. Maybe he was gay. I was about to make my excuses to the overly polite homosexual company man with the busted dick when he put his hand on my leg and my brain stopped working.

He removed it almost as quickly, but the idea, let's say, had been planted. I moved toward him, and he shifted slightly backward, saying, 'I need to tell you something first.'

I leaned back on the couch, tucking my legs underneath me in an effort to look understanding and ready to listen and also, probably, small. Simon took a deep breath and launched into a long, emotional story, the short version of which was that he had cheated on his girlfriend.

Of course! Of course he had. Naturally he was not just some super-bachelor who appeared out of nowhere, rescuing divorced women from low-stakes lawn game accidents. He was a classic bad man, a dirty dog. He had met someone at a vodka-sponsored food festival (for god's sake) and slept with her and lied about it for several months, until confessing and getting kicked out of his apartment by a woman who had done nothing but love and support him (probably) for the last four years of her now-wasted life.

It was a classic tale, and one I knew well, having talked many friends through near-identical scenarios in recent years. For straight women in their late twenties, getting cheated on by a partner is basically jury duty.

I told him this made me think 40% less of him but did not particularly impact my feelings about whether to spend the night in his bed. The relief that spread across his face seemed unrelated to sex.

'Really?'

'You caught me at a good time,' I said. 'I've been reading a lot of Esther Perel.'

He seemed, again, like he might cry. I patted his back and considered telling him about my breakup, but decided it was not enormously relevant and might even, in this instance, be bragging. After all, neither Jon nor I had broken the one mandatory condition of contemporary romantic coupling; we had done the noble thing and slowly fallen out of love over time.

I considered saying something like, *do you want to talk about it?* though this proved totally unnecessary. He did want to talk about it. A lot. It was interesting to hear him wrestle with so many things at once: whether the relationship would have ended on its own some other way (probably), whether he was a good person (unclear), whether he should be dating again yet (unclear but … probably not), and what to do about the 'toxic male paradigm' (his words) in which he had been raised and socialised. His sentences were full of conditions, deferments to his various privileges. He used a lot of therapy terms. This was clearly a man who journaled.

I told him it seemed like a positive sign that he felt bad, that he was doing all this therapy and asking all these slightly lame questions about morality and love and manhood.

'I hope so,' he said.

He looked sweet and nervous and shy, the casually confi-
dent man from the bar punctured and deflated by the great
lawn dart of life. I tried to temper some of the empathy I
felt by thinking about how mad his girlfriend probably was
and would remain for some time. If I was her friend I
would have suggested we burn him in effigy. But I did not
know her, so instead I was in his living room, waiting for
him to stop moping and go down on me.

He finished his beer and said, 'I spend a lot of time
worrying that I'm fundamentally a worse person than I
thought I was. How can you tell if something you did was
a stupid mistake or a real sign of your character?'

I didn't know how to respond to this, so I suggested we
go to his room.

———

The sex was more intimate than I was hoping for – I could
see how this man's style might require some lead-up to a
slap – but also significantly better than average. Like
everything else about him, it was sincere and engaged and
purposeful. I wondered if this was because he didn't know
I was divorced; as far as he was concerned I was just some
woman, single for normal reasons. Maybe what I was feel-
ing was the absence of pity, the way someone touched you
when they didn't know your life was in a shambles.
Whatever it was, I felt connected to him in a way that I
hadn't with anyone else I'd been out with since Jon. This
was annoying, to be sure, but you can't argue with tech-

nique. After a combined four orgasms we fell asleep, the streetlamps outside shining directly into the bedroom.

The next morning, I woke up spooning Simon tightly – a position borrowed from my married life, and something I had been humiliated to find myself doing instinctually with several recent dates. It never felt right: the familiarity of the feeling and the strangeness of the people brought on an unsettling emotional vertigo. I tried to remove my hand without jostling him. He muttered something, half asleep, then turned me over, the crook of his elbow on my waist, his forearm coming to rest between my boobs. I lay there awkwardly, wondering how long it would take for him to get up so I could leave.

When my eyes opened an hour or so later, I was alone. I dressed quickly and came out into the kitchen, my mouth tasting stale and feeling textured. Simon was making coffee in a robe.

'Morning,' he said amiably. The robe was mono-grammed.

'I think I'm late for work.'

I walked into his weirdly clean bathroom and rinsed my mouth with toothpaste, jamming my finger clumsily around my gums and teeth and the sides of my tongue.

'You can use my toothbrush if you want,' Simon yelled from the kitchen.

'What? That's ... no thank you.'

Simon popped his head around the door: 'Doesn't seem less hygienic than anything else we got up to, but suit your-self. Coffee?'

'I have to get going.'

'Sorry for oversharing last night,' he said. 'I've been struggling with how to be transparent about my past with new people while also being mindful not to, you know, emotional dump.'

I had no idea what he was talking about.

'It's really, um, don't worry about it,' I said distractedly, my eyes scanning the living room for things I'd dropped the night before. I grabbed my phone from where he'd plugged it in (!) on his nightstand and put my hair up in a bun. When I came back out to the kitchen, there was coffee on the counter in a to-go cup.

'You just have these in your apartment?'

'A friend of mine manages a coffee shop,' he said. 'Slips me a sleeve every now and then. I mostly use them to take beer to the park.'

I picked it up and took a sip. It was delicious.

'Are you a serial killer?'

He laughed and leaned toward me, pressing his lips to mine with a surprising amount of force for eight a.m. and pushing me up against his open front door. For a second, I thought he might try to take me back to the bedroom, but he pulled away, looked at me, and said, 'That was nice. I'd like to see you again.'

This was very off-putting.

'Were you raised in a cult?' I asked. 'Are you American, or something?'

A neighbour opened the door across the hall, and I was suddenly conscious of my smudged mascara, my conspicuously backcombed hair. Simon made a conspiratorial face at me, then waved at the neighbour, a hip dad who looked

put together, if sleepy. It struck me that this man was probably five years older than me at most, and yet I felt like a teen caught necking at the movies by a grown-up. I wondered if he considered me a peer or a young person, if he waved at a lot of women in this hallway. The neighbour disappeared down the stairs and I turned to Simon, my ridiculous paper cup hot in my hand.

'Thanks for the coffee.'

'Any time.'

————

Three days later, Simon texted me a screenshot of an online purchase: ONE (1) – PAIR LINED GROMMET TOP CURTAINS in DARK GREY. I spent a few days trying to think of something clever to say back but couldn't come up with anything, so I left it.

From: Lori@JansonParkerStevenson.ca
To: m——@gmail.com
Sent: 18 October, 12:04 p.m.
Re: re: some questions about the invoice?????

Hi Maggie,

Thanks for your email, received last Thursday, 11 October. I'm sorry to hear you were surprised by our most recent invoice and thought you might like to see an itemised breakdown of each charge (copied below). As a courtesy, you will not be charged for this email, but please note, per the invoice, that emails do come with attendant fees.

On the topic of correspondence, I think we should address the phone calls. I know this is a difficult time, and I appreciate that you, like anyone going through major life upheaval, are under a great deal of pressure. I am happy to answer calls from my clients at any time, to talk them through the separation and divorce process or receive any relevant information pertaining to forthcoming litigation. However, calls made to my office or personal cell phone are billed at my standard rate of $215 per hour, and, as you will see below, the charges can add up over time. If you are looking for ways to curb your legal fees, finding a family member or other confidant with whom to discuss your experiences and feelings might be a wise place to start.

Thanks and all the best,
Lori

Disbursements and Time Billed, 10 Aug.– 10 Sept. 2018

Photocopies ... $50.75

Fax ... $3.50

Call re: *spousal support law, explained to client that the marriage had been too short to entitle either party to collect support following dissolution of the marriage* (7 mins) ... $25.06

General Couriers/Messengers ... $10.43

Call re: *inability to find 2017 tax return; informed client an estimate as to income based on previous years' returns would suffice; conversation regarding difficulties filing as freelancer, hassle of keeping receipts; request for couples counsellor referral* (12 mins) ... $42.96

Call re: *having found 2017 tax return* (3 mins) ... $10.74

Call re: *the 2017 return actually turning out to be missing several pages; inquiries regarding husband's legal representation and communication with counsel; request for 'worst' stories from counsel's career; lengthy digression regarding state of app-based dating today* (28 mins) ... $100.33

Litigation Support Vendors – Immediate Process Serving ... $30.00

General Couriers/Messengers ... $18.90

Call re: *feelings of despair, exhaustion with the legal process, and distraction at work; reminded client divorce is a marathon, not a sprint, and suggested an increased focus on self-care as petition has not yet been filed and many stages remain; several minutes of cursing* (30 mins) ... $107.40

Emails, various ... $48.35

Litigation Support Vendors – Immediate Process Serving ... $30.00

Call re: *apology for previous day's call* (1 min) ... GRATIS

TOTAL ... $478.42

Merris, presumably sick of hearing me complain about the vultures of the Toronto rental market, offered me the basement suite in her *Golden Girls* house, saying I could have the first month free if I agreed to walk her roommate's Great Dane, Lydia, while the roommate recovered from a foot operation.

It was no beach house or New York loft, and I was not particularly interested in occupying the basement of even a very erudite retirement community. But dating was turning out to be almost as expensive as divorce, and I'd been getting a lot of skincare treatments with Amy, and it struck me that I could go on even more dates and blast my dermis with even more discount lasers if I was living somewhere that wasn't eating up 80% of my income each month. Also, the lawyer calls were adding up. I protested for a few days then accepted, allowing Jiro to ask me taunting questions about the arrangement, and accepting an aspidistra from Olivia that I knew would die instantly.

I asked Merris if she worried that having me as a lodger would affect our professional relationship. She rolled her

eyes and told me to email her about a move-in date; there was a broken aquarium she'd need a few days to get rid of before the place was habitable. I gave my landlord notice. She wrote back, Sorry to see you go! then listed the place online for $400 more per month.

I moved on a grey Saturday a few days before Halloween. Both Laurens came to help (Amirah couldn't find someone to take her shift; Clive had a hangover). We had agreed to meet at ten thirty, and they surprised me by showing up almost on the dot. I was not ready. They found me in the middle of the living room, trying to wrestle a pile of hideous vintage coats into a bag.

Still, the apartment was less than half full, and the three of us made fast work of it, taping boxes closed, finding places for a dish rack or oven mitt I had failed to pack in my admittedly poor efforts to prepare for this day. While wrapping bowls in old magazines, I told them about an unpleasant date I'd been on the night before, with an older man who had complimented my breasts, asked my age, then told me they had 'probably five or six good years left'.

'Jesus,' said Emotional Lauren. 'What an asshole! I've seen your boobs and they've got a solid eight to ten in them – I mean, as long as you don't have kids. What happened to Dart Guy? He sounded like … not that.'

I told her I wasn't sure I wanted to see him again. Through dating apps and Instagram and parties and bars, I had access to so many potential romantic or at least sexual partners, it was hard to know if I cared about any of them. Even if it seemed like I had connected with someone, I was

not particularly interested in that information. My carousel of weeklong adventures was working fine for now.

'There's also the option of, you know, being alone,' said Lauren. 'Nothing wrong with taking some time to yourself.'

Emotional Lauren nodded, adding that the sex shop near her house was promoting a cool new vibrator that was 'essentially a production-grade suction cup'. We agreed that it did sound pretty cool, then got to work disassembling my wretched couch.

Leaving my apartment was less emotionally wrenching than I'd expected. 'Continuing to live in the mausoleum of your old relationship was maybe not the healthiest option, all things considered,' Lauren said, lugging a decrepit coffee table to the kerb for someone younger and more desperate than us to take.

Stripped to its bones, the place was revealed for the shithole it was, all cheap flooring and badly plastered holes, with a bathroom that was almost certainly an illegally converted screened-in porch – in the winter, the toilet water would freeze.

Once, right after we were married, my grandmother had come over for dinner. As we showed her around, she was delighted to see a few pieces of hand-me-down furniture she'd thought were gone forever, sold or lost to time. 'Very charming,' she'd said, eyeing our old couch and scratched end tables, the kitchen chairs we'd picked up on the side-walk. 'It's just like the place your grandfather and I lived in when we were first married.'

I reminded her that when she and my grandfather had been newlyweds, they'd been nineteen and living in post-

war Hamilton, in tenement housing where the heating was operated with nickels. She hadn't even had a job. We were both pushing thirty, worked more than full-time, and could barely afford to live here, in this place where the kitchen 'tiles' were easy-peel stickers, and the landlord locked the thermostat in a small plastic box to avoid us turning the heat on before November.

'Still,' she'd said. 'Nice to see my old dresser again.'

I thought about where my parents had lived at my age: in a little house they owned, with a baby on the way. Jon and I had once talked to a mortgage broker to see what we'd need to buy a home. He'd suggested saving $80,000 and leaving the city.

The Laurens broke my bed frame trying to take it apart, so we put the headboard on the lawn with the rest of the sale items. To avoid spending money on a moving van and hopefully make some money on the side, I'd decided to hold an impromptu garage sale, spreading my possessions in front of the house and offering them to anyone who stopped to check them out. So far, a hair dryer and a clothing rack had earned us $12.85, which we immediately put toward pastries.

We spent the day alternating between manning the items for sale on the lawn and driving boxes and bags and poorly protected plants over to Merris's in Lauren's car, depositing them roughly in my new digs before heading back to pick up the rest of my garbage. After our last trip, Lauren and I returned to find Emotional Lauren victorious and overwhelmed. Some students had come by and cleared out the lawn. 'Their house full-on *burned down* a few weeks ago,

and they didn't have insurance, and they were starting over with nothing,' she said.

She'd offered them the lot for $50. 'They were so happy, you wouldn't believe it,' she said, beaming. 'We did a good thing today.'

Back at Merris's, we unpacked and ate falafel wraps, and Lauren noted that I might have preferred to make more than fifty bucks for a similar percentage of my possessions.

'Do you have any records?' Emotional Lauren asked. 'When Nour put his out at our yard sale, all these men materialised from nowhere. They were *drawn*. We made, like, hundreds of dollars.'

I consulted a box labelled VERY MISC. The only records in it were Alanis Morissette's *Jagged Little Pill*, an Ella Fitzgerald live album, and something called *NONSTOP DANCING 1600*, which was a compilation of seventeenth-century reels and jigs, curated by two different men named Siegfried. We decided to sell some of my old clothes instead.

Lauren had recently received $80 for a beat-up Gucci belt of her mother's at a secondhand store on College. I did not own any Gucci but thought maybe they would have some interest in the approximately three hundred pairs of too-small denim I'd ordered online and could not bring myself to return, because to do this was to abandon the fantasy that one day they might fit, and perfectly. I resolved to drop by the secondhand store tomorrow, after first trying on all the jeans one final time, to see.

'I want to stress that these problems make it sound like I am not very beautiful, but I think we can all agree that I look pretty good, possibly even great, and it is the contemporary method of manufacturing, sizing and marketing clothes that is the problem,' I said.

The group obliged.

We sorted through my clothing and accessories, throwing anything I was tired of that neither Lauren wanted in a big plastic bag. At some point I came upon my wedding and engagement rings. I chucked them in too.

'Maybe … wait on that,' said Lauren.

I told her I couldn't imagine ever wanting them again, that surely if I did it would be a sign I'd succumbed to full derangement. What could I do, string them on a chain and make a miserable necklace? Repurpose them for a second time around when I finally gave in to everyone's pressure and decided to get married again? Anyway, the entire set had cost under $400 from a pawn shop near Jon's office. I did not like to guess the resale value of a twice-used wedding ring, but it felt safe to assume: not high.

Lauren touched my shoulder, then reached in and fished out the small box. 'Tell you what,' she said. 'I'll keep them for a bit. You can tell me if you want to do something with them later.' She slid them on the ring finger of her right hand. 'Okay, these look great on me. Maybe I should call Jon?'

Emotional Lauren screamed, which made Lauren cackle. I threw a pillow at her and told her to keep the rings. They did look pretty on her, and someone should get something out of them.

'Will it bum you out to see them?' she asked.

I shook my head.

'Dope,' she said. 'Free diamond. When I helped my brother move, he just gave us pizza.'

We kept sorting until Merris arrived with a box of welcome cookies. 'Children are always coming to our door with something or other,' she said. 'The only way to get rid of them is to buy whatever little trinkets they're selling. Cookies today, so here you are, *bienvenue*.'

The cookies were the superior mint chocolate kind, and we were happy to have them. Merris and the Laurens got along great, though she departed after her first cookie, promising not to come downstairs often.

'Your space is your space; your business, your business,' she said. 'I don't want to learn anything that might make me view you differently.'

I told her she was more confident in the wildness of my lifestyle than me. Lauren made a joke about hosting an orgy and inviting the gals upstairs for an air of authenticity. Merris rolled her eyes and shut the door, yelling over her shoulder that those only happened in the suburbs. The Laurens left soon after, headed to the launch of some doomed magazine, and suddenly I was in my new apartment, alone.

I looked at my boxes and bags and various piles. I sorted through some general MISC. I applied a face mask and sat in different corners of the room and thought, *this is a place to become yourself*. Then I saw a mouse, cried, peeled the mask off with great effort and not insignificant pain, and went to sleep.

The next morning, the unfamiliar setting had me awake early and disoriented. I made coffee, climbed back into bed, and drank it while attempting some 'morning pages'. I abandoned this effort almost instantly: journalling felt embarrassing and pointless. Why write my feelings down when I could tell them to my loved ones or write a too-long, fake-deep caption under a picture of some clouds? At least then there would be feedback. Keeping a journal seemed like a slower, somehow more tedious way to think about the things I had already bored myself with by overthinking. No.

The apartment was really a studio, compact but bright. Big double doors led to a backyard covered in a thin layer of six a.m. mist. Unlike my old place, the quiet felt intentional here: the sound of an apartment for one. I did not feel an absence; there was only room enough for me.

I went upstairs and called for Lydia, who came bounding around a corner, toweringly large and covered in drool. I attached her lead, and we wandered around my new neighbourhood – quieter than my old one, with weirder coffee shops and expensive independent clothing boutiques that seemed to exclusively sell outfits for ageing psychics heading out of town on a cottage weekend.

Lydia was a well-behaved dope with no idea how huge she was, deferring instantly to the much smaller, more confident dogs that strolled right up to get in her face or sniff her butthole. I bought a coffee and a cardamom bun from a cash-only place decorated in black-and-white pictures of lattes.

When I got home, I let Lydia off her leash and said hello to Betty and Inessa, Merris's housemates. They were old

and vaguely bohemian and politely uninterested in me; Merris had told them all the relevant details, and they were engaged in a heated argument about whether an arborist needed to be called about a worrisome fungus Inessa had found on the big tree in the backyard. Betty, to whom Lydia belonged, had her foot in a plastic boot.

I went back out the front door, walked around the house, and entered the basement through my dingy little side entrance. I filled a large trash bag with several pairs of size 33 jeans and some other old clothes and headed to the secondhand store.

The shop door made an aggressive honking sound when I opened it, and the woman behind the counter looked up. She was tall and slender and had a bunch of little tattoos on her long, graceful hands. She looked like she lived in a pottery studio on a boat, or a van she'd painstakingly renovated with her freelance model boyfriend, or maybe just an enormous downtown condo her parents had purchased. I did not really want to show her my clothes.

There was no one else in the store. I considered pretending to browse for a few minutes then leaving, but was conspicuously carrying a translucent bag full of old clothing, which made it implausible to suggest I was on my way somewhere else. I reluctantly heaved the bag onto the counter and began an Idiot's Monologue about how I'd never done this before, wasn't quite sure how it worked, and hoped she'd be interested in some of my wares. I said 'wares'. Actually, I said 'wares, as it were'. I wanted to die.

The woman sighed. She was impeccably dressed, with a haircut I recognised from Instagram. Only cool girls had it,

and it seemed like you had to go to San Francisco to get it done, but she had probably cut hers herself, with scissors rescued from an old shipwreck.

She dumped my items in front of her, pulling at seams and evaluating labels, occasionally tutting or raising an eyebrow. Everything was sorted into three piles according to some opaque proprietary system. Occasionally she would say 'nice' or 'cute', and I would grin monstrously and stammer something about where I'd acquired it and why I no longer wanted it: 'Oh yeah, hahaha, I got that at Topshop, my mom was with me and literally thought the store only did tops, isn't that … ! Anyway, it's too small now, because of what birth control did to my boobs.'

The woman smiled a tight-lipped smile, leaving her eyes out of it. She pawed through the rubble of my life: ambitiously tall heels I'd worn exactly once, a bunch of those woven belts that makeover shows basically sutured to the bodies of big girls in the mid-aughts, a long chain necklace with an owl on it. Twenty-nine years on earth, and this was what I had to show for myself. I had argued many times with my Catholic grandmother that there was no such thing as hell. I wanted to call her and apologise: hell was real, and this was it.

Finally, the woman had sorted everything. 'We'll keep these,' she said, gesturing to the two largest piles. 'And we can donate the rest of those if you want, but I'm going to have to give you back these trousers.' She slid a pair of corduroy pants across the counter with a sympathetic expression. 'The thing is, we can't accept clothes that have been soiled.'

My ears flattened against my head like a cat's.

'*Soiled* ...?'

'Not laundered.'

'That's not what soiled means.'

'Well, there's a stain on them.'

I grabbed the pants, nervously examining the relevant areas. I found nothing. I turned them over and saw a small purple dot near the hem.

'The stain is on the *leg*,' I said. 'And it's juice or something.'

'It's none of my business what it is,' she said. 'No judgement, obviously, but we can't accept them.'

The woman blinked at me to indicate that the conversation about the pants was over. I was shoving them hurriedly into my tote bag when a man's voice said, 'You shouldn't shit in your clothes.'

Simon was smiling too widely, unable to hide how pleased he was with himself for the joke. The smile took some of the bite out of his initial cool guy move (appearing behind me with a gently teasing line) but added to the overall impression of him (a straightforward, almost weirdly affable man).

'Exactly, sir, thank you,' said the woman. 'There's a policy.'

I dropped my bag on the floor and turned to Simon. He was looking at me with the same unembarrassed interest he'd shown at axe throwing.

'You got curtains,' I said.

He laughed, and I realised with some anxiety that I was happy to see him.

'I did.'

There was a silence. To break it, I told him work had been busy, and I'd been moving apartments, and I had a lot on my plate right now, and I was sorry I hadn't texted.

'Oh, don't worry about me,' he said. 'My bedroom's pitch-black, and I'm loving every minute.'

'Excuse me, ma'am, can you also take this?'

The woman was holding up a T-shirt the Laurens had made for my bachelorette party, featuring my face photoshopped onto a sexy undead body wearing a wedding dress. Above me they'd scrawled in Sharpie, MAGS' BOO-CHELORETTE 2016 and, beneath, LAST DICK EVER. My zombie hand was holding a severed penis.

'It was inside out before, and now that I see it – I mean, realistically speaking, we probably can't sell something so crude,' she said. 'Like on the back it says "RIP", but the R stands for—'

'"Rim in Peace", yeah,' I said quickly. 'It's not serious. It's a funny, um— I just thought, maybe, it might be funny to someone. Like someone might buy it ironically, you know… to be funny.'

I stopped talking, defeated. I could feel my face getting hot and red, which I knew from experience would only make it redder and hotter. What was this woman's problem? I was just trying to make a few extra bucks selling old clothing I no longer needed. Was that a crime, wanting to pass things along for someone else to enjoy, instead of fulfilling the toxic prophecy of fast fashion and consigning them to landfill? For fuck's sake, I was trying to *recycle*.

The woman turned to Simon: 'Do you think it's funny?'

'I do, I'm afraid.' Simon smiled.

I protested heavily, though it was no use. He fished $5 out of his pocket, bought the shirt, and pulled it on. 'So,' he said, making a big show of primping in the mirror. 'You're married!' My undead eyes and big zombie boobs stared back at me.

'Divorced, actually. Well, separated.'

Simon's eyebrows raised. 'Ah.'

'It takes a while to make it official, like a full year and then some,' I said. 'Still kind of … serving my time. The good news is we already cashed everyone's cheques.' I smiled weakly.

The woman behind the counter looked confused. 'The shirt says 2016 … How long were you married?'

'Like five seconds, basically,' I said, too high and too quickly. 'Thank you for asking!'

'No need to get defensive,' she said, busying herself with a pile of old bathing suits.

To avoid yelling at her, I refocused on Simon. He looked curious but not angry. He looked kind.

'I don't know why I didn't tell you,' I said. 'I was having a really nice time and didn't want to be a downer, but it *is* a downer, there's no way around it, and then I felt weird about not telling you, so I didn't—'

'Don't worry about it,' he said, seeming to mean it. 'Divorce is, well … that's a spicy meatball.'

I didn't know how to respond to this, so I suggested we get a drink.

Reasons I Cried, 12–23 November

Bus too full and too hot

Neck looked busted

Dogs, generally

Took a taxi home from a date's house late at night, and the window was open and the city looked empty and beautiful, but I knew it was full of people and I felt connected to them all, and also I was incredibly drunk

Tried five times to remember my password for the App Store, couldn't do it, tried to reset it, couldn't do that either, and eventually remembered it was my own name with an exclamation mark

Jiro saw me open a granola bar at work and witheringly asked if I was 'treating myself', and I was

Thought about how much effort my parents put into teaching me how to read

Had sex with Simon and it was lovely and caring, and the tears surprised us both

One of my students called me 'tall' in a charged way

Saw pictures of an ancient mosaic floor, discovered four feet under an old Italian woman's backyard, perfectly preserved, waiting

Had sex with Simon and cried again, and then he asked about it, and I cried more

Watched a documentary about how many kinds of animals are extinct now

Someone stood me up during the wrong bit of my cycle

R. Kelly came on the radio in Clive's car, and I said the song reminded me of high school, and Amirah said it reminded her of 'the prevalence of sexual assault in the music industry', and I felt like the rest of the car was judging me, and also Jon and I used to dance around the apartment to 'Ignition (Remix)' all the time before we knew a) that R. Kelly was a rapist and b) that we were no longer in love

Used one of those calculators to determine how soon you can retire if you make X amount and save Y amount each month; found I could reasonably begin retirement in 238 years

Steve from *Sex and the City* yelling, 'There's good stuff here!!' at Miranda, who cannot yet accept his love

This description of tomato sauce, in a magazine: 'The genius of Hazan's sauce lies in the fact that, although it's basically a convenience food, made of only inexpensive, shelf-staple ingredients, it can't be improved upon. Add fancy olive oil or fresh Genovese basil if you're moved to; they won't make it any better. The sauce is already as good as can be'

Thought about running into Janet in the street the way you might encounter an ex-lover and try to maintain a distinguished distance while telling them they 'looked well'

Found a postcard Jon sent me from Florida with a big pair of tits on it that said FAKE BOOBS & REAL ATTITUDE

Read all my Facebook Messenger chats from July 2014, when Jon went to Florida

Sex with Simon

Sex with Simon

Remembered everyone I love will die someday, many of them before me; that I will either know their deaths or hurt them with mine, and no matter what I do, the end is coming for all of us at a time we cannot know; that in the meantime my body will rot around my bones, getting creased and mottled and less efficient each day, and that this moment, right now, is the youngest and healthiest and most beautiful I'll ever be, and I don't feel that young or healthy or beautiful – I feel, actually, like I am losing a war with my own posture,

and is it worse if my sister dies before me, or if I die before her, and what will I say at my father's funeral?

A Tim Hortons commercial where some gay dads bring doughnuts to their daughter's hockey practice

The futon frame Merris had provided broke almost as soon as I moved in, but IKEA was backed up with holiday orders, so the SKÅRNSK I'd sent for was not scheduled to arrive until Christmas Eve. I used its delivery to justify skipping a large family event on the twenty-fourth and promised to take the train up the next morning.

Friends, loved ones and popular wisdom had suggested that the holidays might be difficult this year, that every 'new first' without my husband would be gut-wrenching in its own way, but things had been alright so far: Simon and I had gone skating at City Hall like middle-aged tourists, campus had taken on a yuletide glimmer, and the group chat Secret Santa had gone down in classic style, with Clive over-boozing a traditional plum pudding and nearly singeing an eyebrow when he set it alight. There had been a potluck at work, to which Olivia brought 'protein snicker-doodles', and the ladies upstairs had decked the house in nondenominational holiday decorations.

Exam season meant less trekking to my office and more sitting in bed wearing a floor-length turtleneck, eating stew

from the pot and writing 'SOURCE???' on tenuously ecocritical readings of *The Revenger's Tragedy*. Though Betty's foot was getting better I continued walking Lydia most mornings. It got me out of bed and outdoors, and it was gratifying to have a big, silent buddy who was always excited to see me.

Lydia was an ideal companion, a peaceful being whose only interests in this life were being fed and scratched on the head – I related. Sometimes the old gals wouldn't hear her barking at the upstairs door, and she'd saunter down to my entrance, scritch at it with her paw, and whimper until I let her in and gave her a bite of whatever I was eating. I liked our hangs – me working or dyeing my eyebrows or noodling around online, her sprawled across my lower half, farting. I had so far not succeeded in convincing her to sleep in my bed overnight, but I was working on it.

On the twenty-third, Amy took me for a festive mani-cure. We drank cheap eggnog, flipped through magazines, and talked about whether we had the bone structure for those big hats women were always wearing in California. Amy was in a great mood. She had recently been promoted to charge nurse on her floor at the children's hospital and was seeing someone new: a therapeutic clown from the juvenile oncology ward. 'He took off his nose and the whole floor flipped out,' she said. 'It was pandemonium, girls falling all over themselves, but competition brings out the best in me, so.'

They'd been on three dates in two weeks, including one where he'd packed a winter picnic, complete with a hot water bottle for each of them. He'd serenaded her with

gentle acoustic covers of popular R&B songs while she sipped mulled wine from a thermos.

'It was a dream,' she said, though she was describing my nightmare. 'He's an amazing singer and great with the kids … such a Pisces.'

I congratulated her on the promotion and the new man and admitted I didn't think astrology was real.

'Probably not,' she said, examining the jewelled holly on her index fingernail. 'But someone's relationship to the *idea* of their sign is still interesting information to have. Plus, I blame anything bad I do on being a Cancer.'

I asked what traits made up a Gemini. She told me they were 'the real psychos of the zodiac'. Amy said you could tell a man had been in a heavy-duty relationship if he knew what house his Venus was in.

Later that night I went to Simon's, to drink cider and show off my sparkly new nails. We had been seeing each other often, grabbing coffee between my classes, eating for free at restaurants Simon was reviewing, texting each other where u at last call. Initially, I'd worried he might be a book-ish-presenting himbo, because of his face and hair and tidy little outfits, but he was smart and funny and didn't even go on about 'sous vide' despite being a bona fide Food Guy.

He was surprising, too. One morning, hungover and wearing sunglasses at brunch, I noticed him staring at me intently. I examined my scrambled eggs and flagged the server down for ketchup. She brought some, and I dumped a pile of it on the edge of my plate. When I looked back at Simon, he was still staring, a small, moony smile on his face.

'I'm sorry,' he said. 'I can't not do this.'

He reached across the table and grabbed the glasses off my face. I steeled myself for whatever romantic bullshit he was about to pull, complimenting my eyes or telling me he wanted to be able to look – really *look* – at me, when he pulled a small square of white cloth from his pocket and started cleaning the lenses.

'These are disgusting,' he said, still smiling. 'You're an animal.' He blew on them and gave the bridge a final wipe before settling them back on my nose.

'You carry a shammy around with you?' I asked. 'All the time?'

Simon smiled. 'Sure,' he said. 'Why not?'

This slightly fussy thoughtfulness turned out to be his calling card. He once figured out I had used his cologne because I'd returned it to the shelf with its label turned inward. When he called me out on this, he gave me a small sampler bottle to keep in my purse.

'Relax,' he said, when I started stammering that I didn't think we were at a gift-giving stage. 'I got it for free when I bought my face wash.'

These incidents in mind, I took my shoes off in the hall when I got to his place. I walked in on socked feet and found him steam-cleaning his couch cushions, intently focused.

'What's your star sign?' I asked. 'Or like, what are all your star signs? Rising and stuff.'

Simon paused, steamer in hand. 'I'd have to call my mom for my exact birth time,' he said. 'But I'm fairly certain I have a lot of Virgo placements.'

We had sex and watched old episodes of *The Simpsons*, and he prepared a very simple meal with an almost impossible amount of concentration, like he was worried that if he looked the wrong way, the pre-made gourmet ravioli would take its moment to fall spectacularly and purposefully apart. He protested so long about me doing the dishes that it threatened to turn into our first major argument, then eventually relented and settled for hovering behind me with his hands on my hips while I cleaned two plates and a large pot with a strainer attachment.

'You smell good,' said Simon, nuzzling my neck.

I told him it was the funk of my hopes and dreams rotting inside my body (one of my lacklustre essays had been rejected by a third academic journal that week).

'Christ,' he said, pulling his arms away.

I turned around, bubbles on my hands: 'What is this … what's happening right now?'

'I wish I could say one sincere thing without you turning it into a joke,' he said. 'Take the compliment, man.'

'*Man?* Okay, dude.'

'That's exactly the deflective stuff I'm talking about,' he said. 'Just let me be nice to you.'

I rolled my eyes. Over the past few weeks, Simon had been lecturing me with increasing frequency about my alleged 'aversion to kindness'. He cocked his head with a pensive expression, and I could see that we were in danger of repeating the waterfall situation.

To sum up: Simon had a car. When he'd first told me this, I'd said, 'Of course you do,' and he'd looked at me quizzically and I had not elaborated. It was an old, beat-up

Volkswagen Golf in a subdued dark green, with scratchy carpeted seats and gummy cupholders. Occasionally he would pick me up and take me on a kind of drive-through buffet, hitting up Tim Hortons for a breakfast sandwich, McDonald's for hash browns and coffee, and Wendy's for a shake to dump our coffees into, something 6Bites had recently termed a 'dirtbag affogato'.

Last week he had driven us to Elora, to look at a waterfall. It being winter, there was no swimming or anything, so we admired the partially frozen natural attraction for about thirty minutes, then climbed back in the car to drive home. On the way we scanned for local radio stations, listening to Moose FM and Canoe 100.9 as they pumped out easy listening songs I remembered from family road trips past. I hadn't realised I was singing along until Simon chuckled quietly to himself. I stopped immediately, eyeing him with suspicion.

'What?'

'You're always, like, four beats ahead of the lyrics,' Simon said, drumming his fingers against the steering wheel. 'It's cute. Like you're rushing to get to the part you're most excited to sing.'

He laughed and I felt sick to my stomach.

'I don't do that,' I snapped. I turned off the radio and we drove without speaking for a few minutes, both of us focusing too hard on the passing landscape. I knew I was being an asshole and wished I wasn't. I couldn't help myself when he got like this, all observant and dopey. I didn't want him looking at me. I barely wanted me looking at me.

Simon sighed. 'Do you like this, what we're doing?' he asked, sounding a bit annoyed. 'Because I do, and I thought

you did. You're always texting me, and calling me, and asking me to hang out, and I don't know how else to read that.'

I muttered that I was enjoying it – obviously I was – but it was complicated. Simon asked if I wanted to talk about it. I turned the radio back on and rushed weakly into the bridge of a song about loving the nightlife, needing to boogie, etc.

Now in his kitchen I felt the same creeping discomfort, an outbreak of hives on the inside of my body. I wanted to tell him he was being a loser. I wanted to yell *NO!* I wanted him to understand that it was very stressful to experience this kind of thoughtful attention, knowing as I did how it could gnarl and twist into something unrecognisable, or disappear altogether. I wanted to tell him I had once woken up in his bed and thought in the dark that he was someone else, someone who had noticed all kinds of lovely things about me, and who more recently had said that being with me felt like drowning in another person's need. On further reflection, I did not really want to tell him about that.

I grabbed a tea towel and started drying dishes, badly. 'Fine,' I said. 'I smell amazing. I'm like laundry fucked a bakery and gave birth to a rose.' On the counter, my phone lit up with a new Tinder match. I flipped it over before Simon could see.

'That's more like it, bro,' he said, taking a plate from my hand and pulling me toward him. 'Next time we'll see if you can manage some eye contact.'

I could see that Simon was no longer worried. The crisis, as he saw it, was over. Why give it another thought? Simon

was a man who felt that things in life generally worked out, because, for him, they generally did. He was the kind of person for whom flights waited, to whom baristas gave free coffee and bartenders an extra shot. I had once seen him sweet-talk his way out of a speeding ticket when he also was not carrying his driver's licence. I wasn't going to be the one to break it to him that this was not normal. He kissed me and I thought, *this is so doomed.*

———

The next morning I sat alone in my big turtleneck, wrapping the identical sweater I'd bought for Hannah and considering posting an Instagram Story of myself in the cat filter with the caption meowwy christmas ... is that anything, which I knew was lame but didn't mind, because in the photo my jawline looked sharp.

I decided against it, posting instead a blurry image of discarded wrapping paper scraps that I hoped exuded a harried popularity. My windows were foggy with condensation, and I could hear some neighbourhood kids playing in the snow outside. I'd decided against a tree – what would I put on it? – but had propped up a few holiday cards on my dresser in a gesture toward festivity. A strand of tinsel dangled limply above my pile of dirty laundry.

I rewatched *White Christmas*, fast-forwarding through the musical number where all four leads expressed longing for the good old days of minstrelsy, then moved on to lesser (though no less enjoyable) holiday offerings, comedies about house swapping and mistaken identity and finding

love with a festive twist. During these I graded exams and made a satisfyingly disjointed lunch of cinnamon oatmeal, miso soup from a packet, and a rice cake covered in mustard and deli meat. For dessert, I put cheese on a cookie.

Around four thirty, I felt loneliness threatening to creep in. I went upstairs to see if Lydia was around. The house was deserted, everyone off with their respective families or, in Inessa's case, an exciting younger boyfriend (he was sixty-seven, but still). I went back downstairs and checked my to-do list, though everything was already ticked. Solitude makes a person too efficient. I attempted to nap, which only meant I had my eyes closed for the last of the winter sun. When I opened them again it was five p.m. and pitch-black outside. I lit a candle and opened a book, resting my phone between the pages.

At 8:30, the doorbell rang. The delivery driver shoved the package into my hands with a brusque 'Happy holidays'. Fair enough. This man probably had somewhere to be – a loving family or devoted partner waiting for him at home, missing him terribly. It was unfair that he had to work on Christmas Eve, delivering packages to lone morons who, if they'd had their life even remotely together, could easily have borrowed or rented a car, driven to IKEA, and picked up their mid-range bed frame themselves. As I tried to express some garbled version of this, he took what I assumed to be the world's least flattering photograph of me, unwashed and be-turted, balancing the cardboard box on one hip like a long, bad baby.

I went back inside and cut it open. A little baggie of screws and plastic fittings fell out, along with the instruc-

tion booklet. On the first page, an angular cartoon figure stood with a pencil behind his ear and an X over his entire body. He was looking down at a pile of furniture parts and frowning. Beneath him was the caption: 'Best completed with two.' Farther along the page a pair of angular cartoon friends – or lovers, the relationship was unclear, but they seemed to have an understanding – smiled together, ready to finish the job as a team. I decided to construct the bed frame later.

I'd spent the Christmas Eves of my childhood staying up late with Hannah, eating cookies and clementines, deliberating about how early we could reasonably run downstairs and expect our parents (parent, later) to join us. We continued sharing a room on Christmas Eve well into our teens, stopping only when the omnipresence of her boyfriend made the arrangement undesirable. She was still with that boyfriend – a sardonic, lanky boy called Ed. They shared a rickety apartment off Princess Street that they sublet for long stretches, travelling to Colombia and Thailand and New Zealand, taking beautiful photos of beaches and each other and strangers on ethically complicated boat tours. They did not have individual nicknames for each other but referred to themselves as a unit as 'Mom and Dad'. They were in no rush to get married but would clearly be together forever.

I ate a few clementines and got back in bed, wishing I'd gone home to be with Hannah tonight. I dragged my laptop onto the pillow next to me, the SKÅRNSK looming in the corner as I watched a talented young baker realise she was the spitting image of a beautiful, world-weary duchess,

and holiday hilarity ensued. I drifted off sometime after an averted crisis at the televised baking competition, but before the festive double wedding.

The next day I woke early and took the train to Kingston. The automated voice announced the cities we'd arrive at in English and in French as the carriage rocked us slowly back and forth like infants in a bassinet on a dryer. The lake looked beautiful and cold, the sun glinting off the ice at its edges. I knew the city itself would be a mix of bad grey (brutalist libraries, melted snow) and beautiful grey (old limestone, smoke from chimneys curling up through the sky), all quiet and emptied out of students from the universities. My dad met me at the station in an enormous knitted hat, and we drove to his place to open presents and eat bagels and drink mimosas with Ed and Hannah. When I got there, Ed said, 'How you holding up?' and Hannah slapped him hard on the knee, then came toward me with a cup of coffee and a hug, saying, 'I panicked and bought you jeans at the last minute. *Risky* move.'

The year my parents split up, they were appalled to learn that each had modified Christmas in the exact same way: 'Since you're having turkey at your dad's,' our mom had said, 'I thought we'd do ham this year.' The next day, the smell of pork wafted out of our father's kitchen, greeting us before he did. Each of them bought us plush new slippers as gifts. Both of their plans for Christmas 2.0 involved breakfast booze.

Though they'd now been separated longer than I'd known them together, I was often struck by the similarity

of my parents' advice, how many values and first instincts and turns of phrase they still shared. They had been together thirteen years, after all. The love had gone away, by my calculation, sometime around my eighth birthday, but their impact on each other was not so easily undone. They did not seem to relish hearing this, which I understood better now. I was still buying eggplant on autopilot and had only recently realised I did not favour the left side of the bed. Without Jon's playful sparring, my daily life had become less argumentative, and I discovered I preferred it that way. It was hard to learn traits I'd considered mine alone had been forged with or borrowed wholesale from someone else. How embarrassing, to have to figure out what was Me, what was Him, what was Us. How much more embarrassing, to find out you'd got it wrong.

By now our broken family had a practised routine, alternating an intimate Christmas morning with one parent and an extended family dinner with the other. This year was Mom's turn for dinner. My mother's family is huge and, like the families of many caucasian North Americans, passionately if theoretically Irish. You could tell me any white person in Canada was my cousin, and I would believe you. I had many childhood memories of my mother dragging me over to some stranger in the grocery store, shoving my hand out to shake theirs, and telling me this person I would never see again was secretly a dear relative – such and such level of cousin, so and so amount removed. Holidays with her clan started early, ended late, and involved a lot of Drambuie and affectionate yelling. Typically, three to six people cried.

This year, these were the highlights:

- a cousin's husband I hadn't seen since last Christmas asked where Jon was before I had even taken off my coat;
- the turkey was put in the oven two to three hours behind schedule, which meant 'cocktail hour' extended well past eight p.m., which meant Uncle Jamie fell asleep at the table;
- while slopping potato onto my plate, thrice-married Auntie Gillian told me we were part of a sacred sisterhood of jilted wives;
- two middle-aged people had an argument about whether free speech still existed;
- a twenty-three-year-old second cousin announced she was pregnant, leading an older first cousin once removed to accuse her of 'trying to make Maggie feel bad';
- when I took the first cousin aside to tell her I was okay, she started crying and told me she was 'barren';
- a great-aunt asked the cousins to go around the table and say whether we had Jesus in our lives;
- my sister got drunk and told me her 'Christmas wish' was that I would one day 'find happiness again';
- the great-uncle who usually played piano at these things had recently died, so instead of carols there was a very maudlin YouTube-based karaoke sing-along;

- oldest cousin's new girlfriend sat in a *different* cousin's lap for an entire verse (!) of Ariana Grande's 'Santa Tell Me';
- my grandmother asked if I was seeing anyone special (I thought of Simon but told her no), then suggested I try to avoid 'shacking up with another vegetarian';
- I ate so much of the cheese board I briefly considered pretending the dogs had got at it; I did, in the end, pretend this.

When my mother and I left for midnight mass, a small but committed contingent was still going strong, cheerfully arguing over card games, encouraging others to make speeches, and getting emotional about the Pope. Soon they would fish a harmonica out of a cupboard and scream-sing folk songs and dance around the kitchen.

My sister stayed, hoping for the revelation of some major family secret, or at least more almond shortbread. Christmas was the one time of the year my mother went to church, and we usually traded off who accompanied her. This year was Hannah's turn, but after watching Auntie Gillian corner me to warn that it was tough out there for a single gal in her thirties, that gravity came for all of us, and no matter my moisturising routine, my neck would be my downfall, she suggested I go in her place. I thanked her and headed out to the driveway, where my mom was trying and failing to defrost the windshield. She fished the ice scraper out of the back seat and passed it to me out the window. I cleared a little peephole, her side only, and got in.

'I hope Jesus appreciates that I stayed sober for this,' she said, reversing into the street.

I reminded her that newborn babies can't recognise colour or faces, so the concept of designated driving was probably over his head.

'Oh God,' she said, sounding exhausted. 'Not tonight, okay? Please.' She patted my thigh lovingly so I would know that although she sometimes found me maddening, she would also, literally, die for me.

The church was soothingly grand, candlelit and cavernous, with that nice Roman Catholic smell (you can't say much for the institution, but they do have an eye for drama and a nose for incense). I only ever went to church with my mother at Christmas, though my wedding had been in one, at Jon's parents' insistence. They had been more traditional than expected about the ceremony – his mother and I even had a clipped, tense exchange about why I did not want to wear a veil.

In the end, I lost the veil argument, and the vintage lace my mother-in-law found was gorgeous. I wore it with a simple bias-cut silk slip that was more expensive than anything I'd ever owned, and now sat in a box in my studio apartment, judging me from a garment bag. It had been beautiful, and I looked beautiful in it, but walking down the aisle that day I still felt enormously stupid. What was I doing, veil or not, tottering around a church in a virgin costume in front of everyone I knew, toward a man I'd been living with for years? Why did we need to validate our commitment with this showy little stroll? Should I copy the gait they did in wedding movies, one-and-join, two-and-

join? But however stupid the procession, it had been thrilling to arrive at the front of the church, grab my boyfriend's sweaty hands, and make him my husband in front of everyone.

I pushed the unwanted images – Jon's big smile, our friends and family tittering as I instantly flubbed the first line of our 'modernised' vows, that kiss – out of my mind. Mass carried on, and Mom got bored sometime around the blessing of the crib. I could tell, because she started flipping through the hymnal like it was a nail salon gossip magazine.

'"Guide Me, O Thou Great Jehovah" … a classic,' I whispered.

She rolled her eyes and shut the book, then put an arm around me and asked if I was feeling okay: 'I know the first Christmas can be hard.'

I told her I was angry that Jon's parents hadn't reached out. I knew he probably wouldn't say anything, but I had been part of Christmas in their house since I'd been an adult. Didn't that merit a card, or at least an email? My mom told me anger was not useful, that there was no sense in holding on to resentment about people who were no longer a part of my life. I told her she had recently told me, in detail, about a fight she and my father had had about vacation plans in 1997.

'That's different,' she said.

'How?'

'Because he's an asshole.'

She motioned for me to keep my eyes up front and launched into 'Silent Night' with avoidant vim. It snowed as we drove back to her house, picking up Ed and my sister

from Aunt Linda's on the way. In the car they gave us the debrief: the Ariana Grande girlfriend had left with a different cousin than the one with whom she'd arrived; Nana told everyone she could see the ghost of the pianist uncle, and he was mad; the teen cousins got in such a hard-core tussle in the basement that one of them seemed to have sprained something.

'Fantastic news,' Hannah said. 'Psychic Cousin Sheila says you'll find love again in eight years.'

That night I lay in my high school bedroom, staring at a picture of my teen self with friends I no longer knew but saw sometimes on Instagram – one was a lawyer, another ran a record store in Vancouver. Several had babies. I didn't even have that bucket hat anymore. My oblivious baby face smiled out from a frame that said GIRL POWER 4EVA in a curly font. I thought about leaving Jon a voicemail, just to wish him merry Christmas; maybe he was finding the holidays hard too. I fought against a few exceptionally devastating mental images – Hannah exchanging a surreptitious look with Jon as she took the paper crown off his head and left the room; the look on his face as he told me he knew I was not the kneel-down type; him kneeling nonetheless, tiny gold ring inside a broken-open Christmas cracker – and pulled my laptop into bed, scrolling through pictures of Christmases past on Facebook.

At midnight, Simon texted, merry christmas, hope you're having a better night than this guy, attaching a picture of one of his young cousins covered in gravy and crying, hard. I looked at the message on my phone and the pictures on my laptop and could not muster anything

better than a haha yeah. I couldn't tell what he was looking for and didn't have the energy to figure it out.

I spent Boxing Day on my mother's sofa, playing board games and eating hot turkey sandwiches with Hannah. My mother was seeing someone – a friendly but nervous man called Jeff who had dropped in for lunch and was now trying a bit too hard to make us like him. When he left the room, promising to return with hot chocolate like we'd never had, Hannah leaned over and whispered, 'Does he think we're going to try to *Parent Trap* her back with Dad or something? Aren't we all a bit old for this?'

Ed came in and squeezed her waist. They hadn't said anything to me, but at Linda's place I'd overheard Ed tell Auntie Sara that they'd started trying for a baby. I was happy for them and excited about this next step in their lives together, though I was humiliated by their tact, which was also their pity. I imagined Hannah hiding her pregnancy like they did on TV, the two of them holding an increasingly improbable series of tote bags and hat boxes in front of her abdomen at all times, desperate to conceal from me that other people had happy, meaningful lives, full of milestones I would never achieve. My sister snuggled her feet under me and asked what I was up to these days. I rolled away, pulling the blanket tighter around my head, to hide her from my peripheral vision.

The next day I took the train back to Toronto, crawled into bed, and stayed there for days, rewatching casually misogynist old sitcoms and reality shows about beautiful people getting out of and back into emotionally abusive relationships. The period between Christmas and New

Year's always feels long, but this year it had taken a sedative. Time was moving even more sluggishly than usual, and I had been doing reckless things: double and triple delivery days where all my meals were takeout I couldn't afford, biking in the snow with no lights or helmet, sending risky texts riddled with typos.

On 28 December, I texted Simon, wyh do you like me.

He wrote back the next day: off the top of my head? you're beautiful and you make me laugh.

I thought, *Fuck off.*

I texted, fuck off, adding: men don't care if women are funny. i think they actively dislike it.

ok, he wrote, you're beautiful and i find you dull, which is exciting because it does not threaten me.

Three hours later, when I had not replied, he texted, ... i was kidding.

I tapped the message so a little thumbs-up appeared and went back to bed.

———

Suddenly, and against my will, it was 31 December. I woke up and thought, *No.* I texted the group chat that I wasn't up for a big New Year's thing. They were understanding if a bit icy. you don't have to stay if you hate it, Amirah wrote, adding that I could borrow something from her if I needed an outfit. (Smaller friends were always promising to lend me beautiful clothes that wouldn't fit in a million years.)

Clive said the guys hosting the party had promised an 'all dips buffet' and heated backyard experience. I said I knew it would be fun, but that I also had a 700% chance of crying at midnight and wanted to do it alone. do what you want, Lauren wrote back, but next year it will be 20-fucking-20 and mark's inflatable hot tub will almost certainly be broken.

Simon texted to say he would be spending the countdown with friends at the Horseshoe Tavern, watching a cover band play one song from each year starting in 1919. He was, however, available after midnight, to start the new year with a bang (sex). I told him that sounded lovely, but I was doing my own thing and offered to meet him for brunch the next day. He wrote back, as you wish. I couldn't tell if he was making a *Princess Bride* reference or just talked like that.

———

So: a solo New Year's Eve, my first ever. I went to the fancy grocery store and picked up some supplies: blood oranges, calla lilies, herbal tea, and a candle with base notes of vetiver and 'library'.

Everyone else at the store was picking up last-minute party offerings: boxes of leftover holiday chocolate, pre-made cheese and meat platters, nine limes. My reservations about spending this popular group kissing holiday alone melted into a feeling of gentle superiority: I was not even going to get drunk tonight. I was going to exfoliate and set intentions.

While browsing the aisles, I was overcome with a desire to *create*, to have something to show for myself, and decided after a quick search to purchase the ingredients for a beginner-friendly bread recipe I found on 6Bites. I had never made bread before, but it seemed like it would be fulfilling to occupy my hands, to work basic ingredients into something nourishing with only time and effort. Plus I thought it would be nice if the apartment smelled like bread.

I walked home at a clip, my breath forming satisfying little clouds ahead of me. The sky was pink and the air was cold, and people were rushing around full of purpose. I felt proud of myself for accepting my limits: Christmas had been okay, but I didn't want to spend tonight surrounded by happy couples and groups of people excitedly flirting in sparkly outfits all sharing sloppy midnight smooches. I didn't want to have to tell anyone that my New Year's resolutions were to cry less, figure out if I liked being outdoors, and experiment with breakfast salads. A night in was exactly what I needed.

I got home, unpacked my groceries, and changed into my most sophisticated/least dirty pyjamas. I put my phone in a bowl with a plate on top of it, like I was trapping a spider. I boiled some water for tea ('a soothing blend of herbs for women') and took out flour, salt, olive oil and fast-acting yeast. I looked around for a measuring cup. The best I could do was a branded plastic wineglass from a music festival with 150 ml and 250 ml marked on the side.

I mixed my ingredients and rolled the resultant dough into a ball, channelling an ageing celebrity baker I sometimes masturbated about. I kneaded my bread ball and left

it under a dishcloth to rise. I went into the bathroom and lit my library candle. I filled the tub with Epsom salts, essential oils, and a few dusty petals from a grocery store bouquet that had been mouldering in the corner of my bedroom for three weeks, why not. I put on a playlist called 'Relaxing Piano' and ate a clementine, naked. I looked at my body in the mirror and thought, *you know what, fine.*

I lay in the tub for what felt like hours, semi-successfully clearing my mind. As my fingers started to prune, a timer went off in the kitchen, and I ran dripping through the apartment to check on my dough. It was much larger than I'd left it – a result. I put my new, larger dough ball on a baking sheet, covered that with a clean cloth, and left it alone again. I had some slightly basic thoughts about 'being left alone to rise'.

After mopping up the wet patches I'd left around the kitchen, I went back to the bathroom and moisturised myself into oblivion. I was slicker than a baby seal, oilier than the bowl I'd put the bread in. I shone. I also couldn't touch anything without leaving it streaked in residue. I wandered around the apartment, avoiding skin contact with any of my possessions and waiting – for my dough to prove, for my body to dry, for a sense of peace and personal empowerment to wash over me. The drying took longer than expected, and the empowerment, if it planned to arrive at all, was slow going too.

I ate a cookie and experienced some light FOMO. My friends were probably in a hot tub right now, dipping breadsticks into sour cream and laughing their heads off, creating amazing memories and inside jokes I'd never quite

be part of. I wondered if maybe this entire thing had been a bad idea. I went to my bookshelf and opened some Pema Chödrön, heavily dog-eared.

I had acquired the book last summer, while purchasing a bunch of novels – about change, travel, the moon, and how badly famous figures in American literature treated their wives – at a local bookstore where I liked to flirt with the cranky old man behind the counter. When I brought my selections to the register, he said, 'Bad breakup?' and threw in *When Things Fall Apart* for free. A few weeks later we went on a date where we both got incredibly drunk but only one of us talked about our experimental poetry collection for too long.

I flipped through my Chödrön, taking in highlighted passages that had, I guess, been important to me a few months earlier: 'Rather than letting our negativity get the better of us, we could acknowledge that right now we feel like a piece of shit and not be squeamish about taking a good look.' Sure. 'When things are shaky and nothing is working, we might realise that we are on the verge of something.' Maybe! 'So even if the hot loneliness is there, and for 1.6 seconds we sit with that restlessness when yesterday we couldn't even sit for one, that's the journey of the warrior.' I did not feel like a warrior, but I did move the bowl with my phone in it to the bathroom.

Looking for direction, and with time to kill while the oven warmed up, I kept reading until I found this: 'Relaxing with the present moment, relaxing with hopelessness, relaxing with death, not resisting the fact that things end … that is the basic message.'

I was attempting to relax with death when Merris came downstairs. Despite her move-in day promise about keeping to herself, Merris visited my apartment fairly regularly, to drop off leftovers, or ask who Chet Haze was, or complain about a recent interaction with a student ('Honestly, and I hope you won't find this offensive, I'm just not certain we need to queer *everything*'). This time, she was bringing twelve grapes.

'To eat at midnight,' she said. 'You have one at each stroke of the clock. They do it in Spain, for luck.' I asked her if she had Spanish heritage. She did not, but had spent several New Year's Eves there and kept up the tradition on her own.

I told her I welcomed anything that might make this year better than the last.

'Oh, you're not having such a bad time,' Merris said. 'I've heard you down here giggling with that curly-haired fellow, Sinjin or whoever.'

'Simon.'

'Simon, sure, that's what I said. How's it going?'

'Oh, too fast,' I said. 'Heading for disaster, almost certainly.'

Merris looked surprised. 'And what makes you think that?'

'Isn't it supposed to take half the time you were with someone to get over them? I've got another three and a half years of basement wallowing, if that's the case.'

'That's ridiculous. Where did you read that?' Merris said. 'Inessa's husband died last July, and she's been the scarlet lady of her birding group. Though I suppose she doesn't

necessarily have the … what would it be … fourteen required mourning years left.'

All the upstairs ladies talked about death like this – like it was an appointment they knew was coming up but had forgotten exactly when they'd booked it in for.

'It's no bad thing to fall in love,' said Merris, and I snorted.

'I am *not* in love,' I said. 'But I do like him. A lot. He's infuriatingly difficult not to like.'

I had been surprised, lately, by the intensity of my fondness for Simon, and had indeed wondered in private if I was falling in love with him, which was unnerving. The last time I'd felt like this I married the man, so had assumed the experience was unique to finding one's soul mate. But here it was, more or less the same, with some guy I'd found in a bar: the tension and warmth and sense of shared momentum. The feeling of being looked at, of wanting to look at someone more than I wanted to do anything else. The sudden realisation that this human being is in possession, somehow, of the best and nicest brain, the warmest torso, the sexiest legs. The follow-up realisation that you're into men's legs now, that this person has made that so. I knew, of course, that eventually I would reveal the part of myself that made him recoil, and he would go, and I'd be despondent, so for now I was just trying to enjoy the view.

'I've never been with someone so straightforwardly handsome,' I said. 'I keep taking these languid photos of him lying around down here.'

Merris said it sounded like I was in love, or possibly reading too much Alan Hollinghurst. I said it was too early

to call it and reminded her I was still seeing other people. Sort of. I was talking to them, anyway, in my DMs and on the apps, making flirty little comments then retreating when they suggested meeting in person. It was important, I said, to know there were options, to have a frisson at the bus stop. Merris said that sounded exhausting and invited me to spend the countdown with her and the ladies upstairs.

'If we make it that far,' she said. 'Betty's fading already. Inessa's mixing some Irish coffees to pep us up.'

I thanked her but declined; the plan was to go it alone.

'How alone can you be, with all those sordid direct mails?' she said, her haughtiness undercut by the near-ly-there wrongness of the words she was using. When she opened the door, I could hear Betty telling Inessa that her New Year's resolution was to 'smoke more, why not'.

I put my godforsaken bread in the oven and blew out my candle to let the baking smell fill the studio. Half an hour later my windows were fogged from the heat, and the tray I removed from the oven had a gorgeous, loafy-looking loaf of bread on it. I felt proud, then *very* silly, then proud again. I looked at the clock: it wasn't even 10:30.

I decided to watch *Titanic* the way I had when I was younger, stopping when the boat hits the iceberg. As a child this habit had arisen from necessity: the first VHS finished with Jack and Rose in love, startled by the sound of ice grinding against metal. To see the rest of the film you had to eject the tape, put it away, and insert a second one, which seemed like a lot of work just to watch all the char-acters you'd grown attached to drown in the freezing

Atlantic, so mostly I didn't. To me, James Cameron's masterpiece was a rom-com about two young misfits from different social classes who meet, decide not to commit suicide, and, against their family's wishes, have sex in a car.

Kate Winslet's hand smacked the window at 11:27. This seemed impossible. It felt like an entire year had passed, like I was staring down 2020. I looked at my unassembled SKÅRNSK, the pieces piled in a corner, and my mattress on the floor. Panic or determination rose in my throat. It was this or try again to journal.

The single cartoon figure frowned up at me from the instructions sheet. Further into the instructional booklet was a diagram labelled 'EXPLODED PARTS'. It was a drawing of the bed frame's component pieces laid out individually, all the little bits of metal and wood that would combine to make something useful and, if not stylish, more appealing to the eye than a loose pile of junk.

I took a picture of the page and composed an email to Jon about what such a diagram would look like of our relationship. Knowing I would never send it, I allowed myself to get a little flowery, describing a day on our honeymoon where crappy free wine and a frankly spectacular sunset had moved him to tell me that he felt 'safe in my arms', and I told him he was 'my home', and it didn't feel hackneyed or embarrassing, because although it was without question both of those things, it was also, and more importantly, true.

Merris came back downstairs at ten minutes past midnight, two flutes of prosecco in her hands. She peeked around the half-open door to find me on the floor,

surrounded by bits of cheap Scandinavian wood. I had a wet, red face and nine grapes in my mouth. Merris sighed. 'I'll get Lydia.'

I curled around the dog's gargantuan body, letting her soft ears slip in and out of my hands. Merris had made an overture toward assembling the SKÅRNSK herself, then thought better of it; now she was sitting on a chair at the kitchen table while Lydia and I lay in bed.

'There is a touch of the analyst's couch to this arrangement,' she said with a wry smile. Then, more seriously: 'I hope you're taking care of yourself.'

I told Merris I was practising all the self-care I could handle. She scoffed.

'Please. I don't mean your moon rocks or whatever you've done that got oil all over everything down here. That's fine; so is the messaging. But at a certain point it becomes running, when most of moving on is just getting out of bed and plodding forward. Call it what you must, but you need to practise walking around and living life and being heartbroken at the same time. Not in an exciting way, where you're in the thrall of some new person, or buying something outrageous, or terrorising Jiro, but in the way you still have to go to work when you have a toothache.'

I told Merris it was fear of lectures like this that had stopped me from seeing an actual therapist.

She frowned and folded her hands in her lap, then looked at me over the rim of her glasses like a wizard in a children's movie finding out the Potions Turret had been breached: 'You're not in therapy?'

I said I didn't know why everyone was so obsessed with this, but no, I was not. I was not traumatised; mostly I was embarrassed.

'What about?' Merris asked.

I had a sip of her prosecco and thought about where to begin. I was embarrassed:

- that I couldn't do journalling properly;
- that we hadn't given back the money friends and family had given us at the wedding;
- that everyone knew I was struggling – worse, that they knew I'd been rejected;
- that I had been rejected by the person who knew me better than anyone else on earth, to whom I had shown every part of me, been as vulnerable as it was possible for me to be … and that person had decided I sucked;
- that despite the fact that I technically had enough perspective to understand that none of my problems were 'real' compared with any actual problems that could and did exist in other people's lives, my pathetic non-problems still occupied my entire headspace and felt enormous, bordering on insurmountable;
- that I would do anything to simply have been better at being married – to have properly applied myself toward being a sweeter, sexier, more fun, less challenging, properly good wife;
- that this was quite a retrograde way to think, and probably Said Something About Me as a person;

- that I was having increasingly persistent fantasies
 in which singing the correct song at karaoke
 would somehow fix it all;
- that, that, that, that …

Sharing any of this out loud seemed like it would be the start of a Thing, and I didn't want to subject Merris to any more of those, so I said, 'You know what, it's stupid,' and told her I was feeling tired. Although we both knew I was lying, she politely got up to leave. To my dismay, Lydia followed.

I turned off the lights and lay on my mattress in the dark. Last New Year's Eve Jon and I had had a massive fight, the cause of which I could not remember. It was a bad one, both of us retreating behind our favourite defence mechanisms: stony silence punctuated by a bitchy comment for the lady, furious yelling with a side of stomping around for monsieur. Not a cherished memory, exactly, but I wasn't sure lying here alone having alienated a septuagenarian with my refusal to seek counselling was a better alternative. I looked over my email to Jon, added a few lines about forgiving him for whatever had made us so furious with each other on 1 January 2018, and sent it. When my phone buzzed minutes later, I scrambled over to it, but it was just someone I'd been on a few dates with asking if I was 'out'.

As the night grew later, these kinds of texts rolled in from others, wishing me a Happy New Year and subtly or not subtly probing about my whereabouts – it was 1:30, any party prospects had long since been claimed. People were going through their mental Rolodexes, hoping not to

greet the first morning of the New Year alone. I ignored them, sent the group chat a picture of myself making a kissy face at two a.m., then at two thirty received these, from Amy:

U up?

hahaHA Saw the bread you posted on instagram ...

vERY sad

@party near ur house, COME!!! everyone sooooo chiLL :P

k random meant 2 say :) not :P

;)))))

Selected Advice from Amy's Friends, in Ascending Order of Relevance to Me

'Being single this time of year is awful, isn't it? I mean, if I think back to being single, this was the absolute worst time for it. That's why it's so important to remember that it could be worse. Even if it feels like the worst year of your life, it could always, always get worse. You're divorced, sure, and that feels bad, but what if you drowned? Anyway, that's my boyfriend in the blue, don't flirt with him.'

'I think you can't force it. Like you find love when you least expect it, right, so if you're dating too much, and you're trying trying trying, that's gonna take too much out of you. The apps are a dead end, trust me. I've been with my husband for seven years, without going on them ever. He was my boss, and now we're married. So ... maybe try that?'

'Honestly don't change a thing, babe. This is your year. This is your FUCKING *YEAR*. I swear, I have a sense for stuff like this, and I can TELL you are gonna be A-OK. You got this, girl! Have the baby, why not?!'

'You know what's good for us pear-shaped gals? Wrap dresses. Sorry, what was the question? Mmm, yeah, there is dairy in that. Or gluten or something. One of the Bad Ones, for sure.'

'I think if you hate her Instagram Stories so much, just, like, stop watching them? But I think you should cut her some slack. It can't be easy to raise a diabetic dog in a plant-based way.'

'When my mom's friend got divorced, she honestly went nuts, but in this totally badass way where she quit her job and fucked off to Europe and, like, found herself, and had this steamy affair with this guy and had sex in this, like, little bamboo house, and … fuck, you know what, that was Elizabeth Gilbert, I think, not my mom's friend Marie. But Marie did read her book, so that's something you could try.'

'Don't go in the upstairs bathroom, I – *somebody* – threw up all over it.'

Something changed after the holidays, the way it always does, but worse. The snow and the salt stains and the sweating-on-the-subway of it all loses its festive tinge every January, and the emancipatory effect I'd been hoping for from a 'clean slate' had not arrived. Even Amy's party had been a bust. After dragging my ass out of bed and putting on some light makeup, I had arrived to discover a room full of couples having arguments and a few single people who mostly appeared to be on MDMA. Amy was in an upstairs bathroom making out with a guy named 'Maxton'.

I left shortly after arriving, to go home with an ostensibly straight friend of Amy's called Tamara, who told me she 'never did this'; I got the impression she never did this a lot. I had been attracted to Tamara because she was tall and had a kind of horny glint in her eye, but when we got back to her apartment she became probing and intense, asking me about my emotional baggage and star sign and feelings about my place in the universe. (What was it about me that attracted this type of person? Why was it so hard to just go home with a stranger and get railed?) When I told her

about the divorce she made a noise that sounded like an empathy orgasm, then pulled me to her chest and cradled my head like a child's.

'You must be *devastated*,' she said, petting my hair in a way that was not unenjoyable but was not the romp I had hoped for, from the glint. 'This must be such a dark time for you. I'm a Highly Sensitive Person, so you don't need to tell me, I get it.'

I did not think it required a person to be highly sensitive to know that divorce was painful, but more than that, I did not want to talk about it with Tamara. I kissed her for a minute or two, and it was going well until she made the noise again, then pulled away and said, 'Poor little bird.'

I told her I was okay, mostly, that I knew nothing worthwhile came easy and was taking it one day at a time. In reality, life since my mom's house had felt very dark indeed, more or less blurring into one long nap punctuated by cereal and episodes of *Housewives*; but I did not share this, because I did not want to be this woman's bird. She poured us each a glass of water and told me a lengthy anecdote about her friend's bike accident, labouring particularly hard over the doctor's instruction that – should this friend ever find herself hurtling over her handlebars on Roncesvalles Avenue again – she not brace for impact.

'You have to go limp and let it happen,' she said softly. 'You can't fight it, or you'll break every bone in your body.'

She was rocking me back and forth at this point, but getting a cab at that hour, on New Year's, would have been impossible, so when she slid her hand under my shirt, I pretended to be asleep.

The next morning we lay around in her bed, where, to avoid further cycling metaphors, I asked her to tell me the twist endings to every episode of an anthology series she had recently watched about the dangers of social media. In one episode, a man was apparently framed for murder by his hamster, due to technology. In another, a media teacher bludgeoned her students to death with an iPad. Fine.

I left Tamara's house and met Amy at a nearby greasy spoon, where we bought a six-pack of hash browns and coffees the size of our heads. She wanted details about the rest of my night, but there wasn't much to tell, especially since she was against television spoilers. Amy's New Year's resolutions were to finally commit to the 30 Day Shred programme, set up monthly donations to some good causes, and smile more. I told her she already smiled a lot.

'Ultimately, I think you can always do more,' she said, blotting a hash brown with a paper napkin until it was translucent and heavy with oil.

I told Amy I wanted to burrow.

'That's okay,' she said. 'It takes as long as it takes.'

I told her that her skin shouldn't look so glowy on a hangover, and she explained how to rub frozen spoons over your face until it depuffed back to normal, like you hadn't pumped yourself full of poison the night before. I was thinking about how wise she was, how much she had life figured out, when she gave me a book of poems by a man from the internet who was always telling women to wear their wounds like wings.

'You'll love this,' she said, completely sure. 'I'm obsessed with the one about skinny-dipping in your own power.'

Amy walked me to a different diner where I had promised to meet Simon for breakfast, stopping in to say hi before heading to a New Year, New Booty HIIT cardio class. Simon did not look hungover either. I slid into the booth across from him and pretended to consider the sticky laminated menu before ordering another round of hash browns.

I realised he did not know I'd gone out last night, that he thought I had stayed home to be alone and bake bread. I thought about Tamara's cold hand on my boob and wondered if Simon had gone home with someone too. I didn't ask, but decided on my own that he had, and she had been elegant and gorgeous and very good at drawing or something. I was distracted by this imagined rival throughout our meal.

'Everything okay?' Simon asked, his fork hovering over a plate of eggs slathered in salsa. Whenever he encountered them on a brunch menu, Simon made a point of ordering huevos divorciados, winking at me when they arrived. He often made little jokes about my marital status, making a big deal about having a 'married woman' in his bed or quipping about my future second and third husbands. I knew he only did this because I responded with loud, enthusiastic laughter and because I often made jokes like these myself, but coming from him they made me feel exposed and uncomfortable, emotionally nude.

'I'm alright,' I said. 'Just the old ... New Year's blues.'

I had never heard this phrase in my life and realised almost instantly after saying it that this was because it was not one. Simon's lips stretched into a restrained smile and

his eyes twinkled with amusement. 'Ah,' he said. 'Of course.'

He poured tiny plastic containers of cream into his coffee, stacking the empties on top of each other in a neat pile as I ate my eighth hash brown of the day. Whether because of my hangover, or the mild deception about the night before, or some other reason unknown to me, I couldn't join Simon on our usual register. It suddenly felt ridiculous to be at breakfast opening packets of jam with some other, different man, as if this time it would work out, as if it could ever go another way. When the bill arrived, he seemed to understand that I wouldn't be coming back to his place, kissed me primly on the cheek, and promised to text me that evening.

I boarded the streetcar, cried a bit, and arrived home. I pulled on a second pair of socks, got into bed and opened the book Amy had given me, which instructed me to let myself 'dream wild'. I closed the book and went to sleep.

―――

My friends were not happy with me for skipping the dips and hot tub party and were further disappointed by my flakiness in the weeks that followed. I tried to fake a sudden devotion to work, but my waning interest in my job had long been registered. Pretending I was doing Dry January kept them off my back, until I outed myself by tweeting something about a five-alarm hangover and a need for spaghetti that felt like an emergency. I ended up sending a text saying I was taking time to commune with the Physics

of the Quest, something I had read about in *Eat, Pray, Love*, which I had downloaded as an e-book and was about halfway through. Clive texted back, gross, with a heart emoji.

Truthfully, I was feeling depressed and broke, two things I was not really entitled to feel, but which nonetheless had become dominant emotional presences in my life. I dealt with these feelings by buying dumb garbage I didn't need and not looking at my bank balance, ever. Other than the online shopping, I was not doing anything that was not 100% necessary to keep myself alive and my rent paid. The days of meditation and self-improvement efforts were over. I walked everywhere with sunglasses and a pair of big wireless headphones on, though they played no music; I had lost the charging cable months ago. I could no longer bear to stop and talk to people, give them the cheery CliffsNotes of my life, smile and promise I was doing great – really good, actually – then carry on, to eat soup and cut my toenails and watch TV in a basement, alone.

This was probably better for everyone, as I was awful to hang out with. All I wanted to do was dissect my breakup, on some days the worst thing that had ever happened to me and on others the very best, a blessing straight from god that would surely lead to all kinds of positive developments I could not quite yet imagine. I knew if I saw my friends I would have to care about their lives in return, and I simply … did not. What I wanted was to spend my time monologuing about love and tragedy and whether the size of my calves had anything to do with my being now divorced.

The only person I saw with any regularity was Simon, because he loved to talk about his breakup too, and we could go on and on together about where it had all gone wrong, absolving each other of our various relational mistakes. My doubts from the diner ebbed and flowed. I could usually overwrite them with a few beers or a solid orgasm. Also, I had clogged my shower drain and now could not use it for more than five minutes without nasty grey water pooling at my ankles. Simon had a lovely shower.

Occasionally I would meet up with someone from one of the apps, so I could do first date makeup and tell my best anecdotes and ask my most interesting questions to some- one I would never see again. Seeking connection was lovely in theory, but mostly it felt better to sing the hits for a dazzled new audience, to kiss outside a bar and part ways, to leave them wanting more.

Although I was shunning them, I still wanted my friends to invite me to things. Eventually they stopped, carrying on as though I had moved away or had a baby. So one overcast February afternoon, after a few too many Instagram Stories of everyone hanging out without me, I took out exactly $40, selected 'no receipt', and texted my friends that I missed them, and would they please join me at a trivia night we sometimes went to, hosted by a man we were absolutely certain was the worst person alive but who had a genuinely impressive store of general knowledge.

They agreed, and a reunion was scheduled, with a plan to combine our intellects in pursuit of a free bar tab (or one craft beer-branded tote bag split five ways, results pending). On the day of the quiz – running thirty minutes behind for

absolutely no reason – I texted Amy, who I also hadn't seen in a while, to tell her to come along. When I got to the table, the group chat was fully assembled, and I was overcome with a wave of affection for my funny, stylish, oddball friends. I hugged them all and told them that Amy would be joining us.

'Oh,' said Amirah, sounding not particularly pleased. 'That's fun ... We've never really hung out outside of work.'

I told Amirah I hadn't known this and in fact had assumed they were close based on how highly Amy spoke of her.

'Amy speaks highly of everyone,' said Amirah. 'She'd find something nice to say about Stalin.'

'That's not hard,' said Clive. 'Have you seen that picture of him when he was younger? Step on me, comrade.'

Everyone pulled out their phones, something that would shortly be disallowed by the rules of the quiz. It was agreed that the picture of young Stalin could get it, but that it was obviously a more complicated moral quandary to have sex or not with the man himself. Lauren suggested Stalin between 1897 and 1901 was 'the sweet spot' and that she would do it with him during those years only. I proposed an elaborate time travel scenario wherein my powers of fellatio caused a young Joseph to abandon his political ambitions and devote himself to gardening. We caught Emotional Lauren with her phone under the table, googling what did Stalin do.

Amy rocked up as Amirah was telling us about a dog she and Tom had fallen in love with on an adoption website.

'What are we talking about?' she asked, sliding in between me and Clive with an out-of-character bottle of IPA.

'Amirah and her boyfriend are getting a starter baby,' I said. 'Guess it's pretty serious.'

'It's not that serious,' Amirah said, rolling her eyes and turning to Amy. 'But look at him! What were we supposed to do?' She held out her iPhone, which displayed the adoption page for a tiny puggle called Jeremy.

Amy yelped. 'That's the cutest fucking dog I've ever fucking seen,' she said. 'You *have* to get him, oh my god.'

'I think it's a bad idea,' I said. 'What if you break up?'

Amirah made a face like she'd tasted bad milk. 'With Tom? No.'

'Well,' I said, 'you never know. You said yourself it's not that serious. Plus, I think I changed my mind on the concept of pets in general. A puppy is basically a down payment on a future dog funeral.'

Amirah put her phone in her pocket and went quiet. I nudged my chair closer to hers as Amy cheerily introduced herself to the rest of the table, shaking hands with Clive and Lauren and reaching awkwardly across the table to meet Emotional Lauren's outstretched arms. Next to us, a team registered loudly as 'Les Quizerables', then looked around to see if anyone was jealous.

The first round of questions was themed around 'Nineties Names' – the cloned sheep (Dolly), Phoebe's twin sister on *Friends* (Ursula), the Princess Diana memorial Beanie Baby (somehow, incredibly, 'Princess'). Our interest had started to wane by the music round; Les Quizerables were being annoyingly hard-core, and their furtive huddles and loud,

urgent calls for clarification took the casual shine off the evening, revealing us to be engaged once again in Adult Hobbies.

'This is how I know we're getting old,' said Lauren, as the Quizerables captain pulled his group in for yet another showy consultation. 'Genuinely fun people do not need someone to organise fun for them.'

Amirah agreed, pointing out that we were probably the youngest people in the bar – a bad sign.

'I don't know,' said Amy. 'I wouldn't want to be in my early twenties now. I have a few young gals on my floor, and they are stressed as hell.'

Lauren asked what they were stressed about.

'*Everything*,' she said. 'They get anxiety about literally everything. This one girl, Kitty, she had to turn in a report to our floor manager last week, and she straight up … didn't do it. When I asked her about it, she said, and I quote, "Deadlines give me anxiety."'

The rest of the table was unsure how to respond. On the one hand, it was probably very annoying to have to do someone else's report. On the other hand, anxiety is a real and often serious mental disorder affecting millions of people every day. On some third, more embarrassing but most important hand, nobody wanted to sound old for complaining about this stuff. We were about to turn thirty, not fifty-seven.

'I feel a lot of pressure to spit in Simon's mouth,' I said, to change the subject. 'Or at least put a finger in his butt. Do you guys do that? I feel like everyone is doing that except me.' Nobody responded, so I explained that

although I'd asked him a lot of times about it, and even drunkenly offered to peg him without fully understanding what that entailed, he insisted that the normal sex we were having was fulfilling and good. I wondered aloud if he was seeing someone else who did all the ass play he secretly craved. 'In general,' I said, 'I just want to figure out what he's getting from this arrangement. He's always doing such actively thoughtful stuff, and I'm like … *why*.'

I sat back and waited for someone to speak. Emotional Lauren yawned, and I thought I saw Amirah roll her eyes. Normally this was the kind of talk that really got my friends going. When had they all become such prudes? Was there something going on with the moon?

'Do you guys think we spend too much time talking about sex and dating?' Lauren asked.

I felt my shoulders creep up in the direction of my ears. 'I just think, like, what else is there?' I wanted to sound wry and knowing but could tell I'd landed somewhere between vacant and defensive. Instead of trying to fix it, I turned to Amy for help with a question about a recent episode of reality television in which two wealthy women had bullied a third, who'd called them bad feminists and fat.

Amy got it right away. 'It's so sad when they get at each other's throats like that,' she said. 'Because at the end of the day, the management staff of that restaurant is a family.'

The remaining rounds passed calmly if quietly, and eventually we placed third, the prize for which was a waived entry fee at next week's quiz. As the nerds who'd defeated us wasted their bar tab on 'spiked kombucha', I asked, somewhat desperately, what I'd missed during the early weeks of

2019. My friends gave me the headlines as I snapped the elastic of my tights against my knees and took big gulps of water and wine: Clive had 'recently reengaged with leeks' and was keen to determine the Herb of Summer in advance of the weather getting warmer (he was leaning toward dill). Emotional Lauren was moving in with Nour; they'd so far had seven arguments about the definition of the word 'credenza'. Amy had seen a financial adviser and decided to invest in weed. Lauren had finally pulled the trigger on owning a fanny pack. Amirah stayed quiet, looking at her phone and fidgeting in her chair.

I tried to think of something to share, something new that had happened to me. 'The other day …' I started, then stopped. I had been about to tell a story, the climactic moment of which was that I'd accidentally swapped non-dairy milks with Olivia. I did not want to describe the pathetic details of my day-to-day life, and they had been responding poorly to sex and dating stories. But those were all I had. I tried another: 'The other day Simon came into his room and was like, "Can I show you something?" and I said sure, and then he took out this deck of cards and it dawned on me: *this man is going to do a magic trick.*'

This did not receive the roar of laughter and recognition I had hoped for, but I persevered, describing my mental and emotional turmoil at the idea of this handsome man I was coming to care about ruining it all by pulling the ace of spades out of my ear.

'But the twist is that the trick was really impressive,' I said. 'Against all odds it made him even *more* attractive,

something I think a magic trick has never done at any point in history. Wild, right?'

Lauren made a little noise to acknowledge that I'd finished speaking. Clive raised his eyebrows and ate a French fry. 'Sounds like you're the one getting serious,' said Emotional Lauren.

I assured her we were taking it slow – we had slept apart once already this week.

'It's Friday,' said Amirah.

Lauren got up to go to the bathroom.

'Right!' I said brightly. 'Well, better to get all this Simon talk out of the way before he gets here.'

'I'm sorry, what?' Lauren sat back down, unsmiling. I told her I'd assumed this was a more-the-merrier situation. Amirah often invited her boyfriend to things without telling us, and shouldn't we all have the same privileges?

'Name one time I have ever, ever done that,' said Amirah, annoyed to be dragged into this. 'Also Tom is not a *stranger*—'

Emotional Lauren's Incoming Confrontation alarm went off, forcing her to get involved: 'I think it'll be fun!' she said. 'Amirah, you should text Tom too, if you want. Everyone's welcome!'

Clive swooped in to assist. 'I know it's been a rough year,' he said, putting his hand on my arm. 'We're so happy that you're happy with Simon, he sounds great.'

'He is great,' I said. 'You guys are gonna love him.'

'Oh, you totally will,' Amy said supportively. 'He's a babe. Great hair.'

'You've met him?' Amirah asked. Eye contact pinged around the table.

'Yeah.' Amy smiled, walking further into the trap she didn't know was there. 'We went for a little walk on New Year's, after the party!'

I had not told my friends about the party. Emotional Lauren set down her drink and stared into the bottom of it like a deep truth lurked within. Lauren sighed, and Amirah did a faint, furious laugh. Clive breathed in through his nostrils and turned to me. 'I want you to keep in mind, somewhere in there, that you're going through a big thing right now. It's not like you can instantly parachute out of your marriage and into another relationship.'

'God, he is so wise,' Amy said. 'I'm always saying I need more gay friends, and like, this is what I mean.' Clive let this slide.

'The thing is, I think maybe I can!' I said cheerily. 'Jump from one thing to another, I mean. I wasn't expecting it to be this easy, but I feel very okay. Good, even. I know you're worried, and that's really sweet, but you don't have to be. I'm actually meeting up with Jon soon to finalise everything, so it's like, pretty much totally over.' I tipped my glass toward my mouth and discovered it was empty.

'He's talking to you again? When did that happen?' Amirah sounded pissed.

I chewed on some ice as I told her we hadn't had a *conversation*-conversation, in the sense of two people talking, but that I'd made an appointment with a therapist and sent him a link, so we were going to meet for a post-breakup

counselling session, at which we would say our final good-byes and wish each other well.

There was a long pause. Finally, Emotional Lauren cleared her throat and leaned forward, pensive and serious. She looked like Oprah. 'And has he said he wants to do this?'

'Basically,' I said. 'When he was moving out, he suggested we see a breakup counsellor together. I thought it sounded stupid, but now that I've had some time to think about it, I want to be a good partner – ex-partner, whatever – and help him process things however he needs. Especially since I'm moving on and stuff. Anyway, enough about me! Amirah, any cool *frissons* lately?'

Amirah crossed her arms but did not say anything.

Simon arrived moments later to a fully silent table, deposited a bottle of wine and a basket of French fries between us, and hung his coat on the back of my chair. His face was flushed from the walk, and the mineral smell of the cold outside clung to his beard. 'Hope it's okay I got white,' he said, smiling nervously. 'I texted you, but I guess your phone was in your bag.' He did a dorky wave to the group and unscrewed the cap on the top of the bottle.

Amirah leaned forward. 'So, Simon,' she said. 'I hear you do magic.'

Simon handled this gamely, and the conversation moved on to other things. Tom did eventually join us, and the group settled back into its usual dynamic, all rude jokes and dumb theories, and the revelation that while Stalin (and indeed the entire line of questioning) was not to his taste, Simon would, if pressed, do it with a pre-atrocities

Imelda Marcos. Although I felt a certain chill in the air when I was speaking, everyone took to Simon immediately, and it was a genuine pleasure to watch him blossom under the group's interest, doling out witty jabs, asking thoughtful follow-up questions, and being charming in his slightly studied though nonetheless effective way.

I zoned out for a minute and watched my friends and sort-of boyfriend discuss a recent scandal involving the prime minister's socks: to some commentators they had been too political, and to many enraged online presences, not nearly political enough. Simon said he didn't consider the PM a leftist, but he guessed he was more left-leaning than the average voter.

'I did hear you lean left,' Clive said with a sly smile. It took Simon a second to realise Clive was talking about his penis. He did eventually and followed up with a 'huge caucus' joke that didn't technically make sense but was enormously successful as a vulgar pun.

'And *this* is the man you're bringing to Emily's wedding?' Emotional Lauren asked, feigning shock.

'Emily and Patrick?' Amy chirped. 'No way! I'm going to that! The groom and I were both on stu gov at Western. I actually gave him an HJ once, but it was at a stoplight party, so I feel like that doesn't count. Maybe don't tell the bride, just in case.'

I promised I wouldn't. 'I'll barely know anybody there,' I said. 'I'm mostly going to show off my fancy new man. Look at this: face of victory. Right?' I patted Simon's thigh like he was my trusty steed. 'You could be a war criminal and I'd still take you to this wedding.'

A loud wail broke out from the table nearby, and I realised that someone on Les Quizerables was wearing a baby. I was horrified to find myself in the company of young parents, but grateful to their offspring for breaking yet another long, awkward pause. I looked at Simon and could not read his expression. Amirah avoided my eye contact by fussing with Tom's hair, Lauren and Clive were texting, and Emotional Lauren was gazing intently into the middle distance with a strand of hair in her mouth. I shifted my eyeline to Amy, who smiled nervously. For the first time since she'd arrived, she seemed unsure how to proceed.

'I'm excited for you to meet Ryan,' she said to me, then turned to include the rest of the table. 'Yesterday I told one of my patient's moms that my boyfriend is a clown, and she looked me dead in the eye and said, "*Aren't they all?*"'

Clive laughed first, then the rest of them joined in. I could have kissed her. In an effort to ride the wave of goodwill Amy had created, I let out a flurry of complimentary non sequiturs, praising Clive's culinary abilities and Amirah's trivia contributions and the outerwear of both Laurens. They accepted these gamely, then moved along to other topics, asking Simon about 6Bites and letting Tom talk to us about Bitcoin. I used a credit card to buy a round of drinks for the table, and when the rescue puggle came up again, I kept my mouth shut.

As the night progressed I felt a bit better, though if I was silent for too long a panic would creep in and I'd blurt a self-deprecating anecdote or joke, realising too late that someone else at the table was in the middle of their own story or conversation. I could tell my interruptions weren't

winning anyone over, but it seemed better than doing nothing. I felt suddenly desperate to impress this group of people who had known and loved me since we were teenagers, who I'd seen barf and betray people and figure out that they were wearing the wrong-sized bra. It was a destabilising feeling and I wanted it to go away.

We demolished a final round of fries for the table and called it a night, complaining already about how bad our headaches would be tomorrow. Because it was winter in Toronto, the decision to leave meant extensively preparing ourselves to be cold. Base layers were supplemented with scarves, hoods pulled tight around faces, mittens layered on top of gloves, and then we were outside, the frigid air hardening the snot in our noses as we discussed the merits of various bus routes versus the streetcar.

Street mush was already seeping into my cheap winter boots; my toes would be damp when I got home. Amy, whose sublet was nearby, skipped away after putting her number in Emotional Lauren's phone and promising her 'mimos, on demand, any time'. Tom was holding Amirah close to him, his hands in the pockets of her big down coat. Lauren was trying to use the tip of her nose to unlock her iPhone, unwilling to take off her gloves. Clive took in the scene and yelled, 'Fuck this, XL for the girls,' ordering a van to whisk everyone to their respective homes. After a quick head count, I offered – gallantly, I thought – to give up my spot. Nobody protested.

Three minutes later, a grey van pulled up. Everyone piled in, and Amirah said a stilted goodbye and tried to hurry the automatic door closed, which made it fully open again,

then judder and glitch when she tried to pull it back, which she did several times, until the van's driver yelled at her to stop touching it. They looked out at me, unspeaking, as the door inched shut incredibly slowly, emitting a high-pitched, whiny beep. When it finally closed, the van pulled away, and Emotional Lauren did a tentative wave at Simon and me out the back windshield.

I reached for Simon's hand and said, 'Shall we?' in a sort of Cary Grant voice. He put his mitten on mine, and we set off down Dundas. Snow started to fall in fat, thick flakes.

'Sorry about tonight,' I said. 'They're a lot more fun than that, usually.'

'They seemed fine to me,' said Simon.

When we got back to mine, he was quiet in a way that indicated he was mad.

The Fight (Abridged)

He said, 'Is everything alright?' and I said, 'Everything's great' then ranted for several minutes about how nobody made bathing suits with the back and sides on them anymore, and how were you supposed to go on a family holiday with most of your ass and part of your labia hanging out, a bit of majora at minimum. He said, 'Did you tell your friends I was coming' and I said I didn't need to, and he said, 'People like to be told if you're bringing someone somewhere' and 'I wanted to make a good impression.'

At this point the fight had not started in earnest and was more of a light tension somewhere around my lower back. I returned to the bathing suits, and he said, 'You called me your boyfriend earlier,' then explained that he wasn't against the title necessarily, but was surprised because we had not talked about it, and maybe that was something to—

I interrupted to tell him he could still sleep with other people if that was his concern. He said it was not, and the tension crept up my back and into my shoulders. 'You can do whatever you want,' I said, 'but everything is easier if I can say, "This is my boyfriend."' He asked why, and I sighed and described in great detail an orange-brown powder I often mixed with water and spread on toast in place of peanut butter.

When he did not understand what I was getting at, I picked up a dark chocolate and almond butter treat and showed it to him. 'I pay extra to eat this instead of a Reese's,' I said. 'Like, what the *fuck* is a Snacking Cup?' He still did not get it, and I saw that the moment had arrived. I was being forced to take him on a tour of my insanities, to show him their contours and detail their depths. We were going to have a fight and he was going to hate it.

I explained to him that I was busting my ass every day to stay just a little bit beautiful, like maybe seven out of ten, because everyone was looking at me and feeling sorry for me, and I could not deal with their pity about my body or my face as well. 'Do you remember when we ran into that girl Liz on the bus?' I asked. I told him Liz had given me a particular look when she realised I was with him, a look people used to give when they heard I was engaged, like they were proud and happy and, most importantly, not worried.

He was sitting in a chair by the window and had been jiggling his left leg up and down since I'd started talking about Liz. My head and ears were hot, and he said, 'Is this why you were talking about my coming to that wedding like I could have been anyone?' I said I liked him a lot, but it was complicated, and he sighed. The conversation had gotten away from us and now could only be as bad as it was or worse. We slipped into cliché, and he said maybe we needed some space, and I said it was a Me thing, not about him at all, and he said he wanted me to 'let him in', which unfortunately was the last straw.

I yelled, 'I don't know what you're talking about' and he yelled, 'Why do you cry every time we have sex' and I screamed, 'It's BIOLOGY' and he quieted down and said he knew breakups were hard, that his had been the darkest period of his life, so he understood if I was struggling with my divorce. He got up from his chair and looked at me with almost comically sympathetic eyes, and I felt sick to my stomach and started saying things I didn't mean.

Things like: 'You don't even know me' and 'I'm completely over Jon' and 'Men who are obsessed with therapy are always the biggest psychos'. I said, 'I looked up your ex and she's so thin' and he said, 'So?' and I said, 'So what are you doing with *me*?' and he said, 'Why do you keep asking me that?'

My heart started beating too quickly, and I did not stop myself from saying, 'If you're so emotionally healthy, why is the first person you dated after your ex an emotionally fucked-up divorcée who cries all the time?' and 'I don't have to be a therapist to see that you have very intense commitment issues' and 'You'd be so scared if I was taking this even a little bit seriously. You'd probably have to run out and cheat on me too.'

After a very long and very awful silence, he said, 'This is not an emotionally hygienic conversation,' and I told him he was not better than me because he paid someone to tell him his feelings were valid. He sighed, and I accused him of gaslighting me, and he started to define the word 'gaslighting' and I absolutely lost my shit. I told him it was unfair

that he could treat his girlfriend that way and have another woman line up right behind her. He asked me to please leave his relationship out of it, and I said, 'Why should I?'

My intestines twisted in on themselves, and I told him I knew dozens, maybe hundreds of gorgeous, funny, smart, amazing women, none of whom *needed* a boyfriend, but none of whom could *get* a boyfriend, and the fact of that was slowly corroding their belief in themselves from within. 'They're not even allowed to talk about it,' I said. '*We're* not allowed to talk about it. Even though the whole world is set up to cater to couples, and it's more expensive and danger- ous to be a woman on your own, and the only thing you're unequivocally rewarded for is finding someone – a man, preferably – who wants to be with you. And if you can't you have to walk around knowing that people are judging you – often out loud, to your face – and blaming you, and find- ing you wanting, and you have to smile and say something bullshit like, "I'm never lonely because I love my own company!" or "This tastes JUST like peanut butter, only it's half the calories!!"'

Seeing that we had come back to the peanut powder, Simon grabbed his coat and said he was leaving. I sat on the edge of my bed, and my chest hurt and my head throbbed. I dripped big, stupid tears onto my duvet and said, 'I'm sorry, I'm sorry, I'm sorry,' as he took his scarf and the extra toothbrush from my bathroom and said, in a resigned and gentle tone that made me want to rip my hair out, 'I hope you have a nice time at the wedding.'

The mornings were so dark it was almost impossible to get out of bed. Even if you did manage it, and sunlight did appear, it lasted for about three hours total, so if, for example, you went into a drab concrete building at three p.m. to lecture fifty-eight undergraduates about the Long Parliament's banned plays, you would emerge to the same late-evening blackness you had woken up to, and the urge to never go outside again, or to move to Sweden where they understood how to manage these conditions, or possibly to end it all, was almost overwhelming.

I couldn't tell if this semester felt so bad because of the weather, or my deteriorating personal life, or my students seeming genuinely dumber and less engaged than usual. I had been a little stern with them, maybe, but they needed discipline! This was a difficult field! The professor who wrote my letter of reference for grad school had attached a sticky note to the envelope warning me, and I quote, 'The humanities are a sinking ship, just as you are starting to set sail'!

The students responded to my small acts of tough love by becoming somehow even less dedicated, arriving to class

late, ice jangling in their keep cups, teeth clinking against metal straws as they airily announced that they had not done the reading. There were a few kids who showed up early and read everything, but I didn't like them either. I gave everyone an extension on their midterm papers and made my office hours appointment-only.

I sat at my desk on a long Wednesday and ate a pot of yogurt that claimed to provide an experience as delicious and indulgent as lime cheesecake. Products like this produced in me a deep melancholy, but also I could not stop buying them, in case one ever made good on its promise. Every time I ate a dessert-themed yogurt, I felt like a stupid little bitch.

I took out my phone and looked at my message history with Simon. After our fight he had been silent for four days, then sent a Long Text saying that although he cared about me and had enjoyed our time together, he did not think he was ready to be seriously involved with someone new, and he hoped I understood. I wrote back, ok. He wrote that he also hoped, after some time apart, that we could try to be friends. I wrote back, lol. He did not write back to that, and now it was over. It was the least fun way I had ever been proven right.

I checked the group chat, which had been quiet since trivia, a deviation from our usual routine (constant messaging all day long in a barely intelligible shared dialect) that set me on edge. Whenever I looked at the chat, a voice in the back of my head said, *you are a bad friend and a worse person*, and I thought, *maybe, yeah*, but had no meaningful ideas about how to fix that. I was very, very embarrassed by

how difficult I was finding everyday tasks, ashamed of my sudden reversion to teenage-style low self-esteem, the way I poked and prodded at my body in the mirror before work every morning. I didn't want to inflict this version of myself on anyone, let alone people who were used to the old, normal Maggie. She had been so fun.

Instead of putting out feelers with a screenshot or meme to the group, I input the yogurt into a calorie-tracking app I'd downloaded a few days prior. I had run out of gratis fitness opportunities in my neighbourhood, and the app had been free and promised I could lose weight in a swift but sustainable manner, while still eating the foods I loved. Also, I needed something to do when I opened my phone and there were no messages on it. I read a few emails, then slammed another yogurt, which I did not enter into the app.

I checked my email for something from Jon. As usual there was nothing. I ignored a message from my sister and several from students. Below my new emails was one Emotional Lauren had sent after trivia, containing a list of therapists she had compiled, in case I was looking for myself, alone. I opened my spam folder and clicked through the usual mix of newsletters, phishing scams and branded content.

I cycled through a few blogs and websites I liked to waste time on and let a series of seemingly unconnected words wash over me: Twelve of the Best Vases; Experience: I Got Seasick on Dry Land; These Women Are Defying What It Means to Have Cancer in Taiwan. I looked at vintage chairs and pictures of women before and after a

specific type of noninvasive neck lift. I ate a third yogurt and looked at more neck lifts.

I had not mentioned my recent fascination with cosmetic surgery to anyone, though since New Year's it had taken up an increasingly large portion of my waking thoughts. Although I always sought information about it on Incognito Mode, my phone ('the algorithm'?) had figured it out anyway, so my feed was saturated with alluring images of expensive medical procedures that made women in their forties and fifties look ten years younger merely by cutting their faces off and sewing them back on higher up. I knew I was not supposed to be interested in this kind of thing, that it was possibly unfeminist and definitely unhealthy, but I couldn't stop myself. I'd bookmarked all sorts of treatments: a little pen that burned you over and over, activating some tightening impulse in the skin; injections to dissolve a double chin or fill under-eye hollows; an incredibly tempting grafting process that promised to take fat from one place in the body and put it somewhere fat was more allowed to be.

I thought about it for a long time and concluded that, even leaving aside the issue of my self-esteem, my life would be easier in almost every way if I just had smaller upper arms. I didn't invent beauty standards, and I would not take them down on my own, simply by existing and sometimes posting photos of myself 'unapologetically' baring various body parts. The few times in my life when I had been conventionally thin, the change had been immediate: people were nicer, clothing myself was easier, people on the street stopped making weird comments about my body.

The world opened to me. Because of twenty pounds! How was it possible? Why *not* buy into bullshit beauty conventions, if doing so carried such rewards? Yes, the trends cycled in and out – things had happened with desired ass size in my lifetime that I'd never dreamed possible as a large, awkward adolescent – but I was tired of waiting for my exact body type (innkeeper's wife in bawdy eighteenth-century cartoon) to come into fashion. If thin privilege was so arbitrary, why couldn't I just … have it.

I started running the numbers: a few thousand dollars, plus a month or so of healing time, and nobody would ever be rude to me in an Aritzia again. For the cost of a weeklong stay at a mid-tier Mexican resort, I would never have to manage my double chin in another photo – surely a state of affairs more relaxing than any holiday. What was the point of saving for, like, a car, when I could have inarguably perfect tit texture? Was it so wrong to want to buy back a little ease in this life, or to define ease as 'thighs made perfect via the application of highly concentrated radio waves'? Would it not be easier, all things considered, to recover from surgery for one six-month period than to struggle with buying pants for the rest of my life? Basically, it seemed like a very good investment.

I could see I was entering a Bad Area. What was worse, I knew that I had brought this on myself. I'd recently followed dozens of professionally beautiful women on Instagram. Thin, stylish influencers – actors' children, or dancers, or vintage pickers from banking dynasties – with full lips and pert, somehow glowing noses, who were always doing something perfect and ten degrees off-kilter: eating

lavender marmalade from a wonky goblet, say, or wearing two brioche buns as a bra. I scrolled through my new friends and experienced mild body dysmorphia and thought, *Jesus, am I going to buy lace gloves?*

I'd had to follow a bunch of strangers, because everyone I knew in real life was ageing, disconcertingly and before my eyes, which presented the uncomfortable possibility that I was doing the same, that sometimes someone I didn't know anymore saw my photos and thought, *yikes, time sure is passing*, even if I posted it because I thought I looked great, maybe even very supple. It seemed impossible that I was supposed to keep loving – even revering – my body as it decomposed in slow motion. Why not give in and have low self-esteem? Maybe I could slay in that way instead. *Inspiring: This Woman Hates Herself.*

You can see how I ended up at the Instagram Women. They had a lot to teach me (that you could turn a sweater into a crop top by tucking it into a belt; how much stuff there was to do to curly hair), which was convenient because I needed guidance. I had been striking out hard on the apps of late, a situation Amy – my only friend, or at least the only person returning my texts – attributed to my being a bit intense lately, tb-totally-h!! Nobody on Instagram was intense; they focused on the positive and owned milk froth-ers. I made careful study (and bought a low-quality whisk). From what I could gather, men loved women who were creative but not interesting. Women loved women who knew how to style twelve different earrings per lobe.

I opened Instagram and watched one of my Professional Thins explain how she was living her dream life, travelling

the world with her boyfriend in an old school bus they had turned into a tiny house. I found it hard to believe anybody's dream life involved a bathroom where the shower and toilet were the same thing.

'Oh my god, I follow these guys!' Olivia said, appearing behind me and gesturing toward my phone. I would rather have been caught watching porn. 'I love their little kitchen,' she cooed. 'We're considering something like this for our honeymoon. Aidan's never been to Kelowna, which is, like, wild to me. Yogurt?'

I ate my fourth yogurt of the day as Olivia said 'we' a hundred thousand times, with other words related to honeymoon planning in between. 'We' were going to stop at greasy spoons as we drove our love bus across Canada. 'We' couldn't wait to try a hike that was essentially three vertical kilometres of natural stairs. 'We' had finally settled on a way to make our wedding invitations fun. 'They're going to be watercolours in the shape of our pug, Bosley,' she said, smiling at the very idea of such jocund stationery. 'And they're going out soon, so keep an eye on your mailbox!'

I liked Olivia. I knew she was only trying to be friendly. I wanted her, in this moment, to drop dead.

I asked Olivia if she'd heard about the girl who went missing in Guelph. She said she had (hadn't everyone? the missing girl's face had been on the front page of all the major newspapers all week) and that she hoped the various search efforts underway would be successful. I said it was annoying that her disappearance was getting so much press just because she was tiny and blonde. 'That's true,' Olivia

said. 'So many women go missing every year and don't get that kind of coverage, because—'

'That picture they're using is essentially a glamour shot,' I said, louder and faster than intended. 'If I was her, I'd be like, *hope my ex sees this!* Though I guess if something bad did happen to her, in all likelihood it was her ex who did it.' I smiled and absentmindedly closed a tab, revealing the contact page of a local plastic surgeon. I closed that as well.

Olivia sucked her entire lower lip into her mouth. 'Hey, is, uh, everything okay?'

I told her everything was no more or less okay than usual. I guessed I was frustrated that, since every other area of my life had fallen apart, I now had to be defined by my work, which I did not feel particularly passionate about. 'But that's life,' I said. 'Nobody *likes* their job.'

Outside in the hall, a cluster of students perused a shabby corkboard for book sales, poetry nights and families in need of tutors or nannies. An older professor passed by with his arms full of envelopes. Olivia ran her spoon around the empty inside of her yogurt container, scraping metal on plastic.

'I like my job,' she said shyly.

'Me too,' said Jiro, not shy at all.

He stood in the doorway looking carefully tousled and holding a small espresso cup with showy delicacy. 'I'm very passionate about the history of block printing.' One of the students at the corkboard made eye contact with him and giggled.

Jiro went on about a 'startling frontispiece' he had recently seen as I tried to remember if I had ever been

passionate about anything, least of all my profession. Honestly, I had just been not terrible at it, and the idea of working toward a PhD seemed sort of impressive, and having a 'real job' with a traditional schedule and money on the line and targets (?) to meet sounded onerous and boring. Why shouldn't I discuss ancient plays for my living? What else was I going to do, learn to code?

Being half interested in my work had seemed fine when it was only one part of my life. If I wanted meaning, I could find it in my relationship or, if things became very desperate, have a baby. When I first got married, it had been scary to think that the rest of my life (this part, anyway) was fully planned out. But it had also been comforting – one less thing to worry about. At least that was sorted, no more romantic choices to be made. With that piece removed, the entire puzzle looked wrong: did I have to re-choose everything?

I thought about the long nights working on my master's thesis at our kitchen table, Jon covering our rent and groceries to give me space and time to pursue my alleged dream. It had felt exciting and important then, like I was going to contribute meaningfully to the world's knowledge. Jon had joked about me stepping forward on an airplane: *'Are there any doctors on board?' 'Yes! What part of* Coriolanus *is he struggling with?'* I had been so lucky and so stupid.

I tuned back into Jiro's story in time to hear him and Olivia say, 'Movable type!' in joyful unison. Both laughed like it was the funniest thing they'd ever heard. I told my colleagues it was easy for them to like their jobs. They had other things to define themselves: fitness, a dog and a

fiancé, for Olivia; being a pretentious asshole who spent too much time at board game cafés, for Jiro. Olivia's mouth dropped open. Jiro merely sighed in a louche way, finished his coffee, and walked off. I made a face to Olivia like I was kidding. Maybe I was.

'If you're not feeling connected to work, maybe it would help to get a bit more involved,' she suggested, rising from her chair and adding self-consciously, 'I'm standing up now, but it's not because I want to leave, I just need to recycle this.'

It was pretty clear that she did want to leave, but Olivia was a good sport in every sense. She trotted back to the chair beside me after disposing of the yogurt cup and told me about an upcoming conference in Ottawa – 'Belaboured: Birth and Other Women's Work on the Jacobean Stage' – that had recently put out a call for papers. She had submitted one linking midwife characters to the seventeenth-century textile industry. I found the conference's website and browsed some of the upcoming presentations. They felt as nonsense as clicking through my tabs: Twelve of the Best Fools; These Women Are Defying What It Means to Find Love in Illyria; Experience: I Avenged My Father the King and Died in an Ill-Conceived Final Scene Where Literally Every Prop Onstage Is Poisoned.

I told her I resented the idea that I had to love my job or even like it. It was not providing me with a pension, or dental benefits, or a competitive salary, or much life satisfaction. My hours were random and solitary, the path to publication opaque and arduous, and department functions had instituted a two-glass maximum on complimentary

wine. Why, then, should I like my work, or try hard to be good at it, or even show up on time? The version of this job that I had heard about and imagined, getting into it, was not the version of the job currently available.

I asked her to think about air travel.

'Air travel?'

'Have you ever seen a picture of an airplane in the seventies?' I asked, though I did not want an answer. I wanted to do my little speech. 'It's like a fancy restaurant in there. Like a private club. In the nineties airplanes started looking like buses, but they still fed you and gave you that dry little pillow, and you could move your legs without jostling the person in front of you. Now you don't even get a free checked bag. Every human element of the air travel experience has been taken away, and you have to buy back each individual thing. Let's be honest: "premium economy" is a contradiction in terms.'

Olivia said she did miss the free cookies Porter Airlines used to give out.

'Exactly,' I said. 'Late capitalism at work.'

I sounded like my uncle when he got drunk and talked about being tracked by his credit card company. Still, wasn't I right? Didn't she see what I was saying? Olivia said she did, but wasn't sure how the erosion of the in-flight dining experience related to marriage, or anything else we had been talking about.

I told her it was not only planes that had been made terrible over time. This was true of basically every aspect of modern life. Home ownership was totally out of reach. Adulthood would not involve a lot of vacations or week-

ends away or even single-occupancy one-bedroom apartments. Screaming in the streets would not force anybody important to do anything about climate change, and all the body positive messaging in the world would not alter the fact that my favourite store stocked something called a 'triple zero' but did not make sizes larger than a ten, and even that you had to buy online, like a thief in the night. The only thing that really offered what it said on the tin was marriage.

'That's why it's so tempting,' I said, feeling like we were finally getting somewhere. 'I understand why you want to do it. It's like the only hallmark of what we think of as an 'adult life' that's still accessible. And it's so accessible! You can do it for $300 as long as you find someone else willing to sign the papers.'

'That's not why—' Olivia started, but I wasn't finished.

'And you get to stand there in front of your parents, even if you still take money from them sometimes, and say, *respect me as an adult*. Right? And the wildest thing is they do it, because they recognise the ceremony and the moment and everything. It feels so good to have your aunts and uncles act like you're a real human being, to file joint taxes, to tell some rude landlord that *my husband and I* are looking for some extra office space … like, yes, you're buying into the heteropatriarchal state apparatus or whatever, but everybody gives you money and you get to sit at the grownups' table and own a fancy blender.'

Olivia paused for a moment. She furrowed her brow and said she wanted to marry Aidan because she was in love, but she respected that it was complicated and that there

was a lot going on around the concept, maybe in particular for me at this phase of my life. She said that there were lots of reasons to get married, and that she saw the appeal of ritual and even of the blender, but at the end of the day it sounded like I was talking about commitment and community through a perhaps overly bleak lens.

'Maybe,' I said. 'But who cares? Nothing matters, everything ends, the world is ruled by greedy misogynist racists, and all the affordable furniture looks like shit.'

I picked up my bag and strode out into the hall, encountering one of my keenest students, Sara. She had a canvas tote bag from the drama department over one shoulder and her hair in its usual messy bun. 'Still on for our meeting?' she asked, all optimism and young-person pep. I told her something had come up. She looked disappointed in a way that made me hate her.

'Why don't you email me,' I said. 'It's easier for me to answer questions over email.'

Her face clouded. 'I *have* been emailing you,' she said. 'You told me to come to your office. You said it was easier for you to answer questions in person.'

'Right,' I said. I had a vague memory of her many follow-up emails.

We stood together in the hallway, saying nothing. Sara bit her lip and looked as though she might cry. She was not much younger than me, but clearly still in the dreaming-at-the-kitchen-table phase of this career. I tried to think of something useful to say, a bit of advice to make the trip to my office worth it, but really did not try very hard. Eventually I said, 'Well,' sighed in a way I hoped seemed

world-weary, and walked away.

Outside I found Jiro smoking some of his slender, illegal mint cigarettes. Why were all his possessions so small? What was he trying to prove? 'Fun bit about capitalism,' he smirked. 'Is John Oliver hiring?'

'Please, please fuck off,' I said flatly.

Jiro stubbed out his cigarette and regarded me thoughtfully. 'I'm sorry,' he said. 'I shouldn't be teasing you like that today. Have a good night, okay? And don't stress. It's a fake holiday anyway.'

My cheeks flushed. Despite constant reminders from online ads, couples in the street, and drugstore windows, I had worked very hard to ignore the fact that today was Valentine's Day. I didn't need this right now. I turned on my heel and walked down our building's front steps at speed. At the bottom I paused and looked back. Jiro was still standing there, wearing a jocular expression and a fucking cummerbund. It struck me suddenly that Jiro was hot.

'Hey,' I said. 'Do you want to go to a wedding?'

Google Searches, 16 February

normal coverage bathing suit

test for narcissism

psychopath assessment

which Friend are you quiz

what's wrong with ross

why does everyone's hair on TV look like that

BMI fake officially?

spaghetti squash recipes

ped egg videos

is PAWG a compliment

loose waves tutorial

infrared sauna groupon

infrared sauna scam?

divorce poems

divorce books

divorce movies

is joni mitchell alive

is joni mitchell okay

greek island apartments to rent

is the internet a series of tubes

what terrazzo

stage one lipedema or cellulite

early signs of breast cancer or period

6Bites editorial jobs

kimchi loaded nachos cultural appropriation?

problematic foods

anti-anxiety yoga under ten minutes

industrial revolution mistake

REALLY GOOD, ACTUALLY

plastic surgery covered by insurance

blepharoplasty recovery time

low carb fondue

therapist rating site

professor rating site

ratemyprofessor.com trolls complaint

three-legged dogs

yeast infection or ovulating

can a vagina be depressed

The therapist opened our session by explaining the meaning of the word 'liminal' for almost ten minutes. I couldn't tell if she felt this was important information for me to have – a legal separation being, fair enough, a definitively liminal period in one's life – or if she was stalling for time, since Jon was late, and I was getting increasingly agitated looking at the clock.

Eventually I cracked, telling her that I was a graduate student, so knowing how to use the word 'liminal' in a sentence was one of my only concrete skills. She smiled with her lips closed and said, 'How do you feel about your work, are you happy there?' This is how they get you.

Having never been to one before, I could not confirm whether all therapists' offices looked like a *New Yorker* cartoon of a therapist's office or if it was just this one. The walls were a beige colour you could tell was called something like 'Silken Sand' or 'Meaningful Pebble'. A framed print on the wall depicted a barren cityscape, presumably deserted after some kind of emotional apocalypse. I was dismayed to see a sheer silk scarf draped over a lamp in the

corner; I'd done something similar in my bedroom in high school, inadvertently causing a small fire. Wasn't therapy supposed to be a definitively adult space? Surely there were more mature ways of creating ambience than the one I'd discovered in *CosmoGirl* at fifteen.

For her part, the therapist was also pretty classically 'therapist', first, because her name was Helen, and second, because of every other thing about her. She had a soft voice and 'fun', design-y glasses. Her unstructured blouse was covered in an abstract print that suggested she could at any time be coming from or going to a life-drawing evening.

A dark bob framed her round, friendly face, which was open though not revealing: you could tell her your secrets, but she'd never betray how she felt about them. She had an easy demeanour, and her comfortingly drab website had listed many certificates, workshops and other accomplishments in addition to the standard qualifications she required for her practice. She seemed personable and like she had probably helped many people through difficult times. Still, I did not like her. This was inconvenient, as I'd come early to the appointment so that I could a) position my body in a flattering way on the couch for when Jon arrived and b) build a rapport with Helen that would lead her to side with me when we both presented our cases for why things were going the way they were going.

I assumed couples therapy would be something like high school debate club. We'd each defend our position, and then the therapist would tell us who was wrong (him) and who was right (me) and what was to be done about it. I was looking forward, in a way, to hearing Jon's perspective. I

imagined him squirming and stuttering as he tried to explain his radio silence for almost seven full months, the realisation spreading across his face in real time that he had behaved badly. Maybe he would beg for forgiveness. At the very least, he would apologise. After five more minutes, Helen offered to make us some tea.

Two cups of Earl Grey between us, she moved on to ask the usual things: how I'd been sleeping, if I was making an effort to eat well and move my body, how else I was spending my time. She asked if I'd been to therapy before, and I told her I'd tried, many millions of times, to convince Jon to go, but couldn't interest him in the idea. She adjusted the little chain that dangled from her glasses. 'But you've never been yourself?'

I said I hadn't, but only because I hadn't needed to. My childhood had been more or less emotionally stable. I had a small but supportive social circle in high school and got along well with Hannah. My parents' split had been relatively amicable. My friends were great, my work was fine, a moderate level of fear and ennui crept in during moments of boredom or change, but that was normal, surely, especially these days.

'And why did you want Jon to seek therapy?'

I told her about Jon's weed habit, his changeability, the way he got agitated when things weren't how he wanted them, yet was capable of leaving something rotting in the crisper drawer for weeks. His furious response to losing at video games, the oddly close relationship with that girl from his office, the sneering superiority about the practical and financial value of his work compared to mine. I

mentioned one of my favourite wrongs: how, after that girl had been rude to me at a work party, I'd tried to complain to him about it on the streetcar home. He'd brushed my concern aside, telling me it was 'unfeminist to tear other women down'. When we got back to our apartment, I slept on the couch.

Telling this story, to myself or others, gave me a painful twinge, like snapping my feelings with a rubber band. Yet I repeated it often, loving how clearly it cast our roles: him the asshole, me the long-suffering wife. Not all our arguments were so clear-cut.

'Jon was a difficult man,' I said. 'But I honestly wanted to love him forever.'

Helen paused meaningfully. All her gestures felt obnoxiously potent.

'And have you ever had any feedback, from Jon or anyone else, that you might be difficult yourself?'

I laughed, hard. A funny therapist! What an unexpected turn of events. I explained that I was not difficult; although I had been a slightly dramatic child and teenager, my feelings were now more or less under control. I was sometimes, maybe, *circumstantially* difficult, around big deadlines or stressful events like moving, travel, or unexpected changes in plan. I had been known to need extra time to process thornier emotions – grief, say, or hunger – but I understood this to be normal, and in fact I had been told just the other day that I was holding up nicely amid all the recent turmoil in my life.

Actually, Jiro had said I was 'holding up okay', 'considering', then declined to join me at Emily's wedding, but I did

not need to tell Helen everything. I silently congratulated myself on having some of those boundaries everyone was always talking about. Helen was sitting serenely, her hands folded in her lap, trying to bait me into revealing something terrible about myself. Not today.

I told her it was a shame that Jon had not arrived yet, because I had really organised all of this for his benefit. Truthfully, I had found processing the divorce very easy. I was saving money on my new apartment. And I was dating – if anything, I needed to relax a little bit on the dating, because it had been *too* successful. I had fallen in love already! I was more active than I had ever been, and a new friend had shown me how to move a piece of green stone around my face in a way that meant I would never age. 'So, yeah, things are pretty good,' I said. 'But I worry about Jon, you know, he doesn't have as many people to talk to. Men's support networks are not as strong.'

Helen wrote some things down. 'You say you've fallen in love?'

I laughed again. 'I said I *fell* in love, but you know how it goes … Not great!' I laughed more, but it didn't sound how I wanted. 'I met this guy, and he was lovely. He had some stuff to work on, though – commitment issues, you know how it is.'

'How is it?'

'We don't really talk anymore. It's only been … eight, nine days maybe? Nine and a half days. Ten tomorrow. Or something. So, you never know, we might rev it back up.'

We sat in unbearable stillness for what felt like forty minutes. (Per the clock, it was three.)

'Look,' I said. 'Do I have to pay for the full hour if I don't use it?'

Helen indicated that I did.

'Right, of course. I'm sorry if that question was offensive.'

Helen assured me it wasn't.

I told her I was also sorry I didn't have better stuff to say.

'Better stuff?'

'You know, divorce is supposed to, like, rip through someone's life, but I'm mostly okay. What do people usually talk about in here, like, mania and eating disorders?'

'Sometimes.'

'Yeah, I'm alright there. Honestly, I could use some of the discipline I had during my eating disorder!' Why was my laughter coming out like that? I sounded like a haunted doll.

'You had an eating disorder?'

'That was a joke. I mean, I did have one, sort of, in high school. I think everyone did. Do you remember that show where women would get liposuction and nose jobs and stuff before their weddings, and then reveal their new bodies and faces to their husbands for the first time as they walked down the aisle?'

Helen cocked her head to one side. 'I think so …'

'An eating disorder was basically a rational response to the world at the time,' I said. 'But I'm okay now. I'm almost thirty. I feel like you can't be trying to save for retirement and still focusing on how you thought cellulite was going to be a thighs-only thing.'

It was hard to be looked at this intently. It reminded me of Simon, except worse, because I could not stop it from happening by having sex with Helen. It was not pleasant to think about Simon, so I tried to imagine the sincere faces he would make in therapy, how actively he would engage with the soft, probing questions, loving this chance to dig deeper into any somehow-uncovered childhood trauma. Everything was trauma with that guy.

'It's not uncommon to fall back on old coping mechanisms during a life change, and divorce is a major life change,' said Helen, adjusting positions. 'I'm not a big fan of the word "normal", but I want to assure you, it's very normal to have a hard time during a transition like this.'

'It's been almost a year, though,' I said. 'The first few weeks were tricky, but now I just feel, like, nothing, about it. It's almost as if we were never together. When I try to imagine it, there's nothing there.'

'You can't remember your marriage?'

I told her I had flashes, sometimes: the two of us laughing over coffee, singing along to the radio in a rental car, frantically gripping each other's hand under the table at a dinner party where someone was saying something idiotic; an afternoon doing the crossword in bed; a running joke that he might one day piss on me in the shower; the feeling of walking home from work, knowing he and the cat would be there. But these flashes didn't feel like memories, really. They felt like a movie, or – god forbid – an Instagram Story. They felt like something that had happened to someone else.

'You know,' I said, 'I don't know if it's super useful to even talk about it.'

Helen cocked her head. 'Why is that?' She was good, which was annoying. To buy some time, I made a big show of not having anywhere to put my tea bag.

I'd had enough of discussing my marriage, at least without Jon there, so I distracted her by listing my life's Top Shames. These included:

- thinking Ezra Pound, Evelyn Waugh, and e. e. cummings were women until well into my undergraduate degree;
- peeing my pants, fully, after being scared by a loud noise, age nine;
- getting caught by a family friend completely giving myself over to song while pretending to be a mermaid, perched on a rock, aged slightly too old to be doing so;
- my preferred way to eat macaroni (the entire package, oversalted and cold, in a large congealed lump that had been left out overnight in the pot);
- allowing my classmates to bully a close friend in elementary school, out of fear that without this distraction, they would turn on me instead;
- the time I tried to give Jon a lap dance, got upset about whether I was doing it right, cried, and briefly attempted to keep going through the tears;
- the fact that I've never been moved by a painting.

'I've liked a lot of paintings,' I said, 'and found them beautiful and sometimes even arresting, but I've never seen a painting and felt any emotion other than "interested or not

interested in the painting in front of me", which feels wrong and embarrassing and like I am not fully participating in being human. Oh, and the other big one is whatever's going on with the shape of my pinkie toes.'

Helen responded gamely to all of these, making a probing remark here and there, noting things down on a yellow legal pad like the ones in Lori's office. She did not try to move the subject back to Jon or our marriage or divorce. In fact, she let me speak mostly unbroken for almost half an hour.

At 5:45, she leaned forward and suggested we might want to try 'sitting with the possibility' that Jon would not arrive. 'I'm sure this is a disappointing turn of events, but we can rebook for next week,' she said gently. 'Maybe you could leave me some of the other dates the two of you discussed, and I can get in touch with Jon myself.'

I admitted that there hadn't been a lot of back and forth about the appointment. 'Basically, I had to book it without him,' I told her, 'because he hasn't been responding to my emails, but I know he's been opening them because there's a Gmail setting that notifies you when your emails get read, so he's definitely seen the message about today, and I thought he'd want to clear the air, you know? I mean, he still might. We haven't fully ruled out an accident or something. Or he could be using a twenty-four-hour clock and have confused two p.m. with, like, fourteen, four p.m. – you know what, let's call him, just to make sure.'

I took out my phone and discovered it was dead. 'Do you mind if we use your landline?' I asked Helen. 'We probably won't get anywhere. It's worth a try, though.'

I did not mention that I'd tried to call him, twice, from my cell phone in the waiting room. Helen plonked her big grey landline on the coffee table between us, an expression on her face I couldn't quite read. I dialled Jon and, after some direction from Helen, was able to put the phone on speaker. I knew his number from memory. I also knew he never answered. I told Helen it would probably go to voice-mail. She did her quietly understanding nod, and Jon answered on the first ring.

'Hello?'

'Oh, hello, Jon, this is Helen Yim, I'm a relational coun-sellor, and—'

'Ah, yes. Hi. Is Maggie with you?'

I leaned forward and said I was there. I was there, and I was sorry, and I was feeling, like, maybe medically distraught, and it was so clear, now, hearing his voice, that I had made a mistake. I didn't want to do more yoga or watch any more dismal old movies, didn't want to be tactful and mature. It had been hard to be married, yes, but it was so much harder to be divorced. I didn't want to do it anymore. I wanted him to take me back. Helen's breath caught in her throat. On the other end of the line, Jon was quiet.

'Fuck,' I said.

'Yeah,' said Jon. 'Fuck.'

'I mean … what do you think?' I asked.

Jon laughed dryly, incredulous. 'Come on, Mags …'

I hadn't heard him say my name in half a year. The tears felt very reasonable.

'Think about it,' I said, wiping my eyes. 'I am a big

enough person to admit that I still love you, that there's still love in there, for me.'

'I know, you said that in your email.'

'Right, okay, so, what about you?'

'What about me?'

'You know,' I said. 'Do you … ?'

'I really did love you, Maggie, b—'

'Well, then isn't it kind of crazy to throw it all away because – what? It seemed bad for a minute? Because we had a few doubts? I feel like I'm definitely having an equal number of doubts about this whole divorce thing, so maybe that's life, you know, maybe you never feel good about any of your choices and that's normal, in which case we really shouldn't get divorced because actually everything's fine.'

Helen passed me a tissue, and I dabbed at my nose. When I pulled my hand away, a string of milky-green snot came with it. I balled up the tissue and stuck it up my nose. This was not how I'd imagined this conversation going. I realised with horror that what I'd sold – to Helen, to my friends, to myself – as a kind of exit interview had existed in my mind as a do-over. A chance to ask again, 'Is this working?' and have him fight me, say yes.

'I'm not the bigger person,' I said, my voice taking on a bad-part-of-the-psychosexual-thriller quality. 'I've done everything you're supposed to do and it's not working. I'm not going to find myself. I don't even want to. I live in a basement. I'm having nightmares, and I keep spooning people I don't know that well because I'm not used to sleeping with someone casually. I'm used to sleeping with you.'

'One of your voicemails said you had a boyfriend.'

'Oh, yeah, well,' I said, 'I did for a second, but I don't anymore.'

'From your messages it sounds like you've been dating a lot. I'm sure you'll find someone else.'

'I don't *want to*,' I cried, feeling oddly empowered by the depths to which I was sinking. That I could be this pathetic and still breathing was an achievement, in its way. 'We made this big, huge decision, and now we have to go out there and choose *something else*, knowing we did it wrong the first time? Absolutely not, I'm sorry. No.'

Helen's tight-lipped expression was transforming from strained concentration into something more overtly perturbed. 'If I may,' she said. 'Sorry, Helen here. Can I ask, how frequent are these voicemails?'

I sat back as Jon told her the truth. That I'd texted or emailed most days, sometimes several times per day, since we had separated. That he had stopped answering my calls seven months ago, but that had not stopped the messages, which had only become longer and, in his words, 'significantly more batshit'.

'I don't think that's fair,' I said.

'On Valentine's Day you left a three-part voicemail where you sang that Bernadette Peters song in full.'

'I don't know what you're talking about.'

Jon sang a few bars of 'No One Is Alone', from Stephen Sondheim's 1987 musical *Into the Woods*.

'Oh,' I said. 'Well. That's not actually a Bernadette Peters song, she only covers it on *Sondheim, Etc.*, because it's one of her favourites. And I didn't do the whole thing, I just

wanted to show you the chorus and one particularly reso-
nant verse about how everybody makes mistakes, because
they do, and maybe that's not so—'

'I don't care, Maggie.'

'I think it's important to be accurate—'

'I don't care about any of it,' he said. 'I don't want to hear
from you.'

'Why didn't you *say that*?' I asked. 'How could you just
disappear?'

Jon let out a frustrated breath. 'I don't know,' he said. 'I
guess I was mad. I don't know why you thought you could
suggest we get divorced and then have me hold your hand
through it, too.'

'Because you promised!' I wailed. 'You said you would.'

'Did you have sex with Calvin?'

Helen's lips were so pursed I was genuinely worried
about her air supply.

Jon tried again: 'I don't even think you mean it, about
getting back together. I think you're stressed out about
having to make decisions for yourself. Honestly, you might
just be bored.'

I told him I was bored, that being sad all the time was
fucking boring, actually. He was unmoved. I tried to rally,
invoked the promises we'd made, the day at the beach with
the sunset that had made him feel safe, the jokes about
baby names, the life we'd agreed to make happen. Didn't
people have rough patches? Didn't they have rough years?
Was trying to be happy again worth being this miserable?
The words were tumbling out of my mouth, melodramatic
and fast. I wasn't sure I meant them either. I didn't want to

think any longer about what I wanted, or how to be, or who to try to be with. I wanted to go back to how it was.

'We can't do that,' Jon said.

'Fine, then,' I said. 'I want closure.'

'Closure isn't real,' he said.

'Well fucking *WHY NOT?*'

I yelped the question at Helen as much as Jon. Wasn't closure kind of a therapist's purview? Helen had been waiting for her opening. 'That is unfortunately all the time we have for this session,' she said. 'I, um— usually I would suggest we come up with a schedule that works for us all, but—'

'That won't be necessary, Helen, thank you,' said Jon.

I could feel that Helen was looking at me but I could not make myself meet her gaze. 'I'm sorry,' I said. 'I'm so sorry.'

'Me too,' said Jon.

'You can text me any time, you know, if you change your mind about talking. Or we could agree to meet at, like, the midway point of a bridge, maybe …'

Jon sighed. I wondered if he was in bed in the new home he lived in without me, if he had roommates or a lover or had bought Janet a little outfit. I wondered if he was wearing the sweatpants I always stole, if he still smelled like the crappy bodywash he'd used since college, if even a small part of him had feelings for me.

I stared at the floor, chewed a bit of my hair, and waited for him to speak. I sat with Helen, quiet and rigid, hoping she could not hear the weird rumbling sounds my stomach was making, wondering how fast I could get out of here when this was over. I checked the clock. The session had gone eight minutes overtime.

'Jon, listen, I—'

Almost as soon as I started speaking, I realised he had hung up. The dial tone cut in, droning and loud, and I felt something like heartburn, tight and sour in my chest. I kept my eyes on the spot of carpet in front of me, letting it come in and out of focus as I rode waves of shame and nausea and fought a confusing urge to laugh. Helen opened her mouth and closed it again. The idea that I'd freaked out a therapist was very stressful.

'I'M FINE,' I shrieked, to put her at ease. 'DON'T worry AT ALL about me, because as I said, I really am SO fine.' I smiled like a child pageant contestant – blankly, hugely, with frightened eyes. My cheeks stung. I hooked the sleeve of my cardigan over my thumb and poked at the corners of my eyes in short, sharp dabs. Helen leaned forward, resting her forearms on her thighs, interlocking her fingers. Our eyes met. I smiled apologetically and let out a ragged, resigned breath.

She smiled back and said, 'I would really like it if you came back again next week.'

Emily and Patrick's Big Day

9 March 2019

3 p.m. VOWS – Family and friends gather in the (covered and heated!) gardens for a nondenominational commitment ceremony.

The wedding was *Gatsby* themed, which was too bad, and there was a 'winter wonderland' component as well, though that came and went. (Basically, there was an ice luge.)

I had capitulated to the *Gatsby* element by wearing dark lipstick and an embarrassing headband with a feather in it, which I removed almost immediately after arriving. Otherwise, I was dressed in a style Amirah called 'floozy semiformal', in this case a wedding-friendly floral print on a perilously closed wrap-front dress, rented via a website where women wealthy enough to own such things but not wealthy enough not to stress about it could loan out their $400 garments for $20 a day, plus shipping and cleaning. It didn't look right, or I didn't feel right in it. Normally any wardrobe uncertainty could be cleared up with a photoshoot for the group chat, but things were off with my friends right now; it was not the time to send a transparent request for compliments.

I wiped some goo from the corner of my eye, careful not to smudge my unusually complicated eyeliner. The bride and I had been friendly in high school, so I had to put in some effort. Emily, who looked gorgeous, was marrying a man she'd met at work. She had been counting down to their wedding on her various social media profiles for liter-

ally the last five hundred days. Her dress was beautiful: sleek and modern, with a slightly whimsical cape thing on the back. I'd seen images of all ten she'd been considering via Instagram, and this was easily the prettiest one. It clung to her impressive body – honed, as I'd also seen online, via a personal trainer's proprietary #ShreddingForTheWedding programme. Her husband-to-be was wearing a bolo tie.

Though it had presumably been their idea, the couple seemed to have eschewed the twenties theme, which was perhaps why the bridesmaids looked so down about their dumpy sequined sack dresses, ordered in bulk from an online retailer that had recently been outed, to no consequence whatsoever, as exploiting the workers in its factories overseas. They adjusted and readjusted themselves under the rotunda, trying to find a flattering way to stand as Emily and Patrick each expressed how lucky they were to grow old with not only the love of their life, but their best friend too.

'I hate when couples write their own vows,' whispered Merris. 'It takes so much longer than a standard civil ceremony, and no one is ever able to access any gravitas.'

After Jiro turned me down on the department steps I had resolved to attend the wedding alone, and felt good about this idea until the morning of the event, when, in a panic, I went upstairs and asked Merris if she owned any formalwear. The idea of facing it all – the ceremony, the slow dancing, the small talk – without a sarcastic hand to hold was simply too much. We watched as Emily told Patrick it would be an honour to stay out of his way on game day for as long as they both should live. Merris rolled her eyes as the rest of the guests giggled conspiratorially.

There were falteringly delivered readings, and the photographer made them redo the kiss after Patrick dipped his bride away from the camera in a fit of passion. We waited through the awkward document-signing portion, and the happy couple was presented to us, officially, as husband and wife. Everyone clapped. A four-piece band started playing a jazzy cover of a pop song about living forever, and the bridesmaids self-consciously sidled down the aisle, clinging to their respective groomsmen. We blew bubbles as Emily and Patrick passed by, beaming and laughing with relief: *This was it, forever! Maybe!*

4:30 p.m. COCKTAIL HOUR – Enjoy a signature drink and nibbles in the indoor courtyard or try your hand at some lawn games!

'What's this?' Merris asked when I brought her a drink, pink and bright, with something shimmering around the rim. She reached out and felt the granules between her fingers.

I shrugged. 'Salt, maybe? The bartender said it was a Canadian riff on a Mexican classic, so I think it's some kind of maple margarita.'

Merris tasted the powder and made a face. 'Oh dear,' she said. 'Pop rocks.' She took a small sip, then a bigger one. 'How are you, anyway?'

I told her I was doing well, this morning's panic notwithstanding. I did not mention that my closest friends were sick of me and I did not blame them, or that I'd been romantically humiliated by two men in the same number of weeks. Better to keep it positive: I'd lost five pounds

through my tracking app and was trying an intermittent fasting thing, and although my personal life was in a shambles, my tweets about it were doing great.

'You pretty much just have to say some version of 'men are trash' and dozens of women will agree with you,' I said. The other day I had tweeted men really do be garbage without quite understanding what I was getting at, but the sentiment raked in almost eighty retweets – quite good, for me – so it must have resonated.

I'd recently followed a bunch of accounts that churned out similar content multiple times per day, posting screenshots of bad Tinder exchanges, degrading tales of dates gone wrong, crying selfies featuring deep cleavage, etc. Everyone was ostensibly kidding, though I had to admit none of the posts were particularly funny. Still, they provided a certain comfort. I could act recklessly – meet a stranger at his house at four a.m., double text a woman who was clearly not interested – and if it went badly, as it often did, I could dust myself off and turn it into light-hearted content. Someone might even take it and claim it: literally me. Literally, me!! We were in it together.

I liked thinking about my sorority of unhinged internet friends on our respectability rumspringa, single by choice, even if we were sort of hating it. They would understand about the calls and texts, about the therapy mishap, about sometimes still dialling Jon's number from a decrepit pay phone on a corner near campus, never taking my finger off the switch hook – just standing there thinking about it – until I grew too embarrassed and went back inside, to cry in the disabled stall and try something new with eyeliner

afterward. I couldn't tell my real-life friends or family or Merris how badly therapy had gone, and indeed had not even confessed online, but it was comforting to know there were people out there who might get it, in theory.

5 p.m. PHOTOS – The bridal party (and Bacon, the rescue pup!) spend some time with the photographer; guests keep partying!

Amy found me standing next to a lace-swaddled heat lamp, watching the bridal party attempt a 'fun one' (truly odd expressions from the men, a few half-hearted tongues out from the women). An ambitious groomsman, the shortest of the group, proposed that the rest of them moon the camera. The bride looked at the groom with Please No face, and when the moment came, only the instigator pulled down his pants.

'I feel like you're avoiding me,' Amy said. She was wearing a flapper dress and had her lips painted in an adorable twenties-style cupid's bow. 'Why didn't you dress up? You could have done those little flippy bangs.'

I told her short bangs on someone with my hip-to-waist ratio made people feel in danger of a burlesque performance, or a lecture about how Marilyn Monroe wore a size fourteen.

'God, it's so depressing, isn't it?' I said.

'I don't think so,' said Amy. 'If you ask me, beauty has no size. Like I prefer myself when I'm keeping fit and eating healthy, but I think you can look however you want and still be so gorgeous.' She pulled me into an affectionate side hug.

'I meant *this*,' I said, gesturing at the photobooth and the bean bag toss and the couples referring to themselves as the 'Wedding Attenders'. 'It's the beginning of the deluge. It's going to be wedding after wedding. A whole spring and summer of spending money congratulating other people and needing to have something to say about the colour scheme.'

Amy asked if I had a lot of other invites lined up.

'Not yet,' I said, 'but they're coming, and I'll put them on my fridge, and every time I reach for almond milk, I'll have to remember that some girl I went to summer camp with has love in her life and I don't.'

Amy frowned. 'The divorce rate is hovering at, like, 45% these days,' she said. 'Like half the couples you have to buy expensive placemats for are doomed.'

I looked at Amy, surprised. 'That's quite pessimistic for you.'

She smiled happily. 'I know, right? I'm like an empath. I adjust to the emotional output of people around me, even if it's all goth and intense like yours.'

'I'm wearing Reformation,' I said.

'Sure,' she said. 'But you are exuding a gothic energy.'

Across the room, Ryan the therapy clown was wearing twenties-style plus fours that ballooned stupidly below the knee. His outfit was so embarrassing I could tell he really cared for my friend, though I guessed he was also used to wearing ridiculous outfits at work. He did a huge, eager wave in Amy's direction; Amy waved back and indicated that one of the drinks she was holding was intended for him. She turned to me.

'Can you cheer up, please?' she said. 'You already brought an old lady as your date. You can't bring bad vibes too.'

Amy skipped off, and I tried to figure out how to exude happiness or at least confidence, almost instantly admitting defeat and ordering a tequila soda instead. Across the room, Emily let her new husband hoist her onto his shoulders, his head disappearing beneath the huge, fluffy skirt she'd changed into for the party.

6 p.m. DINNER – Please find your seats and enjoy a three-course meal from the couple's favourite eco-friendly farm-to-table establishment, *Recyclage.*

The tables were named after famous couples from history, though the wedding planner had played fast and loose with the definition of 'famous', and 'history', too. Merris and I were at 'Sandy & Danny', along with an extremely ragtag group of professional acquaintances and lesser relatives who had clearly been lumped together after the rest of the tables were decided and only a few randoms remained. I sat between Merris and a lanky man called Jesse, who was there with his partner, a freckled, braless woman called Darragh.

Darragh was so much hotter than her boyfriend it would have been inconceivable had I not encountered three hundred other couples exactly like them already that evening. It was not that Jesse was hideous, just that his girlfriend was more attractive than him by every possible metric: funnier, sexier, smarter and more charming. I remembered a joke I used to make to Simon, that I was

queering the straight relationship by being less attractive than he was. Thinking about Simon was a mistake.

'Me and Patrick worked together at the marina in Port Hope,' Jesse said, attacking a seeded sourdough bun with a too-hard ball of whipped butter. 'Back in the day, obviously. How about you guys?'

An older woman across from us perked up – mine and Merris's relationship was obviously causing some confusion at the table.

'Emily and I went to high school together,' I said. 'And this is my friend Merris.'

Merris waved. 'A bit of a last-minute substitute,' she said, though that didn't seem to clarify things for our dinner companions.

Darragh leaned forward: 'So are you two … ?'

'Together?' I said. 'No, no, it's more glamorous than that. I live in her basement.'

Servers descended on our table with the smallest possible servings of 'cured beet carpaccio', and Darragh smiled at me like Princess Diana visiting those orphans. 'I used to live in a basement,' she said. 'Think I still have my SAD lamp somewhere.'

My stomach growled, and I wanted to eat a roll more than I'd ever wanted anything, but the Eating Window dictated by my fasting schedule did not open until 6:30. Clear liquids were allowed any time, so I had more of my tequila, then went to the bathroom and composed a tweet regarding that feeling when you're at a wedding and want to burn down the entire marquee.

8 p.m. SPEECHES – A chance to hear from Emily and Patrick's loved ones and, of course, the couple themselves!

Everyone congratulated the couple at length. This was the smartest thing they'd ever done; it was meant to be; they were perfect complements to each other and welcome additions to their respective families-in-law. Their parents could not wait to give them money and hoped they would start having sex to make babies as soon as possible, preferably tonight.

The banalities were their own kind of drinking game: drink when the mother-in-law cries, drink when somebody says 'my person', drink when a bridesmaid delivers a joke she clearly found by googling wedding speech humour. It was awful to watch, but I knew from experience that it felt amazing to be on the receiving end of this parade of generic compliments.

Between my private drinking game and raising our glasses to the happy couple, I had quickly drained my glass. I turned to Merris and offered to get her a refill.

'Maybe some soda water,' she said. 'So we pace ourselves.'

'Don't worry,' I said. 'Tequila is an upper.'

I stood and made my way through middle-aged couples and out-of-town cousins and children, so many children, in the direction of the bar. When I got there, I ran into Amy and told her I was going to win Simon back. She listened patiently as I detailed my various plans: I could leave a secret message in the 6Bites comments section, or send him a cookie with his face on it, or maybe get on the Jumbotron at a soccer game.

'I want something big and impactful,' I said, 'to show him I know I fucked up.'

Amy frowned. At the front of the room, the groom's brother told a story that danced gracelessly around the hiring of a sex worker.

'I'm sorry, but I don't think that's going to work,' Amy said, after I confided my best idea: telling his landlord I was his sibling so I could break into his apartment and fill it with balloons. I said that kind of thing worked all the time in the movies.

'Well, yeah,' she said. 'I mean, not to be rude, but those are fictional situations. The only people who want a big public gesture are the women who watch those films.'

I finished my tequila and soda and switched to white wine. The sugar would perk me up, which I needed; although my Eating Window had opened, the main course was a breaded chicken Kiev, and I was trying to avoid brown food. I looked over to my table and saw Jesse pick up Darragh's napkin from where it had fallen at her feet. Amy cleared her throat.

'Hey, um, I just peeped Twitter,' she said. 'And I feel like … I don't know, I saw some of the stuff you said about Patrick's tie and the theme and everything, and I just think, like, those are public, right, and if they saw that stuff they'd be pretty hurt.'

'They're *jokes*,' I said. 'I think that's pretty obvious.'

'Oh, totally,' said Amy. 'Yeah, totally. I just mean, maybe you don't have to live tweet the wedding?'

I grabbed my glass and headed back to my table as Emily took the mic and began an acrostic poem using the word 'COMMITMENT'.

9 p.m. THE DANCE FLOOR IS OPEN! – After the first dance, guests are invited to join the couple on the dance floor. Prizes will be given out for wildest moves (look out, cousin Eddie!).

'My girlfriend thinks you're beautiful,' Jesse whispered as I participated, against all odds, in a table-wide conga. Interesting. This phrase was internationally recognised couple code for *you seem bi and we have always considered ourselves evolved enough to have a threesome.*

Despite our rocky start, Sandy & Danny had been irreversibly bonded by how long it took our main courses to arrive, so by the time the dance competition was announced, most of us were game, which was to say very drunk. Even Merris was a little tipsy – Patrick's bachelor uncle was giving her sips from his flask – and Jesse and Darragh had proved themselves more fun than expected. Jesse had stolen us some leftover canapés from an abandoned tray, and they had both participated enthusiastically in a few rounds of What Did This Cost, which I played about every element of the wedding. We guessed the entire event had a final price tag of $40,000, or approximately two and a half independently funded master's degrees.

At some point in our slurred calculations, we realised that nobody at our table was married. Darragh, who was from Oregon, said her initial position on marriage was that she would never do it herself until it was legal for everyone: 'Then they legalised it for gay couples, and I was like, oh, maybe I think marriage sucks.' Jesse said being divorced was sexy, and Darragh shot him a look, widening her eyes

like, *be cool, man.* She took a sip of her drink and winked at me. *Well,* I thought. *Well, well, well.*

10:30 p.m. CAKE CUTTING – Time to tuck into a four-tiered lavender and lemon cake with mascarpone buttercream and blueberry compote ... gluten-free, like the groom!

Shots appeared at the table and we all did some. Everyone pretended to love it as Emily traced mascarpone down her husband's nose and he pretended to be shocked. I accidentally let out my fake laugh a beat or two late, preoccupied by the prospect of a threesome.

Jon and I had had one once, kind of, but we'd botched it, and the girl, a friend of mine from an early bartending job, mostly ended up reassuring me that I was attractive while Jon did the dishes. There was so much that could go wrong: different levels of interest, experience, or self-confidence. I wasn't particularly into Jesse, but he was so sweet with Darragh. The idea of being part of a couple again, even someone else's, was very appealing. I wanted to zip into their intimacy like a sleeping bag and take a nap.

'You're an addict,' Merris said, leaning toward me.

I jumped. How did she know?

She smiled. 'What could possibly have happened to your phone in the last three minutes?'

'Oh,' I said. 'Right. Yeah, it's bad.'

I told Merris it wasn't just me; everyone's brain was broken in exactly the same way. I did not tell her that I had recently opened my laptop and googled mom when what I had meant to do was call my mother. I covered my phone

with my napkin and tried to seem tranquil and centred. I licked some extra buttercream off my knife, hoping it made me look like Angelina Jolie. Instead, I cut my tongue a bit. To sterilise the wound, I did another shot.

Merris looked like she was fading. 'I won't leave without you,' she said. 'But let's start thinking about our exit, yes?'

I offered her a shot, which she declined, and thanked her again for coming with me. 'It means a lot,' I said, patting her arm. 'I don't know what I would have done without you this year.'

Merris gave me a dubious look and pointedly reached for her purse.

'Oh, let me stay out, Mom, please!' I whined. 'I never break curfew.'

Merris's face softened, and I saw I had bought myself an hour or two, which was all I needed; I wasn't a good sport about wearing high heels, and my Eating Window closed again at one. The older uncle leaned over and started asking Merris about an outlandish vintage brooch she was wearing, so I left her to it, finishing the rest of the cheese puffs we'd hoarded earlier, when the passed hors d'oeuvres were still in transit but we had not yet been served. Under the napkin, my phone lit up. It was a text from Jesse, who had acquired my phone number somewhere after the conga and before the chicken dance: come fuck us in the bathroom.

I looked up from my phone. He was barely a foot away, making an absurd face he must have thought looked cheeky and seductive. I grinned, though it felt a bit stupid. People didn't really have sex in bathrooms, I knew. That was just

something TV writers made up. Still, it was nice to be desired by his beautiful girlfriend, to know their relationship had a hole in it, too, and that tonight they wanted to fill that hole with me.

11:30 p.m. LATE-NIGHT EATS – Hungry after all that dancing? The courtyard will be visited by a pizza fairy just before midnight!

The bathrooms at the venue were fancy but not spacious. The couple (or, more accurately, the couple's parents) had sprung for secondary toilets outside on the sprawling grounds, and it was one of these we snuck off to, with a bottle of amaretto filched from the bar.

I took a swig as Darragh closed and locked the door and Jesse cut up neat little lines. I did not ask what they were or bring up fentanyl and its prevalence in Ontario's powdered drugs. Instead I leaned over the counter, inhaled deeply, and tried to seem like I did this all the time.

'So,' said Jesse, 'do you think you'd ever get married again?'

Darragh hit his arm. 'Babe. She doesn't want to talk about that at a *wedding*.'

'Ding ding ding,' I said. I took a risk and put a hand on Darragh's thigh, to emphasise how right she was. I told her being divorced at weddings made me feel like a shrivelled old crone.

'You're not shrivelled,' said Darragh, fully taking my boob out of my dress.

Jesse, who was kneeling in a corner doing more credit card stuff, stood and came over.

'Look at that, baby,' she crooned. Darragh was suddenly using a totally different voice. Her face looked like someone had approached a caricaturist and said, '*Do horny.*'

The two of them were staring at each other intensely. Jesse didn't even look at my breast, just swiped it with his paw and lunged at Darragh's face, muttering the word 'smooth' under his breath. I hoped I didn't look or sound as drunk as Jesse, though we'd all been drinking the same amount. I reached toward them in an unfocused effort to become more involved, lost my nerve, and withdrew my fingers before they made contact.

Jesse pushed Darragh up on the counter, and they started licking each other's faces, each reaching out occasionally to grope at whatever part of my body was to hand. They were moaning a lot, though neither was stimulating any part of the other that would normally produce that type of reaction. I started playing with Darragh's hair and realised I was dividing it into sections like I was about to start French braids.

I took my hands off Darragh; she didn't seem to notice. I felt that thing where the porn you're watching turns abruptly horrible, and you know that even after you close your laptop, you're going to feel unsettled about it for the next hour at least. Maybe I was just dizzy. I looked over and realised that Darragh had moved to the floor. Unsure what else to do, I crouched down next to her and tried to muster a sexy expression.

Six minutes later, Jesse came in Darragh's mouth while I sat on the ground nearby. He pushed my head toward his girlfriend's, and the idea that he expected me to interact

with his secondhand ejaculate when I still had most of my clothes on and had otherwise barely been involved in our alleged 'threesome' was … not it, for me. I started to make my way to my feet, and realised I was swaying in my heels.

'I should probably get back,' I said, steadying myself on the back of the toilet.

'Eugcht!' said Darragh, putting her arm around me. She held up a finger and swallowed. 'Sorry. Want some weed?'

Jesse fished out his vape pen and passed it to me. He seemed completely unhurried and content. He hadn't even buttoned his pants; I could see his flaccid dick through the break in his boxers. I felt … not stressed, exactly, just very aware of my teeth in my mouth, the bones in my jaw, my temples. At least they were using their normal voices again. I puffed out smoke that smelled like cotton candy and tried to think how I would spin this experience to make it sound fun. I felt certain that, whatever I decided, I would do a great job.

It had been fun, I thought. In a way. Even if it had not been a threesome proper, surely the fact that it had happened at all meant that I was very modern and wild. I leaned back against the bathroom door, savouring the vape aroma like one of my candles and experimenting with holding my eyes open very wide. Jesse started telling me how polyamory was historically a more natural way for animals to live, and Darragh explained that was why they had gotten their tattoos. Everything they were saying was terrible, but I felt very, very good.

I heard the sound of the door opening before I realised I was horizontal on the ground, looking up at Amy as she stood over me.

'*What* are you doing?' she hissed, as Jesse scrambled to cover himself and Darragh yelled, 'Occupied!'

I grinned up at her.

'Self-care.'

1 a.m. CALL IT A NIGHT ;) – You don't have to go home, but you can't stay here!! Friends and family with rooms at the hotel are invited to get on the complimentary shuttle. All other guests, please make sure to arrange safe, sober transportation home!

Amy lectured me through the entire pizza reveal and well beyond. We stood under the dumbass rotunda as I asked her over and over to keep her voice down, and she assured me she was basically whispering, and I'd ask her to repeat herself, and she'd say, 'I'M BASICALLY WHISPERING,' and I'd say, 'Be quiet, please, you're embarrassing me.'

Amy had told Ryan to give us some space, though I could see him lurking a few metres away, watching carefully, picking olives off a slice he was no doubt saving for his precious girlfriend once she was done telling me what an irresponsible idiot I was. I was having a hard time focusing on what she was saying, because it was tedious, and I was wonderful, and my mouth was very dry.

'I'm worried about you,' she said. 'Did you read the book?'

'What book?'

'*Wild Wishes*,' she said. 'There are a few poems in there that I turn to when—'

I knew I shouldn't be laughing so hard. I also couldn't stop it. 'I'm sorry,' I said, 'I'm truly very sorry, but ... obviously I haven't read the book.'

'Why not?'

'Amy, I mean, come on.'

'What happened to your therapist?'

'Just because I didn't like your nightmare poetry book doesn't mean I need therapy.'

'That's not why I'm asking.'

I told her I didn't want to learn about myself. I wanted to say something funny and move on. Actually, I wanted to look good in jean shorts. I explained my theory that firming the skin above my knees with what seemed to be some sort of sonar would have the same impact as therapy and would be significantly cheaper, because it only took two, sometimes three treatments to work.

'These feelings are normal,' I said. 'This really is more normal than anything.'

Amy clicked her tongue, and I muttered something about the Instagram poet's overreliance on enjambment. While rummaging in my pockets for my phone, I remembered my dress didn't have pockets and tried to play it off like I just had a very itchy leg. I dropped my lip gloss on the ground and almost fell over picking it up. I righted myself quickly, but standing up at speed had been a bad idea. I rested both elbows on a nearby table, then helped myself to a piece of half-eaten cake sitting on top of it.

'It doesn't seem—' started Amy, but I'd had enough.

'Maybe divorce stuff is harder for me!' I said, louder than I meant. Maybe I meant it. Amy was pissing me off.

She crossed her arms and continued in that special responsible voice drunk people put on when dealing with

people only slightly drunker than they are. 'Why would it be harder for you?' she asked.

'I don't know,' I said. 'Because I have a critical mind? Because I feel things very deeply? Because I can't just go to Tulum with thirteen of my "closest girlfriends" and share a picture of a sunset with the caption "Te Amo, Mexico" and magically feel better?'

'You're being mean,' said Amy. She pulled her pashmina – her *pashmina!* – around herself. I looked down and realised there was icing on my dress. (I hoped it was icing.)

'You don't get it,' I said. 'We are very different.'

'We're not that different. Anyway, your friends agree with me.'

I told Amy she was full of crap. She didn't even know my friends.

'I know Amirah's engaged,' she said. 'And she asked me not to tell you, because she didn't trust you not to be a jerk about it.'

I tried to scoff and ended up spewing a non-negligible amount of cake and saliva in different directions. I wiped the corner of my mouth and said, 'Not true' a number of times. I shivered slightly, and something warm fell over my shoulders. At some point during all this, Merris had wandered over with our coats.

'Time to make our exit,' she said, giving me a comforting little pat. 'Sandy & Danny has more or less disbanded, anyway.' Merris regarded me with concern, and I felt instantly furious – at Amy, for making us talk like this out in the open; at Emily, for holding this wedding and making

me buy a feathered headband for it; at Amirah for … something.

I told Merris I could not join her. I was heading out for a walk. I needed to clear my head because *somebody* – and I was not naming any names, but actually it was pretty obvious who I meant – was being an ASSHOLE, and one day they were gonna feel reallyfuckingstupid, because I was going to get the fat sucked right out of my chin and put *underneath my eyes*, and then it would be clear how stupid whoever it was – who I was NOT naming – was being.

'Food for thought,' said Merris. 'But for now, what say we put on our coats, and I'll call us a cab?' The words were caring, even if her tone was detached.

I declined the cab, reminding Merris that it was important for everyone – women especially! – to get their ten thousand steps per day. I bid her 'good e'en', which I regretted, and did a little curtsy, which ruled.

'You shouldn't go anywhere on your own right now,' said Amy.

I ignored her and turned to Merris, my real date tonight. My ally. I told her she was a reasonable person, a smart person. The smartest person I knew, in truth, and as a result she surely understood that life was complicated and experiences were complicated, and I was just someone in the middle of what was, you know, really for me kind of a sort of complicated experience. But obviously that was okay, right? Didn't she think?

'I think you and I have a long conversation ahead of us,' said Merris, impatiently scanning the street. 'But I don't think we should have it tonight.'

Ryan sidled over and started showily checking in with Amy.

They could all get fucked.

Merris took out her phone and held it at that old-person distance, regarding it through narrowed eyes. Amy was explaining surge pricing to her when I took off, at speed, inwardly congratulating myself on my genius plan to sneak back into the venue from the other side, to get another quick bump from Darragh before embarking on my walk. Maybe I would walk all the way to Simon's, on the other side of town. I could do my gesture for him now. I looked *great*, after all. Why not?

I skipped around the side of the building, hearing my heels click and feeling the wind in my hair and knowing somewhere deep within that from the outside this looked very cinematic. I could hear Amy and Merris calling after me, the click of Amy's enormous heels and Merris's sensible ones as they gave chase. What were they going to do? I had incredibly fast, good, very strong legs, and they were old and stupid and old and bad and old. I rounded a corner, chuckling to myself, and started scuttling down a set of concrete stairs, gripping the railing, feeling focused and alive.

I was halfway down the stairs when I heard Merris fall.

The hospital was a hospital: depressing and sterile, some-how both too bright and incredibly dingy at once. I picked at my cuticles and looked around guiltily for somewhere to sit. Two middle-aged women who seemed to be sisters were spread out on the last available bench, doing a Sudoku and lightly crying and looking like they'd been awake since they were born. I did not feel high anymore. I felt like the worst piece of shit on the earth.

It had been horrible, every part of it: Merris on the ground; Ryan shining his phone's flashlight in her eyes as Amy asked her to count back from ten; a small crowd forming as I called 911 and repeated the words Amy was yelling at me; the paramedics arriving, briskly checking Merris's wrists, ankles and knees before loading her onto a stretcher. Only one of us was allowed in the ambulance with her, and I said, 'Please, Amy,' and she let me. As they closed the doors, I saw her fall into her clown boyfriend's arms in tears.

Merris had looked so old on the stretcher, although she'd spent the entire ride loudly insisting it was ludicrous that

283

they'd put her in one. It was easy to forget, talking to her, that she was over seventy. Occasionally she made jokes about her arthritic limbs, or how people automatically gave her their seats on the bus, but for the most part she seemed vital, sharper than ever, indestructible. I took out my phone and googled some statistics about seniors and falls, an idea that revealed itself instantly as a bad one.

Down the hall near the reception desk, a man bleeding from his head tried to urinate into a water bottle while two cops spoke rudely to a woman who seemed confused and upset. Everyone the nurses wheeled by looked to me like they could plausibly be dead. I thought about how smugly I spoke to Americans about having access to free health care and decided I would not bring up this kind of thing next time I did. I asked a man holding a toddler in his lap if I could take the seat next to him. He stared back at me, either uncomprehending or angry or too tired to care about some woman wearing open-toed sandals in the middle of winter. The child in his arms said, 'We've been here one thousand and one million hours.'

I bunched my stupid rented dress around my knees and sat on the floor. My phone was on 1% battery; I had no idea how long Merris's various tests would take. There was a plug beneath some benches, between the Sudoku women and a guy in athletic gear who was cradling his left arm and periodically wincing. I tried to reach the socket from a seated position, leaning behind them and sliding my arm along the wall, but it became clear I'd have to lie down on the floor to get there. I was halfway under the bench, my fingertips straining to give the charger a final, decisive

push, when someone stopped in front of me and said, 'Maggie?'

I looked up from the ostentatiously sensible shoes at my eye level and met the aggravated face of Amirah. She was wearing pale purple scrubs and a stethoscope decorated with a small stuffed snowman I recognised from a children's film about not being afraid to be who you are. The hospital she worked at was across the street. Amy must have texted her.

I crawled out from under the bench, jostling the Sudoku siblings.

'Did you yell at Amy?'

'No,' I said. 'Yeah. Fuck, Amirah, it's so bad. It's so, so bad.'

'Is Merris okay?'

'I don't know,' I said. 'She's getting X-rayed. They won't let me in because we're not related.' I brushed a line of fluffy grey dust off my arm and my eyes filled with tears.

'What the fuck happened?' There was an exasperation in Amirah's voice that I didn't care for. She sounded like she was at her wit's end, but she'd just got here.

'I didn't see,' I said. 'She was behind me. It's been so cold out … maybe there was some ice, or she tripped or something … I don't know.'

I ran my fingertips under my eyes, and they came back flecked with mascara. I wished Amirah would hold me and comfort me or grab my hand and lead me out of here.

'Are you engaged?' I asked, sniffling.

Amirah reached into her pockets and proffered a tissue, a kind gesture performed coldly. I took it and blew my nose, then wiped off what was left of my lipstick.

'Yes,' she said. 'I don't want to talk about that right now.'

'Why didn't you tell me?'

'I said I don't want to talk about it.'

'Well, congratulations,' I said. Then, in case it sounded sarcastic: 'I really am happy for you.'

'Thank you.'

Something beeped, and she took out and examined an actual pager. My friend the hero, taking a quick break from saving babies' lives to scrape me off the emergency room floor. I straightened my posture and adjusted the front of my whorishly diaphanous dress. I felt light-headed and wondered if it was panic or the first glimpses of my impending hangover. My jaw hurt.

'I think maybe it was too soon to go to a wedding,' I said. 'I think they make everyone go a bit nuts, just in general.'

Amirah sat down beside me but didn't say anything.

'Especially our generation, you know? Like we were promised these great lives, and they aren't materialising—'

'Oh my *god*, sorry, no,' Amirah said. 'You're not doing your weird rant about capitalism and fucking millennial ennui. I'm not sitting through it again. It's such *bullshit*. And you're, like, smart, right, so you must know, somewhere, that it's bullshit. I don't know what you think you're doing. I don't even know if you *are* thinking about it, which makes me feel, like, completely crazy.'

'I'm sorry,' I said. 'I've been a bad friend.'

'Yeah, you have.'

Although I knew it was true, I hadn't expected her to agree with me. It struck me that I was possibly still a little

high, because I had an abrupt and surprising urge to slap her in the face. I settled for shaking my head in disbelief.

'I'm grieving,' I said. 'I'm having a hard year.'

'Yeah, well, so is Amy,' she said. 'And she's not treating me like shit, or going ballistic on the internet, or talking about her breakup like it's some large-scale societal problem. You and Jon didn't break up because the concept of marriage is broken. You broke up because you couldn't make it work, a normal thing that happens to millions of people. It doesn't have to be some big conspiracy. It doesn't have to be special. It can just be bad.'

'But—'

'No, no. That's all.'

Amirah got to her feet. I figured I should probably look her in the eye before she left and scrambled up to mine as well.

'Lauren suggested we do an Asshole Intervention *weeks* ago,' she said. 'Can you believe I said no?'

I smiled a little. The idea of my friends gathering for a specific conversation about what to do with their messy, pathetic pal was mostly horrible and a little bit nice. I took a risk and pulled her in for a hug. This time she allowed it. Her stethoscope was freezing against my bare skin. She patted my back, and I could smell her expensive hair oil beneath the stronger scent of antibacterial soap.

'I really am sorry,' I said into her shoulder.

'I know,' she said, calmly extracting herself from my clutches. 'Hey, did you do cocaine off someone's dick?'

I told her the coke had not been *on* the dick as such, but someone's dick had definitely been out in the cocaine's vicin-

ity. She said both scenarios were equally gross and that I was objectively terrible at being alone. In fact, she suggested, I had never done it before, ever, in my adult life, and she and the rest of my friends felt that I was clumsily running from solitude, rather than facing it with bravery or grace.

'I'm trying,' I said. 'I know I'm doing a bad job, but I am actually trying.' One perk of being in the hospital was that everyone looked like they were going through it, so it wasn't weird that I was crying like this. Amirah handed me another tissue.

'Try harder,' she said. 'So much stuff is happening and you're missing it. I have to go. Drink water, okay? And text me. Not soon, but text me.'

Amirah walked away, and I slid back to the floor.

I sat alone with myself for either three minutes or nine hours, ruminating on the ways I'd disappointed my friends and what kind of stuff I was missing. Maybe they'd break up with me too. Certainly Amy would be within her rights to never speak to me again. I wondered if I should send an apology email to Emily, or even to Jesse and Darragh. I seemed to spend half my time doing things and the other half apologising for having done them; it was not a dream ratio.

My phone vibrated under the bench, indicating it had a charge. I took the athlete's now vacant seat and opened Twitter, where I deleted (thirty-seven?!) tweets I could not bring myself to read. I opened my photos folder and flipped through pictures from the wedding I'd just been to. Emily looked gorgeous and happy, dancing with her husband while he stared at her with genuine awe. My phone had

compiled the images into a slideshow it called a 'New Memory', lumping some pictures of the three-year-old flower girl sticking out her tongue with a series Jesse had taken of me and Darragh flashing our tits, setting the whole thing to jazzy music.

The other Memories were a mixed bag: a collection of every picture I'd ever taken of food; a slideshow of photos from a cottage trip a few years ago, where a terry cloth leisure suit changed Lauren's personality for the weekend; last Christmas with Ed, Hannah, my mom and sweet, weird Jeff; my own wedding.

I scrolled through the images of Jon and I, beaming and oblivious. Everyone says brides are too stressed to enjoy their own weddings, but I had the time of my life, swanning around my mother's backyard in expensive silk, accepting praise and well-wishes and envelopes full of cash. It had felt so easy to be sure.

Merris had stayed at our wedding only briefly, leaving almost immediately after the reception kicked off in earnest. She wore a jewel-toned tunic thing with a necklace of unknown ethnic origin, and gave us an oddly shaped vase, though we'd asked for cash, ambitiously, to 'put toward a house'. After the ceremony, she pulled me into a hug and said, 'This is a good day. It's important to carry the good days around.'

I thought about her now, in some dank room getting her bones photographed. I should have pretended to be her cousin, her younger lover, her daughter. I should have been in there. Instead, she was alone in some enormous, frightening tube, and I was out here smelling stale coffee and

archiving my wedding photos in a folder labelled whoops. I started googling physiotherapists near Merris's house, inputting various worst-case scenarios, learning about avulsion fractures and bursitis and labral tears. I wondered if I should go home and move out before Merris was discharged. I wondered if I should quit my job. I deleted Jesse's phone number.

As night became morning, the people I'd arrived with were replaced with new pairs: mothers and sons, old married people, roommates, young couples, ageing siblings. Everyone was waiting with or for someone. I hoped Merris wanted me to wait for her. I hoped my friends would wait for me. I wanted more than anything to text someone who cared about me, to talk things through with a loving entity, but I had quite literally exhausted my options. Across the room, a man rested his head on his partner's shoulder while a woman horked something green onto the ground.

A Fantasy

I wake up one morning and start to dissolve. At first it's only a shimmer at the ends of my hair, my split ends glistening as they transform into nothing, but the nothing spreads quickly, up each strand and down into my shoulders. By the time I'm out of bed, my hands are a million disparate particles. My forearms tingle and I know that soon they'll be gone too.

Initially, of course, this fills me with fear; I am afraid to die. But this isn't death. I'm still here, except I don't have upper arms anymore, which is actually a perfect scenario.

My thoughts are there – my feelings too, likes and dislikes, affinity for the colour orange – but as I take what's left of me for a walk down the street, I realise that I am unobserved. As my lower half begins to pixelate and fade, I find myself thinking it might be alright, even ideal, to live the rest of my life as a shapeless fog. Nobody gives fog a hard time for being what it is. Fog can't have a hard time with midrise denim. Fog never said the wrong thing at a party and ruined the vibe.

I let my legs drift up and away, vein-mottled calves first. I will never think about them again. My friends and family will have to adjust to this new way of knowing me. Over time they will come to like that I am everywhere and nowhere, instead of disappointing them emotionally, or forgetting to bring my own wine to the event and then drinking most of theirs, or getting weird about the group photo. Rather than being smothered or put off or bored by my big, stupid feelings, they will find the atmospheric

experience of me calming. My presence will be a warm breeze, like Mandy Moore's after she dies in that religious movie about singing.

A glowing light fills my torso until it explodes, shooting outward like the universe at the very beginning (probably). I feel only relief: I do not have to know what to do about anything. It doesn't matter that I do not stretch in the morning and have never successfully meditated, or that my face is round and my body decaying, or that I am a bad friend, ungrateful daughter, and functionally useless in the face of society's many problems.

I am a delicate mist. No one can look at me or touch me or see me. I do not want to be held, which is fine – no one wants to hold me, and even if they did, it wouldn't help. I am a murmuration, a lightly undulating spray of particles, moving easily around the earth without impacting it. I don't miss anyone and have never fucked anything up.

Merris's hip was bruised but not fractured. She would need rest and a few months of rehabilitative exercises, and to avoid falling again. When she finally emerged from the hospital's interior it was almost five a.m. and she was using a walker. Despite pounding back-to-back bottled waters for several hours, my hangover had set in properly, and I felt as if the waiting room's fluorescent lights had somehow seeped inside my body.

'You didn't have to wait,' she said. I couldn't tell if she was touched or aggravated.

'Yes I did,' I said. 'I'll get us a car.'

Our Uber pulled up, and I folded the walker into the trunk and helped Merris into the front seat. I asked the driver to be careful, to do his best to avoid bumps and potholes. He said, 'Sure,' and did no such thing. We jangled along Dundas in the wintry pre-dawn fog, the street popu- lated by the odd shift worker and a few guys sitting outside an encampment. A couple walked past us at a stoplight, apparently having an argument. (The girlfriend was employing that peerless rhetorical tactic, 'speed walking a

foot or two ahead of your opponent, in heels'.) I decided I would speak only if I had something good to say. I tried to think what that might be and came up with nothing. Wind basically whistled through my empty skull.

I must have fallen asleep, because I woke up with a snort as we pulled into the driveway.

I wiped the corners of my mouth and said, 'We're here,' to Merris, who said, 'Yes,' and opened her door with great effort. I ran around to the trunk and pulled out the walker, thanking the driver and guiding Merris toward the front steps with a transparently guilty abundance of care.

Inside, we worked our way slowly up still more steps. I said, 'Are you alright?' and Merris said, 'You have to stop asking me that.' I helped her to her room, promised to cook for her and clean things, assist with appointments and medications and errands and classes … whatever she needed. 'You're working yourself into a frenzy,' she said. 'I'll be fine.'

I got her into bed with an ice pack and a big bottle of water and some painkillers. I bunched pillows behind her and arranged the duvet just so. She smiled and squeezed my hand. Leaning forward made her wince. I told her I was going to move out.

'Well,' said Merris, and for a second I thought she might stop me. 'Take your time finding the right place.'

As I crept downstairs, I could hear Inessa and Betty at the breakfast bar. It was quarter to six, but they were always up obscenely early, puttering around, folding things, making weak coffee from an immense plastic tub. I stood on the landing, wondering if maybe they would leave once

the kettle boiled. Whether they did or didn't, I could not face them. I would have to wait.

'I never wanted her here,' Inessa said. 'I was on the record, opposed, from day one.'

I heard a cupboard open, the clinking of two mugs brought out by the handles. It seemed like they were settling in.

'Ness, please,' said Betty. 'She can probably hear you.'

'I know she can, she's out there on the stairs.'

I weighed my options: stay silent where I was and hope they didn't check the hall; run out the front door and never look back; walk confidently into the kitchen, taking out imaginary earbuds and pretending I had heard nothing; sneak back upstairs and hide under Merris's bed. Instead, I stuttered, 'Oh, hello, I, well,' speed walked into the room, and started drinking from the sink like a gerbil.

'Sorry,' I said, coming up for air. 'Thirsty.'

I was thirsty. My mouth was dry and tasted terrible. My whole body was sore from spending the night on hospital floors and benches, my nostrils felt thick, my head hurt. I did not want to think about what I looked like. The women considered me briefly, then turned back to each other and carried on.

'She's clearly ashamed of herself,' said Betty, addressing Inessa only. 'And that works for me, she should be, but we don't need to lay it on.'

'Maybe we do,' said Inessa. 'Taking advantage of Mer's guilt like that.'

Unsure what to do with my jittery hands, I grabbed an apple from the counter and started slicing it finely on a

cutting board. The women continued to ignore me. I felt an impulse to tell them about my monthly donations to charity, my commitment to voting Green.

'I've always said, if she'd just call the girl, they could sort it out in an hour,' said Betty. 'Daughters can't stay mad at their mothers, it's not natural.'

I turned away from the counter and toward the two women. Inessa's eyes darted in my direction, then back at Betty. She gave a little cough, but her roommate seemed not to notice. I averted my eyes, pretending to be engrossed in the decorative moulding that hugged the perimeter of the kitchen ceiling.

'I thought when Gene died it might move things along for them, but they barely looked at each other at the funeral,' Betty said. '... what's the matter with you?'

I had abandoned my pretend disinterest and was now standing directly beside the two women, staring stupidly and holding out a plate of wafer-thin apple slices, hundreds of questions bouncing in my brain. I set the apple in front of Inessa, who looked at me like I'd plated a human turd.

'Merris has a daughter?' I asked.

Inessa scoffed and rolled her eyes, though Betty gave me a few facts: the daughter was about a decade older than me; she worked at a bank; she had Merris's features with her father's colouring; the relationship had always been strained, but several years ago there had been a proper falling out; Merris did not like to talk about her; she lived in Spain. Eventually, Inessa stood up and said, 'Enough now,' walking over to the counter with the plate of apple slices. She fished a Ziploc bag out of a drawer, slid the slices into

it, and handed them to me, indicating that our time together was over and they would not be revealing any more of Merris's family secrets.

I went back to my room and stayed there for the rest of the month. I left only for work or food or apartment viewings, and to take Merris to physiotherapy on Thursdays. I'd help her into the car, drive to a little grey building north of the city, and wait in the foyer under a diagram of foot fascia as an overfamiliar Australian man helped her stretch and wriggle in healing ways. Then I'd drive her home. Merris made polite small talk sometimes. If she started, I'd carry on, but I preferred to listen to the radio, look straight ahead, and let shame fill my head like static.

At home I took baths and drank a lot of CBD beverages, hoping they did something but feeling like they probably didn't. I threw a stick around for Lydia and stayed 'California sober'. I tried to read – novels, magazines, student essays, anything – but always ended up back on my phone. My main activity was reading one page of a book, then putting it down and looking at a screen for twelve to forty-seven minutes. There was always something tragic on the screen: details of someone's workplace sexual harass-ment, beloved pets dying suddenly, a brand using slang. Simon seemed to be soft-launching a new Woman of Significance in his Instagram Stories. There had been a feminine-looking jacket on his couch in a photo of some new beers he'd acquired, and I heard a woman laughing in the background of a video he posted of himself bowling a strike. She sounded pretty.

Sometimes I would get an email – a home goods store alerting me to exciting new offers, or updates on a friend of a friend's cousin's brain surgery. I'd discovered a fundraising page for this man one night after taking several melatonin and donated $50 with the note get better pLEASE. Now I got emails what felt like once an hour about how things were going (as a Real Housewife once drunkenly yelled at another: *Not well, bitch!*) and asking for further money. I didn't feel like I could unsubscribe and still consider myself a good person, but I also did not have another $50s lying around, at least not for this.

The only emails I responded to were from prospective landlords or my students, toward whom I had been trying to be more professional. In an effort to butter them up, I had also removed the class participation component of their final grades. I met with Sara in a coffee shop and answered her questions about graduate programmes and let her outline her dream of one day studying in London. Her enthusiasm made me feel like a fraud. I recouped some sense of myself as an authority figure by paying for her matcha latte while she was in the bathroom.

The group chat picked up and carried on without me, a flurry of links and screenshots and questions about what the fuck old classmates, the government, or our bodies were up to. I did my best to give everyone some space without crossing over into the silent treatment, dropping in a supportive haha or sending a heart emoji when one felt needed. After a week or so of 'space', I sent Amirah and Tom an Edible Arrangement to say congratulations. Amirah texted a photo of the ridiculous, brightly coloured

basket with the message tom's allergic to strawberries ... saboteur, then, jk thank you they're delicious. I wrote back, could we get a drink soon? just like green tea and 45–50 mins grovelling, max. Amirah left it for two full hours before replying, sounds good, will see if aritzia's selling hair shirts. Buoyed by this success, I sent an Edible Arrangement to Amy too. I wrote, 'I'm very sorry, please call me' on the card. She didn't.

I drank three litres of water a day, which meant, give or take a few half-hours here and there, I spent the rest of my time on the toilet. I figured this was life: I'd spend the next twenty years alternatingly hydrating and pissing, then all the water on earth would dry up and I would know it was time to die. The apartments I viewed were dilapidated and out of my price range. I started looking at places in Kingston.

One day after physio, the Australian chased Merris into the parking lot.

'M-dawg!!' he said, horribly. 'Forgot your resistance bands, my girl!'

'What a shame,' said Merris. 'They're such fun.'

The Australian did not return her smile. He rested both hands on the roof of the car and spoke to her like she was a child refusing to wear her coat outdoors in winter. 'It's so important that you do your exercises,' he said. 'At this stage in life, if you don't guard your mobility, you really can lose it for good.'

Merris took the bands from him but didn't say anything else. In the car she was quiet too.

'What does he know?' I said, turning up the radio. 'He probably has that strain of super-chlamydia koalas invented.'

Merris didn't respond.

'I'm so sorry,' I said. 'Really, I'm—'

'Enough, Maggie, please,' she said. 'I am tired and sore. I feel about a million years old, and I don't want to go over it all again. It's not your fault.'

'It is kind of my fault.'

'Well, it's not only your fault,' she said. 'Maybe I'm being punished.'

I asked her what she thought she was being punished for.

She flipped down the sun visor and examined her face in the mirror. She sighed. 'Oh, I don't know. Idleness, pettiness, vanity … pick one.' Merris ran her hands over her neck, pulling the skin taut. 'Do you know how much money I spend each year on creams?'

We drove past a Lenten celebration, a cluster of old people lifting the Virgin Mary high over their heads. I realised I'd left my indicator on, that it was still clicking away to warn others about a right turn I had no intention of making. I switched it off. On the radio, a man who owned a furniture warehouse screamed about unbeatable deals.

'Betty told me you have a daughter,' I said. I kept my eyes on the road and tried to radiate a noninvasive empathy. Merris flipped the visor back up.

'Well, there it is, isn't it?' she said. 'Late-onset maternal instinct, misapplied, with unpleasant consequences.'

I snuck a look at her, and someone honked at me for drifting too close to the next lane. 'Why didn't you tell me about her?'

'You didn't ask.'

She was right, which made it worse. I had probably asked her fewer than three questions about herself this entire year, maybe our entire relationship. We pulled into the driveway and sat there with the car idling, the heated seat warming the backs of my already hot legs.

'That's terrible,' I said. 'I'm sorry.'

'Don't be,' said Merris. 'I'm sure that was part of the appeal. Relationships with young people are very straightforward; they basically just want to talk about themselves. Lazy of me, really, to accept intimacy without any risk.'

'What happened with … ?'

'Danielle?' Merris sighed again. 'I don't know. I think I couldn't be what she needed, and she couldn't forgive me for it. Her whole childhood, she was reaching out for something that, for whatever reason, I couldn't or didn't want to give. And then her father got sick, and we handled it in completely opposing ways – it's all a bit miserable. Let's not get into it.'

Merris pulled on her gloves and readjusted her scarf, acting out the beginning of an exit. I wanted to tell her I'd listen to her talk about anything, to march inside right now, make a pot of tea, and ask her to start from the beginning. I told her she'd listened to more than enough of my miserable tales, and if she ever did want to get into it—

'I don't,' she said. 'Thank you.'

'You've been so generous,' I told her. 'I wish I'd been a better friend to you.'

'Oh, Maggie,' she said. 'We're not friends. We're just two people having a hard time.'

I turned the key and the soft hum of the motor went quiet. It was raining a little, and I could see Inessa peering out her bedroom window on the second floor. When she noticed me looking up at her, she snapped the curtain shut.

'I'd like, if you wanted, to try to be friends,' I said. 'I know my living here was probably a step too far, but I wasn't just hanging out with you because I was having a breakdown. I think you're kind of amazing.'

Merris laughed lightly, and I clenched every muscle in my body.

'There's a joke in there about which of us really took the step too far, but I don't have time to think of it,' she said. 'Anyway, must get inside and mess around with these bands. I could lose my mobility, you know.'

She opened the car door and unbuckled her seat belt, slowly pulling one leg and then the other out onto the ground. I helped her into the house, as I did every week. We stood in the foyer and she said, 'Thank you, dear,' and I went down into the basement and lay flat on the floor.

I moved out a few days later, very early in the morning, mostly to avoid Inessa. I left a thank-you card and a box of fancy dried fruit. I had stayed up late the night before, dusting and scrubbing every surface, trying to reset the place to how it had been. As I finished a final round on the bathroom fixtures, Lydia came wheezing down the stairs, jumped on my bed, and stayed there. The next morning I kissed her goodbye, letting her huge tongue go a little bit in my mouth, something I usually fought against, but which she seemed perpetually desperate to make happen. I opened the door to the upstairs, and she scrambled off, to eat and

drool on things and sleep in the sun. I left my keys on the kitchen counter with my gift and took a bus to Kingston, where my dad picked me up.

A week later I used what would have been my rent money to book four sessions with Helen. In the lead-up to our first, I started a note on my phone identifying potential topics for discussion, which seemed like a smart move, until I opened the document in her warm beige office and it read 'legs', 'is inner peace real' and 'having a skull is actually insane'. I abandoned the list and we talked about Merris (relationship to), my body (negative feelings toward), and doorframes.

'I learned recently,' I said, 'that straight men have this compulsion where it's important to reach up and slap the top of the doorframes they pass under. Did you know about this?'

'Vaguely,' said Helen. She adjusted the knot in her silk scarf and took a sip of herbal tea. Her mug was covered in smiling painted bees.

'Well,' I said, 'I had no idea this was happening. I can't believe all men, or even some men, have been doing this my whole life. Do they not have anything better to do?'

Helen wrote something down. 'And what about this behaviour bothers you in particular?' When she turned the mug to access its handle, I saw it had the words BEE CALM on it in block letters dripping with honey.

'It doesn't bother me,' I said. 'I just think it's weird.'

'Seems to me that it bothers you a great deal.'

There followed one of those long and bothersome therapy silences.

'I don't know,' I said. 'I guess I wonder: Is that what it's like to have a brain not filled with questions about whether you're too old or fat or dumb or smart or in immediate danger of some kind? Fucking … doorframes?'

I realised I did sound quite angry. I apologised to Helen; I'd been reading too many threads about street harassment.

'I shouldn't really be mad about anything,' I said. 'Statistically speaking, I'm one of the luckiest people that has ever been born.'

Helen told me that although that was true from a historical perspective, I was still allowed to have feelings, even difficult or ungrateful ones. Those feelings were, apparently, an unavoidable part of life, and it was better to notice and name them than pretend they didn't exist.

'Alright,' I said. 'I'm angry that my threshold for discomfort is so low. Like I can function totally normally as long as there is no uncertainty in my life, but if I'm waiting to learn the outcome of something, the entire day is fucked.'

I looked at Helen. She was doing 'placid' as a charades clue.

'Unfortunately,' I continued, 'my threshold for what counts as "something" is very low, so we're talking, like, responses to emails, likes on a tweet, results of a routine pap smear … This year has been like having a rash, continuously, for months. And also? I'm angry about glamping.'

'Okay …'

'It's not as nice as being indoors. No matter what. And I hate renter-friendly apartment hacks and all these other cutesy ways we've repackaged the conditions we live in. It's not romantic to pay hotel room prices for a camper van in

a wealthy older person's backyard, even if there is a fire pit out there. I have $37,000 in student debt. Why do we have to be the generation that accepts – on top of all the actual indignities – those sliding barn doors on bathrooms?'

'Right,' said Helen. 'Interesting. What emotions are coming up for you right now?'

'I feel embarrassed,' I said. 'I know these are the wrong things to be thinking about. I should be thinking about, like, inequality. And I do think about that stuff. Some days I'll completely forget about how much I dislike my body and toggle around on those maps that show you how underwater everything will be in thirty years. Other days it's exclusively my body, all day, which I know is awful.'

'What you think about is one thing,' said Helen. 'But what do you *care* about?'

I told her I cared about doing the right thing in a very general, almost abstract sense, but I did not have any meaningful ideas about next steps. 'I just feel like, why would I know what to care about, or even what to do? I don't know anything. I didn't choose the right person, and I have no idea what late capitalism actually is.'

The session carried on, me explaining my little theories and dumb preoccupations, Helen nodding and affirming and sometimes writing things down. Although I sounded like a not-impressive issue of *Adbusters*, it felt amazing to say these ridiculous half-thoughts out loud, even better not to have them presentation-ready. It was a thrill to express poorly and inelegantly my small and petty and unuseful ideas. I would not achieve anything by expressing them to someone else, but it was nice to think about them here, the

personal as personal. Yes, all the big bad stuff was happening, but so was all the little bad stuff (and as Helen was quick to point out, a fair amount of little good stuff, though that was unlikely to be the focus of our sessions).

I told her my theory that intimacy was a scam. I told her I wasn't sure I liked my job. I told her how satisfying it felt to tweet MEN and have someone I didn't know respond that they knew, yes, they knew exactly. I told her about the yogurt and the tracking app and the peanut powder. I told her I could not believe I had been brought to my knees by something as quotidian as heartbreak. I told her I was sick of feeling like the biggest woman Emilio Zara could imagine.

'Emilio … ?'

'Oh,' I said. 'That's what my friends and I call the head designer at Zara. I don't think that's his real name, but we needed somewhere to direct our rage.'

I explained that we envisioned him as a kind of sadistic mastermind, like the puppet from *Saw*, except his twisted endgame was to bring otherwise sane women to tears in flimsy dressing rooms. 'Every time I go in there,' I said, 'I feel I'm the worst-shaped person on earth. Honestly, being divorced feels the same.'

'How do you mean?'

I told her getting divorced was like getting stuck in a blouse at Zara: I was struggling, and it was clearly the wrong fit, but maybe it would be more embarrassing to try to take it off, to come out of the dressing room and have to admit, *I tried, but I couldn't make it work*. Maybe it would have been easier not to attempt extraction. Maybe I should

have flung open the curtain and proclaimed it my favourite, insisted on wearing it out of the store and every day thereafter, laughing as it cut off the circulation to my arms.

'Has this happened to you before?' Helen asked. 'Getting stuck in a blouse?'

'Oh, tons of times,' I said. 'You usually realise somewhere around the shoulders that it's not going to fit, but it's so tempting to mash it on and see.'

'And how does that go?'

'Badly,' I said. 'Every time. And you end up sweaty and panicking and desperate, struggling but refusing to call anyone in to help you, and usually the thing gets ripped on the way off.'

Helen squinted slightly and made some more notes on her pad. I leaned forward.

'Look,' I said. 'I know this may not be up to me, but if at all possible, I would love to avoid labelling any of this "trauma".'

Helen shifted in her chair, an amused expression on her face. I wondered if this meant she liked me or if she looked at all her clients this way. I realised I wanted her to like me very badly. She tapped her pen against the side of her face and crossed her legs.

'Do you want to talk about what happened last time you were here?'

'Not really,' I said.

'Alright,' said Helen. 'Maybe a better question is, can you?'

Google Searches, 4 April

how many eggs safe to eat one day
therapist reviews toronto helen yim
marijuana for pain, seniors
how to make weed butter
shakespeare smoked weed yes or no
what do newborn babies know
4L of water really
part-time jobs kingston
cool bars kingston
bernadette peters medley
time share but for cars
vagus nerve real thing
how to wear wide leg pants big ass
quotes about rest and resting
john donne, 'nocturnal upon st lucy's day'
john donne sexy ones
r/relationships
r/friendshipadvice
r/therapy
reddit = incel thing?
best pillows bad backs
alexander technique beginners free
modern resume templates
what is a cover letter
gemini cancer friend compatibility
sell collages etsy
'team player' synonym
single coffee delivery

how to win someone back
pube styles 2019
workout videos under ten minutes
mediterranean diet potatoes
how important is fibre
what is fibre
incognito mode twitter
safest places for solo travellers
eat pray love island
stream love island online free
home bleach kit

The weather turned from hard wet (ice, hail) to soft wet (rain, mush), and I was still living at my dad's, a three-bedroom bungalow near Sydenham he had begun referring to as 'Divorce Club'. I had planned to stay with my mother, historically the more tolerant parent, but things were getting serious between her and Jeff, so Divorce Club it was.

To my surprise, my father and I had settled easily into a cohabiting rhythm, sharing breakfast then going our separate ways until dinner. On Wednesdays I would borrow his car and drive to Toronto, where I would teach and hold office hours, see Helen, and sleep on Lauren's couch. On Thursdays I taught another class and took Merris to physio or to run other errands before driving back to my dad's to pedal a stationary bike in the den and consider my credit card debt. On weekends I worked at a cheese store that smelled terrible.

The house had been purchased after I'd moved to Toronto, so it was not enormously familiar to me. I would occasionally open the linen cupboard door thinking it led

to the bathroom, and I had no idea where pots and pans went in the cheerful, jumbled kitchen. I slept in a single bed in a room with wood-panelled walls that I worked hard to find pleasingly ascetic, if not aesthetic – hygge on a budget. My father was very understanding and gave me a great deal of space and privacy, but I was always on the lookout for the generational difference that would disrupt our fragile peace. On Twitter I followed a few millennials who lived with their parents and were constantly having to school them about how to be good and conscientious people. It seemed easier to live with children; they were always wandering into living rooms saying something accidentally profound – *Mom, it's so important when women vote*, etc. – but I had a male boomer on my hands. Nightmare.

'Look at this,' he said one morning, gesturing to a physical newspaper he had somehow acquired. 'A bunch of fast-food employees want to raise the minimum wage. $15 an hour, to work in McDonald's.'

He tutted and I cracked my knuckles, readying myself to make a speech. I did not relish the idea of yelling at my father, but he was being a small-minded classist, and I knew, as someone who had read more of the right articles, that I had a certain responsibility. '*Dad*—' I started, but he was not finished.

'It's not really enough,' he said. 'With inflation, I mean.'

'Oh,' I said. 'Right.' I looked down and saw I had adopted a kind of Power Rangers stance, my feet wide, my hands on my hips. 'Well, they wouldn't even have to worry about it if we had universal basic income.'

He took a long sip of coffee and looked at me with a placid expression. 'I agree,' he said, and went back to his paper. To purge some of the righteousness I'd built up, I picked a fight about his belief that the property bubble would one day burst, allowing me to purchase a home.

I went back to my bedroom and deleted Twitter, Tinder, Hinge, Instagram, Bumble, TikTok and Facebook from my phone, then redownloaded them a week later, plus an app that would limit the window during which I could access the internet. I downloaded another app to show me where the moon was in the sky, whether it was waxing or waning. I downloaded something called a 'newsfeed eradicator' that promised to claw back my attention span by replacing the endless updates from friends, brands and journalists deafened by silence with motivational quotes. The first one it showed me read, 'Nothing is impossible. The word itself says, "I'm possible"!' attributed to the actress Audrey Hepburn.

I unfollowed the tiny Instagram women having picnics in the sun and started following a 'radical softness'–themed account that was mostly shots of ecstatic fat women dancing around in their underwear. Sometimes their pets featured. I watched a girl in Korea fill in paintings of her friends' gracefully sloping bodies. I listened to a livestream of a tulip field in the Netherlands. I visited a website that let you look out strangers' windows. I cut and bleached my hair and resisted a near-physical yearning to share a photo of it online. As a compromise, I sent seven different Live Photos to the group chat, who all agreed they had been

wrong, this was a great move, and I looked, in Lauren's words, possibly damaged but definitely sexy, so: net positive.

I cut back heavily on posting, though the compulsion was still there – to have something to say or show for myself, to 'share'. When I did say or show or share something (a tweet about my menstrual cycle, a photo of flowers by the lake with the caption ok spring!!), I felt instantly and viscerally ashamed and often deleted what I'd posted. This did not help. In fact, the deleting felt, in many ways, just as white-hot humiliating as leaving the posts up, because it was the act of posting in the first place, the expression of the compulsion, that shamed me. No need to admit this publicly too.

I didn't know where this aversion had come from. No one else in my life seemed to share it. Clive and Lauren had started 'going live' on Friday nights, drinking and laughing and performing very loosely sketched out character comedy for six or seven people. Friends who seemed completely normal IRL were taking slow-motion videos of themselves weeping and putting them on TikTok with messages about how to respect but also push past one's comfort zone. A guy I often saw in the department kitchen turned out to have a famous Twitter account where he tweeted not now babe to various world leaders.

Sometimes I thought: *Why shouldn't I post a little joke, or tell a pundit he was being an asshole? Why not document my life, my face, my moods?* And sometimes I thought that setting up a self-timer in my bathroom, biting my lower lip over and over, then posting the one image I liked from the

four hundred I'd taken was as vulgar and unnecessary as bending over and showing everyone my asshole.

One night I was in the den 'stretching' after a bike ride, which mostly meant lying on the ground with my legs up the wall. Usually I spent this post-workout time trying to sit quietly with myself, but if I did that for too long I almost always became overwhelmed with memories of the phone calls and voicemails and texts to Jon, or the image of Merris on the ground outside the wedding, or how Amy's face had looked when she told me I was being mean. It was horrible to remember these things. I knew, theoretically, that to err was human, but it sort of seemed like there should be a limit on how much erring one human could do.

I thought about that first night with Simon: *how can you tell if something you did was a stupid mistake or a real sign of your character?* I still didn't know, but it was starting to feel like thinking about it all the time was not as useful as just trying not to do it again. I nudged my butt closer to the wall, pushing my legs up higher, and stretched my arms out on both sides until my left hand curled around my phone. Outside the door, I could hear my father plodding around, probably making some wild Dad Snack – he had recently bought us individual his 'n' hers jars of applesauce – or watching the news on both the television and a nearby iPad.

I was looking over old photos I'd sent to/received from Simon when the screen went dark and his name appeared. I stared at my phone for a few confused seconds before realising it was a call. Simon was calling me.

I held the phone to my ear tentatively, like it was a trick. 'Hello … ?'

'Maggie, hi,' he said, his voice as warm and steady as I remembered. 'Sorry to call. I was thinking about you and had an urge, but maybe I should have gone for a walk or something.'

I told him it was not a problem and asked how he was. He was good, of course. Work was busy. His parents had decided to move. He was tuning up his bike in preparation for spring. He missed me and wondered if we could get together and talk a few things over.

'I'm so sorry,' I said. 'About the last time we talked.'

'I'm sorry too,' he said. 'I've been thinking about it a lot, and I feel like we really rushed into things. Like it was nice to meet you, and it was *so* nice to feel something other than incredibly bad about my breakup all the time, but I think I should have been better about keeping it casual, giving us some time to get to know each other. I guess I'd like to take you on a date and see if we want to go on another one a week later.'

'God,' I said. 'Shit.'

'Oh, right, well, don't worry about it,' he said. 'Never mind.'

'No, not shit like bad, shit like good.'

'That famous application of the word "shit".'

I looked up at the ceiling and sighed. 'Well, I guess shit bad, because I can't see you,' I said. 'Helen and I have agreed to put that area of my life on hiatus.'

'Who's Helen?'

He was going to love this. He was going to cream his jeans.

'She's my therapist.'

Simon was quiet, a therapist-acquired trick if ever there was one. It worked, unfortunately, and I went on a long rant about how we were doing the smart thing. The mature thing, even! Ultimately, we were being wise. Yes, I liked him, and he liked me, but nipping that in the bud meant I did not have to disappoint Helen. It also meant neither of us had to disappoint each other, eventually. It had gone bad so quickly the first time.

'Sounds like decathecting to me,' said Simon.

'I don't know what that is, but don't tell me.'

'Okay. Well, call me if you change your mind.'

'Okay.'

Another pause.

'This is embarrassing,' I said, 'but I haven't been alone in a long time, and now I am, and if I don't stay that way for a bit, I will never understand what it is I actually like or want or even, maybe, feel, so I have to be a careful little nun for a few weeks or months, and then who knows? Maybe I'll have missed the window and every person worth dating will be taken and I'll just stay alone for the rest of my life.'

'I think that's unlikely,' said Simon. 'But it sounds like a worthwhile endeavour.'

A non-negligible part of me was screaming, *run, run toward the kindness the handsome man is offering, it may be the last time this ever, ever happens.* But I had meant what I said. It was not a good time. I closed my eyes and said, 'Thank you, Simon,' and I felt like I could hear him smile.

After he hung up, I looked up the word 'decathecting', then spent twenty minutes trying to compose a tweet

listing the events of a decathect-lon – like a decathlon, but for protecting your emotional sanity. I did not even save it to drafts.

I wandered into the kitchen and told my father I was experimenting with interiority. He looked up from the crossword only briefly. 'Oh?'

'This sounds very basic,' I said, 'but you don't have to say everything you think and feel to everyone around you all the time. Even if you want to. You can keep it to yourself. Sometimes, that feels better.'

'"Teaspoon",' he said, filling in 10-down. 'That's lovely, sweetheart. As you know, if you're happy, I'm happy.'

I told him my discovery had inspired some fruitful experimentation. My options, when I had a thought, experience, or god forbid, a feeling, were to write it down and resist the impulse to text or tweet it, or to mentally note what I was feeling and – and this was the thing that seemed impossible, possibly even fake – let it pass.

'Well,' he said, counting out the letters in the word 'petrichor'. 'Could have saved us all a lot of trouble by discovering this in high school, but better late than never.'

'I'm serious,' I said, grabbing some milk from the fridge. I told him I'd realised recently that almost nothing had ever happened to me that I had not shared with someone else. This had, after all, been one of the big appeals of marriage: somebody to say all my stupid bullshit to or run my decisions past, someone to listen to me forever. I poured the milk over an enormous bowl of cereal, letting it crackle and hiss before digging my spoon in and taking a bite.

'Of course, the whole point of a relationship is you've also got to listen to – pardon my French – *their* stupid bullshit,' said my dad. 'I assume you struggled in this area.'

I ignored this, though he was not wrong.

'I saw Mom yesterday,' I said. 'She's still mad at you.'

'Makes sense,' he said. 'I was kind of an asshole.'

I asked what had happened between them, really. He told me he was almost finished with the crossword and would prefer I experimented further with interiority.

'Aside from the fact that it's none of your business,' he said, 'I can't tell you because I don't know. I thought I did, at the time, but the further I get from it the more I see how little I understood what was going on in there. My feelings about it and your mother's feelings about it are very different. Neither of us is exactly right, but both versions are accurate.'

I said this was disappointing to hear. Distance was supposed to give you more perspective, not less.

'I think it did,' he said. 'With time I stopped clinging to my own version of events and accepted that two things can be true, that we might never agree about what exactly went wrong. Though I'm sure she'd agree we should never have had that swingers' night with the Carlsons.'

I stayed poker-faced and waited for him to say he was kidding. He remained focused on the crossword. I peeped over his shoulder and said, '"Prolix."'

He filled in the relevant squares. 'You're telling me.'

I went back to the den and climbed onto the stationary bike. I finished a triathlon over the remaining weeks of April, a laughably modest goal the completion of which felt

better than drugs. While running some of my twenty kilo-metres, I tripped over a root in the sidewalk, falling hard onto the side of my body where a sporty little fanny pack held my keys, phone, and some extra hair ties. I completed a full thirty minutes of running, went home, and got in the shower. Later that night, I went to text the group chat an image of a fish finger that looked like a dick and found the fall had cracked my phone screen. It was still functional, just less pleasant to use, and I worried I might get a glass sliver stuck in my fingertip. *Charlie Brooker*, I thought, *you've done it again!*

The weeks continued this way: more newspapers, more cereal, more driving to Toronto, more driving back. I felt very fortunate and a little bored. I helped Merris with groceries and minor housekeeping and stayed out of her way at work, though we sometimes had coffee when I brought her home from physio. I read a few poems from Amy's book and hated them a lot, but felt fondness for the person who gave them to me, who was comforted by the idea of a woman whose heart was a house fire. Amirah and I had our green-tea-and-grovel session, and I went with her afterward to a hospital fundraiser/musical revue featuring a bunch of a cappella anesthesiologists. It was completely terrible and so, so fun to be there with her, whispering and giggling at the back of the room. I saw Clive and Lauren and Emotional Lauren in real life, one-on-one situations where I tried to be a good listener and better friend. Sometimes I succeeded. This was quietly satisfying but did not do much to quell the shame that would rise in me every few hours like acid reflux – a reminder that I was a failure,

back in the town she grew up in, eating applesauce her dad had paid for.

Still, pleasant moments found ways of sneaking in: finding a solo seat on the bus near a window, having enough coffee left for a perfect top-up, coming home from the grocery store with flowers, to put tomatoes in a different bowl from bananas. In one of our now-weekly sessions, I described these moments to Helen. As I was leaving her office, I caught a glimpse of her notes: 'finding joy in the mundanity of life'.

It did feel mundane. Everything just kept happening.

Emotionally Devastating Things My Therapist Said to Me Like They Were Nothing

'I'm going to start today's session by challenging you not to try to make me laugh during our time together. This is not because you are not an amusing person, but I wonder where we might get if we did away with the idea of trying to entertain.'

'When you say you're "addicted" to buying shirts that don't fit and wearing them anyway, do you feel an actual compulsion at work here, or is this another case of online jargon?'

'I was struck, last time, by your statement that what you were looking for was a kind of exfoliant for the personality. I'd like to look into how it came about that your psyche has melded skincare with morality. There seems to be a real connection between aesthetic effort and emotional effort for you – would you say that's accurate?'

'I admire your interest in authenticity, though I do not think it makes a woman – or any person – a cliché to "also" feel bad about their neck.'

'You say you have no need to tell your family about your dates with women, since none of them have been serious. I wonder if they might *get* serious if you started taking them more seriously, or if you're consciously avoiding doing so to save yourself the administrative hassle of coming out.'

'This urge to throw your phone off a bridge or into some major body of water is one we've found ourselves talking through in multiple sessions. You imagine feeling very free. Indeed, you describe this feeling of total elation at the idea of being parted from your phone by chance or force. What is stopping you from – and I'm sorry if this sounds obvious, but … what is stopping you from simply turning it off?'

'I wonder whether it might benefit us to differentiate between the concepts of friendship, extended community, and imagined audience. I think there is some elision at work, and really these are very different kinds of relationships, with very different obligations and mores. And then, of course, one of them exists in the mind only.'

'What do you think it would feel like … to delete your cat's Instagram account?'

'If you don't enjoy smoking and aren't addicted to cigarettes – as you say, you don't like them enough to buy them yourself and only smoke socially, when your friends or acquaintances are doing it – why don't you quit? And if you don't want to quit, can we dig in a little bit to the source of your reaction just now, when I called you a smoker, because that was quite a strong reaction.'

'The journal-based worksheets I've given you are merely exercises to get you thinking about your feelings and responses to those feelings. I cannot therefore provide feedback or "grade" them.'

'When you say that you feel you'll never find another person willing to be in a long-term relationship with you, that makes me feel very personally sad. I wonder if we might ask whether you are willing to be in a long-term relationship with yourself?'

A one-litre bottle of branded X-Cycle water cost, I'm not kidding, $9. I bought one and registered for the six p.m. Guilty Pleasure class, which promised both the ride – and the time – of my life. The girl at the front desk had found my sign-in request slightly weird, but ultimately gave in. That was what happened when you paid full price (fifty! three! dollars!) for one of these classes: you became a kind of temporary king. I grabbed my clip-in shoes and exorbitantly priced water and headed to the changeroom.

I felt frazzled and anxious. That morning, Lauren had semi-subtly hinted that our couch-crashing arrangement was reaching its close, and Merris's physio appointments were being reduced to once monthly. With spring term ending in two weeks, I would soon be left with no reason to come to the city, and nowhere to stay if I did. I set my bag down and took a bite of a protein bar that promised a 'salted caramel explosion' but tasted, of course, like sand.

Wrestling myself into a sports bra, I eavesdropped on two girls, both partially naked and (respect) filling their bags with free tampons and hair ties.

'Someone needs to have a word with Kira,' said the taller and more nude of the two. 'Her Stories are getting *grim*.'

The other one adjusted her underwear in the mirror, getting on her tiptoes to check out her butt. 'I know. It's like, we get it, you're single,' she said. 'But I do watch them every day.'

The other girl sighed. 'It's getting so bad I don't know whether to mute her or turn on notifications.'

I pulled my leggings up and decided to put on my shoes in the foyer, joining the rest of X-Cycle's Guilty Pleasure acolytes.

The mastermind of the Guilty Pleasure ride was a physically gorgeous person called Blake. Amy had told me so much about their 'butts and guts' glute- and ab-focused rides that seeing them in person felt like a celebrity encounter. They had a dazzling smile and enormous arms and seemed to be roughly fourteen years old. Their X-Cycle-branded T-shirt was cut in a scoop so deep it formed a reverse-bib; they radiated enough positive energy to power a small town. On a corkboard featuring the day's class schedule, a sign-up sheet informed us that Blake was 'not afraid to rock out'. I watched them bounce around the waiting area, air-kissing fit strangers and slapping the butts of friends. I wondered what was keeping me so fearful of rocking in any direction.

Blake embraced a girl in mesh shorts, asking after her dog while she lunged, squatted and touched her toes without any visible effort. The girl looked like everyone else in the bright green lobby: sandy-blonde hair, visible abs, the air of a job in corporate finance. I sat underneath a neon

sign that said LIMIT/LESS and tried to seem casual and unembarrassed. I did not feel that way; I felt like a walking Before photo surrounded by dozens of possible Afters, all of them named Amber. Still, I reasoned, I belonged there as much as any of them. Had I not looked up the class schedule? Did I not also have $53? (Not really, but I had spent it, and surely that was all that mattered here.) Finally, Blake blew a little whistle they wore around their neck and flung open the doors of the studio, reminding everyone to grab earplugs, because 'I am NOT getting off my bike mid-class just because YOU can't handle my play-list!'

Inside, I shimmied past the first row and clipped into spot 23, smack in the middle of the second line of bikes. Usually I was a very-back-row, very-back-corner kind of gal, but today I had other needs. I placed my water bottle in its little water-bottle groove and clipped my right foot to the pedal. When Amy entered, I ducked my head and pretended to be busy adjusting my seat height. She didn't notice me, and I kept my head low as she clipped in, pedal-ling lightly, rocking back and forth on her feet to stretch her hamstrings and calves. It was nice to see her without the risk of finding out whether she wanted to see me. I watched her tighten her ponytail and hoped she wouldn't notice me until I was ready.

Amy and I had not spoken since the wedding, unless you counted the Edible Arrangement and the one post-Ar-rangement apology text I'd sent in case she didn't like pineapple. When that went unreturned, I resolved not to bother her. If I felt an urge to text her or compose one of

my Big Emails, I would open a Google Doc called dots and add a period to the page. Looking at this document (eighty-seven dots and counting) made me feel unbalanced, though I had managed to avoid leaving even one emotional voice message, and surely that was something. Helen would check in with me about it in our sessions, and each week I reported having left Amy alone, Helen would tell me she was proud. I always acted like this was an unnecessary and even babying gesture, but I knew deep down that if she *didn't* tell me she was proud every two or three sessions, I would simply fall apart. I had not mentioned my plan for today, my one last effort to win Amy back; I suspected Helen would not fully approve.

Blake shut the door behind them and flicked the lights on and off. 'Alright, my pretties, time to RIDE!!' they yelled into the studio. 'I'm asking you all to send some energy to your asses right now, because let me be clear: they're gonna need it!' The hot girls on either side of me tittered knowingly. Before I ruined everything, Amy and I would attend fitness classes at many different studios, though I had so far avoided any at X-Cycle. I'd told Amy it was because its West-West location was too far from Merris's, but truthfully it was because of the leaderboard.

X-Cycle was famous for its leaderboard, a large screen at the front of the class featuring a cutthroat ranking of every rider, with live stats about how hard and fast they were pedalling. Instructors would consult the leaderboard and scream messages of support or disapproval to cyclists – by name – in front of everybody. *KylieG, you are not giving me everything right now*, or *FitMom73, yes baby, FEEL that*

resistance!! I could not imagine anything I wanted less than to be singled out during group exercise.

The class started with a low-key warm-up but quickly progressed into challenging, fast-paced choreography. I did my best to follow along, dipping forward and tapping back and bobbing my head side to side in time with the beat. Blake kept telling us we were superstars and encouraged us to 'generate power' with the bodies we cherished, which had done us the favour of carrying us around all day and getting us here, to this darkened room full of top-of-the-line exercise equipment. Blake asked us to think about what we loved about moving our bodies, and I surprised myself by obeying.

It was tempting to make fun of Blake's attitude, their relentless positivity and cutesy sayings about moving your feet to the beat or leaving your stress at the door. But instead I felt my legs working in the dark and thought how much more powerful they were than they had been this time last year. I felt strong. I felt happy. I felt, actually, grateful. Aside from my other purpose, I was in Blake's class to 'push myself', something I had been trying lately, though acknowledging this humiliated me to my weak, untrained core. Blake turned the music up and encouraged us all to add resistance. It was time to climb.

I took a deep breath and pressed into the balls of my feet, pushing down with my left and pulling up with my right, bouncing in time to a song about being an extremely powerful slut. My thighs burned, and I felt sweat bead and drop down the shallow valley of my back. I looked around and saw I was keeping up with the Ambers – not easily, necessarily, but I was doing it.

I had worried, during the long hours on the stationary bike, that maybe nothing was happening. Certainly I did not look any different, which was the only way I knew to measure the progress of a fitness regime. And although over time I rode for longer distances, swam faster, ran easier, I had not gotten smaller. There had been no sudden six-pack, no overnight glow up. I was glowing laterally at best, but I had kept at it, there being not much else to do on long nights in my hometown, and because I had started to feel some of the so-called endorphins that people in tank tops were always promising arrived with strenuous movement.

'Let's get uncomfortable in our breathing!' yelled Blake, though I was way ahead of them. I pedalled harder, my name rising up the class ranking, inching toward Amy's, which had hovered at the top since class began. Blake shouted at someone called TheRealSpinShady: 'I'm sorry, but you do not pun in my class and then coast during a climb! Up that resistance or get out of here, babe!' Blake consulted the laptop next to their bike.

'Okay, we have a cyclist *burning up* the leaderboard. Can I get a big X-Cycle cheer for … AMY-I'M-SORRY?' Blake paused, checked the screen again. 'No, that's— Amy I'm … yep, okay! AMY-I'M-SORRY, damn, here they come! They know what they did, and they are repenting on the BIKE, baby!'

In front of me, Amy slowed her feet and stood hovering above her bike seat. She towelled her face and looked tentatively to her left, then her right. She gulped some water and sat back in the saddle. I cycled harder. The icon with my

username travelled higher up the board … then started to drop. Other, fitter riders were overtaking me. If I didn't make the top spot, I wouldn't get the special shout-out I needed, the moment at the end of class where I could do it right. My name dropped out of the top half of the leaderboard, and the chance at the gesture – the apology in the rain, the boom box overhead, the cue cards at the door in the snow – disappeared.

The track changed, and in the momentary gap between songs I shrieked, 'AMY! IT'S ME!' Amy stopped again and turned around. I smiled ghoulishly at her, hair everywhere, wildly out of breath. 'I'M SO SORRY!' I yelled, gasping for air.

'What the hell?'

'I—'

An insistent techno beat picked up, and the class moved on without us, bobbing in unison as they performed a series of complicated triceps push-ups.

'PLEASE TAKE ME BACK!' I shouted. 'YOU SAID WOMEN LIKE THIS!'

For some reason I was still pedalling. I didn't know if I was feeling a cyclist's high or if this surge of adrenaline was the result of sheer emotional desperation, but I felt incredible. Amy's feelings were harder to read. The music entered another lull, and we locked eyes. Her face softened, and she cocked her head and whisper-screamed, 'Can we please talk about this later?'

'Yes, you can, thanks!' yelled Blake. 'That's enough! Okay, y'all, we're going to pick it up!' They started undulating on the bike, using their abs to push themself up and

over the handlebars like a magnificent, Lycra-clad seal. I followed their lead, clumsily rolling up and back. A few of our fellow classmates were staring. Eventually, the demands of Blake's routine took over, and I was left to myself. I watched my name slip further down the leaderboard.

The last song at X-Cycle was always a slow jam, something vaguely emotional over which the instructors could preach mindfulness, self-love, and the importance of regularly returning to the studio for its copyright-protected blend of cardio, weight training and 'adrene-rock'. Blake told us we should be proud of ourselves, that it wasn't always easy to be vulnerable, to put ourselves out there in a group fitness setting. They encouraged us to close our eyes and groove, to feel free to leave what was holding us back in the studio when we left it.

The instrumentals gave way to a man's voice, speaking softly: 'We all want to help one another,' the voice said into the pitch-black studio. 'Human beings are like that. We want to live by each other's happiness – not by each other's misery.' The music swelled again. It was corny, and I found it comforting. It was too much, and I was happy to be hearing it. Two contradictory things really could be true! And so, robust glutes on fire, I cried lightly in a spin class to a techno remix of Charlie Chaplin's speech from *The Great Dictator*, a situation I found surprising but not, in the scope of the year's changes, impossible.

The class ended, and Blake shouted out the rider who had performed best, a beautiful man in a mesh top and tiny shorts, whose name on the leaderboard was Bry2k. Blake shone a flashlight at him, and the class cheered and twirled

their towels over their heads in celebration of his achieve-
ment. This was when I would have given my big speech to
Amy, had things gone to plan. I looked at my final ranking:
twelfth out of thirty-seven. Not even close.

I unclipped and stood in the studio, bright red and
covered in sweat, still breathing hard. Blake opened the
door and high-fived exiting cyclists as they trickled into the
lobby, making plans for tomorrow, laughing about brunch
sweated off and Bloody Marys earned. I noticed a few of
them staring at me, whispering to each other about the
madwoman who had tried to get her girlfriend back, or
something, in the middle of spin. As the last set of braided
pigtails flounced out of the room, I saw Amy lingering by
the door.

'I really thought you would like that more,' I said,
clomping awkwardly toward her in my special clip-in shoes.

Amy sucked in an impossibly long breath, and I resigned
myself to a future where we were no longer friends, where I
had to block her on social media to stop myself from scroll-
ing through her perfect life without me. Then she smiled.
'Honestly?' she said. 'It should have worked! Or it *could*
have worked. Like I see what you were going for, but the
end result was crazy.'

I told her I was sorry for how I'd behaved at Emily's
wedding, for underestimating her, for not telling her how
much her friendship – the utter surprise and real joy of it
– had meant to me this year. I'd wanted the gesture to say
all this, but it had just made things worse and insinuated to
everyone at X-Cycle that she was involved in some kind of
lesbian personal drama.

Amy dabbed her face, then threw her towel in a designated bin. 'I didn't hate it,' she said, leaning down to unstrap her shoes and put them in a different bin. 'Like it was definitely thoughtful. Plus, top half of the leaderboard is impressive.'

I told her it felt like every ligament in my legs had melted.

'Blake is the devil,' she said, laughing. 'But in a way, they are also my Jesus. Whenever I have an event coming up, I'll do, like, all five of their classes in a week and get *shredded*.'

Amy leaned against the wall and grabbed her left ankle to stretch her quad.

'Also, can I just say, the hair looks amazing,' she said. 'You're gonna love being blonde. It's cliché, but we literally do have more fun.'

Her easy warmth made me panic. I needed to know she forgave me; had to confirm that we were good; wanted a promise, in writing, that she saw I was a ridiculous, needy, petty, cranky, genuinely very odd person and still liked me, still thought going for drinks or dinner and texting sometimes would be nice. I did not like being a person who needed this much, but that was the situation.

Amy pulled me into a clammy hug. 'I missed you,' she said. 'I was going to call you eventually, but I'm glad you came to me first. Also, at the end of class the girl next to me fully farted … out her front. Want to get froyo?'

Journalling Exercise: Self-Knowledge

Sit somewhere quiet with a blank notebook or sheet of paper. Without editing or judging yourself, write freely for 10 or 15 minutes. Try to answer (or at least think about) the following question: What do I want? *If this is difficult, consider the opposite:* What don't I want?

————

I want better posture. I want a good life. I want to *want* to spend less time on my phone.

I want it to matter that I stopped going to Whole Foods. I don't want, particularly, to wrinkle. I want a kitchen with a lot of natural light and a little rack to hang pots and pans on. I want to know if vitamins do anything. I want better-fitting pants. I want to be taken exactly the right amount of seriously. I don't want to know so much about the lives of people I met one time in 2008. I want a closer relationship with my sister.

I want my friends to know I care about them. I want to accept that they care about me. I want to have faith in even one politician and/or human man. I want to feel like I understand the news. I don't want to know anything else about what's at the bottom of the ocean. I want a fulfilling job that pays a living wage. I want to have sex in a fancy hotel. I want to know how much protein I actually need and whether or not I'm getting it. I don't ever want to eat chia pudding. I want another person to look at me with love. I want all of this to happen in a non-corny way.

I want to feel calm. I want a signature scent. I want to be the kind of woman who whips up a galette. I want to enjoy stretching. I want to mean it when I tell someone, 'no worries'. I want to be good at sports or at least *a* good sport. I want a partner who thinks my best qualities are the Real Me and my worst qualities are manageable. I don't want to date someone who thinks I'm only okay. I want to love easily. I want to be gentler. I don't want to drink so much. I want to be open and nonjudgemental and warm. I want to look pretty with my hair wet.

I want to do more than sign petitions and go to protests where I feel shy so I mouth the chants. I want to provide help where help is wanted. I want to be a vegetarian, not someone who talks a lot about the day or two a week she doesn't eat meat. I want to delete Facebook. I want to delete Instagram, which I understand is basically Facebook as well. I want to make things that feel useful. I want to *be* useful. I want to retire one day. I don't want to write any more bad essays about *Hamlet*.

I want to make a positive first impression. I don't want to 'sweat the small stuff'. I don't want to habitually look at the social media profiles of people who have hurt my feelings, or who make me feel bad about myself, or who I think I am better than. I want to have literally no idea what I look like. I don't want to spend all my time telling myself and everyone else that I am 'enough'. I want to know how doomed we actually are, as a species. I don't want to look at my face every day. I guess I want to do something about the earth? I want to know what that something is.

I want to think about anything other than the shape of

my stomach, or if I'm a good person, or who wants to fuck me, or if anyone will ever really love me for me. I don't want to celebrate the pimples on my ass or honour my spider veins. I want to know that I am an alright person trying very hard, who deserves love and has spider veins, sure, they just don't occupy a lot of her time.

I want to know what kind of stuff to want. I want to not be completely embarrassed by this activity and most other things I do in a day. I want my tortellini to cook faster.

Classes finished, and I had even fewer reasons to visit Toronto. I made a few trips out of picking up exams and helping out at Merris's place, but I no longer stayed overnight, so coming to the city meant driving six hours in the same day or taking the very unpleasant bus or very expensive train. It was nice to have somewhere to be, even if I was finding my work uninspiring and certainly not worth the train ride – over two hours and $85 each way.

I went down to clear out my office for the summer and let myself fall into a familiar routine: a cup of weak coffee from the machine in the kitchen, an hour or so of clicking around online, a few minutes of desk-friendly stretches, some filing and organising. I found a crumpled receipt in a copy of *Utopia* and rolled my eyes at the eager marginalia I'd left in it a few years earlier. I closed the never-ending Word doc with my dissertation on it and browsed a few résumés.

I was in the process of finding Merris a new research assistant. We'd both agreed that would be best, although our post-physio coffee dates were getting longer. She had

started telling me about her life, working forward chronologically from an apparently formative skating accident, age eight. We'd recently reached her first marriage, at nineteen, and I was trying very hard not to ask her to skip ahead to the sort-of-secret daughter. I ate a cheese sandwich and forwarded a few applications that looked promising.

Olivia walked by, tote bag brimming with exams. The bag had a poorly rendered cat on its front, and when I inquired about it, I learned it was a gift from the cat shelter at which she was a volunteer. The idea that a person could a) perform a charitable activity in a long-term way and b) keep that information to themselves for any amount of time was incomprehensible and impressive, and I asked if she would take me along sometime. 'Of course!' she said. Then, concerningly: 'Don't wear shoes you like too much.'

A week later I was outside Paws4Thought No-Kill Feline Rescue and Shelter (I had notes about the name), on an east end street full of warehouses and drab dental practices almost directly under the highway. It was either very near a bunch of those trees that smell like cum, or someone had done something awful in the parking lot. Inside it was sterile and harshly lit and loud, the chaos of its animal charges barely balanced out by the insistent tranquillity of the volunteers in their stirrup pants and fun vests.

My trial shift was horrible. Olivia frolicked with a batch of new kittens as I cleared out piss-soaked cages and tried to give sad animals their dinners in a non-traumatising way. My big victory was getting a hulking three-legged beast called Colin to come eat in the centre of the room, apparently an indicator of trust. I tried to give Colin a comforting

pat to show him that trusting humans was okay, even if one had hurt him in the past. He hissed at me and threw up.

Nearby, Olivia played with her litter of tabbies. 'They always give the grunt work to newbies,' she said, just absolutely covered in kittens. 'Weeds out the people who are only here for cuddles.' She giggled and dangled feathers for her fuzzball army while I wiped up Colin's mess and sprinkled deworming medication into chunks of brined tuna.

Other than Olivia, everyone who worked at the cat rescue place was weird, which was fine. Being there probably meant that I was weird too, and I'd already learned my lesson re: adult hobbies. Plus, I liked the cats, even the mean and stinky ones, even big Colin. I understood and could easily meet their needs. I filled in the requisite forms, acquired the requisite branded polo, and was given access to the shared Google Calendar.

It was soothing to be around animals, to have quiet time among people I didn't know, to see kids and couples and old men on their own come in and encounter their future pet. It was gratifying to help a cranky, nervous creature understand that it was safe, its life would no longer be as hard as it had been. When I went home I looked up the adoption profiles of my new friends, which I felt undersold them a little: Don't be put off by Dunstan's scrappy looks; Carrie is a dramatic girl who may seem strange at first; Tomasina is NOT for everyone. Did we need to lead with this information? These animals had already been through a lot. The names were another thing altogether: what kind of disturbed individual calls a cat 'Meaghan'?

A few weeks into my time at the shelter, Olivia took a shine to Tinker, a charming old boy with a grizzled face and one bad eye. (His bio read, A classic grandpa, Tinker is not afraid to give you a nip to assert himself. Whose grandpa behaved like this?) After talking it over with her fiancé, they decided to 'add him to their growing family' and started the adoption process. I was running the front desk when she and Aidan the Egg King came to claim him. I watched them fuss over their new charge and thought, *that cat's gonna have to get into hiking.* As they walked away, I admitted to myself that I was jealous of Tinker.

When my shift ended, I threw my vest in a hamper and pulled on a new, less hair-covered dress. I touched up my makeup in the tiny staff bathroom and tried to make my hair do something normal. Most of the time I went straight back to Kingston after the shelter, but Lauren had given me special permission to stay at hers for two full nights. I was excited to be in the city for a longer haul, to take a stab at a wilder version of existence, or at least one where I went to parties. I'd booked Sunday off from the cheese store and stolen a pair of shoes from my mom, and Clive was having us all over (plus seventeen strangers I hoped to mostly ignore) in celebration of Amirah and Tom's engagement.

I took the streetcar across town and walked up to Trinity Bellwoods, stopping on the way to buy the couple a gift – a coffee-table book? Of large-scale pictures? Of beaches? – and pick up some food. I watched clusters of students eat charcoal ice cream and tried to practise compassionate non judgement toward the too-old slackliners and rich

moms complaining about their colourists being away on holiday. Anyone in the park over age thirty had a dog. Anyone over thirty-five had a stroller. I lingered near a recessed off-leash area called the Dog Bowl and waited for the desire to take a video of the animals to pass. While smugly putting my phone back in my pocket, I spilled the contents of a vegetarian banh mi down the front of my dress.

I didn't want to be the first person at the party, but I didn't want to loiter in the park smelling of carrot and rice vinegar all day either, so I got on the bus, knowing Clive would have a bleach pen or some other tidy man trick to clean me up. I sat by the window, absorbing the late-May sun and reading a book about a woman who kills her entire family but in a chic and feminist way. At some point between Dundas and Harbord, Jon got on.

What happened was this: I became distracted by an odd, insistent noise and looked up to discover its source. Across the aisle, a few seats down from mine, a black gym bag was emitting a long, low growl. A blur of greyish-brown fuzz from inside revealed it to be a cat, furious in its carrier, meowing and throwing itself against the sides of its mesh and canvas prison. Watching this made me miss Janet. She used to do something very similar, scooting around in tiny circles inside her bag until – ah.

It was Janet. Her little face was mashed against the carrier's front window, displaying her signature snaggletooth. The carrier had a smiley face key chain attached to it, one I'd tried and failed to take off several times. And above this, with the bag in his lap, was Jon.

I could feel my pulse in my ears. I was a big bag of whooshing blood. I snuck another look at Jon, who did not notice me – he had headphones on and was absorbed in his phone, ignoring Janet's antics but occasionally patting the bag in a soothing way. He looked good. Healthy. He was dressed up, for him: a light sweater I didn't recognise over a shirt one of his sisters had given him for his birthday last year. He looked like he could be going to a job interview, or a party, or a date.

I had thought about this moment once or twice … a day, for the last three hundred and fifty-three days. There was so much I wanted to say, so many ways I had imagined this encounter taking shape. I could sing the exact right song, of course, or fall to my knees and apologise, or say something clever but devastating, toss my hair over my shoulder, walk away. I could admit that I was angry, still, at both of us. I could explain what I had discovered with Helen: that cutting someone totally out of your life without warning during an ongoing legal process was not a particularly useful application of 'boundaries', and had robbed us of the small moments of exposure necessary to defang moments like these. I could hug him and see how it felt.

The bus stopped again.

I wondered if he would recognise me with my new hair. I wondered if I could grab Janet and run. I took a breath, stood, and walked past them – my cat in the ratty carrier I'd bought at a yard sale, my husband in a shirt I loved – my little family. I stepped down into the street and the doors closed behind me. I leaned against the bus shelter and let my breathing slow. My eyes watered but did not break into

full tears, and when I raised them to watch the bus depart, Jon was looking at me, and I didn't want to say anything cool or do anything right, I just wanted him to know I was sorry it had turned out this way and I hoped he was okay, and to promise that I would be too, probably, or at least if I wasn't, it would not be his problem. I guess I would also have liked it if he'd made the cat wave her little paw out the window, but it would have been unwise to let Janet out of her carrier on public transit. Jon's upper lip twitched, and the bus pulled away, and I watched our old life drive up Ossington Avenue.

Then, obviously, I had to wait for another bus, which was kind of a pain in the ass.

I decided, ultimately, to walk, and got to Clive's an hour or so later, slipping into the crowd as Tom's dad gave a speech about how excited he and his wife were to welcome a woman like Amirah into their family. Amirah's cute parents dabbed their eyes, and Tom smiled bashfully at his father's platitudes. It really was the same every time.

A dark-haired woman holding a baby (there had started to be babies at things) stood in front of me, next to a tall blonde in enviably dramatic earrings. The blonde leaned over her friend's infant and whispered, 'I don't know how many more of these I can do.'

'Rachel, relax,' said the brown-haired woman. 'You always get like this.'

'I'm thirty-two,' she said. 'I'm thirty-two and I've never even been engaged.'

I knew why Rachel felt this way. Wedding stuff was everywhere. Since I'd turned twenty-five, developments in

other people's relationships and families had been the social tentpoles of my year: engagements in the winter, starting at Christmas and continuing into Valentine's Day, then in spring the weddings from the previous year's engagements would start, and by autumn some bitches would be pregnant. My social feeds were similar: girls from elementary school stretching their left hands to the camera in posts that were indistinguishable from the omnipresent ads for engagement rings; photos of friends at quirky, jar-filled venues; babies next to chalkboards proclaiming they were sitting up now. Despite my rigorously clicking NOT INTERESTED every time it appeared, I was being stalked by a sponsored post for something called ModernWeddingHarpist.com.

I did not feel pressure when I saw these items. I had been married – it was bad. I had not considered that it might also feel bad not to have been. The blonde swished past me, looking for the bathroom. She was so beautiful it was hard to imagine her having any problems whatsoever.

I had been reading a lot about intuitive eating and let my intuition guide me toward a plate of mushroom and leek pastry things. I ate seven, knowing they would make me bloated and gassy later, which was probably not what this approach to food was going for, but I figured there would be a learning curve. The event was dry, out of respect for Amirah's parents, who also believed that Tom worked at a 'kombucha brewery', something Amirah thought she had made up but which had blissfully turned out to be a real thing. I poured myself another sparkling water and surveyed the room.

Tom was standing alone at the other end of the snack table, carefully reading the little cards Clive had made to explain each dish. I wandered over to ask some whispered softball questions about craft beer. He was friendly as always and knew an unbelievable amount about hops. Unable to keep up with the yeast filtration chat, I tried to glean if he was the type of man who would be psyched to receive a large book of blown-up beach photography.

'Tough question,' Tom said. 'I love the coast, but I'd say for me the jury is still out on sand.'

I decided the main thing was that he loved my friend and told him I was very happy for him and Amirah.

'Thanks,' he said. 'What do you think, would you ever get married again?'

'She's focusing on herself right now,' said Amy, appearing from nowhere in an expensive-looking boho minidress and steering me toward the balcony. 'And I need to ask her something privately, so, back in a jiff!'

'Please don't tell people I'm "focusing on myself",' I said after she slid the door closed behind us. 'It's so embarrassing.'

'That's literally what you told me you were doing.'

We stood outside, and I wished I'd brought my sweater; the weather was getting warmer, but it was still cold in the shade. Below us in the building's brick courtyard, a woman was losing an argument with a fragile-seeming dog. Amy looked at me solemnly and brought her face close to mine.

'I saw on Spotify that you've been listening to that confidence-boosting playlist a lot,' she said. 'So, I wanted to remind you … it's okay to not be okay.'

One of Amirah's handsome cousins came outside to smoke, giving us a friendly nod of acknowledgement. I nodded back, then lowered my voice and moved closer to Amy, unwilling to let another person know about the playlist. I had tried to change my Spotify settings several times and had no idea how to do it.

I whispered, 'Let's talk about this another time?'

'You said you were trying to mean it when you said you enjoyed your own company,' she replied, so loudly, certainly much louder than necessary. 'And I love that goal for you. You'll get there!'

She smacked me, hard, on the arm, and the cousin looked over again. Amy grinned at him.

'My friend is taking a break from dating,' she said. 'Bad divorce. I'm divorced too, but I'm not that disciplined!'

The cousin looked thrilled and introduced himself. His name was Sam. He was a hockey fan and sometimes-DJ and, body-language-wise, seemed single. He worked in real estate.

'What a coincidence,' said Amy. 'I'm looking for somewhere to live.'

'Fantastic,' he said. 'I should give you my number.'

Sometimes it really was that easy. I told Amy I didn't know she was moving. 'What about the condo?'

'Greg got it, in the end,' she said. 'I got sick of arguing and was like, honestly, take it. He did technically pay for it, so whatever. Plus, now I have a hot little down payment to live somewhere else!'

Amy shot another big smile at the cousin as I searched her face for hidden pain.

'And you're … okay?' I asked.

'Yeah!' said Amy, seeming to mean it. 'I feel like, you know, *que sera*.'

'Totally,' said Sam. 'That's my philosophy 100%.'

'Well, are you going to move in with Ryan?'

'Ryan and I broke up,' she said. 'A few weeks ago. We were on very different journeys. God, I literally haven't seen you in forever!'

Sam saw his opening and took it, stepping forward and angling his body in a way that cut me slightly out of the conversation. I left them talking about how the Leafs were doing (Amy had heard this would be their year) and found Amirah and the Laurens in the kitchen.

'Which cousin?' asked Amirah. 'If it's Daniyal … he's a fuckboy.'

She was more approving of a match with Sam, though warned he had already been out with a former housemate's cousin and a girl Emotional Lauren knew from work. I said I was glad to be taking a break from dating. There seemed to be an endless supply of single women in the city, and I didn't feel like competing with them.

'Everybody's so hot,' I said.

Lauren nodded. 'They're probably more mellow than you too.'

Amy joined us, flushed and excited and holding an ornate mocktail. 'I've been working on a theory,' she said. 'I think your thirties are honestly the perfect age. Like in a way being thirty-one is exactly like being twenty-six, except you're smarter and hotter and you know a bit about tiles.'

I said I would probably enter my thirties on a single bed at my dad's house.

Amy groaned. 'Could you not be a downer for five seconds, please? Sam's taking me to some viewings tomorrow, and it's like a date, I think, so you can't come, but I'll send you pics.'

'Really?'

Amy looked confused. 'What do you mean, "really"? Duh, really! We were gonna look at one-bedrooms, but I'm sure there are tons of twosies.'

'But ... what?'

'Oh my god, bitch, let me be your roommate,' Amy said. 'Or your landlord, I guess, which is a bit rando, but whatever.'

'Very rando,' I said, trying to be sarcastic and somehow sounding very sincere. I could not hide that I was moved; I knew this because Emotional Lauren started rubbing my arms.

'You need to move back to Toronto anyway,' said Amy. 'The Kingston thing is such a bummer. The other day a friend of mine asked what had happened to you, and I swear I almost just told her you died. So, perfect, you'll live with me – okay, he's looking, he's looking, oh my god, don't cry, for god's *sake!*'

Birthday Messages I Did Not Particularly Wish to Receive

At & A HARD PLACE Training Centre, our climbers are family. Which is why we were so excited to hear you've rappelled into another year! Come in any time today and get a Nutrition Ball, Protein Shot, or Grass Powder Top-Up, on us. And don't forget to keep on... Rockin'!!

heyyyy girlie! i know we haven't kept in touch since high school days, but i wanted to say happy thirtieth, because i know this can be an intense birthday, and it looks from IG like you've had a hard year. i hope you have as great a day as possible, and if you want any info about how you can double your income from home next year, let me know! i'm part of a badass community of momtrepreneurs i think you'd totally dig ... sending love and light ❤

• HAPPY BIRTHDAY, MARGARET • THANK YOU FOR BEING PART OF THE TL BANK FAMILY • AVAILABLE BALANCE: $135.33 •

Maggie, NANA here on email!!! – Wishing you a very PLEASANT birthday today, with a reminder to please TRY NOt to get any tattoos.! here is a LInk your mother sent me to a very cheering article in the NEW YORK TIMES about a young Lady who found a new career by going to computer school,. Something to CONSIDER? Love, NANA

HOLLA AT A GEM KWEEEEN – To celebrate your big day (and Gemini SZN in general!), here's a list of famous figures who share your star sign, including Sir Ian McKellen and most serial killers! Much love from your pals at DailyAstroz

happy birthday amiga, hope your gr8 :P let me know if ur out later ... it's calvin, ps

'Seven Ways You Didn't Know You Could Use Birthday Cake (And One Way You Probably Did)' – HBD from 6Bites!

Hi Maggie, Thanks for your inquiry regarding IPL hair removal. Unfortunately, people with your complexion are not candidates for this treatment, as your hair and skin are too fair for the laser to do its job correctly. A shame, as redheads also have some of the coarsest hair types :(But it's not all bad news: Stripp'd Wax Bar offers 15% off Birthday Brazilians! Let us know if you want to book in to make this your smoothest birthday yet! Xoxoxo

Olivia tells me it's your birthday, so just wanted to say: medically speaking, muscle atrophy begins at thirty. Have a good one. Jiro

The morning of my thirtieth was brisk and bright. I decided to 'start the decade right' by going for a run, but ended up taking a light stroll around my neighbourhood in full fitness attire. Hannah sent flowers, and my mother called and gave her traditional speech about the rigours of childbirth, and I gave my traditional thanks for her efforts and my life. She told me one day I'd know what she was talking about, and I said, 'I don't think so,' and she said, 'You'll change your mind.' Ten minutes later my father called, and we repeated the interaction almost word for word, minus the focus on vaginal tearing. I wondered if Jon would get in touch.

I showered and brushed my hair and looked at my face in the mirror, which prompted the ordering of a new ointment, some French thing that the internet said would either burn my skin off or make it perfect. In a small show of restraint, I did not even click on the suggested accompanying purchase, an expensive mucus from Japan that I wanted incredibly badly. I tidied my room and made plans to get some things framed, thinking, *women in their thirties own things that are framed.*

I went to the grocery store and picked up ingredients for the dinner party we were having. Amy had wanted to roast a chicken ('It's the most casually grown-up dinner there is!'), but I was trying to be a proper vegetarian, so we were having spaghetti and garlic bread and a big Caesar salad, like a family in an after-school special.

Having lost the battle over the menu, Amy had insisted on being allowed to do a 'tablescape', covering the rickety wooden table she'd inherited from her parents with an old sheet, then covering *that* with an array of items from other parts of the apartment: old candlesticks, crystals, some dried flowers, etc. I'd been sceptical while she was doing it, but when she stood back, made a few final adjustments to some leaves and the twinkle lights she'd nested around them, there was no denying it was gorgeous.

'Guess where I got the idea,' said Amy. 'Reese *Witherspoon.*'

Living with Amy was surprisingly great. She was tidy and considerate and had her dad's Netflix password. Our only real argument had been over a gigantic poster she bought for the living room without consulting me, a black-and-white print of a female surfer silhouetted against a crashing wave, with the words I NEED THE SEA BECAUSE IT TEACHES ME written in the sky above her. ('Do you surf?' I'd asked. 'No,' she'd said, 'but I *feel* like I do.') I lost the argument, and now it was in the kitchen, on a big patch of wall next to the fridge. Lauren made a privately sarcastic face at me about it when she walked in. Emotional Lauren told Amy she thought it was 'important to think about the ocean sometimes'. Amy agreed.

The apartment's air-conditioning system comprised two boxes perilously installed in our respective bedroom windows, so by the time Amirah and Clive arrived, the kitchen was incredibly warm. Amy looked dewy and gorgeous, moving breezily between the pasta on the stove, the bread in the oven, and the light, zippy salad she'd put in an enormous bowl I'd never seen before, magicked out of a back cupboard.

I was not faring so well. Having blow-dried my hair for the occasion, I'd already been forced to gather it in a high, crumpled bun to stop the strands sticking to my neck.

'Someone's pink,' said Amirah when she arrived, passing me a gift and a bottle of wine. 'Happy birthday.' She kissed the side of my sweaty face and pretended to be disgusted, then kissed the other side.

As he entered, Clive clocked the banner Amy had made, raised his eyebrows, and said nothing. Amy hugged him like an old friend. 'Nobody better have any dietary restrictions they haven't told me about,' she said with a maternal hand on her hip. 'I asked in the side chat, and no one said anything, so if you and gluten have an issue, that is your business.'

'Where do you even *buy* an apron in 2019?' Lauren asked.

'Muji,' Amy tutted. 'Or, like, anywhere. Go sit down.'

The food was perfect, flavourful and rich. I slopped a second helping onto my plate as Clive told us about his latest Grindr disaster and Lauren upped the ante with a story from Tinder: 'The first date was amazing, like, top five dates of my life,' she said. 'He was funny and hot and

smelled like firewood. We texted nonstop the next week, but when we met up on Friday, *he had shaved his beard into a goatee.*

Amy screamed. 'Did he say anything about it?'

'Not a word.'

'And he didn't warn you beforehand, when you were texting?'

'Nothing.'

Amy said this was bad manners. 'You cannot spring a goatee on someone.'

'I don't see what the problem is?' said Emotional Lauren hopefully.

'He looked like a gamer,' said Lauren. 'He looked like a gamer who owns a bird.'

Emotional Lauren came round, and dinner carried on. We drank red wine and laughed loudly and told each other we looked hot. We ate too much and gossiped remorselessly and complained about our jobs and our families and our completely satisfactory lives, soundtracked by a playlist an algorithm had compiled called 'Adult-Ass Dinner'.

Lauren asked when the divorce would be final, and I told her honestly: I didn't know.

'It's out of my hands,' I said. 'All I know is I'm paid up.'

Lauren asked quickly, 'So did Jon call today … ?'

Amirah shushed her as I shook my head no. 'Helen says I should get comfortable with the idea that we may never speak again.' I didn't mention the bus.

'What about Simon?'

'Lauren, please!' said Amirah, taking things into her own hands. 'How's it going at the cat place?'

I told them my manager had let me write some punchier bios of the cats up for adoption. She'd liked them, and her friend, the proprietor of an online-only skincare business, had asked me to do the same for her, writing descriptions of serums and oils and essences. The cat gig had been unpaid, but the skincare lady had given me 200 bucks. I was hoping to parlay that into further work, and maybe take a night class in communications or copywriting or something, in case I wanted to leave academia and make an actual living one day.

'Ironic,' said Lauren, 'since that was Jon's j— OW!'

Amirah released her grip on Lauren's leg and said copy-writing sounded like a good door to keep open. Sometime after we ran out of garlic bread, Amy clinked her fork against her wineglass like a maid of honour.

'Okaaaaaaaaaaaaaay!' She smiled and straightened her already extremely straight posture, too prepared for some-thing. 'So, in my family, on birthdays, we go around the table and everyone says one thing they love about the birth-day perso—'

'No.'

Amy didn't even look at me, just kept talking. 'Everyone says something they love about the birthday person, and it's very cute, and we all like it. Okay? I'll start. When I met Maggie, she was a *mess*—'

'Amy, please.' I stared at the napkin resting on my lap as Amirah, Lauren, et al. suppressed their laughter with vary-ing degrees of success. This was my worst nightmare, and theirs. It could not stand.

'She was a total mess,' Amy continued, undaunted. 'So

heartbroken and cranky, and she still had those bangs. I was like, *who is this girl?* But I gave her my number anyway, and I'm glad that I did, because she's actually super sweet and has, like, a heart of gold, and she slays a back-to-back Super Saturday at X-Cycle better than anyone I know, except Laura, or my friend Sidra from work, she's got these quads that are just … anyway. I also think – I mean, I know, from experience – that it's hard to go through what she went through this year, and it's very brave to, like, keep going and try to figure out what life looks like on your own, when you thought you'd already figured it out with someone else. I know she's worked hard to do that, and I feel lucky that we get to figure that out together.'

The rest of the table was quiet for a minute. My friends shifted uncomfortably in their seats, and I moved my tongue across the surface of my teeth. I swallowed a few times. It didn't help. I opened my mouth to say something, but it would have been impossible to speak without my voice cracking, so I sat there speechless and fixed my eyes on the ceiling.

'Well, everyone's sick of watching Maggie cry by now, right, so I'll jump in,' said Clive, refilling his glass while I discreetly dabbed at my eyes. Amy beamed from the end of the table, visibly thrilled with this result.

'She's a lot, right? She's very loud, terrible to share fries with, and she talks during movies,' said Clive.

The table erupted with a list of films I'd single-handedly destroyed for them: times I'd spoiled the ending, asked the name of a character who'd just been introduced, pointed out when someone said the title of the film *in the film*.

Clive continued: 'I don't understand what she does for a living, and when she tries to explain it, it's like, those people have been dead for centuries and I hope they stay that way, shut up! She's a nightmare, top to bottom, but being mad at her is technically biphobia, so. Happy birthday, you dumb bitch, we love you.'

I smiled at Clive, grateful to him for cutting through the sincerity of the moment. Emotional Lauren opened her mouth and immediately started tearing up, so the other Lauren stepped in, telling a story of a particularly busted birthday we'd shared in university at a bowling alley. The night had ended in romantic disaster for several of us, horrific hangovers for most of us, and one instance of being charged $50 for ruining a pair of bowling shoes in a beer-pong-related mishap. It had not been the highlight of my twenties.

'Still, you went home with a really cute guy that night,' Lauren said. 'And isn't that what's most important?'

'I think that was you,' said Amirah.

'Yeah, it was you,' said Emotional Lauren. 'I remember because Maggie puked taquitos on my duvet.'

Clive and I agreed it had been Lauren's story, not mine.

'Well. I guess what I was trying to say is: happy birthday, Maggie, and congratulations to me.' Lauren raised her glass: 'To the hottie from the bowling alley, wherever he may be.'

There followed some debate about whether he had been all that good-looking – Lauren insisting, of course, that he had; the rest of us finding this account revisionist. Amirah took a sip of water and composed herself for her turn.

'The main image I remember of your wedding—'

'Oh, here we go.' Clive folded his arms. 'We *just* stopped the waterworks.'

'No, no, it's good, I promise,' said Amirah, turning back to me. 'The main image I remember of your wedding is you in your dress – and it was beautiful, let's be honest here, whatever else happened around that event, the dress was fucking gorgeous – you were sitting in this fancy dress, chowing down on those burgers that came out at, like, one, and you were crying your face off.'

I snorted, surprised and a little embarrassed. 'I don't remember this ...'

'Well, it happened,' Amirah continued. 'We had snuck off to have a snack and debrief a bit, and you started crying – for context, I mean, I'm *sure* you were drunk – but you were so upset because you thought it was unfair that there wasn't a ceremony for pledging love and commitment to your friends.'

Emotional Lauren burst out laughing: 'I remember this, oh my god! You got ketchup on your tits while telling me I meant as much to you as any partner.'

'I think her actual phrase was "friends can be husbands too",' said Clive.

'You were very worked up,' Lauren added.

Amirah nodded. 'You made us all hold hands and promise to love each other forever,' she said. 'You called them "our vows".'

My face was flushing a deeper red than the wine and heat and food had made it already. Amy's eyes were enormous: 'I can't believe you don't remember doing this.'

'The bartender kept feeding me G&Ts!' I cried. 'He had a special stash for me underneath the bar that I could get any time I wanted, without waiting! He kept calling it "bride juice"!'

The faces around the table registered a deep disapproval of the phrase 'bride juice', and Amirah wrestled back control of her anecdote: 'All of this is to say, I think you were right, and—'

'I'm so sorry,' I said quietly. 'For everything, the whole—'

'Relax, it's almost over,' Amirah said. 'My god, no more big apologies, we get it, you were a little garbage tornado, and now you're not … as much.' She laughed and so did I, but I worried I might throw up or prostrate myself before her or burst into embarrassed flames. 'I want you to know,' she continued, 'I meant what I said while you were drunk and eating that burger: you're someone I promise to love forever.'

I looked across the table at Amirah. She looked a little bit bashful and exceptionally beautiful. She took a bite of some remaining pasta and her engagement ring caught the candlelight, and she said, 'Amy, I hope you're happy. That's all my sincerity for the year.'

Amy did look happy. She pushed her chair away from the table, wiped her mouth daintily with a napkin, and said, 'That was the moment this tablescape deserved.'

We cleared the table, and Lauren brought out a cake. It was very homemade, a lopsided green heart covered in thick pink globules.

'Rosettes,' Clive said. 'There's rose water in the icing. It's called a *theme*.'

Between the rosettes was a message, piped in slanting orange icing: BETTER LUCK NEXT YEAR. They didn't sing the song, just cut the cake and yelled, 'Birthday!' in unison. Amirah's gift was a dark brown Italian drink, for sipping from a set of impossibly small glasses, gifted by Lauren.

We poured a round and toasted again, this time to nothing. The brown drink was herbaceous and sweet and thick. Savouring it in small sips made me feel restrained and elegant, though after our first glasses we poured huge amounts of it over ice and mixed it with bourbon, an idea we stole from the website LibationNation. com.

Amy got me a necklace that said JOY, and Clive promised to cook me an enormous meal at his house on a date of my choosing. Emotional Lauren gave me a gift voucher for a pedicure. 'The employees are extremely rude, and they go so hard on your foot calluses it's genuinely painful,' she said. 'I love it there.'

We ate second servings of cake with our hands, and Hannah and Ed FaceTimed at a moment of extreme commotion: Amy was outsourcing witty responses to the dozens of men clamouring for her attention on dating apps, and Lauren had convinced her to message hot toilet to a man whose profile comprised four identical images of him in the bathroom.

'You guys are the worst!!' she screamed, smiling wide to show us that she didn't mean it.

The man replied moments later with haha, absolutely, and they planned to meet up next week.

Clive told us his sister was pregnant and threatening to call the baby 'Khaleesi', Lauren announced she was considering going back to school, Amirah told us we could wear whatever we wanted as her bridesmaids, and Emotional Lauren admitted she had already started a Pinterest to brainstorm outfits for all our future weddings. Stuff was happening, and I was glad to be there for it.

Amirah left at midnight, to catch Tom at the end of a work thing. The rest left an hour or so later, when the candles had burned to their wicks and the bedsheet on the table was covered in crumbs and wine stains and the remains of an aborted group effort to roll a joint. Billie Holiday crooned from the kitchen where Amy sang along as she clanked away at the dishes. I picked at a piece of wax on the table and tried to avoid what I knew was coming: the Sudden Turn. When I realised there was no fighting it, I put on my shoes and told Amy I needed to grab something from the twenty-four-hour drugstore.

'Ah,' she said. 'Tummy troubles? I've noticed you and dairy have a tumultuous relationship.'

I told her no, it was a gynaecological thing – annoying.

'Ugh, *so* annoying,' she replied, empathising incredibly hard without any specifics to hand. I thought, not for the first time, how lucky I was to live with someone so invested in my emotional, digestive and sexual health.

'Thank you so much for tonight,' I said. 'The food, the table … everything was amazing. I'm glad I gave you my number too.'

'Oh god, my pleasure!' Amy said, smiling. 'Now go fix your pussy.'

I did not need pussy medication. I needed to have a big, unpleasant cry. Not a cute, tender one like I'd done with my friends – a cry I could only do alone, in a specific place I had designated for precisely this type of tears. I had discovered this spot shortly after moving in with Amy, when it became clear she could hear everything I said or did in my room, even if I hid under the duvet to do it.

'I'm not a doctor, but your vibrator is on its last legs,' she'd said on our first Sunday afternoon together, when I'd finally emerged from a long morning alone with a series of videos where two women wrestled and the winner fucked the loser. I didn't mind Amy knowing about this; I had heard her and Sam's entire protracted negotiation regarding whether he meant it when he asked her to sit on his face. It was fine, people had sex. But Amy was too sweet to know about the Sudden Big Cries – she would come in with mint tea and an awful, thoughtful expression, ready to tell me how Jennifer Lawrence coped with the 'Sunday Scaries' – and they were happening too regularly for me not to have a place for them.

Embarrassingly, this place was a graveyard. Well, a churchyard with a few graves in it. There was a certain spooky appeal to the headstones, sure, but mostly it fit my purposes because the church and grassy lawn around it were surrounded by a high stone wall and next to a busy road, so a person – any normal, mature person in need of a bit of privacy and emotional catharsis – could enter the yard, duck behind the barrier and let 'er rip. Passing traffic drowned out any sounds, the wall was cool to the touch and hid you from sight of anyone walking past, and I did not have to risk anyone coming into the churchyard, because as a society we had just about fully lost God.

I had been going to the churchyard a lot, despite being sick to death of crying. How was there more of it to do? I was feeling better and better! This actually seemed to be the issue. Lately, whenever I perceived something beautiful or felt pleasure or experienced joy, I was hit with an instant, aching sadness. My throat would constrict and my face would flush, and I would need to go somewhere private very quickly, to be alone and bawl.

I walked down Dundas and the bars were emptying out: clusters of people showing off conspicuously new outfits bought in anticipation of summer; pairs deciding shyly, finally, to kiss; a group of women trailing behind one shoe-less, sprinting friend, all yelling, 'Tiff, come ON!' and agreeing they hate it, they *hate* when she does this; men slapping each other's backs as though they'd triumphed at a difficult challenge instead of sat together drinking beer for six hours; beleaguered bartenders kicking people out as they lit post-shift cigarettes. Inside a bakery that sold $9

cookies and nothing else, an old man wiped down racks of trays. He caught me looking, and his jokey little wave made me jump, startled, and run off.

I turned left, heading down a curved and quiet residential street. It was leafy and dark and deserted, and my big, weird sandals slapped the sidewalk too loudly. A raccoon skittered across the road and dived into a garbage can, tipping it over. Farther ahead a car passed, an incredibly popular song about tonight being the most important party of our lives blaring from its windows. Eventually the church loomed in front of me. Seeing it quickened my breath and tightened my chest, Pavlov's dumbest baby. I passed under the churchyard's stone archway, trying to remember if it was in through the nose and out through the mouth or out through the nose and in through the mouth. Whichever it was, I seemed to be doing the opposite.

I leaned against the rough surface of the wall and felt the damp from the soil seeping through my skirt. I rolled my eyes and gritted my teeth, but it didn't matter, the tears were coming. *How silly*, I thought. *How unnecessary.* I had survived the big, bad thing – more stressful than moving, only slightly less stressful than death, people said – and was doing my little therapy sessions and getting my steps in and drinking my endless glasses of water. I was experiencing delight and seeing beauty in life. The good things were back! And yet they were happening – now would always happen – without the person I'd hoped to share them with. Tonight was merely another in an endless parade of birthday parties he'd miss, news he'd never celebrate, gossip I couldn't come home and tell him after expressly promising

not to tell a soul. I had worked so hard to get my head above water, only to look around and discover I was in the big, freaky ocean, alone.

A truck rumbled past, leaving silence behind it. I stuffed the collar of my T-shirt into my mouth and sobbed. In the interest of speeding things up, I lay down on the grass and tried to think about positive things. I was healthy and safe. A new career direction was emerging, and the carnations on my dresser were still alive. Tomorrow I would have a late lunch with Merris at a Polish place she liked where everything tasted like cabbage. After that I could do anything: lie around, read, walk down to the lake and just look at it. The weather was supposed to be beautiful all week, and until we ran out there would be cake for break-fast; I could even eat it in bed, if I wanted.

During my marriage I had taken to calling our bed 'The Restaurant' because I liked eating in there so much. Jon thought this was disgusting and appointed himself city councillor, always trying to shut The Restaurant down for health code violations like crumbs or spills. As time passed, I knew, little details like this would fade from my memory; I would fixate less often on our relationship and the low-grade horror of its ending. One day I would climb into bed with a sandwich and think, *I used to have a name for this*, and not know what it was. I snorted at the idea of pulling this off for a day, even a few hours. It was taking so long. It would take so much longer.

I sighed at the thought of all the unsexy time ahead: nights in with my thoughts and feelings, earnest efforts at knowing and possibly (ugh) loving myself, the utter hassle

and enormous privilege of deciding what I wanted to do with my life, my weekends, my heart. The karaoke fantasies and app-based mania of early divorce days were giving way to the reality of it: a quiet, slightly undignified plod toward … what? Eventually pulling my head out of my ass and realising there were other things to worry about? I knew that already. It had been driving me to distraction all year.

I stayed on the ground a little longer, looking up at the sky and trying to take my losing-it level from an eight down to a more manageable five or six. Helen had taught me some brain exercises and I tried a few of them now, taking in my surroundings and naming textures, shapes and colours. I did some humming and gargling, secure in the knowledge that no one outside the wall could hear me desperately stimulating my vagus nerve in secret. I started to feel more settled and present very quickly. (The most annoying thing about these exercises was their efficacy.) I sat up and let out a big, declarative exhale, bringing my knees to my chest. Inside my bra, my left boob vibrated. I fished out my phone and looked at the message: wasn't sure if i should text, but wanted to say happy birthday xS.

I opened my mouth and ran my fingers along the ridged, wet collar of my T-shirt. I stared at the message, adjusting the brightness of my phone so my face shone in the dark, and let out a surprised sound somewhere between a gasp and a hiccup. The little *x* with the initial was classic Simon: soft and sincere and a bit officiously formal. He had once told me he composed all important text messages in the Notes app first, only copying and pasting when he knew

exactly what he wanted to say. I imagined him trying out different sign-offs: (it's Simon, by the way); xo Big S; your erstwhile lover, Simon. I reached down to scratch a mosquito bite on the back of my ankle and began to laugh.

What now?! What fucking now? The temptation to call him or go to his house was very strong. But he had not invited me there, he had merely said happy birthday. He was not actually asking to see me at all, but he *was* reaching out with affection after twelve a.m., which was not nothing. I would just … text him tomorrow, then? See if he wanted to 'catch a movie'? Ludicrous. I laughed as loud as I'd cried, my shoulders shaking, my head in my hands. *You little idiot*, I thought. *You sweet, deranged moron.*

I tried to centre myself, to find some calm. But how could I? My phone glowed white blue, and my butt felt soft on the earth, and I was sitting in an actual graveyard having some tiny private epiphany. If it wasn't Simon, now, it would be somebody else someday, and wasn't that insane? I would have to figure out how to love them without freaking out, and some small part of me would have to believe that it was real. More outrageous than this was the possibility that one day, it might be.

I thought about next year, how I had no idea what it would be like, who I would meet, what they would do. Things would happen to me, and I would make decisions, and sometimes they would work out and sometimes they wouldn't. It would carry on like that, over and over, until ideally, I got incredibly old and died in my sleep, maybe with somebody nice nearby, or a cat that would definitely eat part of my face, but what would I care, I'd be drifting

around in that endless nothing space I could not think about for too long without becoming sweat-drenched and queasy. It was a funny idea, my existing for years and years, shit happening all over the place, everything seeming so Big and Meaningful. And it was, but also it wasn't. I would feel one way for a while, and then I would feel another way, and it would never be forever, because nothing is.

I wiped my nose and did a bit more humming. A warm breeze moved through the trees above me, dislodging a fat chestnut that clattered to the ground near my feet. I looked up at the empty church, then past it at the moon, full and gorgeous and absurd. I clicked the side of my phone and the message disappeared. Then I got up from the ground, still laughing, and went home.

An Epilogue

The papers arrived on a Tuesday, bundled with a magazine, a utility bill, and a postcard from one of Amy's friends ('Dallas ain't the same without you, slut!'). I opened the envelope carefully, leaving the dense stack on the counter while I made coffee and toasted an English muffin.

The places I needed to sign were tabbed. I considered reading the entire thing over, but Lori had walked me through it already: satisfactory division of assets, refusal of further financial liability, mutual desire to dissolve the marriage ... I got the gist.

It crossed my mind that it might be best not to get a buttery fingerprint on important legal documents. I put down the muffin.

Flipping to the first of the tabbed pages, I noticed Jon's signature was different. It seemed larger, loopier, the *P*s in his last name more ostentatiously *P*-like. Possibly he had jazzed it up for the occasion, or maybe I had misremembered or forgotten it. It looked like the handwriting of a stranger.

I wrote my name under his and finished the muffin. Later that day I would do something else.

Acknowledgements

The acknowledgements for my essay collection rambled on for three pages and thanked basically every person I'd ever encountered, so I am going to try to keep things concise here, but I am very grateful to a lot of people so we may end up with a ramble no matter what we do. Thank you for your patience (we've begun).

Enormous thanks to my wonderful agents, Marya Spence and Claire Conrad, as well as their assistants at Janklow & Nesbit. Their support during every stage of this process has made impossible things possible; I would never have found Merris without Marya. It is also through my agents that I ended up with the dream team of Kishani Widyaratna and Jessica Williams, who guided the book to its final form with such wisdom and humour. I'm very grateful to them, their assistants, and to Liv Marsden, Laura Meyer, Naomi Mantin, and the publicity and marketing teams of 4th Estate and William Morrow, as well as to the many, many people involved in printing, distributing, and selling this novel. Thank you in particular to Mumtaz

Mustafa and Jo Thomson for designing the book's beautiful covers, and to Sari Shryack for making us an original painting. I'm also grateful to Louise Glück for the use of her gorgeous poem as an epigraph.

Many people provided early feedback that made this book better than I could have managed on my own. Thanks to Katie Baker, Emma Herdman, Nathan Foad, Adam Howard, Marisa Meltzer, Liz Watson, Amy Reed, Catherine Liao, Helen Gould, Neha Patel, Emily Whalen, Hali Hamilton, Emily Stubbings, Celeste Yim, DJ Mausner, Sarah Hagi, Mark Lund, Rose Johnson, Caroline O'Donoghue, Dolly Alderton, Adam Burton, and Josie Long, for conversations, emails, and advice that changed the book's shape. In particular, Tess Degenstein, Kathryn Borel, Laura Dawe, Lauren Oyler, and Joel Golby fielded a LOT of texts about the book and still read it, in full, in some cases several times over. Thank you so, so much.

Thank you to Paul Bogaards for his support and advice throughout the unfamiliar process of putting something like this out into the world. Thanks to Abby Singer and Rob Kraitt of Casarotto Ramsay & Associates, Cara Masline and Katie Newman at 3 Arts, and their assistants for their continued support.

I am most grateful to my close friends and family for their support during crises fictional and real. Special shout out to the original Five Poots group chat; my almost comically supportive parents, Peter and Janice; my kind and funny sisters, Alice and Melissa; and Stephen Carlick, who hears every idea and joke the first (and fortieth) time, and whose calm care has been one of the great surprises of my life.